WHEN THE PIPER CALLS

"Two million dollars in nonsequential bills. I will call in twenty-four hours to confirm you have the money."

Having learned his lesson, Scott kept quiet.

"Do you understand?"

"Sammy." Scott paused for a second, expecting the line to go dead at his interruption, but it didn't.

"What about him?"

"I want to speak to him."

"When you have the money," the Piper said, then hung up.

The Piper wouldn't be calling back tonight. Scott surveyed the agents entrenched in his home.

"You did well," Sheils said. "We need to discuss the ransom. I'm assuming you don't have two million."

"No," Jane said, shaking her head. "The Piper has to know we don't have that kind of money."

"I'm sure he does. This is where our negotiator will come into play. He'll bargain the price down."

"Wake up, Sheils," Scott said. "The Piper purposefully picked a figure out of our reach. This isn't a normal Piper kidnapping—or haven't you gotten that yet?"

Other *Leisure* books by Simon Wood:

ACCIDENTS WAITING TO HAPPEN

SIMON WOOD

PAYING THE PIPER

LEISURE BOOKS NEW YORK CITY

A LEISURE BOOK®

November 2007

Published by

Dorchester Publishing Co., Inc.
200 Madison Avenue
New York, NY 10016

ISBN-10: 0-8439-5980-0
ISBN-13: 978-0-8439-5980-2

Visit us on the web at www.dorchesterpub.com.

ACKNOWLEDGEMENTS

My thanks goes, yet again, to my wife, Julie, for all her hard work. She helped turn this from an idea into a story. Special thanks goes to Supervisory Special Agent George Fong of the Federal Bureau of Investigation for his help and generosity. I think I listened to what he had to tell me. Finally, congratulations to the winners of my "Casting Call" contest for letting me immortalize their names as characters in this book. They know who they are, even if no one else does.

PAYING THE PIPER

ONE

Scott leaned on his horn and roared through the red light. Six lanes of traffic on Van Ness with the green light on their side lurched forward, then slithered to a halt in the same breath. A barrage of blaring car horns trailed after him.

Geary Boulevard rose up on the other side of the intersection. Scott tightened his grip on the wheel and braced for the jarring impact. His Honda sedan bottomed out on the steep incline, but maintained its speed. With the gas pedal floored, the car accelerated and closed in on a slow-moving SUV switching lanes. Scott jumped on his horn again. The SUV froze, straddling both lanes to block his path.

"Idiot," he snarled and shouldered his way past the other driver.

Traffic was everywhere, but when wasn't it in San Francisco? He weaved between two cars, jerked out from behind a muni bus, and still had a stream of vehicles ahead.

His cell phone rang. He snatched it from its holder on the dashboard. "Yes."

"Scott, where are you?" Jane squeezed out between sobs. "You said you'd be here."

Hearing his wife cry split him in two. His own tears welled, but he bottled them for later. He needed to be strong. If he let this overwhelm him, then what good was he to his family?

"I'm nearly there." His hoarse voice cracked in the middle of his short reply.

"Just hurry."

"I am."

He hung up and tossed the phone on the passenger seat next to him.

How could his life have changed so irrevocably? Just twenty minutes ago, he'd been living a normal life. A good life. He was a reporter for the *San Francisco Independent*. He and Jane had a loving marriage—a miracle in this day and age. They owned a house in a good neighborhood in the city, even with its insane real estate prices. It was the perfect place to bring up kids—and they did. They had two great kids.

Had two great kids.

It had only taken a moment to lose one of his children. Some sick freak had snatched him out from under them. How could that happen? He and Jane took every precaution. They'd entrusted their children to a good school—the best they could afford with their two incomes. They'd gone private to prevent this kind of thing from happening. He palmed away the tears clouding his vision and swerved around a UPS truck.

He felt the guilt spreading through him, eating away at his spirit. He'd failed his son, Sammy. Abduction was a parent's worst fear, but he hadn't wanted to be one of those parents who saw phantoms on every street corner. Putting bars on the windows and dead bolts on the doors didn't keep them out, it kept you in. But that cavalier attitude had led to this. His worst fears had been realized. Someone had taken his son.

"I'm sorry, Sammy."

A new sensation swept away his guilt. Imagination,

strong and invincible, assaulted him. He'd always been
able to conjure up images from secondhand accounts.
That's what made him such a good reporter. He didn't just
relay facts. He told stories—living, breathing stories. He
turned readers into eyewitnesses—transporting them to
the actual locations, inserting them inside the people present at the celebration or the tragedy. Now that talent
turned on him. From the meager facts available, Scott con-
structed a nightmare. Sammy appeared to him, his smiling
face melting into a scream as the abductor dragged him
kicking and screaming inside a van. His imagination
blinded him with these false, but true, images. The abduction was true, but the events were lies, just images his fear
conjured up. He would know nothing until he reached the
school. He stabbed down on the gas again and frightened
a hybrid hatchback out of his way.

At the cost of a door mirror snapped off against the corner of a Safeway trailer truck, he made it to the school.
Half a dozen SFPD cars were staked out in front. Was that
all his son warranted—six patrol cars? Not that these cops
were any good now. Talk about closing the stable door after the horse had bolted. Where were these bastards when
Sammy was being snatched?

He ground to an untidy halt in front of the cop cars and
abandoned his Honda in the roadway. *Let the city tow it*, he
thought. He spilled out onto the asphalt, gathered himself
up, and raced toward the school gate. He hadn't gotten ten
feet when his cell rang. He darted back and snatched it off
the car seat. He hit the green key on the run.

His antics drew the attention of two uniformed officers
protecting the school's perimeter. Seeing him charging
toward the school gates, they moved as a unit to intercept
him.

Scott put the phone to his ear. "I'm here, babe. It's okay.
I'm here."

"That's good to know."

The voice on the line chilled him. Instead of his wife's

soft tones, he heard a voice that was harsh, blunted by an electronic disguise. The words came out robotic and demonic. Scott recognized the voice, but he hadn't heard it in eight years. The raw adrenaline left him as swiftly as it had come and he ground to a halt with the cops still racing toward him.

"It's been a long time, Scott. I thought I'd reintroduce myself."

"What have you done with Sammy?"

"Nothing—yet."

Scott feared asking the obvious question, but there was no way around it. "What do you want?"

The cops caught up to him. They bombarded him with questions and threats. He ignored them. He listened to the distorted voice on the line until it hung up.

He lowered the phone. A wave of nausea swept over him, taking his legs out from under him. The two cops caught him before he hit the ground.

"He has my son." Misery clung to his words. "The Piper has my son."

"Jesus Christ," one of the cops said.

Two

Eight years earlier

"*Independent*, Scott Fleetwood."

He'd answered his desk phone out of reflex and he cursed himself for it. He was late finishing up a feature piece for tomorrow's deadline and some two hours past the time he'd told Jane he'd be home at his last update. No doubt she was calling to chew him out about leaving a pregnant woman expecting twins alone. Only last night they'd agreed on names—Sammy and Peter if they were boys, and Emily and Rachel if they were girls.

When no one answered, he said, "Hello?"

"This is the Piper," the garbled voice said.

Yeah, right, Scott thought. There were plenty of freaks out there eager to see their name in print. What better name to use than that of the infamous serial kidnapper? It was common knowledge that the Piper used an electronic voice disguiser. It wasn't exactly a difficult item to obtain these days with all the spy gadget stores around.

He leaned back in his seat. "You won't be insulted if I ask for proof?"

"Of course not."

"Put Nicholas Rooker on the line. I'm sure his parents would like to know that he's all right."

"Can't do that. He's not with me."

What a surprise, Scott thought. He checked his watch. If he left in fifteen, he'd get home by eleven.

"That's disappointing," Scott said. "Look, I've got to go."

"And miss out on the story of your career?"

Scott smiled. He had to give it to this guy. He had plenty of cool. He sounded just like the Piper. Scott sat up in his chair.

"Look, I don't have to travel far in this city to find someone who'll tell me they're the Piper if I give them a buck. If you really want me to take you seriously, you're going to have to do a lot better than you're doing. Tell me something no one else would know."

Silence. Just what Scott expected. He was about to hang up when the Piper spoke.

"I sedate the kids with chloral hydrate. You won't find that in any FBI press releases."

Hairs stood up on the back of Scott's neck. There'd been plenty of publicity surrounding the Piper and his seven kidnappings in as many years. The Piper targeted the families of Bay Area millionaires. The Piper's current victim, Nicholas Rooker, was the son of San Francisco's premier property developer, Charles Rooker. A lot had been said about the kidnapped children, but Scott couldn't recall any mention of doping. Even so, that didn't make it the truth.

"I'll need to check it out."

"Then check it out."

"Give me a number where I can call you back?"

An electronic laugh came from the phone. "Nice try. I'll call you. You've got an hour."

Scott hung up his phone and hit the Internet. He

combed story after story and found no mention of chloral hydrate. Even the *Independent*'s own morgue kicked up nothing.

He called Keith Ellis on his cell. Ellis was a reporter who was tight with the cops, since he had family in the SFPD and Oakland PD. Ellis tried shooting the breeze, but Scott shot him down. He had fifteen minutes before the Piper called back.

"Okay, what do you need?" Ellis asked, sounding put out. He was in a bar, judging by the burble of voices and music in the background.

"The Piper. Any mention of him using chloral hydrate on any of the kids?"

"Not that I know of. Why?"

"Can you ask someone? Now?"

"What is all this?"

"I can't explain. Can you do it?"

"Sure. I guess."

"Get back to me in ten. Okay?"

Scott hung up in the middle of Ellis's protests. He eyed the clock at the right-hand corner of his computer monitor, then his desk phone, then the clock again. If he really did have the Piper calling him, it was the story of his career. He tried not to let his imagination run away with itself.

Ellis called back with three minutes to spare. All of the Piper's kidnap victims had been doped. The Piper drugged them to keep them docile. When the FBI ran blood tests on the children, they found chloral hydrate in their blood. The feds were keeping the knowledge from anyone outside the investigation.

Scott's excitement left him panting. Ellis pushed for details, but Scott hung up on him and ignored his subsequent calls.

The voice claiming to be the Piper called back exactly one hour from his previous call. "Well?" he said.

"You have the benefit of the doubt. You're either the Piper or someone very close to him."

"Caution. I like that."

"Why come to me?"

"I had to call someone. You answered the phone."

Scott deserved that. He was hoping for a little ego stroking. If anyone was going to get his ego stroked, it was the Piper. He'd come out of the shadows to talk after all the speculation about him. Scott wasn't going to blow it now.

"You know I'm going to have to go to the FBI with this."

"I want you to. I want someone to document this kidnapping. But I don't want you to go just yet. We have a lot to talk about. Are you okay with that?"

The implication of what the Piper was asking of Scott hung in the air like smoke. "Yeah, I'm okay with that."

The present

That decision eight years ago had cost Nicholas Rooker his life. When Scott looked back on that night, his involvement with the Piper seemed so tenuous. If he hadn't stayed late that evening, he wouldn't have picked up the phone. If the Piper had picked a different newspaper, a different reporter's life would be in shreds. If he'd only gone to the FBI right away, then . . . So many ifs.

That night had led him here. He was in the principal's office with Peter on his lap, the boy's arms wrapped around his neck. Jane sat beside him, leaning into him as if body heat would make things better. They'd all been crying. Clare Donnelly, the school principal, kept telling them how sorry they were, as did the two SFPD inspectors. Their condolences failed to penetrate. Scott was numb.

"It's my fault," Scott murmured. "I'm being punished."

The Piper hadn't made a threat after Nicholas Rooker's death, but it hung there in the air unsaid and unseen. A lot of people blamed Scott for botching the Nicholas Rooker kidnapping. He'd started writing his own ticket when the Piper came to him. The infamous kidnapper had selected him out of all the reporters out there. The Los Angeles and

New York *Times* were courting him. Book offers were falling through the mail slot daily. A Pulitzer Prize had been put aside for him when the next round of awards came around. He was talking to the Piper, kidnapper of children.

But he wasn't. He'd been conned. He'd been talking to Mike Redfern. Redfern wasn't a malicious hoaxer or some deranged lunatic who claimed responsibility because his cat told him to. No, Redfern was a sad, lonely man who lived out elaborate fantasies. He'd read and absorbed the theories about the Piper's identity and put himself in the kidnapper's shoes. He'd gotten the Piper's identity down pat. Scott hadn't been the only one fooled. The FBI believed Redfern was the Piper, which only fueled him to keep going with his fantasies. Only when the FBI caught him did it sink in that they'd been suckered. Worse still, while everyone had been focused on Redfern, the Piper had been overlooked, his demands disregarded, and his ultimatum ignored.

Nicholas Rooker's body had been found in Golden Gate Park the day after Redfern's arrest. The Piper had been humane. He'd sedated the child first before smothering him.

Nicholas's face from that night flooded Scott's memory. The image became so vivid it hurt his vision. Sammy's face bled into Nicholas's until Nicholas no longer existed and Scott stared at his son's dead face.

The world had pointed a finger at Redfern. His childish antics had led to Nicholas Rooker's death. The finger pointed at Scott too. The Los Angeles and New York *Times* stopped calling. Hate mail replaced the book offers. The Pulitzer went to someone else.

And the Piper? He never made a public announcement. He didn't call a competing newspaper or send a note to the television stations. He simply disappeared. After seven kidnappings netting him in excess of ten million dollars, he went underground.

"Mr. Fleetwood," a squat inspector said. "You've got nothing to worry about. The FBI is on the way."

The FBI. The mention of the illustrious name was meant to fill him with confidence and hope. Unfortunately, there wasn't a lot of hope to be had, considering the bureau had failed to catch the Piper on all the previous occasions. Only one thing could make things worse.

"Who are they sending?"

"You're in safe hands, Mr. Fleetwood. They're sending their top guy."

"Would that be Tom Sheils?"

"Yeah. You know him?"

"You could say that."

THREE

Sheils pulled up in front of the school. SFPD didn't give him any grief at the scene. They looked more than happy to off-load this case onto the bureau. He welcomed another shot at the Piper. The thought of finally bringing the bastard down filled him with excited determination. His hand trembled when he presented his ID to the cop protecting the school entrance. The officer seemed not to notice and directed him to the principal's office.

Thoughts of Nicholas Rooker tempered his excitement. That boy weighed heavily on his conscience. Circumstances had worked against him, but he'd let Nicholas down. He should have done better. Now he had another chance. If he failed, he doubted he'd get another.

No one ever blamed him for failing to catch the Piper. No one faulted his methods, but the fact remained he'd worked every Piper kidnapping, and he'd never even gotten close to catching him. That single fact affected him more than his stalled career. Pride ate into him. He'd closed a lot of high-profile cases, but he'd lost to the Piper every time. Statistics said he'd lose again, but he didn't think so. This time the Piper had screwed up.

He'd made it personal.

The Piper was a "for profit" kidnapper. He kidnapped for the income his victims earned him. He went after prominent Bay Area families who could rustle up a million or two without a second's thought. But Scott and Jane Fleetwood didn't fall into that category. They could bankrupt themselves and still not come close to the Piper's usual ransom demand.

But that wasn't the point.

This was payback. Scott Fleetwood had derailed the Nicholas Rooker kidnapping and now the Piper was dishing out a little retribution. Sheils could relate. He'd wanted some of that action himself. If Scott hadn't given Redfern his fifteen minutes, then the FBI wouldn't have been sidetracked. The Piper blamed Scott for botching the Nicholas Rooker kidnapping and so did Sheils. If Mike Redfern's bullshit hadn't suckered Scott in, the Piper would have gotten his money and Nicholas Rooker would be alive.

This was personal for the Piper, which was good. Until now, the kidnapper had kept things businesslike and detached. But if he was making this personal, that made this kidnapping emotion-driven. That made him reckless. Reckless people were easier to catch, but twice as dangerous. Emotion would bring the Piper down. His desire to destroy Scott would distract him from the business of kidnapping.

Thoughts of the Piper's emotions turned him to his own. He didn't like to think he hated Scott, but he did. His interference had killed Nicholas as sure as if he'd suffocated the boy himself. Scott had brought this pain upon himself and he deserved every miserable minute of it. Sheils's bitterness drew him up short. He couldn't face the Fleetwoods with that attitude. Regardless of how he felt about Scott, there was a frightened boy out there who needed him.

While he took a moment to compose himself, his cell rang.

"Have you spoken to the Fleetwoods yet?" Bill Travillian asked. Travillian was the special agent in charge of the San Francisco division and Sheils's boss.

"No, I'm just about to."

"Just take it easy on them."

"You mean take it easy on Scott. Bill, I can separate my personal feelings from my job."

"I hope so, Tom. I'm assigning you to the Piper because you know more about this prick than anyone and you've earned the right to bring him in, but I won't if there are going to be problems."

There weren't going to be any problems. His duty came way above his grudges. He wanted Samuel Fleetwood back safe and sound, irrespective of who his father was. Samuel was priority number one with the Piper's apprehension a close second, but Sheils couldn't deny he'd enjoy watching Fleetwood squirm during this case.

"You have nothing to fear. I'm here for the Piper."

Travillian paused, mulling over Sheils's response. Travillian wasn't a bureaucrat. He was an old-school agent who'd come up through the ranks and had twenty years of fieldwork under his nails. He knew his stuff. Sheils felt the man pick through his reply, analyzing it for its truth content.

"Okay, Tom. I'm trusting you on this one."

"Thank you, sir."

"Don't thank me. Just stop this bastard."

Sheils found the principal's office and knocked on the door.

Scott's stomach tightened when Sheils entered the office. He never expected to cross paths with the FBI agent again. After Nicholas Rooker's death, Sheils had pushed for Scott's arrest. The charges ranged from wasting police time to accessory to murder, but Sheils's pleas fell on deaf ears. The denial only fueled Sheils's contempt for him.

The last eight years had taken their toll on Sheils's hair, skin, and waistline, but not his resolve. The agent burned with the same purpose Scott had encountered eight years ago.

Sheils introduced himself and said, "I won't patronize you by asking how you're holding up."

"Thank you," Jane said.

"Are you going to get Sammy back?" Peter asked.

Neither Scott nor Jane made any move to admonish their son for his question. They needed the answer as much as he did.

"We're going to do our very best to find your brother."

"That doesn't answer his question," Jane said.

Sheils squirmed under the intensity of Jane's stare and turned back to Peter. He put out his hand to the boy. "You have my word as an FBI agent that I'll bring your brother home safe and sound."

Peter shook Sheils's hand and smiled.

"I would like to get Samuel's picture on the evening news."

"Sammy," Jane corrected.

"Yes. Right. Sammy."

"I can get you a photo. We have them of all the children," the principal said and left her office to get it.

"Peter, I'd like to talk to you about what happened. Would that be okay?"

The question was directed at Scott and Jane more than Peter. They gave their permission and everyone sat down. Sheils dragged over a chair and pulled it in front of the boy. He sat forward in the chair so that he met Peter at eye level and spoke in a calm and soothing tone.

His questions were open, friendly, and nonaccusatory. Peter answered as best he could, but the answers were vague and uninformed. They were those of a frightened eight-year-old who'd witnessed his twin brother's abduction. Sheils reasked his questions, rephrasing them in the hopes of getting an answer. This worked against the agent.

He crowded Peter and Peter retreated into himself. His replies went from simple sentences to one-word answers to shrugs.

Scott felt time getting away from them. As soon as the Piper reached the freeway, he could be hitting sixty miles an hour. That was a mile a minute. For every minute they wasted, Sammy was another mile farther away from them. The bastard would have Sammy out of the Bay Area in the next twenty minutes. Once he was free of the congestion, his escape velocity would increase. But while distance was Scott's enemy, it was also his friend. While the Piper was at the wheel, he couldn't hurt Sammy. Scott shut out the image forming in his head and willed the bastard to keep driving.

"Let's take a break from the questions," he said.

Peter sagged, then clutched his mother.

"Can I have a minute alone with my family?"

Sheils nodded and left the room.

Scott knelt before his son. "Peter, we need to know everything that happened, okay?"

Peter jerked his head up and down.

"It doesn't matter what you tell us. You aren't in trouble. Sammy isn't in trouble. The man who took him is the one in trouble. Okay?"

"Okay," Peter said in a quiet voice.

Scott called Sheils back in.

"I want to try something different, Peter," Sheils said. "If that's okay with you?"

Peter nodded.

Sheils asked Peter to reenact his final steps leading up to Sammy's abduction. Peter took them to his classroom.

"The bell rang for you to go," Sheils said. "What happened from there?"

Peter seemed to put his fears aside. Holding on to Scott's and Jane's hands, he ran through the school, calling out what he and Sammy had done. He led them down the school steps toward the main gate and stopped at the sidewalk.

"This is where we spoke to him."

"We?" Sheils asked. "You spoke to the man who took Sammy?"

Peter's expansive mood dried up.

"C'mon, Peter. This is really important," Jane said. "Did you speak to this man?"

Peter backed away. Scott saw they were losing him again. His boys might have been twins, but their personalities were very different. Peter was the timid one of the two.

Scott knelt down in front of his son. "I know we told you not to talk to strangers, but it's okay if you did. Agent Sheils just needs to know."

"No. Sammy did."

Scott smiled at Peter to let him know everything was okay. Sheils ventured toward Peter. "So, what happened?"

"We were waiting for Mommy."

"Waiting?" Scott asked. Jane got off work in time to be outside the school before the bell. He turned to her. "Why were you late?"

"Flat tire. A strip of wood with nails through it was placed under my wheel and I backed over it."

"The Piper wanted you out of the way," Sheils remarked and turned back to Peter. "Okay, your mom was late. So you waited for her?"

"Yeah. We waited here." Peter pointed to the spot where he was standing. "A car pulled up in front of us."

Sheils interrupted. "It was a car, not a van or SUV?"

"No, not a car, a minivan. A blue one."

"Good boy," Jane said and hugged Peter.

"Did you get a license plate? Do you know if the minivan was a Dodge or Honda or anything?" Sheils asked.

Peter shook his head.

"That's okay," he said. "What about the driver? Did you get a good look at him?"

Peter scrunched his face up. "Not really. He was wearing a red hoodie with the hood up."

"Could you see whether he was white, black, Hispanic?" Sheils asked.

After seven kidnappings, thousands of FBI man-hours, and six surviving victims, no one had ever seen the Piper's face.

"White. I saw his hands."

"That's great," Sheils said. "How about age? Young? Old?"

Peter hemmed and hawed. "Old," he replied, but sounded uncertain.

Scott saw how subjective the question was to an eight-year-old. College grads were senior citizens in Peter's eyes. "As old as me, Peter?" he asked. "Or as old as Grandpa?"

"As old as you," Peter said.

"That's good," Sheils said. "Now, did this man say anything?"

"Yes. He told us that Mom had sent him to pick us up. Sammy asked who he was. He said a friend. He said he knew you. He used your name." Peter stared up at Scott.

Scott's stomach clenched.

"What else did he say?" Jane asked.

"I told him we don't talk to strangers and he laughed and said that he wasn't a stranger and he told Sammy to get in."

"Did Sammy get in?" Sheils asked.

"Yes."

Jane broke into tears and pulled Peter tight to her. This started Peter crying again. Sheils gave them a moment before interrupting. Jane wiped Peter's tears away with her hand.

"Peter," Sheils asked, "did you get in the minivan?"

Cracks appeared in Peter's resolve. Tears welled up again and his chin wobbled.

Scott hated seeing Peter in so much pain. He couldn't imagine how Sammy was doing right now. He moved toward his son to comfort him. "Tell us, buddy. It doesn't matter what you did. We just need to know for Sammy."

His reply came out small and tight. "Sammy told me to

get in. I didn't want to and he told me I was a wimp." He wiped away his own tears. "I went to get in and he told me no."

Scott thought he'd missed something. "Sammy told you not to get in the minivan?"

"No. The man. He said Sammy only. Then the door closed and he drove off." Peter's grip on himself came to an end and he broke down. Jerking sobs racked his body and he buried his head into his mother's shoulder. "He didn't want me."

Then it made sense. Scott understood his son's reluctance to tell them the whole story about Sammy's abduction. Peter was ashamed. The Piper had chosen Sammy over him. Peter hadn't been good enough to be kidnapped. He should have been counting his lucky stars, but instead, he was mourning his unpopularity. Scott put a hand to Peter's head and murmured words of comfort.

Sheils signaled to a pair of men in suits walking toward them. "I want to get you home. The Piper will call with his demands tonight. I want to be ready."

Sheils pulled Scott to one side while the two agents led Jane and Peter away. "What's the world teaching our kids if they're ashamed when a kidnapper looks them over?"

"Life is a popularity contest," Scott said.

This was the first nonacrimonious conversation they'd had since they met. Scott took that as a good sign.

Sheils frowned. "We both know this kidnapping is personal. The Piper wants to hurt you. You need to be prepared for the worst."

"Do you think Sammy's still alive?"

Sheils didn't answer him.

FOUR

Scott expected a horde of FBI agents to pour into his home. This was a Piper kidnapping after all. Instead he got Sheils and three agents. Sheils read Scott's expression and moved quickly to dispel any fears.

"Sammy's abduction isn't being taken lightly. We're the tip of the iceberg. The public, the press, and the Piper won't see the FBI machine at work. This investigation's heavy lifting will be taking place back at the division office."

Sheils introduced the three agents who would be assigned to the family—Shawn Brannon, Terry Dunham, and Lucy Guerra. Brannon, a tall and serious-looking guy around Scott's age, was Sheils's second in command. Sheils dismissed them and they swept through Scott's home with the might of an occupying force. They commandeered the entire first floor with the exception of the kitchen, and set up their command post in the dining room. In a matter of minutes, his home was no longer his. There was little for his family to do except stay out of their way.

He, Jane, and Peter took refuge in the kitchen. They sat around the table like they did every day, except for the unoccupied chair. Peter stared at the space that should have been filled by Sammy.

"It's going to be okay," Scott said to his son.

He and Jane explained to Peter what would happen. They put the most positive spin on events that they could. If they could convince Peter that everything would be okay, then maybe they could convince themselves.

Sheils came into the kitchen. He sat in Sammy's seat, unaware of the sacrilege he'd committed. Scott felt like telling him to stand.

"We need to talk," he said. "A lot will happen before the night is through."

"The ransom demand?" Jane asked. "There will be one, won't there?"

"Yes, and in the next few hours, while we're still mobilizing. That's why we have to work fast. I need to ask you more questions. Okay?"

He received a round of nods.

"Good. Peter, I'd like you to help identify the type of minivan you saw. Can you do that?"

"Okay."

Agent Guerra shook hands with Peter. She was a slim, attractive, Hispanic woman in her late twenties. She immediately won him over with her warm smile and good looks. Peter took Guerra's hand and she led him from the room.

Jane stiffened. Scott recognized her fear. She'd lost one child to a stranger today and she didn't want to let her remaining child out of her sight. He leaned in and whispered, "It's okay."

"Normally, we'd have a negotiator coach you on phone techniques, but he won't be here for a few hours, so I need to prep you," Sheils said. "With today's technology it's very easy to trap and trace a phone call, but it's still important to keep the Piper on the phone. I expect he will want to talk to you, Scott, so I want Jane to answer the phone. Any requests he makes, ask for them to be repeated or say you don't understand. Ask questions. Even if the Piper doesn't answer, you've bought us vital tracking time."

"Okay," Scott said.

"An even more important factor is to build a rapport. If the Piper starts to bond with you, it will make it hard for him to hurt Sammy."

"The Piper isn't most kidnappers. This isn't even a typical Piper kidnapping. He's not here for the money. He's here for me. He's looking for any excuse to hurt Sammy."

"Oh God," Jane said.

"That's an even bigger reason to build a rapport with him," Sheils said.

"I don't know how well we can do this," Jane said.

"That's okay. Whatever you can do will help. I might not need you to deal with the phone calls at all. When the negotiator arrives, we can have him take over, pretending to be a close relative."

Jane looked relieved at the news.

"Our negotiators are trained to string the conversation out, listen for inflections and background noise, and ask for proof of life."

Scott knew Sheils had said the wrong thing the moment the words left his lips. Panic ignited in Jane's eyes and spread across her face.

"You think Sammy's dead," Jane said.

"I'm not saying that. It's a term that you're going to hear a lot. Don't let it frighten you." Sheils smiled to settle her nerves. "If the Piper has Sammy with him when he calls and we trace his location, then we'll find Sammy at the same time."

Sheils needed statements. He sent Jane off with Agent Brannon and drew the door shut. The move unnerved Scott. Eight years ago, Sheils had warned him that he couldn't be held responsible for his actions if they ever found themselves alone with each other.

"Thanks for playing this down with Jane," Scott said.

"Playing it down?"

"We both know this kidnapping is about revenge. And what finer revenge would there be than to kill Sammy?"

"At least you're being realistic."

"This is no time for delusions."

"I agree." Sheils leaned against the countertop. "There's something I want to ask you. Is this your first contact with the Piper?"

Scott had thought Sheils was going to keep his personal feelings out of the situation. He wanted to be the bigger man, but the snide remark dug deep. "What's that supposed to mean?"

"After Nicholas Rooker was killed, did the Piper get in touch with you?"

"Don't you think I would have contacted you?"

"I don't know. You were pretty lax about picking up the phone the first time."

"Jesus Christ. Do you really think I wanted that kid to die?"

Sheils's hands balled into fists at his sides. "You know what? I don't know. You seemed as hung up on being a headline as writing them. I'm not saying you wanted the kid dead, but if it bleeds, it leads. Isn't that what you bottom feeders say?"

"You're unreal, Sheils. Do you know that?"

"Enough about me. Back to the Piper. Has he ever contacted you?"

"Why would he?"

"You got his story wrong. Maybe he wanted it told the right way."

"Okay, say he did, why kidnap Sammy now?"

Sheils smirked. "It would make for a great publicity stunt for you. Ever finish that book on the Piper?"

Scott lost his fingernail grip on his temper and threw a punch. Sheils easily sidestepped it, but not his charge. Scott dropped a shoulder and drove it into Sheils's stomach. Sheils absorbed the impact until Scott smashed him into the countertop, its edge cutting into his back like a knife. Sheils yelled out, then bottled his pain, using it as fuel to fight back. He thumped a fist down on Scott's spine between his shoulder blades to loosen the reporter's grip, then trapped his head under his arm and peeled him off.

Jane ripped open the kitchen door. "What the hell do you think you're doing?"

Sheils held Scott in place while Brannon appeared in the doorway behind Jane.

"Grow up," Jane shouted. "Settle your grudges later. My son is in danger. Deal with that first."

Sheils released Scott. He slumped onto all fours.

Guerra forced her way past Brannon. "Sir, we've got an incoming call."

FIVE

The brawl was forgotten. Sheils ushered Scott and Jane back into the living room. There was no fancy equipment on show. Scott and Jane had just to answer the phone. FBI technicians were monitoring all calls from the division office. A second handset had been plugged in to allow Sheils to listen in.

Scott looked around for Peter. He was with Guerra in the dining room. He'd taken to the woman and was acting like he was her sidekick, which was great. It kept him involved and out of the way of the more difficult decisions.

The phone rang again. Scott went to answer it, but Sheils stopped him. "Let Jane answer it. Remember what I told you about keeping the conversation going."

"Yeah, we know," Scott said. He didn't want to lose the call if it was the Piper.

"Brannon, you're playing the part of the relative," Sheils said.

Brannon nodded.

"We'll do our best," Scott said to Jane and smiled at her. She smiled back.

The phone rang again.

"Jane, if he asks for Scott, tell him he's too upset and hand the phone to Agent Brannon. Okay?"

Jane looked nervously at Sheils and snatched up the phone. "Hello?"

Scott leaned in next to Jane to listen. "May I speak to Scott?"

The familiar sound of the Piper's doctored voice leaked from the phone. Scott glanced over at Sheils. His expression had turned grim-faced. The Piper had damaged a lot of people.

Jane tried to respond, but a whimper replaced her words. Scott wanted to tell her it was all okay, but he couldn't break his silence.

"We know you took Sammy to get at Scott. He's not up to speaking right now."

"Is that right?" The Piper's contempt for Jane's lie punched through the electronic device disguising his voice. "You don't sound up for it either."

"I'm not. Do you mind speaking to my brother?"

The line went dead. The burr of the disconnected line sounded like the end of the world.

Jane jumped up. "What just happened? He's gone. He's gone."

Scott embraced his wife to calm her.

"It's okay," Sheils told her. "He'll call back."

"He knows," Brannon said, defeat thick in his voice. "He knows we're here."

"Of course he does," Scott snapped. He locked stares with Sheils. "He's dealt with you guys seven times before. Why would this time be any different?"

"It was worth a try," Sheils said.

"It's okay, Jane." Scott kissed her. "He'll call back. He wants me."

Everyone retook their seats and clustered around the phone, waiting for it to ring. Peter broke away from Guerra and jumped into Jane's arms.

The phone didn't ring. The minutes ticked by.

"Why hasn't he called back?" Jane asked.

"He's testing us," Sheils replied.

"He's punishing us," Scott corrected.

"He'll call."

Dunham, a slight and fresh-faced guy for his age, removed his cell phone from his ear for the first time since the Piper had called. He frowned and hung up. "The call's been traced to a broadband Internet provider."

Sheils cursed.

"What's wrong?" Scott asked.

"He's calling in through the Internet and more than likely he's using a wireless connection."

"Are you saying you can't trace the call?" Jane asked.

"No. It's just going to take longer. We need to nail down the IP address, then triangulate his position using cell phone towers."

This act was all supposed to instill confidence. *What a crock*, Scott thought. They might be buying it, but he wasn't. The Piper was on top of things. He knew the feds would be in charge of this case. He knew a negotiator would be flown in and how long that would take. He also knew if he called now, they wouldn't be ready. Scott couldn't help but feel like the Piper was toying with them.

The phone rang again after ten minutes. Sheils started reeling off instructions, but Scott snatched up the phone.

"Hello?"

"Good," the Piper said. "We don't have to play games. Let's keep things honest. You have the FBI with you, yes?"

Scott tried a delay tactic. "Screw the FBI. What about Sammy?"

The line went dead again. The Piper wasn't going to fall for Sheils's tricks. Everyone had to play it his way. Any deviation resulted in punishment. "I don't think he likes your tactics."

Sheils said nothing.

The Piper's time-out lasted exactly fifteen minutes. Scott answered the phone again.

"Answer my questions and I'll stay on the line," the Piper said. "The FBI is with you—yes or no?"

"Yes."

"I want two million dollars in nonsequential bills—"

"I don't have that kind of money," Scott interrupted. He wasn't employing one of Sheils's hopeless delay tactics. It was genuine shock, but regardless, the Piper hung up.

"Damn it," Scott shouted and threw the phone down.

"Stay calm, Scott," Jane said. "He's doing this to irritate you."

"Well, it's working."

"For Sammy, please try."

And for Peter, he thought. The poor kid was clinging to Jane. He looked petrified. "Okay."

The Piper called back thirty minutes later. Scott reported for punishment.

"Two million dollars in nonsequential bills. I will call in twenty-four hours to confirm you have the money."

Having learned his lesson, Scott kept quiet.

"Do you understand?"

"Yes."

"Good. Good night."

"Sammy." Scott paused for a second, expecting the line to go dead at his interruption, but it didn't.

"What about him?"

"I want to speak to him."

"When you have the money. Start breaking open your piggy banks," the Piper said, then hung up.

The Piper wouldn't be calling back tonight. Scott felt his tenuous grasp on the situation slither out of his hands. He surveyed the agents entrenched in his home. They'd yet to come to this realization. They were surplus to requirements and they didn't even know it.

"You did well," Sheils said. "We need to discuss the ransom. I'm assuming you don't have two million."

"No," Jane said, shaking her head. "Even if we sold

everything, we wouldn't come close. The Piper has to know we don't have that kind of money."

"I'm sure he does. This is where our negotiator will come into play. He'll bargain the price down."

"Wake up, Sheils," Scott said. "The Piper purposefully picked a figure out of our reach. This isn't a normal Piper kidnapping—or haven't you gotten that yet?"

Sheils stiffened but didn't retaliate.

"Can't the FBI lend us the money or something?" Jane asked.

"Sorry, no. It's against government policy."

Scott looked over at the clock. Time had slowed. He would have sworn it was deep into the night, but it wasn't even 9:00 p.m. Scott knew the feds were doing their job, but it was starting to get claustrophobic. Their house had never seemed so small.

"I'd like to speak with my family—alone."

"Sure. Good idea." Sheils got up and directed his agents into the dining area to confer with them.

"Time for bed, buddy," Scott said to Peter.

"Okay, Dad," Peter said. For once there was no argument about bedtime.

He hopped off the couch and Jane took his hand as they climbed the stairs. Scott and Jane helped Peter change into his pajamas and watched over him while he brushed his teeth. Scott expected difficult questions from his son that he wouldn't be able to answer, but Peter said nothing about his brother. Like all of them, he needed a break from the nightmare. Scott found himself wanting Peter to ask him about Sammy. He needed the pain. Pain gave him drive.

Scott and Jane walked Peter to the room he shared with his brother. Without Sammy, the room seemed cavernous. His empty bed was a nasty reminder of his absence.

"Are you going to be okay in here?" Jane asked Peter.

The boy stared at Sammy's side of the room. He nodded and climbed into his bed. Scott and Jane sat by his side.

"Do you want to talk about anything?" Scott asked.

"No." He rolled over and within minutes he was asleep. Scott led Jane to their bedroom and closed the door.

Jane fell into his arms. "Where are we going to come up with two million dollars?"

He'd been totting up their assets in his head, converting their possessions into dollar figures. They had savings, stocks, bonds, and pension funds. Their cars were only a couple of years old. Their house was a million-dollar asset in the current housing market, but the mortgage ate into a large chunk of the equity. The plus side looked rosy, but the total came nowhere near the Piper's figure. "We'll come up with it."

"How, Scott?" She pulled away from him. "How?"

He sat her down on the edge of the bed and knelt before her. "We'll mortgage the house."

"It's already mortgaged."

"We'll sell it, then."

"Be serious, Scott. Even if someone bought our house to-morrow, it's not worth two million."

He looked her directly in the eye. "I'll raise the money. I don't know how, but I will. If I have to sell everything I own, mortgage my future, and live in a box for the rest of my life, I'll do it to get Sammy back."

Jane pulled him to her, kissed him, then hugged him. "I love you so much."

Scott had desperately needed to hear this. Sheils could promise the might of the entire FBI, but it didn't compare to his wife's support. He hugged her tight to prevent her from slipping away.

"Can they do it? Can they get Sammy back?"

Scott pulled back from her. Her need for reassurance that her son was coming home scarred her face. As much as Scott recognized this and wanted the same, he couldn't lie. He hoped that was enough for her. "I don't know. I have to believe Sheils and his people can get Sammy back."

"Believe? That's not enough, Scott. They've never even come close to catching this bastard. He killed the last child. I don't know if these people can save Sammy."

What Jane said scared him. He feared for his son's life, but he had hope. If they complied with the Piper's demands, Sammy would be returned to them. The only danger came from an FBI screwup. He couldn't let that happen.

"What are you saying?" Scott asked.

"We can't rely on the FBI. We have to get involved."

"No, we can't do that. It's too dangerous."

"So we'll sit back and do nothing, is that what you're saying?" Jane's voice had risen. He shushed her in case someone overheard.

"No, I'm not. The Piper has targeted us because of me. I'll do everything possible to get Sammy back."

Jane latched on to his words and fixed him with a burning stare. "Do you promise that? Do you promise to bring him home?"

"I promise," Scott said. "It'll happen. Whatever it takes, I will make it happen. There's nothing I won't do."

Six

By 1:00 a.m., calm had descended over the Fleetwoods' house. The Fleetwoods were in bed. Sheils sat around the dining table with Brannon, Guerra, and Dunham.

"Thoughts and impressions?" Sheils asked.

"The Piper is back with a bang," Dunham said.

Sheils concurred with this point, but something still itched where it shouldn't have. Why the eight-year gap between kidnappings and why target Scott Fleetwood?

"Fleetwood bothers you, doesn't he?" Brannon said to Sheils.

"Yes," he admitted. "I don't like that the Piper broke with tradition by singling him out."

"But it makes sense," Brannon said. "The guy screwed up the Piper's last kidnapping. Killing Nicholas Rooker made the Piper one of America's Ten Most Wanted. Kidnapping Fleetwood's son seems like a fair trade."

"Do you think Fleetwood is involved with the Piper?" Dunham asked.

"I can't rule it out. Fleetwood played things to his own ends before. Why not now?"

"Because his kid is at risk," Guerra said.

"Not if this is a setup," Sheils said.

"If you're right, then Fleetwood is a first-class prick," Dunham said.

"I've thought that for eight years," Sheils said.

Jane cleared her throat, startling the assembled agents. Sheils had no idea how long she'd been standing in the doorway. Embarrassment swept across them all. She smiled but there was no doubting the fatigue in her pale face.

"Could I speak to you for a minute?" she asked Sheils.

"Of course, Mrs. Fleetwood," Sheils said.

"Call me Jane."

Sheils guided her into the kitchen and closed the door. She pulled out two chairs and they sat.

"What can I help you with, Jane?"

"You blame Scott for Nicholas Rooker's death, don't you?"

"It was an error in judgment on your husband's part."

She smiled. "Don't play coy. I blame him too."

Her remark shocked him, but he respected it. No one, not even a spouse, could turn a blind eye to what Scott had done.

"Scott let his ambition get the better of him and it cost that boy his life, but he didn't kill him. His mistake was thinking he could deliver the Piper. The Piper killed Nicholas. He knew you would catch Redfern. He could have waited, but he didn't. He killed that boy for no good reason other than spite."

It had been a long time since someone had shamed Sheils. He regretted his outburst in the kitchen. "I'm sorry. I deserved that. I do hold Scott responsible for what happened to Nicholas, but I hold Redfern and the Piper responsible too. They all made bad choices."

"Don't you think Scott knows that? A day doesn't go by without him blaming himself for his mistakes. He wouldn't be human if he didn't."

"Again, I'm sorry for my earlier behavior. I'll apologize to Scott in the morning."

"I don't want your apologies. I want you to get my son back."

Sheils liked this woman. She was strong. "You have my word."

"Good." She smiled at him. "Can I make you any coffee? Sleep isn't going to come easy tonight."

"Thanks, but no, thanks. I was about to go home. I want to check in with my family."

He wrapped up for the night and saw himself out. The drive didn't take long at that time of night. He drove with the window down to refresh himself. The night was mild, the air cool.

Sheils pulled up in front of his garage and let himself into his house. He loved coming home. Being with his family shut out the cruelty he had to deal with on a daily basis. Years ago, he'd made a conscious decision that when he closed the door to his home, he would slough off the pressures of the job. But tonight it wasn't working. He'd closed the door and Sammy Fleetwood's abduction remained tied around his neck.

Angela emerged from the living room to embrace him. She smiled at him, but there was pain behind the gesture.

"Is it him?" she asked.

He nodded.

She sighed. "Why now after so long?"

"I've been asking myself the same question."

"Have you eaten?"

"I grabbed something earlier."

"I'll make you something." She released him and went into the kitchen.

He followed her. "It's too late to eat and you've got work in a few hours."

She raided the fridge, pulling out eggs, cheese, vegetables, and sausage. "You won't be on a nine-to-five for some time. You're going to have to eat while you can."

He surrendered to her good sense and she put together one of her massive scrambles. It was protein on a plate—

something she'd been making for him since before they were married.

While she cooked, he stripped off his gun, phone, and jacket. He fell into the chair at the kitchen table to watch her cook. He couldn't remember the number of times he'd told her not to stay up. He didn't bother anymore.

She set the plate in front of him and watched him eat. "So he went after Scott Fleetwood. This is going to be messy."

He put down his fork. "Yes. I'm frightened he's going to kill that kid just because of what his father did."

She shook her head. "He won't even be able to hide in hell if he does."

"No, he won't."

"How much is he asking?"

"Two million."

"Do they have that kind of money?"

He shook his head. "They're liquidating their lives as we speak."

She looked around their home. "I can't imagine what that would be like. They should make an appeal for donations. This city would give to stop this bastard."

"Considering who Sammy's father is, I can't see many people donating."

She frowned. "How are you with Scott?"

If he said fine, she'd call him a liar. She'd listened to his rants after Nicholas Rooker's death. She knew how he felt about Scott. "I'm professional," he answered.

"That's good. That boy needs you. You're the one who's going to save him."

He picked at his food and failed to make eye contact with her. "I got a little rough with him tonight. I made it personal. I crossed a line."

"Tom, you can't do that. You can't have one eye on Scott when both should be on the Piper."

"I know."

He pushed his plate away. He didn't want to get into a

fight. He'd come home to be away from Scott and the Piper. There wouldn't be many moments like this over the next few days, maybe even weeks, depending on how things went. "I don't want to talk about this right now. I just want to be home with you guys and sleep."

She got up from her seat, went over to him, and kissed him. "Don't let the Piper get to you. Do your job and you'll nail him."

He wished he had her faith. The need for sleep pressed him, but he had to draw a line between his work and rest. If he didn't, he'd spend the night tossing and turning. He went into the living room and switched on the TV. Angela joined him.

"I tried calling Jen this afternoon, but she didn't answer," Sheils said.

"Oh, she forgot to charge her cell."

"She forgot? What if it had been something important?"

"It's okay. She just forgot to charge it. It's no big thing."

"I bought the damn thing for her protection. I didn't buy it so she could let it run flat. Is it on the charger now?"

"I don't know." Irritation crept into her tone.

"Where is it?" He jumped up from his seat. "I'll do it."

She grabbed his arm. "Tom, she's asleep. Do it in the morning."

He nodded and she released her hold. Instead of sitting, he went to the front door.

"What are you doing?"

"Locking up."

He latched the security chain and snapped the dead bolt home, then went to the back door and did the same.

"Where's Matt? I didn't see his car outside."

"San Jose. He was catching that concert with Julie."

"Has he checked in?"

She came into the kitchen. He brushed past her to lock the connecting door to the garage.

"No. He's eighteen. He doesn't need to. I know where he is and I trust him."

He went into the living room and flipped the window locks. "He's a good kid, but I like him to check in."

She followed him into the living room. He went to sweep past her, but she blocked his path.

"Tom, it won't happen."

A flush of embarrassment swept over him. "What won't?"

"The Piper won't come after our kids."

Could she be that sure? He knew he couldn't.

SEVEN

The Piper had hoped a midnight run along the beaches of Half Moon Bay would help him sleep. It didn't. The day's events left him too excited and frightened to sleep.

He poured himself a drink and sat in front of the TV. The kidnapping was still all over the news at this ungodly hour. It had been a long time since he'd heard his name. No, not his name. His persona. His neighbors saw someone completely different. They saw an easygoing guy who kept a nice home and attended barbecues every Fourth of July.

The TV pundits pretended they understood him. What pricks. He'd heard better theories scrawled on a men's room wall.

Channel after channel dredged up the same potted history with nothing of note. They all painted him as a monster, of course, all pouncing on the Nicholas Rooker angle. Poor kid. He hadn't wanted to do it, but he had no option. The FBI had bought into Mike Redfern's fantasy after he'd gone to that reporter. That had screwed everything. The Piper kept his kidnappings to a timeline. They all worked to a critical path. They had to. The cops and feds weren't dumb. They learned and adapted. Nicholas Rooker's kidnapping had to work to a clock and Redfern burned up all his time. On his critical path, there were only two choices. Expose himself to discredit Redfern or cut his losses. Exposing himself was cutting off his nose to spite his face. No, he had to cut his losses, which came at the expense of Nicholas Rooker's life. He hadn't wanted to do it, but he had to send a message. He made it painless. He wasn't a sadist, despite what the newsmen said.

Where other so-called criminal masterminds went wrong was they didn't know when to quit. They got greedy. They stopped looking at the numbers, the percentages, and the probabilities. All crime was entrenched in mathematics. Risk had to be justified. Too many people ignored the adage "Don't do the crime if you can't do the time." He hadn't wanted to do the time. That was why he quit. Once he crossed that line with Nicholas Rooker, retirement was his only option.

The FBI could search for him for a hundred years and they would never find him. Profilers postulated that he was a thrill seeker who would keep trophies. But they were comparing him to serial killers. He was nothing of the sort. He was a businessman. It was all about the money. Once he finished a job, he destroyed all evidence. He kept nothing. If the feds busted down the door right now, they wouldn't find anything linking him back to Nicholas Rooker. Not a thing.

But that had all changed. Now there was Sammy Fleetwood. The feds would be on their A game this time around. Before Nicholas Rooker, no one feared for their child in a Piper kidnapping. The threat was always there, but he always returned his children—as long as he was paid. But Sammy Fleetwood was different. Sammy could die at any time.

The Piper looked around his home with the ocean view. He'd leave in the morning for his ranch. He hadn't expected the media firestorm to catch so quickly. If any suspicion fell upon him, there were too many people who knew him around here. The ranch would be perfect. There would be no one around to watch him up there.

Jerky images of FBI agents hustling Scott Fleetwood inside his home flashed across the TV screen. This guy had to be sweating bullets—.45 caliber and bigger. He had to know he'd brought this shit storm upon himself.

The Piper lifted a glass of bourbon to his lips and drank.

Well, if Scott Fleetwood thought he was suffering now, it was nothing compared to what was to come.

The Piper lifted his glass to a freeze frame of Scott Fleetwood and toasted him. "To pain and suffering."

Eight

Scott awoke to the sound of his cell phone ringing. The previous day's events failed to penetrate the fog of sleep. He rolled over and grabbed the phone. Only as he put it to his ear did Sammy's kidnapping penetrate his skull.

"I need you to come in," George Moran said. George was the *Independent*'s executive news editor and Scott's boss.

"George, I'm a little tied up today if you haven't noticed."

Scott rolled out of bed and went to the window. He edged the drapes aside to view the media amassed outside his home. Many of the faces he knew. Under normal circumstances, he'd be amongst them. He let the drapes go before someone noticed him watching.

"You're going to want to hear me out. We want to help with the ransom. I've got clearance to buy your story. We'll pay big."

He wanted to tell George to go to hell, but George was a good guy. "How big?"

"Six figures. Can you get here now?"

"Sure."

He showered and dressed, then slipped from the room

without waking Jane. It had been a long night. They'd spent the evening on the phone hitting up family and friends for loans and donations, calling their banks' twenty-four-hour lines to cancel certificates of deposit, and selling their stocks through the Internet. That yielded a hundred thousand, which was a long way from the two million they needed. But it was business hours again. The next few hours would make the difference. They planned on trading in their cars today and meeting with the bank on how much they could borrow.

As Scott padded down the stairs, Sheils let himself in. He frowned at Scott's appearance. He'd put on a sport jacket over a button-down shirt and a tie, a notch up from his usual office attire, but he had to look the part today. If he was selling his story to the paper, then they'd need pictures. He couldn't look like a total wreck.

"Going somewhere?" Sheils asked.

"Yes. The *Independent* is going to contribute to the ransom in exchange for my story."

"You're selling your story?" Sheils said scornfully.

"Yes, I need to raise a ransom and they need a headline."

Scott wasn't about to get involved in a pissing match. He brushed by Sheils on his way to the garage. Sheils stopped him and called to Guerra.

"Agent Guerra is going with you."

"I don't need a babysitter."

Sheils flashed Scott a look that said privacy had ended at 2:35 p.m. yesterday. "I wasn't giving you a choice. You don't go anywhere without an escort. This isn't just a kidnapping. It's a grudge. Sammy's abduction may only be the beginning of what he's got in store for you."

Guerra led Scott to one of the bureau cars parked in front of his house. The moment Scott ventured outside his door, the media clamored for a sound bite. Sheils and the SFPD uniforms kept the reporters and cameramen in check.

Sheils pulled a couple of sawhorses aside and Guerra drove through the gap. Scott's colleagues from TV and newspaper swarmed Guerra's car. They slapped microphones and digital recorders against the windows. Their collective voices exploded into unrecognizable noise. He recognized the hunger in their expressions.

Guerra accelerated away and fell in with the morning traffic. Congestion slowed their progress. On the radio, DJs tried to make light of Sammy's kidnapping. Scott switched it off.

"Sheils really doesn't like you. You want to tell me about it?" Guerra said.

"Ask your boss."

"I'm asking you."

Scott guessed she was sizing him up to see what kind of man he was. At least she was objective. He needed people like Guerra.

"The Piper contacted me. He wanted his story told and he wanted me to tell it, so I did. The *Independent* brought in the FBI. The Piper insisted I act as intermediary. I even delivered the ransom."

"But you weren't talking to the Piper. You were talking to Mike Redfern."

Redfern's face appeared in Scott's mind. "Yeah, I'd been talking to a dumb wannabe."

"You were duped. You all were. It was hardly your fault."

If it was only that simple, he thought. "Your boss has just cause to detest me. When Redfern first contacted me, he told me not to involve the FBI and I agreed. I met with him in Golden Gate Park." They'd stood across the park from each other, talking on cell phones. Redfern talked while Scott took notes. Scott had made a big deal of the park meeting in his article. The Piper had obviously read it. He placed Nicholas Rooker's body dead center in the no-man's land between where they'd been standing. "I didn't contact Sheils until after that meeting. Sheils believes if I'd brought him in at the beginning, they would have caught Redfern that night and the Piper wouldn't have killed Nicholas."

Guerra was silent for the rest of the journey.

She grabbed a parking spot on the street and they crossed Mission, then fell in with sidewalk traffic. Sammy, the ransom, and the Piper preoccupied Scott's mind and he banged into some guy, lost his footing, and collided with the woman next to him. He regained his footing at the expense of the woman's. She went down in a tangled heap. He apologized and Guerra helped her up.

"Look where you're going," the woman tossed over her shoulder as she stormed off.

It was the best advice anyone had given him. He needed focus. His thoughts were directionless, pinballing off each other. Two things mattered. Sammy and the two million. When he raised the two mil, he got Sammy. He couldn't let what had happened to Nicholas Rooker distract him. It wouldn't happen to Sammy. He'd promised Jane.

As he and Guerra passed through the *Independent*'s hallways and offices, his colleagues fixed him with sorrowful stares. Some offered their condolences and best wishes and he accepted them with good grace. Their compassion did nothing to lift his spirits. It just reminded him of his hopeless situation. Guerra's hip-holstered automatic kept well-wishers to a minimum.

George Moran emerged from his office to meet him. He put one hand on Scott's shoulder and pumped his hand with the other. "Scott, I don't have the words."

George bundled Scott into his office. Guerra went to follow, but Scott put up a hand and shook his head. She frowned but didn't argue. George closed the door and adjusted the blinds. He pointed to his conference table in the corner of his office. Various papers were spread out across the table.

"Bodyguard?" George asked.

"From Sheils, with love."

"Not surprising." George slid the papers in front of Scott. "I'm not going to waste your time with details. It breaks down like this. The *Independent* will pay two hun-

dred and fifty thousand dollars for exclusive rights to your
story and the right to resell the story to other media out-
lets. The check's cut already. I just need your signature."

Scott didn't bother checking the contract. He plucked
the pen from George's hand, then signed and initialed.

George handed him the check. "I got it made out to cash."

"Thanks."

"Now for the hard part. Showtime."

They photographed him at his desk as well as shooting
more traditional portrait shots. Then he sat down with two
senior staff writers who quizzed him about the story so far
and the history of the Piper, Redfern, and Nicholas Rooker.
All this was conducted under Guerra's watchful eye.

It was strange being on the other end of a story. The reporter in him wanted to report on what was happening,
but the father in him had to focus on saving his son.

When it was over, George whisked Scott back to his office.
"I won't keep you long, but I wanted you to know that for
story balance, I've sent someone over to Charles Rooker for
a comment. His wife died last year. Cervical cancer."

"I didn't know."

"I hear the Piper wants two million. Is that right?"

"Yeah."

"That's a lot of money, Scott. Can you raise it?"

"I don't know. The FBI called to say they have a bank to
underwrite the ransom, but we need to put up collateral.
The house will cover most of it, but we're still half a million
short."

"The Piper must know you don't have that kind of
money—not like Charles Rooker and the others."

"This isn't just about the money. He wants to see me
sweat. He knows two million is out of my reach and that
I'll have to spend the rest of my life working off the debt."

"Indentured servitude." George pulled out a bottle of
Jack Daniel's from his desk. He offered to pour Scott a
glass. Scott declined and George put the bottle away.
"How's the FBI?"

"Tom Sheils still hates me."

George nodded. "I'm going to say something incredibly stupid, but I believe it has to be said. Stop blaming yourself for Nicholas Rooker. You aren't alone in your responsibility. When Redfern sold us his dog and pony show, I told you to go for it. In hindsight, we should have called the feds right away. We've all got a little shit on our shoes."

Scott owed George a lot. When the FBI had found Nicholas's staged corpse, Scott took on pariah status. The corporate level wanted him fired, but George fought for him. He argued that the *Independent* had elected to cover the story the way it did, not Scott. Everyone bore a responsibility. It was a fine argument, but fine arguments weren't worth shit when a scapegoat was needed. Thankfully, George had a strong reputation in the business and it carried enough weight for Scott to keep his job.

"I accepted my part in Nicholas's death a long time ago. I'd even begun to forget about him. I could walk through Golden Gate Park and not base my position on where the FBI found his body. What is eating me up alive is knowing that my mistake has put Sammy in peril."

"I just hope they catch the bastard this time."

Scott's cell vibrated in his jacket pocket. Instinctively, he reached for it, but knew something was wrong. His cell was clipped to his belt. The phone he pulled from his pocket didn't belong to him.

NINE

"Are you alone?"

The Piper's voice slammed a fist in Scott's ear, leaving him dazed. The Piper asked his question again. "No, I'm not," Scott answered.

"Then change that."

"Are you okay?" George asked.

"I need the men's room."

Scott burst from George's office with George in tow. Guerra sprang up from her seat. They pursued him across the newsroom. When he reached the men's room, they tried to follow him. Scott stopped them.

"I'm okay," he said. "I just need a minute alone."

They read his stricken expression as a sudden bout of nausea and backed off. Scott closed the door and locked himself in. He collapsed into a stall, the phone hot in his hand.

How had the Piper gotten the phone to him? He remembered the collision outside. Had the man he'd collided with slipped the phone into his pocket? Was that man the

Piper? He tried to conjure up the man's face in his head and came up blank. He hadn't taken much notice of him. His focus had been on the woman he'd upended. She'd been conveniently there to catch the ricochet. Maybe the Piper didn't work alone. It made sense. Kidnappings were hard to pull off solo. Then again, these two strangers could be totally innocent. Maybe the Piper had seen the woman go down and had pounced. Scott had felt a number of people brush by him when he helped her up. Any number of them could have been the Piper.

This was crazy. What did it matter who had slipped him the phone? The deed was done.

"I'm alone."

"Good, a few ground rules about this phone. It stays on at all times and you don't tell anyone about it. Not your wife and not Sheils. You always pick up. If you fail to comply, I will take it out on Sammy. Are we clear?"

Scott wanted to reach down the phone and tear out the Piper's throat. He ground his teeth together to keep his thoughts confined. "Yeah, we're clear."

"I thought we'd chat without Sheils and company listening in. How are you getting on with the ransom?"

"We're close," Scott lied.

The Piper whistled. "You've done well. I didn't think you'd get that much so quickly. I suppose you sold your soul to your newspaper."

"Anything for my son," Scott snapped.

"Don't get sore, Scott. This is business. It's not personal."

"Bullshit."

The Piper's electronic device disguised his voice, but not his tone. Anger and disgust cut through. "You're right, this is personal. You're the only person who can give me what I need."

"Money?"

The Piper laughed. "I thought you understood. I couldn't have made the message any clearer."

What's he talking about? Scott thought. *What message? What have I missed?*

"I misjudged you. You might not be the right person for this."

"For what?"

"For the real ransom demand."

Suddenly, the air disappeared from the room, leaving him light-headed. He was suffocating in the cramped confines of the men's room. "What do you mean?"

The smugness returned to the Piper's voice. "The money is only a diversionary tactic to keep the FBI busy. I don't want them getting in the way of our real business."

Scott was afraid to ask, but he had to. "Which is?"

"I have scores that need settling and you're going to be settling them for me. That's the ransom. Understand, if you tell the FBI about this, I'll kill Sammy. Fail to comply with my demands, I'll kill Sammy. Do anything to annoy me, I'll kill Sammy. And, Scott, I won't be as compassionate as I was with Nicholas. Sammy will know pain like he knows breathing and he'll know that his father caused it all. Do I make myself clear?"

Scott felt sick. This was his fault. His doing. It wasn't fair. Not to Sammy, Jane, or Peter. "Let Sammy go. Take me. I'll do whatever you want me to, but let my son go."

"Scott, it doesn't work like that. Killing you in the most painful of ways would be very satisfying, but it wouldn't sate me, not fully. I'd get hungry again the moment it was over. I need something substantial. Seeing you squirm will satisfy me. Are you squirming now, Scott?" He paused for an answer that didn't come. "C'mon, Scott, don't be a spoilsport. Admit that you're squirming."

"What do you want me to do?" Scott asked.

"I want you to find Mike Redfern."

Scott and Guerra drove back to his house. He held the check from the *Independent* in his hand, its value worthless.

The two million was window dressing. The Piper wanted his pound of flesh torn from Scott, not cut. How the hell was he going to find Mike Redfern? Worse still, how was he supposed to do it under Sheils's nose?

It was obvious the Piper wanted him to suffer, but how much? Did the Piper even want him to succeed with this demand? Finding Redfern might be an act of futility designed to provide an excuse to kill Sammy. Scott's stomach clenched at the thought, forcing him to lean forward.

"Are you okay?" Guerra asked.

"Yeah, fine."

She didn't look convinced. "You look terrible."

"It's just the stress. I'll be fine when I get out of this car."

The media were still waiting when Guerra pulled onto his street. SFPD cleared a space for them to pass through. A Mercedes S600 filled his driveway. The owner's identity became apparent the moment Scott stepped from the car.

"What is the significance of Charles Rooker's arrival?" a reporter asked.

"Are you going to apologize to him, Scott?" another demanded.

Nicholas's father? Scott didn't need this on top of everything else. Rooker had called Scott a hero after he'd announced contact with the Piper. He hadn't called him anything after Nicholas's death. Scott couldn't imagine what the man wanted, not at a time like this. He ignored the questions and disappeared inside the house.

He found Sheils and Brannon seated at the dining table in deep conversation with Jane and Rooker. They stopped when Scott walked in. Jane jumped up and engulfed him in a hug.

"Charles is giving us the two million. We have Sammy's ransom, Scott."

Rooker rose from his seat. When Scott had last seen him,

he had been a big man in every sense—height, girth, and persona—but he wasn't anymore. The death of his son and the loss of his wife had diminished him. Scott had contributed to this man's decline. It made Rooker's gesture all the harder to stomach.

"Scott, this is a terrible thing," he said.

"I don't know what to say. Mr. Rooker, why are you helping us?"

Rooker smiled and pumped Scott's hand two-handed. "I can't stand by and let that man terrorize another child the way he did Nicholas. Our differences mean nothing as of today."

A lump grew in Scott's throat, cutting off his air and his words. He didn't know what to say to Rooker. He'd ruined this man's life, robbing him of his only child. Scott didn't deserve this. This man's generosity humbled him.

"Thank you. I'll pay back every penny."

Scott's emotions got the better of him and he broke into tears. He released Rooker's hand to hug Jane. She was the only thing holding him up. He wept for Sammy, Nicholas, and all the people he was going to betray by working for the Piper. The fist clutching at his insides tightened its grip.

"It's okay, baby," Jane cooed. "This is a good thing."

It took a minute for Scott to regain control. He sat next to Jane. She held his hand under the table, squeezing it tight.

"I'd like to caution you about paying the ransom," Sheils said.

"Why?" Jane demanded.

"As soon as you pay the ransom, Sammy is no longer of value."

"Not paying the ransom got my son killed," Rooker said.

"We're paying the ransom," Scott said. *For all the good it will do*, he thought.

Sheils conceded without fuss. "I can't stop you. I can

only advise you," he said. "Now that we have the ransom covered, the banks will work very quickly."

"I've already spoken with my bank," Rooker said. "They're preparing the money now."

"That won't be necessary," Sheils said. "The bureau has ties to a number of banks. They keep specially prepared kidnap cash aside for us. We have several million dollars' worth of nonsequential bills recorded. We'll exchange your bills for ours. Even if the Piper detects our tracking devices, we know every one of the serial numbers."

"Tracking devices?" Scott said. "I'm not taking any chances with Sammy's life."

Scott realized too late how that must sound to Rooker, having taken risks with his son's life.

"The Piper already knows we're here. He just has to switch on a TV."

Scott couldn't make out if there was a slam aimed at him in that reference, but he didn't care.

"The Piper would think something very strange was going on if he didn't find any tracking devices," Brannon said. "We want him to focus on the trackers and not our other tactics."

"You do want him caught, don't you?" Sheils asked.

"All I care about is Sammy."

Jane squeezed his hand again, her signal to him to cool down.

"So, what are these trackers?" Scott asked.

"We have a variety," Brannon said. "We'll have them built into the drop bag and the paper bands as well as between the bills."

"You're saying these are decoys. What else do you have planned?" Jane asked.

"We'll have surveillance teams in the air and on the ground," Sheils said. "We'll have a number of ways to catch the Piper."

Rooker's expression turned stern. "How is any of this

different than what you told me eight years ago? You didn't catch the Piper then."

Sheils shifted in his seat. "There were complications last time."

"You mean Redfern?"

"Yes."

"Redfern had no involvement in the other kidnappings. What's your excuse there?"

"Mr. Rooker," Sheils said, "I understand your frustration with our failures."

"I don't think you do."

"Charles," Jane said, "please hear him out, for Sammy's sake."

This seemed to soothe Rooker and he relented.

"Technology has changed since the Piper's first kidnapping. Our procedures are more refined and this kidnapping is different from all the others. I believe that's the thing that's going to trip up the Piper."

"How so?" Rooker asked.

"The Piper has singled out Mr. Fleetwood. This is personal, which means it's emotional for him. His won't be as fixed on the prize as with previous kidnappings and that's how we'll get him."

Rooker nodded and smiled. Scott got the feeling that he didn't entirely believe in Sheils's plan. Scott felt the same way. The Piper was too well organized to fall prey to his own emotions.

"Let's hope you're right, Agent Sheils," Rooker said. "For Sammy's sake."

Peter wandered into the dining room. Scott's stomach lurched at the sight of Sammy's twin. To see Peter was to see Sammy. Peter was a constant reminder of Sammy's abduction.

"Hey, kiddo," Scott said.

Peter came over to the adults and Scott slipped an arm around his shoulders.

Rooker got up from his seat and approached Peter.

Rooker's movements were relaxed, but Peter retreated from the property developer.

"It's okay," Jane said. "Mr. Rooker is a friend."

Peter glanced at Scott for confirmation. Scott nodded that everything was cool. Peter still looked wary, but stayed his ground.

"Friends don't call me Mr. Rooker. They call me Charles." Rooker knelt before Peter. "You must be Peter."

Peter nodded.

"I'm here to help you get your brother back."

"Are you with the FBI?"

Rooker shook his head.

"Charles"—Scott found it hard calling Rooker by his first name—"is lending us the money to get Sammy back."

"Not lending. Giving. Banks lend money. Friends give it."

Jane released Scott's hand to palm away a tear.

"Mr. Rooker," Sheils said, "we need you to come to the bank to sign for the money."

"Of course." Rooker stood. "I think it might make a nice outing for Peter."

Peter's eyes went wide. "Can I?"

"I don't know," Jane said, but Sheils shrugged.

"Sounds like a plan," Rooker said.

Peter took Rooker's hand, his trepidation now forgotten.

The meeting was breaking up and Sheils was issuing instructions to his team and explaining the procedure to Rooker when Scott's cell phone rang. He pulled it off his belt and checked the caller ID. The display showed George Moran's number.

"I need to answer this," he said to Jane. "It's George."

Jane frowned.

"I'll just be a second." He shifted to the living room. "Yes, George."

"Rooker is at your house. What's going on?"

"He's putting up the ransom."

"That's fantastic."

Scott didn't know who'd responded—George, the friend, ecstatic that the ransom was raised, or George, the newspaper editor, ecstatic with a great human-interest angle for the story.

The Piper's cell phone vibrated in Scott's pocket. Scott started at the sensation and panic rushed through him. What was the Piper playing at? He had to know he'd be in the company of the FBI. Didn't he want Redfern? If the Piper carried on screwing with him like this, he'd blow it and he'd have to find the bastard himself. There was no way he could answer the call, not with George on his other phone.

The Piper had said to always answer the phone. There was enough hubbub in the house to disguise the cell's vibrating, but a second's lull and someone would hear it. He couldn't let it continue ringing. He had to switch it off, but if he did, the Piper would hurt Sammy. If someone discovered the phone on him, then Sammy was dead. The choice was simple. He slid a hand into his pocket and pressed the phone's END key. The cell stopped vibrating and he thought he'd puke.

"Can you get Rooker to meet with us?" George asked.

"We're just leaving for the bank."

"Can you bring him by afterward?"

He needed time alone to find Redfern, and George had just given him his excuse. "Charles, the *Independent* would like to interview you. Could you come by the paper after we're done at the bank?"

"Why?" Sheils asked with suspicion.

"Because of Mr. Rooker's generosity."

"It would be my pleasure," Rooker said. "I want people to know why I'm doing this."

"We'll meet you at the *Independent*'s offices," Scott said to George and hung up.

"I'll have a car brought around," Sheils said.

"No," Jane said. "I don't want Peter riding around in police cars with men with guns. He needs stability and familiarity. We'll go in ours. You can follow."

As they headed toward their cars, Scott tried to look pleased when all he could think about was what the Piper was doing to Sammy.

TEN

Scott stood at the entrance of the bank vault. It looked utilitarian compared to the gleaming examples found in the movies. Still, Peter was getting a kick out of being allowed inside. Bank staff had taken him and Jane into the vault while Brannon supervised the two million being counted out and bagged. According to Sheils, the money would remain with the bank until the drop.

Sheils sidled up next to Scott. "Unbelievable, isn't it?"

Scott thought he meant the immense amount of wealth being put aside for him until he noticed Sheils's gaze was on Rooker. The property developer was sitting at a desk behind the tellers. Rooker was on the phone while he and the bank manager examined a computer screen.

"What is?" Scott asked.

"That man is putting up the ransom for Sammy, despite what you did to his son."

Scott guessed Sheils's goading wasn't going to let up. He kept a tight grip on his temper. He wouldn't give Sheils the satisfaction of losing it in public. "I didn't do anything to his son."

"You're right. You didn't. That's what killed him."

"There's one thing we can both agree on."

"And what's that?"

"Charles Rooker is a better man than the both of us put together."

Rooker and the bank manager concluded their business with a joke. Rooker rejoined Scott and Sheils. He clapped his hands together and smiled.

"We have the Piper's ransom," Rooker said. "Now, shall we tell your newspaper how he can choke on it?"

"Yes," Scott said.

They drove to the *Independent*. As they entered the building, Peter announced he was hungry, so Jane took him in search of a restaurant with Brannon in tow. George Moran set Rooker up in the boardroom with the reporting team. He even managed to entice Sheils into the interview. Suddenly, Scott found himself unattended.

He'd been wondering how he'd wangle some alone time to check out Mike Redfern's whereabouts for the Piper and now he had it. He estimated he had an hour at the most before George had enough to work up a story. Was an hour enough to find Redfern?

He grabbed a city directory and disappeared inside George's office. Redfern had owned a house in Piedmont at the time of his conviction, but had sold it to pay his legal fees. Scott logged on to a Web site listing property information and ran a search for Mike Redfern. The database came up blank on all fifty states. Considering the kind of legal fees Redfern had run up, Scott doubted he could afford real estate anywhere.

The only person who had stood by Redfern was his younger brother, Richard. Richard was listed and Scott called him on the Piper's cell. The phone wouldn't be traced back to Scott and knowing the Piper, it wouldn't trace back to him either.

While the phone rang, he worked up a cover story. Considering the purpose of his call, he couldn't identify himself.

"Richard Redfern."

"Mr. Redfern, my name is Sims and I'm trying to locate your brother, Mike Redfern, regarding outstanding college loans."

"College loans?" Richard said skeptically.

"Yes, he obtained two loans in connection with his CPA accreditation."

"Bullshit."

"Excuse me?"

"I'm getting pretty sick of you people harassing me in an attempt to contact my brother about this damn Piper business. Leave us alone."

Richard hung up before Scott could say anything more.

So he wasn't the only one trying to find Redfern. No doubt every news organization in the country would be seeking a quote from him.

Scott didn't know who else to try. There were people he could contact—Redfern's parole officer, staff writers at the *Independent*, even a couple of contacts in the SFPD—but they were all off-limits. If he were to contact any of these people, it would get back to Sheils. Whoever Scott contacted had to be independent and outside of the authorities.

Scott ran a search for Redfern on the *Independent*'s archive. All the stories kicked up by the search dated back to Redfern's capture, arrest, and trial—except for one. The most recent story dated back to a year ago and covered Redfern's release. The story went with a "man who hoaxed the *Independent*" slant, which would have been hard to pull off with Scott's byline, so Dale Murphy had covered it.

The photograph accompanied the story. It showed Redfern being met at the prison gates by a man identified as Kenneth Katz. According to the story, Katz was a friend. The article featured a quote from Katz saying, "Mike has done his time and now he wants to live his life in peace."

Katz sounded like a stand-up guy, until Scott ran a search on him. Katz had sold his story to the *Independent*. He wasn't Redfern's childhood buddy. He'd been his cell mate for three years. Katz was a small-time crook from all accounts, Redfern's only friend.

Scott looked across the newsroom at Murphy's desk. He wasn't there. Scott went over and took a seat. He asked casually if Murphy was around and got a no. He feigned disappointment. He didn't want Murphy interrupting him.

Murphy was old school. He kept all his contacts on two twin spindle Rolodexes—contact info for almost a thousand people. Scott looked up Katz's name. There was no address, just a San Francisco phone number. He scribbled the number down and dialed it when he returned to George's office.

"Yeah," a less than interested voice answered.

"Kenneth Katz?"

"Yeah. Who is this?"

"It's the *Independent*. I wanted to talk to you about the latest Piper kidnapping." Scott did well to sound upbeat and professional and not like a parent coming apart at the seams.

"You mean you want to talk about Mike." Sudden interest entered Katz's tone.

"Yeah, I was hoping to get a quote from Mr. Redfern."

"Five hundred bucks."

"Excuse me?"

"You want Mike's contact info. It'll cost you five hundred bucks."

Some pal, you are, Scott thought. "Okay. Come to the *Independent* and I'll have your money."

"No, no, no. You come to me."

Going to Katz wasn't an option. Sheils and Rooker would be through with their interviews in less than half an hour, closing his window of opportunity. Scott didn't know when he'd get the chance to be alone again. "If it's a question of transportation, I'll spring for a cab to bring you here."

"It don't work that way, friend. You want something from me, you come to me."

"I don't really have the time to make the trip. It would be so much more convenient if you could swing by here."

"No doubt, you'd consider it a personal favor."

"I would."

"I don't do favors. It don't pay."

What a prick. Scott couldn't believe this guy was flexing his muscles over five hundred bucks. His gut told him to blow the guy off, but he needed Redfern's information.

He checked his watch. He guessed he had twenty-five minutes before Sheils came looking for him. "Okay, where do you want to meet?"

Scott left George's office and crossed the newsroom floor. He walked in the direction of the men's room. No one engaged him beyond a head nod or smile. He returned the greetings while praying Sheils wouldn't suddenly appear.

He took the stairs to avoid bumping into anyone and slipped from the building through the parking lot. He was thankful Jane had insisted on driving their own car to the bank. He got behind the wheel and drove to the location Katz had given him. He hit the ATM on the way and withdrew the five hundred.

Scott parked in a red zone on the corner of Bryant and Gilbert. He didn't see Katz and couldn't afford to wait. If he could get this over and done with, he stood a slim chance of getting back before Sheils finished his interview. He pulled out his cell and punched in Katz's number.

"I can see you," Katz said in his lazy tone.

Scott scanned for him and still didn't see him. "Where are you?"

"Leave the wheels. I'm in the alley across the street."

Scott spotted a service alley for a building. Dumpsters blocked a clear view of anyone lurking within. It bore all the hallmarks of a trap. Scott groaned.

He left his Honda with its hazard lights flashing. He jogged across the street, but slowed when he entered the alley. He called Katz's name before venturing beyond the alley's mouth.

Katz stepped out from behind a Dumpster. He was an

untidy mass of flesh, barrel-chested and thick-necked. He ambled toward Scott with his hands down and away from his sides.

Scott brought out the wad of bills from his pocket. "I've got your money."

Katz snatched the money and counted through the bills. "I'm going to need more."

"We agreed on five hundred."

Katz pocketed the five hundred. "That was until I realized who you are. Your face is all over the news, Scott. Now, why would you be interested in contacting Mike Redfern when your kid is in the Piper's clutches?" He shook his head. "It stinks, Scott. It stinks worse than this alley."

Scott bridled against his anger. This small-time creep had put it all together in a matter of minutes. God knew how quickly Sheils would join the dots if he got wind of this. "How much do you want?"

"It depends what you want Mike for."

"How much do you want?" Scott repeated.

"Watch the tone, Scott. Just remember who is calling the shots."

"How much?"

"Ten thousand." Katz smirked. "To begin with."

The smirk and the "to begin with" tipped the balance. Scott was already living under one threat. He wouldn't live under another, especially from the likes of Katz.

"No," Scott said. "Five hundred is what we agreed to and five hundred is all you're getting."

Katz's smirk developed into something ugly and he brushed past Scott on his way to the street.

Scott didn't know why he hit Katz. Maybe it was his need to strike out at someone when he couldn't strike out at the true source of his pain. All he knew was it felt good when he drove his fist into Katz's kidneys. Scott expected the big man to absorb the blow and turn on him, but instead he crumpled, collapsing against the side of a Dumpster. Katz possessed more bravado than muscle. Scott pushed him down and kept him in place with a glare. "You're going to give me Redfern's address and phone number."

Katz nodded and reached into his jacket pocket, but pulled out a switchblade instead. He slashed the air with the knife and Scott leapt out of the blade's arc.

Scott had made an error. He'd jumped deeper into the alley, putting Katz between him and his escape. He knew he was faster than Katz, but the narrow alley and the Dumpster constricted his escape route. He could outrun Katz, but not his knife.

"You just doubled the payment," Katz snarled and held the knife out at Scott.

Katz struggled to his feet, his bulk working against him. He rolled onto all fours, putting his knife hand on the ground. Scott saw his opportunity. He sped forward, stamped his foot on Katz's knife hand, and kneed him in the side of the head. The impact cut Katz's strings and he went down hard.

Scott dropped his weight on Katz's back, forcing the air form his lungs. He wrenched the knife from his hand and pressed it against his throat. "Got any other surprises?"

"No. Just the knife."

Scott patted him down anyway and found nothing.

He yanked Katz's head back by the hair and jammed the knife against the underside of his throat. He pressed so hard the blade nicked the skin. "There's a man out there who has my son. He's likely to kill him even if I pay him the ransom. Do you think I have time for your petty bullshit?"

Katz didn't answer.

"I asked you a question."

"No," he stammered, "you don't have time."

"Now we understand each other. Do you have Redfern's address?"

"Yes."

"Then give it to me."

Scott climbed off Katz's back and stood back.

Katz rolled over and fumbled in his pocket. He yanked out the cash he'd just extorted. His hands shook so badly he dropped the money. He gathered it up and offered it to Scott.

"That's yours. You earned it. All I want is Redfern's address and number."

Katz reached into his pants pocket and brought out a folded scrap of paper. He held it out to Scott with a shaky hand.

Scott snatched the paper and unfolded it. It listed an address in Lebanon, Oregon, but the name on the paper confused him. "Who's Ray Banks?"

"A new identity. That's what I do. Social Security numbers. Driver's licenses. You come to me. Mike got threats after he got out. He needed a new start and I gave him one."

Scott snatched the paper away. "This better be right."

"It is. It's golden."

Katz looked too scared to be lying, but Scott had to make sure. He yanked him up into a sitting position and slammed him against the Dumpster. "You aren't going to warn him and you aren't going to tell anyone else. If you do, I'll know and I'll find you. Do you understand me?"

Scott left Katz slumped against the Dumpster, sitting in his cash. He tossed the switchblade in the Dumpster on the way back to his car. He got behind the wheel and started shaking. He'd done what the Piper had asked, but he didn't like how he'd done it. Intimidation was something the Piper did. Not him. He had to cling to that. No matter what happened from now on, he had to remain himself.

He reexamined the scrap of paper with Redfern's new identity and address written on it. Never had a death warrant looked so cheap.

His cell phone chirped and he pulled it out. Time had

run out. He had messages from George, Jane, and Sheils. There was no going back to the *Independent* building. He had no excuse for his absence. He needed to be found elsewhere and he thought he knew just the place.

ELEVEN

The Piper turned into the driveway of his ranch and stopped his F-150 in front of the house. He'd last been up here a couple of months ago to repaint the exterior of the house, but the place had changed. This was no longer his weekend retreat. It was a place where he kept children against their will. It had taken him a long time to dislodge that feeling after Nicholas Rooker. Now all that hard work was ruined. Nicholas seemed like only yesterday.

He let himself into the house, bringing his provisions with him. He stacked the pantry and refrigerator with enough food to last him close to a month. He didn't expect to be here that long, but it paid to be prepared. He'd brought a camp stove and a bottled water supply in case of a standoff scenario.

He removed the leather pouch from a box and unzipped it. The 9mm automatic slid into his hand. It felt cold and alien in his grip, but regained familiarity as he loaded the weapon and stuffed it into his waistband.

He propped the door open and opened up all the windows to flush out the stale air. He liked the ranch house but rarely used the place. It was the reason why he'd gotten rid of the horses. He had someone in to take care of them when he wasn't around, but it wasn't fair to the animals. He left the house to air and crossed over to the paddock. He'd considered trying again, moving to the ranch and renting out his home in Half Moon Bay, but Sammy Fleetwood had changed everything.

Sammy's kidnapping was a mistake. Sheils would stop at nothing this time. He'd turn the country upside down before he gave up on the boy. There was a chance he'd find this place—not now or even soon, but in the long term, there was a chance.

He didn't like the morbid funk settling over him, and he turned away only to be faced with another reminder of the past. The barn stood pressed up against the line of eucalyptus as if trying to hide. It could try all it liked, but it couldn't hide. It had all happened in the barn.

He recalled the faces of the kidnapped children he'd kept here. They'd been good kids. None of them had caused him any trouble, although the chloral hydrate helped there. His recollection settled on the face of Nicholas Rooker. On the night he'd smothered the boy, he had gotten the feeling Nicholas sensed something wasn't right. Nicholas stared right into him as if he were made of glass. Had he known what was going to happen? Had he seen the hypodermic filled with a larger than normal dose? The Piper wasn't sure, then or now. He just knew Nicholas was extra quiet when he had gone into the barn that final night and placed the pillow on the boy's face.

He walked over to the barn and inspected the padlock before opening it. No one had tried to force it. The last thing he needed now was a vandal or someone looking for a place to crash. He swung the doors open. He flicked on the light switch and a single fluorescent tube ignited but failed to illuminate the vast expanse beyond a dull glow. He didn't need light to find what he was looking for. He'd built it, carved it out by himself.

He grabbed the shovel leaning up against the wall and picked a spot on the ground. He dragged the shovel's blade across the dirt. After eight years, it had settled, squeezing out the air to form a crust. He chipped away at the soil, finding the corners easily. He continued until he exposed the entire edge, then shoveled the few inches of dirt off the surface of the trapdoor.

He reached for the iron ring and took a breath before yanking the wood door open. He snapped on a flashlight and aimed it into the depths. The light fell upon the cramped confines. The cot had stood up well over time.

His trepidation left him in that instant. He'd feared time had corroded him and blunted his razor-sharp instincts, but just one look into the cellar changed that. Eight years of dormancy was eradicated. He was the Piper. He was and always would be. The realization struck him hard, harder than he expected. When the moment had passed, he descended into the cellar where he, the Piper, kept other people's children.

TWELVE

Eight years earlier

The rain hammered down on Golden Gate Park. The downpour beating the ground sounded like galloping racehorses. Storm clouds had cloaked the city since dawn.

Scott followed the police officer through the park toward the gathering. He hunched his shoulders against the relentless rain, but it still got underneath his jacket collar. Its chilling touch failed to match the chill he felt from within.

The congregation turned toward him when he drew close. Several of the assembled cops and agents cursed him under their breath.

"Let him through," Sheils barked and a path opened.

The FBI agent glared at Scott. His hands were balled into fists and looked ready to throttle him. Instead, he pointed at Nicholas Rooker's body lying on the ground.

The boy was too still to be asleep. His chest failed to rise and fall and he didn't flinch when the raindrops pounded his eyelids. He looked so peaceful. His head lay on a small rise in the park as if it were a pillow. His legs were placed together with his hands interlaced across his stomach and he held a note between his dead fingers. The rain's onslaught had smudged the words, but they remained legible.

YOU'RE TO BLAME

Sheils grabbed a fistful of Scott's jacket and jerked him closer to the corpse. None of the assembled law enforcement agents made any attempts to stop him.

"I wanted you to see this. The Piper and I don't agree on much, but we do agree on one thing." He pointed at the smudged note. "That boy is dead because of you."

"I know," Scott said. He was responsible. There was nothing he could ever do to repair the damage. Nothing.

"Good. Then write about that."

Charles Rooker's voice cut through the roar of the rain. "Where is he? I want to see him. I want to see my boy."

Sheils released his hold on Scott with a shove.

Rooker burst through the perimeter of people surrounding his dead son. Alice Rooker and two agents restrained him. The moment he set eyes on his murdered child, his legs went out from under him. Only the agents prevented him from falling to the ground.

"Oh God, Nicholas."

He shook free of the agents and crawled on all fours toward his son. Alice stood transfixed at the sight of her dead child, frozen in place by her own private hell, but the sight of her husband crawling on his hands and knees galvanized her. She dropped to her knees next to him and embraced him.

"Stop, Charles. Please, just stop."

The sight of the Rookers turned Scott's stomach and he had to look away.

Sheils swept in to stop Rooker from contaminating the

crime scene. With Alice's help, he lifted the man to his feet. The harsh tone he'd used with Scott only moments before had been replaced with sincere compassion.

"Mr. Rooker, I can't let you touch him. We need to check for physical evidence. I don't want the Piper getting away."

"Why'd he do it? I was going to pay. He didn't have to do this."

Sheils struggled for a reply. How did anyone answer a question like that? How did anyone explain someone like the Piper?

"Let me hold him," Rooker pleaded.

"I can't. Not yet. You can be with him later."

Suddenly, Rooker became aware of himself and the people around him. He stood back from Sheils and palmed away the tears.

"You're right," Rooker said. He spotted the note, seemingly noticing its presence for the first time. He nodded. "We are to blame. We let Nicholas down."

The present

Scott stared at the spot where Nicholas Rooker had lain. He'd visited here several times over the years when guilt compelled him to return to the scene of the crime. If he focused on the spot, he swore that he could make out the indentation left in the ground by Nicholas's body. It was crazy, he knew. There was nothing after eight years to mark the event other than his memories of that night.

His fingers rubbed the Piper's cell phone in his pocket, willing it to ring. He'd phoned the Piper repeatedly on the drive to the park, but the son of a bitch hadn't answered. Scott had the information the Piper wanted. The scrap of paper was a slug of molten lead burning in his pocket and he wanted to hand it over. The Piper was fucking with him for no good reason other than that he could.

A vehicle crunched to a halt on the street behind him followed by someone's hurried footsteps. Scott didn't have to turn around to know it was Sheils.

Revisiting Golden Gate Park gave him a cover story. What could he say? I skipped out for twenty while I beat the crap out of a known associate of Mike Redfern? No, he needed something else. The park gave him that excuse. But he hadn't come here purely to muddy the waters. As the messages on his phone mounted up and he saw his options running out, something occurred to him. Something Sheils needed to understand. Eventually, he'd answered the phone and told Sheils where to find him.

Sheils clamped a hand on Scott's shoulder, spinning him around. "What the fuck are you playing at?"

"I wanted to get away."

"This isn't the time to play damn fool games."

Scott turned away and returned his stare to where Nicholas had lain. "You spend too much time worrying about me and not enough about the Piper."

"I have to worry about you. You're the target of this bullshit or haven't you worked that out yet?" The fight went out of Sheils and he fell in next to Scott and examined the same spot. "I come here every year."

Scott looked at Sheils. This boy's death had scarred so many. The scars might look different, but they were all made with the same weapon. "I come now and then. Usually when I think about it all."

Sheils nodded.

"Jane doesn't know I come out here. I'd appreciate it if you didn't tell her."

"Sure."

"You still blame me for the boy's death."

Sheils opened his mouth to object, but stopped. "Yes. Yes, I do. You got caught up in the drama and the attention. You did nothing malicious, I know, but you were a contributing factor in Nicholas's death."

"I know and I live with that every day. You don't have to keep following me around like a criminal."

Scott knew the hypocrisy of what he was saying, but he also knew that even if the Piper wasn't pulling his strings, he would be telling Sheils this.

"I'm just doing my job."

Scott shrugged the weakhearted answer away.

"You're to blame," Scott said. "Remember those words?"

"Of course."

"You think that note was meant for me and the kidnapping of my boy is my punishment, yes?"

"You said it."

"Consider this. I'm not the only one who screwed up the Piper's plans."

"Sharing the blame. How nice of you."

"For Christ's sake, Sheils, put your grudge aside for a second. It's blinding you to something here."

Muscles in Sheils's jaw flexed. "And what's that?"

"You bought into the hoax too. We all did and it cost Nicholas his life. I don't think he's just punishing me. I think he's punishing you too. This was aimed at everyone who fell for Redfern's game."

"Bullshit."

"Maybe. But you're here again, stumbling about in his tracks, making the same mistakes you did on all the other investigations. If the Piper gets his way, you're going to lose again. But this one is going to crush me as well as you. My son's life is in your hands. You get it wrong and the blame will be all yours."

Scott knew he'd struck a nerve. Sheils's jaw muscles flexed as if he were gearing up to challenge the accusation, but he bottled his reply. "Let's forget the blame game, I need to get you home. The negotiator has arrived. He wants to prep you before the Piper calls back."

THIRTEEN

An air of expectancy greeted Scott when he walked through the door with Sheils. The Piper could call at any time. Sheils's people were dialed into their tasks at hand. Jane, Peter, and Rooker were deep in conversation with Brannon. Scott had no objections to Rooker's presence. He had a stake in this kidnapping. His two million dollars was sitting on the dining table in a black duffel tricked out with the latest in tracking devices. More importantly, Scott owed the man. Rooker had never seen closure. Sadly, he wouldn't today.

Scott's arrival ended the conversation with Brannon. Jane wanted an explanation for his disappearance. He promised answers later, but she wasn't about to be sidelined. Sheils came to Scott's rescue, interrupting the burgeoning argument.

"Scott, this is David Dunn, our negotiator. He's worked a lot of kidnappings. He's top-notch."

Dunn was around forty, with a boyish face but a heavily receding hairline. He smiled benevolently. "I'd like to talk through some tips with you to help us the next time the Piper calls."

"Sure."

Like Sheils the night before, Dunn stressed the importance of building a relationship with the Piper. The greater the bond between the kidnapper and victim, the greater the chance he wouldn't take action against his captive. Scott saw this working in more conventional kidnappings, but not on this occasion. There were much more powerful motives at work here.

"Keep the dialogue going," Dunn said. "It gives us time to trace his location as well as building the bond between the two of you."

Scott had built his bond already. Just not the kind Dunn was hoping for.

"Really push to speak to Sammy," Dunn said. "You need to personalize the conversation. Remind him that you're the target, not Sammy."

"But don't worry if he doesn't let you speak to Sammy," Sheils said. "Our belief is that the Piper keeps the children stored at a second location during the drop."

"How do you know that?" Jane asked.

"He made a mistake during negotiations on the fourth kidnapping. When proof of life was asked for, he remarked that the child wasn't with him."

This information gave Scott no comfort. He hated to think of Sammy stashed somewhere alone, but then again, if he was alone, then the Piper couldn't hurt him.

"I'd like to do some role-play to see how you handle yourself and suggest improvements," Dunn said. "Sound good?"

It sounded like a waste of time, but it beat waiting for the phone to ring.

Dunn made a stage production of the role-play. Scott would play himself and Sheils, the Piper. Dunn handed Scott and Sheils a cordless handset and sat them down in front of each other. Scott felt like he was part of some bad improv skit.

Dunn pulled out a stopwatch and clicked it. "Take it away."

Sheils put the handset to his ear. "Have you got the ransom?"

The words sent a chill through Scott. Sheils injected the sense of superiority that the Piper did. It startled him how easily Sheils took on the Piper's persona.

Scott's sense of role-play disappeared. This was serious. This was his one and only chance to practice before the real thing. He tuned out the burble of conversations coming from the FBI agents in the other rooms. He saw only himself and Sheils.

"I want to speak to Sammy," Scott demanded.

"Very good, Scott," Dunn said. "Avoidance. I like it."

"I asked you a question. Have you got my money—yes or no?"

"I have the two million. I have every penny you asked for."

"Nice," Dunn said. "Substituting twelve words when only one was necessary."

"Good. I want you to bring the money to the corner of Market and First."

"Will Sammy be there?"

Dunn gave Scott the thumbs-up.

"I know what you're doing."

"What's that?" Scott asked.

"Stringing this call out."

"I just want to know that my son's okay. Please don't hurt him. He's innocent in all this. This is about what I did to you."

"No, you're playing with his life, but that's what you like doing, isn't it?"

The remark hit Scott hard. Sheils fixed him with a stare that cut through steel.

"Watch for this, Scott," Dunn said. "The kidnapper is trying to control you through fear."

Sheils's remark had nothing to do with demonstrating

the Piper's need for control. It was all Sheils. He wanted to needle him. Scott should have guessed Sheils would retaliate for running out on him.

"I would never play with my son's life."

Sheils leaned forward in his seat. "No, you'd do that with someone else's son."

"Fuck you."

Dunn cleared his throat.

"Not so cocky now," Sheils said.

"Where's my son?"

"Safe and sound, as long as I get my money."

"You'll get it."

"Come alone. If I see cops, I'll kill the boy."

"You harm Sammy, I'll kill you."

"Then you'd better do the right thing, hadn't you?" *Click.* Sheils put the handset on the coffee table and stood.

No one spoke for a moment. Everyone was focused on the role-play. Dunn broke the deadlock.

The negotiator cleared his throat. "Very good, Scott, you did very well at stringing out the conversation. Don't take the harsh comments to heart." He eyed Sheils. "The kidnapper will say hurtful things when cornered." He checked his stopwatch. "A minute twenty. We could get a significant trace in that time, but if we can get that to two or three minutes, we'll have him."

Scott put the handset down on the arm of the chair. He'd been gripping it so tightly it had marked his hand.

"Let's take five and try that again."

Sheils pounded him for another hour, but it had the desired effect. Scott got better at turning the conversation personal and putting Sammy on a pedestal. Eventually the punishing role-plays with Sheils lasted seven to eight minutes.

When it was over, Brannon came over to Scott. "We expect a call in the next hour. You should get changed. You'll be doing a lot of running tonight."

Scott was getting changed into sweats and running

shoes when the Piper's cell vibrated. He went over to the bedroom door and locked it.

"You didn't pick up earlier."

"I was busy finding Redfern."

"And have you?"

Scott sat on the bed. "Yes. He's changed his name to Ray Banks and lives in Lebanon, Oregon. I have his address."

"Oregon? That's a problem."

"Not for me. I got you his information. Now I want Sammy back."

"Scott, I think you've misunderstood."

"What do you mean?"

"You have to bring Redfern to me."

The Piper was crazy. What he was asking was impossible to achieve. Scott saw the machinery coming apart and any chance of recovering Sammy disappear.

"The FBI won't let me take a piss without their company. They aren't going to let me run off to Oregon to find Redfern," Scott said.

"Let me worry about that."

"They're gearing for the money drop tonight."

"The FBI isn't running this. I am. The drop will follow my schedule. Not theirs."

Scott went to speak, but heard footsteps outside his door.

"Scott, it's Dunham. Agent Sheils needs to go over tactics."

"I'll be down in a minute," he called out.

"Okay."

"Poor Scott. His back is up against the wall. Don't worry, it's going to get a lot worse before it gets better."

Scott accepted that he wasn't in the driver's seat. While the Piper had Sammy, he was a passenger. "What do I do?"

"Wait for my call."

Scott didn't like the helpless situation the Piper had put him in, but what choice did he have? He pocketed the phone and rejoined everyone downstairs.

The effort taken to descend the single flight of stairs robbed Scott of his remaining energy. He was exhausted already and this nightmare was less than thirty hours old. The whole scenario seemed so unfair. The FBI was just jumping through hoops. He debated telling Sheils about the Piper's facade, but the Piper said he'd know if Scott squealed. How? Was his house bugged? Did the Piper have an agent on his payroll? As much as he wanted to play straight with Sheils, he couldn't.

It was all so futile. They couldn't beat this bastard. He already had the drop on them for tonight. The money wasn't even part of the equation. The FBI was just pissing in the wind. Scott wondered how many mistakes Sheils's team had made, how many kidnap victims had died, and how many bungled money drops they had been part of to attain their proficiency.

The phone rang and the house went silent. Brannon came into the kitchen. "It's him."

Sheils guided Scott into the living room. Dunn reeled off last-minute advice. Scott glanced over at Jane, who had Peter in her arms. Rooker had his arm around her shoulders and was telling her everything was going to be okay.

"Any time you're ready, Scott," Sheils said.

Scott picked up the phone. "Hello."

"Do you have the ransom?" the Piper's garbled voice asked.

"Yes, I have it all. All two million. Just as you asked."

Dunn flashed him the thumbs-up.

"Well done. I didn't think you'd do it."

Scott glanced over at Rooker. "I have a generous benefactor."

"So I see. You must feel like a real shit considering what you did to him."

Scott contained a sneer. It sounded as if Sheils and the Piper went to the same insult school. He wouldn't be goaded. "I want to speak to Sammy."

"When I've got my money."

"No, now."

"Don't make me hurt your son, Scott."

Dunn performed a hand gesture. He looked as if he were pulling taffy between his fingers. He was telling Scott to stretch the conversation out.

"I want assurances that Sammy is okay."

"I don't hurt kids. That's your assurance."

"You hurt one last time."

Scott glanced over at Rooker. He hadn't wanted to go here, but he couldn't ignore an opening like that. Rooker squeezed out an encouraging smile.

"You left me no option, Scott."

"You always had an option."

"Scott, would you like me to recite the Pledge of Allegiance?"

"What?"

"I'm guessing the feds and the phone company are working hard to trace this call. You insult me, Scott. Really you do. I'm going to make this simple. I'll contact you later about where to leave the ransom."

Scott didn't have to act. Panic tore through him. He knew this was part of the Piper's plan, the diversion to get him to Oregon, but it still scared him. The Piper was a runaway train with everyone else trapped aboard. "No, I'm ready to do this. I've got the money. Just tell me where."

"Eugene, Oregon. Be there tomorrow."

The line went dead.

FOURTEEN

"Oregon? There is something seriously wrong here," Sheils announced.

After calming down the Fleetwoods and Rooker, he'd brought his key team back to the division office and called in Travillian to regroup. The Piper had thrown everything into confusion. Brannon, Dunham, Guerra, and Travillian sat around the windowless confines of the situation room.

"Maybe the Piper is trying something new," Brannon suggested, "and he's taking the runaround to the next stage. This might be the beginning of a state-hopping tour."

"What would be the purpose?" Travillian asked.

"It stretches our resources. As soon as we've got a team on the ground, he's got us on the move again," Brannon said.

It was a nice theory but Sheils didn't buy it. "It stretches his resources more than it does ours. Also, he's upping the risk by shunting this kid from state to state."

"That's if the kid isn't already in his final location," Travillian said. "He may lead us from Oregon to Idaho to Utah when the kid's been in California all along."

Sheils hadn't brought in Travillian just because he was

the boss. Sammy Fleetwood's kidnapping was gathering momentum in the media. Heat from Washington was only a call away and there was only so much time they'd get before results were demanded, not just expected. He'd brought in Travillian because he possessed great instincts.

Dunham tapped a printout. "The rough triangulations we've gotten on his WiFi connection so far have put him in the East Bay, San Jose, and the city."

"Which illustrates my point. He's making us run while he stays still. He's conserving his resources and energy while expending ours."

Fatigue pressed down on Sheils's shoulders like a lead weight, leaving him feeling tired and old. He was losing the Piper again. Everyone considered him the foremost expert on the Piper because he'd been allowed to fail a lot. He went to the coffeemaker and poured himself a cup to inject some life into his body.

Sheils retook his seat to silence. There was another scenario, but no one wanted to be the first to mention it. He decided that he'd point out the pink elephant in the room.

"Sammy Fleetwood was taken thirty-six hours ago. We all know what that means. The recovery rate after twenty-four hours dwindles. So we're looking at the possibility that he's dead."

"The Piper doesn't kill if you play ball with him," Brannon said.

"But this isn't a normal Piper kidnapping," Sheils said. "The Piper wants to hurt Fleetwood. What better way than to put him through some epic goose chase and then deliver his kid to him dead?"

"That's one hell of a fuck-you," Travillian said.

"Why the eight-year gap?" Dunham pressed. "I mean the Piper could have spent a year planning this snatch, but an eight-year gap has to be significant."

The answer jumped out at Sheils. It surprised him that he hadn't thought of it earlier. "Yes and no. The gap is significant, but the meaning might not be. The Piper might have been in prison serving a sentence for something totally unrelated. I want a check on known and suspected kidnappers who've been paroled in the last twelve months after serving six to eight."

"I'll get on it," Dunham said.

"What about Scott Fleetwood?" Travillian asked. "He played on the wrong side of the street with Redfern. Any belief he'll do it again and work with the Piper?"

Sheils knew Travillian had aimed this question at him, but he kept quiet. He wanted to hear what everyone else had to say before he responded.

"I don't think he's working with the Piper," Brannon said. "I don't see what he has to gain."

"I don't even see how," Dunham said. "The guy hasn't been out of our sight."

"He'd have to be pretty dumb to contact the Piper now, but that's not to say the guy hadn't preplanned this," Travillian said.

Sheils wondered if Travillian had said this for his benefit. Everyone knew how he felt about Scott Fleetwood. The point bore more validity if someone emotionally uninvolved said it.

Guerra stopped doodling in the margins of a legal pad. "My read on the guy is that he's genuinely frightened by what's going on. I think he gives off a cagey air, but that's because of his past association with the Piper. The guy is embarrassed. His family is on the rocks because of his bad instincts and who comes to his rescue? Rooker, the one person he screwed over. The guy's in turmoil."

"Your thoughts, Tom?" Travillian said.

Sheils had thoughts, but doubts too. About Scott. About himself. He was trying to give Scott the benefit of the doubt, but he was struggling with his feelings. He wanted Scott to pay for the past and he would love to find a link between him and the Piper, but that thinking would get him into trouble. He'd already blown it once, compounding his unprofessionalism by losing it in front of his team and Scott's family. He could pretend there wasn't anything to it, but he was twisting the blade for cheap thrills. Was this the behavior of a senior bureau agent? No. The smart thing to do was to remove himself from the investigation, but he couldn't. He wanted the Piper. If his capture dragged Scott down too, so be it.

"I don't like the man, but I don't think he's deceiving us," he said and left it at that.

If there was a right answer to Travillian's loaded question, Sheils had reeled it off. Travillian smiled, genuinely pleased with the response.

Travillian capped his pen and folded his case file. "I think we're playing this one by the book. I have no complaints. The Piper is a first-class sadist who's putting the Fleetwoods through hell. We just have to make sure he doesn't do the same to us. He's obviously got a new wrinkle to his plan, but what I'm hearing is that we have a lot of theories and no clear lead as to his identity."

Travillian paused. No one disputed his claim.

"Okay, then. Let's wake up some people in Portland. It sounds like you're off to Oregon."

Sheils's predawn departure didn't faze Scott. He'd barely slept and was glad of the excuse to get up. From the looks of Sheils, he hadn't gotten much sleep either, but his casual dress of a polo shirt and chinos softened his usually officious FBI persona.

"Ready?" Sheils asked.

Scott hefted his overnight bag to show that he was. He hoped this trip didn't warrant an overnight stay.

Sheils led him out to a convoy of three unmarked bureau vehicles. Brannon, Dunn, and half a dozen other FBI agents Scott recognized made up the traveling team. Guerra was the notable absentee. She remained at the house to keep watch over Jane and Peter.

Jane came out after him with Peter in tow. Scott hugged him before embracing her. Usually, public displays of affection embarrassed her, but not this time. She clung to him as if they were stranded on a cliff ledge. He kissed her and she made it linger long after it should have ended.

"Bring Sammy home." It wasn't a plea, but a demand, born from fear and need.

"I will." He knelt before Peter. "Think about something neat we can do for Sammy when he comes home."

"Sure, Dad."

"We need to hit the road," Sheils said.

Sheils put Scott in his car with the two million sitting on the backseat as the only other passenger. Obviously Sheils wanted some alone time with him during the drive. Scott braced himself for a long ride, but Sheils kept it civil and coached him on the ransom drop. Just as Scott thought Sheils was going to leave the third degree out, he brought out the thumbscrews.

"Why do you think the Piper's bringing us up here?"

"I don't know," Scott replied, his lie sounding convincing.

"It doesn't make any sense to move the switch to Oregon."

"I don't know what he's thinking."

"Sure you don't?"

"How many times do I have to tell you I'm not involved?" The lie tasted bitter on Scott's tongue.

Sheils didn't answer and let the point fester for the rest of the journey.

Scott ran the Piper's demand over and over in his head, trying to make sense of it. He expected him to find, abduct, and deliver Redfern to him, all under the nose of the FBI. How the hell was he going to do that? Sheils wasn't going to let him out of his sight for a second. Even if he were to give the feds the slip, he didn't have a vehicle to go after Redfern. The Piper was leading the FBI to Eugene, but Redfern lived an hour away from there by car. Scott didn't stand a chance.

The motorcade stopped for gas outside Redding. Scott hadn't realized how stiff he'd gotten until he had to walk. The air came ice-cooler chilled and Mount Shasta dominated the skyline. Sheils and his agents clustered around the gas pumps to talk. Scott caught the "feds only" vibe and made for the restrooms. He locked himself into the bathroom and called the Piper.

"Where are you?" the Piper asked.

"Redding. Look, there's no way I can ditch the feds."

"Do they suspect you?"

"No, but I don't go anywhere unescorted."

"Don't worry about that. I'll take care of them."

"How?"

"Always the reporter, Scott," the Piper lamented. "It's all what, where, when, why, who, and how. None of that applies. There are no answers. You're in the realms of faith now."

"With you as God?"

The Piper chuckled. "Now you're learning. For now, play along with everything the FBI tells you."

"But how am I supposed to lose them?"

"You'll see."

Those words preyed on Scott and carried him all the way to Eugene.

The FBI Portland division played host with the support of the Eugene resident agency and had set themselves up in a hotel room. After introductions, there wasn't a lot to do other than wait. The hours of inactivity wore Scott's nerves raw. The feds burst into action when the Piper called at 8:00 p.m. They were a machine. Scott couldn't see how the Piper was going to dispose of them.

"Any time you're ready, Scott," Brannon said.

Scott took his cell phone from the agent. Sheils listened in on a separate phone.

"Scott, I want you to drive out to South Twenty-eighth Street in Springfield and stop when you reach a bridge," the Piper said.

"Where's that?"

"Ask Sheils. I'm sure he's got a map. You've got twenty minutes. If you're not there, I start hurting Sammy."

"No, don't. I'm on my way." But Scott was talking to a dead line.

Play along, the Piper had told him. Obviously, it was time to start playing.

"Right," Sheils said. "This is it. Everyone knows their role. Now let's catch this bastard."

The agents pounced on phones, hurling calls out to a covert operations team holed up at a separate location. Conversations went on with the phone company, the local and state cops, and the pilots they had in the air. Sheils had this thing covered. There was no way in hell Scott was giving them the slip. The Piper had screwed up this time. He was getting too cute for his own good. Hands pressed into Scott's back, ushering him out of the hotel room and down a corridor.

Brannon flung open the door to the hotel's underground parking lot. One of the Portland agents clambered behind the wheel of a brand-new, white Toyota Camry. He popped the trunk and hopped from the car, leaving all the doors open.

Sheils put the duffel with the two million on the front passenger seat. "The trackers are activated. You're good to go."

Sheils introduced Jim Taggart. "He'll be with you every step of the way, Scott."

Taggart was a Portland FBI agent. He was in his mid-thirties and athletically built. He was clad in a blue-black jumpsuit with a heavy Kevlar vest and the letters FBI across the front and back in gold letters. A fearsome automatic pistol hung off his belt. He climbed into the Toyota's trunk and squeezed himself into its tight confines.

Scott had objected to having an agent ride with him, but Sheils overruled him. Now Scott feared for Taggart. The Piper would surely put a bullet in the agent when he found him. Scott didn't want another victim on his conscience.

"I've got your back, Scott," Taggart said, before an agent slammed the trunk lid down.

"Right, Scott," Sheils said. "This is where the wild-goose

chase begins. He's going to bounce you all over town. Don't worry about it. Just follow his directions. The car has a tracker on it. Our teams will be close behind. Okay?"

Scott nodded and got behind the wheel. He'd lost the feeling in his fingers and toes, despite gloves and thick gym socks.

"You've got eighteen minutes to make the rendezvous," Brannon said.

Scott stamped on the gas and the Toyota's tires shrieked on the polished concrete floor. The Camry came equipped with a GPS navigator. The navigator's mechanical voice called out directions and he followed them.

He eyed his rearview mirror and scanned the road ahead for the legion of FBI vehicles Sheils's teams had on tap. He saw no one and wondered how far back they had distanced themselves from him.

"Scott," Taggart said from the trunk, his voice muffled. "Got bad news, buddy. The cloud cover is too thick for the plane to see us on the ground."

That was one factor taken care of. Scott tried to sound disappointed.

"Don't worry about it, Scott. It's a minor setback. We've still got the surveillance teams, the electronics, and me. The Piper isn't going anywhere."

"Great."

Scott pressed ahead. The directions took him out of the college town. Trees soon outnumbered properties. Even if the clouds hadn't been a problem for surveillance aircraft, the tree cover would have been.

He drove east across Eugene crossing I-5 to get to Springfield. He passed through the town and into an unincorporated area. This made sense. There'd be fewer witnesses and it forced the FBI to hang back, but their trackers covered that slack. The Piper was still far from shaking Sheils.

The navigator told him he'd arrived at his location, which proved to be a stretch of road crossing over a creek with an aged Buick Century parked on the bridge. His heart skipped a beat when he saw the car. Was this it? Was this where he was supposed to act? Was he coming face-to-face with the Piper? His heart rate quickened and his blood pressure spiked.

He pulled up behind the Buick. The Toyota's headlights lit up its driverless interior.

"What's happening, Scott?" Taggart asked.

"I've reached the destination. There's a car parked in front. It looks empty."

Scott checked the dashboard clock. He'd arrived a minute early.

"Agent Sheils says don't leave the car. Wait for the call."

Scott peered into the gloom and wondered how close the Piper was to him. If he was close by, he would know that he'd arrived and call, but he didn't. He was waiting until the prearranged time. That still didn't mean he wasn't hiding in the trees. Scott grabbed the cell from the passenger seat and thought about the Piper's cell hidden in his pocket. He wondered which would ring first.

The moment the twenty-minute time limit expired, his cell burst into life.

"What do you see before you?" the Piper asked.

Scott decided the Piper wasn't close if he was asking this question. "An old Buick Century."

"Well done. You made it. Take the Buick. The keys are in the ignition. But first, dunk the ransom money in its bag."

"What?"

"Scott, the money is electronically tagged. Don't deny it."

"What about the money?"

"That's the great thing about the U.S. dollar. Waterproof inks. Now dunk the money in the creek. Sammy's waiting."

The creek crossed under the road. Scott dragged the duffel from the car and clambered down the bank. He slipped on the wet grass and fell on his face. He held on to the cell, but the ransom flew from his grasp. The duffel rolled end over end, crashing into the water. He gathered himself up and snatched the duffel before it disappeared from sight. He let the money remain submerged to ensure that every one of Sheils's tracking devices shorted out. After a minute, he yanked the duffel free. It weighed twice what it did dry. He hefted the bag over to the Buick and dumped the sopping mess on the backseat.

"Now what?" Scott asked.

"Drive your car into the creek."

Scott hesitated because of Taggart. "Is that necessary?"

"Does it matter? It's not like there's someone hiding in the car with you, right, Scott?"

Scott didn't answer.

"I have my eyes, Scott. I'll see if you let him out. Now drive the car into the water."

Scott cursed and ran back to the Toyota. This was why he hadn't wanted anyone riding with him. Sheils couldn't blame him for this. Taggart was on his own.

"Scott, toss the phone too. You won't be needing it."

Scott hurled the phone into the creek and got behind the wheel. He jerked the selector into reverse and backed up.

"I'm sorry, Taggart," he called out.

Taggart said something, but it was lost under the screaming tires when Scott floored the gas. The Toyota leapt forward. Scott kept the door pushed open with his hand, popped the trunk release, and bailed out when the Camry crashed over the curb. He struck the ground hard, sending jolts of pain up his arms and legs.

The Toyota smacked into the water. The impact stopped the car's forward motion. Water engulfed the car's cabin, dragging it down. The fast-moving current grabbed the sinking car and dragged it along.

Scott didn't wait to see if Taggart had escaped from inside the trunk. He needed to delude himself. Taggart was okay. He was already swimming to the surface, safe and well. Scott got behind the wheel of the Buick and powered away.

The cell phone in his pocket rang.

"Where to now?" he asked the Piper.

"Drive to Oakridge. You've got thirty minutes. Follow the directions I left," the Piper said and hung up.

A map lay on the passenger seat next to him. He flicked on the dome light to check his directions, never once taking his foot off the gas. Oakridge took him into the Williamette National Forest. His destination seemed simple enough, as long as the FBI didn't intercept him.

Could they, though? Taggart was gone. The trackers were disabled. The plane couldn't fly. No one had a make on this Buick or the cell. What tricks did Sheils have left? He'd have to fall back on the old-fashioned methods, roadblocks and cops on every street corner. Sheils couldn't mobilize in time. Scott would slip through his net. He relaxed his grip on the steering wheel and settled into his drive.

As he racked up the miles, his thoughts drifted from his driving to Jane. She had to be worried sick. He wished she were here. He considered calling her and eyed the cell phone.

He didn't see the moving van until it was too late. It ran the stop sign and broadsided the Buick. The impact sounded like a bomb going off inside the car. The Buick's passenger side deflated and glass showered the car's cabin. Scott's head slammed into the door pillar and his vision clouded over, leaving him dazed. Reflexively, he held on to the steering wheel as if he had some control over the car. Both vehicles slithered to an untidy halt on the roadway.

Panic ripped through Scott's haze. The Buick was toast. He couldn't deliver the ransom. The Piper would kill Sammy. The idiot truck driver had killed his son. He scrambled amongst the broken glass for the cell phone. He had to call the Piper and explain.

The truck driver jumped down from the cab and shouted at Scott to get out. His tone suggested the accident was Scott's fault.

Scott's fingers fell on the cell and he grabbed it. He shouldered the door open and clambered out. Blood from a head wound ran into his eyes. He palmed it away. "I need a ride."

"No, you don't," the trucker said.

The trucker was wearing a ski mask. Everything clicked. This was no accident.

"Scott, get the money," the Piper said.

Scott staggered over to the rear door, wrenched it open, and rescued the still sodden duffel.

The Piper carried a plastic gas can with a rag trailing from the end. He lit the rag and tossed the can on the Buick's backseat. Fire spread through the car.

"Where's Sammy?"

"Wrong question."

The Piper drove a fist into Scott's gut. The air in his lungs evaporated and his legs buckled. He leaned against the Piper for support.

A sharp pain flared in his neck for an instant. He looked up to see the Piper jerk a hypodermic free. The drug worked with immediate effect, unconsciousness claiming him before he struck the ground.

FIFTEEN

Sheils walked up to the burning wreck of a Buick sedan sitting in the middle of the road, halfway between Jasper and Pleasant Hill. The stink of melting radials ensured that he didn't get too close to the conflagration. Smoke curled from the tips of the flames into the night. The symbolism wasn't lost on him. The ransom drop was going up in smoke. Yet again, the Piper had grabbed an operation and turned it on its head, and he was forced to pick up the pieces. State and local cops were setting up roadblocks without any idea of who or what they were looking for. The word *shambles* sprang to mind.

Brannon had arrived before him and was in a heated discussion with the fire chief. The fire chief wanted to put the fire out. Brannon wanted the fire to burn itself out so as not to disturb any physical evidence. Sheils inserted himself into the argument and the fire chief backed down. Not that the argument was necessary. The fire was almost out, having eaten through the car's interior. Most of the paintwork was scorched off, but what was left was dark blue. It looked as if they'd found Scott Fleetwood's second car.

"Fleetwood?" Sheils asked.

Brannon shook his head. "Could be in the trunk."

Possible, but unlikely, Sheils decided.

"Look at this." Brannon showed Sheils skid marks coming from the Buick's right. "It looks as if a large truck T-boned him."

Sheils recognized the tactic. The kidnapper has the ransom courier jump through hoop after hoop. The courier becomes comfortable with the procedure, and then the kidnapper turns everything on its head with a smash and grab. The courier is left immobilized while the kidnapper makes off with the ransom. That tactic had served many kidnappers well. The Piper had added a new wrinkle. Usually the kidnapper took the ransom and left the courier.

"This doesn't make sense," Brannon said. "Why take Fleetwood and the money?"

"To make him squirm."

"Do you think he's offered to swap places with his kid?"

"It's possible. Tell the fire chief to put this out. I don't think we're going to learn anything here."

They stood back to let the firefighters do their job.

Sheils's driver came over with a radio unit in his hand. "They've picked up a signal."

Sheils listened to the tech back at the resident agency explain that they'd picked up a faint stationary signal from one of the money band trackers only three miles from the wreck. Finally, a break.

Sheils instructed the deputies to secure the car after the fire department had put out the fire. He and Brannon raced over to the location of the signal. On the way, he requested that the Lane County sheriffs set up a perimeter around the signal to prevent anyone from getting in or out of the area.

Sheils set up a staging area two hundred yards from the signal's coordinates. It came from a parking lot belonging to an out-of-business burger joint. The place was in darkness and nothing moved inside. As soon as he saw it, he got a sinking feeling.

"Maintain positions. I'm going in," Sheils told Brannon.

He approached the burger joint with a flashlight in one hand and his 9mm drawn. He wasn't afraid. He knew what he'd find, but he could feel his pulse racing in his temple. Even in the darkness, he spotted the immobile shape lying in the parking lot. He recognized it immediately and jogged over to it. He raised his weapon as a precaution and slowed his pace when he got within ten feet of the object. He shone the flashlight on it.

It lit up the duffel, minus two million dollars.

"All clear," he said into his radio.

The task force closed in. Sheils ordered an agent to book the duffel into evidence and have it examined. He doubted they'd get any usable forensics from it, but they had to try.

"He might have the money, but he can't spend it," Brannon said. "I've released the serial numbers. Banks, stores, they're all expecting them."

Brannon's cell rang a couple of seconds before Sheils's did.

Sheils unclipped the phone. As he lifted it to his ear, he watched Brannon's expression change. It froze, then cracked as if someone had dropped a heavy weight on it.

"Agent Sheils," Sheils said.

"Long time no hear, Agent Sheils," the Piper's disguised voice said.

"How did you get this number?" Sheils's question came out tight and clipped.

"Mrs. Fleetwood gave it to me," the Piper replied. "She's a very scared lady. She wanted details, but I spared her. Some things should be kept from the innocents."

"I couldn't agree more."

"I'm sure you have someone frantically telling you to expect a call. I thought I'd beat them to the punch."

Brannon hung up and hushed the agents around them. He motioned to a local agent to put a trace on Sheils's phone.

"Where's Scott Fleetwood?"

"He's with me."

"Is he unharmed?"

"For now, yes."

"Sammy Fleetwood?"

"He's good too."

"Are they together?"

"Agent Sheils, stop wasting my time. I have a simple message for you. Go home. When I've decided what to do with Scott, I'll call you."

Before Sheils could get his next question out, the Piper ended the call, severing any link to Sammy and Scott.

Sixteen

Scott awoke on his back in the middle of a field. It was still night. He sat up and a note tumbled from his chest. He opened the twice-folded sheet of paper. Written in black Sharpie and smudged by dew was a simple message.

FIND HIM

Printed out on the other side of the paper was a MapQuest map of the city of Lebanon with a circle around Mike Redfern's address. He pocketed the map and trudged across the field. When he reached the road, a sign welcomed him to Lebanon.

It took half an hour to find Redfern's tiny, ranch-style house on a dead-end street. Mildew streaked the ancient wood siding. The place looked so damp that it needed wringing out. Unkempt brambles and vegetation provided unwelcoming barriers to strangers. A worn gravel path marked out a driveway.

I'm here. Now what? He supposed he should have developed some sort of plan to apprehend Redfern, but none had come to mind. He was worn out and emotionally drained, which weren't the kind of credentials to boast of under these circumstances.

At first glance, Redfern didn't look to be at home. Scott tried the doorbell, but the lack of movement from inside the house confirmed his suspicion. He peered through the living room window and saw no one.

He considered breaking into the house. He'd lie in wait for Redfern armed with something sharp from the kitchen. Suddenly, he felt the heat of an unwanted stare burning into his back. He turned to find an elderly man standing on the sidewalk.

"Didn't mean to startle you," the old man said.

"That's okay." Scott jerked a thumb over his shoulder. "Do you know when Ray comes home? I'm supposed to be hooking up with him, but I think I missed him."

"You're not a close friend, are you?"

Scott held in his shock. "What makes you say that?"

"If you were close, you'd know he spends his evenings at Ed's Bar. Alone."

Scott nodded with sad understanding while he pieced together a cover story. "I was afraid of that. His family sent me. I'm a counselor. They're afraid his drinking is a problem again." He kept his distance. He didn't want the old man getting a good look at his face. "I'll see if I can catch him there, then. Thanks for your help."

The old man stood his ground, then asked, "Do you need directions?"

"In my line of business, you know where all the bars are."

The old man lingered on the sidewalk. To not move meant drawing attention. Scott couldn't put it off any longer and walked toward him.

Just as he got within good identification distance, Scott glanced skyward. "Looks like a rainy night."

The old man looked up to examine the sky and Scott breezed past. It was a cheap trick but it worked.

Scott looked up Ed's address in a phone book. The place

looked how he imagined—barfly territory. Style came in the form of neon signs for Budweiser and Miller glowing in the window. The interior wasn't much better. It relied on forty-watt bulbs and a couple of wall-mounted TVs for lighting. For a dive, Ed's was packed and conversation drowned out the TVs.

Redfern wasn't at the bar, so Scott searched the booths. He recalled how Redfern had looked when Sheils arrested him. Scott pictured this man, not the man whom prison had eroded. He would have missed him if he hadn't recognized the guilt in Redfern's face. It was the same guilt that plagued him.

Redfern had aged, looking nearer fifty than forty. He was twenty pounds lighter than Scott remembered. Age lines sliced his face more deeply than they should have. A ragged scar ran under his chin, disappearing behind his ear.

Redfern looked up at Scott from his beer. He showed no signs of recognition. That made things easier for Scott and he slid onto the bench seat opposite him.

"I don't like company," Redfern said.

Redfern had been a mild-mannered claims adjuster for an insurance company before his arrest. Not anymore. Hardness edged his words. His request sounded like a threat.

Scott had expected Redfern to be someone he could overcome easily, not a prison-hardened ex-con. He felt his confidence wane. "Do you remember me, Mike?"

"Yeah. I figured someone would come looking, eventually. Look, get something from the bar. We're drawing attention."

Scott bought two beers and put one in front of Redfern.

"How do you sleep?" Redfern asked.

Scott didn't have time for this, but decided to play along. Redfern wouldn't simply go with him to the Piper just because Scott said so, but he might if he got drunk enough. "Fine. I sleep fine."

"That's a whole lot better than me. You see this?" Redfern jerked his chin up and pointed to the scar. "Happened two weeks after I went to prison. An old door hinge sharpened into a razor. Anything can become a weapon if you have the imagination."

"Imagination is what put you there. Why'd you do it? You had to know you'd get caught."

Scott's remarks dulled Redfern's sharp edges. "You probably think I'm pathetic. Don't deny it. That's how I see myself looking back. Your dreams are all you have when you don't have anything. They help you get up in the morning, go to the day job, pay your taxes, and generally put up with crap, because those dreams could come true."

"And your dream was to be the Piper?"

"No. Not really. I wanted to be powerful. The Piper was powerful. His name meant something."

"But you knew things about the Piper that no one else did."

"Don't you think I researched him? To pretend to be him, I had to understand him. I carried out my own investigation. I saw the connections. Made assumptions."

Redfern blew Scott away. This guy, this nobody, with no police training had pieced things together from secondhand accounts. He didn't know whether to be in awe or disgusted.

"Did you keep any of your findings?"

Redfern didn't answer for a minute. "The FBI thought they got it all, but I kept copies."

"Could I see them?"

Redfern shrugged. "Everything's back at the house."

"Show me."

Scott followed Redfern out to an aged Ford Escort. The guy was over the limit, but Scott wasn't about to argue with him. Redfern drove them back to his small home. The house was cold and smelled musty.

"I've got the stuff in my study," Redfern said and disappeared into one of the bedrooms.

Scott went into the living room. Redfern owned the bare minimum. Something to sit on. Something to put his meals on. Something to watch for entertainment. A couple of picture frames sat on the mantel above the fireplace. Scott picked them up. One was a studio shot of a smiling woman in her early thirties. The other photo pictured a vacation shot of the same woman with a man and a couple of kids around Sammy's and Peter's age.

"My sister and her family," Redfern said, returning to the room carrying two bulging cardboard file boxes. He set the boxes down on the floor.

Scott set the picture frames back on the mantel. "Do you see them much?"

"What do you think?"

Scott let the subject drop. He opened up one of the file boxes and yanked a fistful of file folders free.

Redfern padded into the kitchen to make coffee while Scott sifted through the files. A lot of what Redfern had collected was what Scott expected—newspaper clippings, online news reports, and even videotaped recordings from *60 Minutes*, *Dateline*, and just about every other news magazine show on TV. Redfern went the extra mile with screen dumps from various Internet conspiracy sites. There was a lot of crap that wasn't worthy of Scott's time and he almost lost interest in what he had before him.

Then it got interesting.

One file revealed a transcript of telephone calls the Piper had made to the kidnap families, all on FBI letterhead. Redfern had annotated the transcripts and highlighted repetitive words said by the Piper. Essentially, he'd created his own Cliff's Notes on the kidnapper. No wonder everyone had bought his act.

"How did you get these transcripts?"

"When you tell people you're from the FBI, they tend to believe you," Redfern said proudly.

Scott set about putting the jumble of information into some semblance of order. He separated out the Internet bullshit. Any official documents, and there were a lot, he kept separated from the media stories. These were all of note, but the stuff Scott really wanted to get at was Redfern's own notes and the journals he'd put together. He'd managed to accurately mimic the Piper from reading between the lines.

"So," Redfern called from the kitchen, "why did you track me down? You never did say."

Scott expected the question. "You seemed to know a lot about the Piper, so I thought you might be able to help me get something on him."

Redfern returned to the living room carrying a mug of coffee in each hand. "Funny that you should come to me, when you've supposedly been abducted by the Piper."

Redfern stood over Scott with steam unfurling from the mugs.

"I escaped."

Redfern shot Scott a questioning look. "Is that right? And you came to me and not to the cops."

"Yeah, well, if I can give the feds any info, it'll help them stop him."

Redfern nodded. "So it was lucky you had my address at hand."

Scott had created a facade from spun glass. It was pretty to look at, but fragile as hell, flawed by beginner's errors. It stayed intact as long as no one touched it. Now it was crashing down. He anticipated Redfern's move a fraction of a second before it happened.

Scott dropped the papers and lurched out of the way of the hot coffee Redfern hurled at him. The scalding liquid slashed across one leg. He ignored the searing heat and scrambled across the couch.

Redfern jerked out a steak knife from the back of his pants and threw himself at Scott. He landed on Scott's back and both men bounced off the couch and crashed into the coffee table, upending it and all the stacks of paper Scott had placed on it.

Redfern locked his legs around Scott's waist and snaked an arm around his neck. He pressed the knife up against Scott's throat. "Do you think I'm that stupid, Scott?"

Scott held very still.

Redfern jerked Scott's head back. "I asked you a question. Do I have to give you a scar like mine to get an answer?"

"No," Scott croaked.

"Where's the Piper? Outside? Waiting?"

"I don't know."

Redfern dragged the knife an inch across Scott's throat. No additional pressure was necessary. The serrations took up Redfern's cause and the blade cut through Scott's skin. He felt the jagged edge invade his flesh and his blood run down his throat. He choked down a scream.

"Lie to me again and I won't stop," Redfern threatened.

"I'm not lying. The Piper sent me, but I don't know where he is."

Redfern repositioned himself to gain a better lock on Scott. He pressed his knees down on Scott's arms to pin them to the floor. Although Redfern had him, the man had no strength. His prison time and whatever life he'd led since had given him a certain intuition, but not physical power. His hundred-and-thirty-pound weight went only so far.

"And what were his instructions?" Redfern asked. "To kill me?"

"No. Just to bring you to him."

"But you don't know where the Piper is?"

"I have to call him."

Redfern had made the mistake of only pinning Scott's upper half. Scott's legs were free and he snapped them back. His feet slammed into Redfern's back, pitching him forward.

Free of the deadly threat, Scott thrust up onto all fours, bucking Redfern off. The force pushed Redfern into an untidy somersault, sending him crashing onto his back. Scott snapped to his feet. It was his turn to pin someone to the floor.

Scott was upon Redfern before he had a chance to recover. The Piper wannabe slashed the air with the steak knife. The blade sliced through Scott's sweatpants and slashed his right calf. He didn't stop to check the damage. He swept in and kicked Redfern in the face, snapping his head around and leaving him dazed.

Scott grabbed Redfern's knife hand at the wrist and twisted hard, until Redfern yelled out and the knife went slack in his grasp. Scott snatched the knife away and disabled Redfern with a kick to the ribs.

Suddenly feeling the pain in his injured leg, Scott staggered back, collapsing onto the couch. He examined the damage. He wouldn't need stitches if he taped it up tight enough.

Redfern groaned and squirmed on the floor.

Scott called the Piper and told him, "I have him. Where do I bring him?"

SEVENTEEN

Scott guided Redfern's Escort down the winding track toward the disused sawmill ten miles south of Redfern's home. Light spilled from windows and splits in the siding. He stopped the Escort next to a pickup, the only other vehicle there.

He put his hand on the pickup's hood. It was cool. The Piper had been here awhile. He'd have everything choreographed. Every move Scott made would have been anticipated before he even thought to make it.

He went to the rear of the Escort and popped the trunk. Redfern lay in the fetal position in the cramped confines. Scott had had a hell of a time fitting him in there. Unconscious and bound, Redfern had been a deadweight to lift, but he'd managed it. The ride from Redfern's house had been silent except for the drone of the car's engine and his thoughts. With Redfern so quiet for so long, Scott had feared he'd killed him, but two frightened eyes now stared back at him.

Scott leaned in, yanked the duct tape from Redfern's

mouth, and tugged the gag free. Redfern gasped for air like he'd been underwater.

"Don't bother screaming," Scott said. "We're miles from anywhere."

Redfern said nothing, putting all his effort into sucking air into his lungs.

"Now, I'm going to cut the tape around your ankles. Start any shit and it won't be me you'll have to worry about."

His words sounded cold. He didn't like the person he was becoming. He wasn't turning into the Piper, but a servant of the Piper without will or independent thought. It was a role he accepted for Sammy's sake.

Scott didn't wait for Redfern's answer. He sliced through the triple-wrapped tape around his ankles and hoisted him from the trunk. Redfern's legs buckled when he tried to support himself unassisted. Scott held him while he stamped the circulation back into his lower extremities.

"Let's go," Scott said.

Redfern hesitated and Scott pressed the tip of the steak knife into his back. As if he was a wind-up toy being started with a key, Redfern lurched forward. Scott grabbed a fistful of Redfern's collar in case he bolted. Now that he was so close to the exchange, he wasn't about to lose his ransom.

"You realize he'll kill us both," Redfern said.

Scott had accepted this eventuality. For his son's safety, it was a price he would pay willingly. If he were to die tonight, he hoped he saw Sammy beforehand. He wanted one last look at his child, a chance to tell him how much he loved him, his brother, and their mom. He wanted him to carry a message back to them, to tell them how sorry he was for this and how much he would miss them all.

"You don't know that," Scott said to pacify Redfern.

Redfern whipped around to face Scott, illuminated in the light from a busted window. His eyes scanned every inch of Scott's face. "You're crazy if you believe that."

"Whatever happens to us in there happens because we deserve it. We caused a child's death. Now we're being judged."

"By the person who killed the kid."

"Does it matter who judges us?" Scott said and spun Redfern back around. He marched him in the direction of the nearest door before his nerve gave out.

Redfern pulled on a side door that hung by one hinge. Generator-powered spotlights illuminated an area on the main floor between two large table saws. Instructions weren't required and Scott shoved Redfern toward the light.

"Are you armed, Scott?" the Piper asked. His voice came from high up in the building.

Scott held the steak knife aloft, then tossed it away.

"Is that all?"

"Yes."

"You wouldn't be lying to me, would you, Scott? A lie will get Sammy killed."

Sammy screamed out to illustrate the point. Until now, Scott had feared that Sammy was already dead and that all the hoops the Piper had forced him to jump through were an elaborate hoax. But Sammy was alive. Still not safe, but alive.

Scott lunged forward. "Don't you hurt him, you bastard."

"I'm coming down, Scott," the Piper warned. "Don't move."

His words nailed Scott's feet to the floor.

"Move from the light and I will put a bullet in Sammy's head."

"Daddy," Sammy screamed out. "Help me."

It tore Scott in two to hear his son in pain, but he stayed in the illuminated area.

A shot rang out. The bullet ricocheted off the concrete floor to Scott's left, but it wasn't intended for him. Redfern had tried to bolt. He hadn't gotten six feet. The warning shot kept him in place as successfully as the threat against Sammy had stopped Scott.

Footsteps rang out on a metal catwalk in the direction of the offices. The Piper, still dressed in black and face hidden by the ski mask, descended the stairs. He moved with the grace and speed of a dancer. He kept a gun trained on them, changing his aim with every step. He slowed when he reached the circle of lights. "There's two of you and one of me, but let's remember who has the gun."

From where the Piper had been, Sammy's whimper dripped down. Scott looked up in the direction of his son, imagining him tied up and helpless.

The Piper moved in close to Redfern and examined him. He cocked his head and looked Redfern up and down, like an animal trying to make sense of an object it had never encountered before.

Redfern stepped back and the Piper pressed his revolver to his forehead. Redfern winced and shrank from the weapon's touch, but he didn't move from his spot.

"So, you're Mike Redfern. You thought you could be me."

Redfern squeezed his eyes shut.

The Piper ground the revolver's muzzle against Redfern's head. "Didn't you?"

"Yes."

"What audacity. How did you, a spineless worm, honestly think you could impersonate me?"

"I'm sorry." Redfern broke into tears. "I'm sorry."

"Sorry isn't going to cut it. Your stupidity cost a child his life and cost me two million dollars. Now, I want to know what you're going to do about it."

"I don't know."

"You don't know? Scott here knew what to do. I said find me Mike Redfern and he did it. Now what are you going to do for me?"

"Anything. You tell me and I'll do it."

"Would you rob a bank for me, Mike?" the Piper berated. "And steal my money back?"

"Yes."

"Scott showed great initiative in tracking you down. I

need to know that I can expect the same from you. How would you do it?"

"I . . . I don't know."

"C'mon, Mike, I need better than that."

"Okay, okay, give me a second. I'd go in there with a gun and tell them to empty the vault."

"That's it—your master plan? You thought you could be me. Is that what I would do?"

"No," Redfern whimpered against the weapon, "you'd do better."

"Then you're no good to me. I'm better off sticking with Scott." The Piper tightened his finger on the trigger.

"I'll do anything. Just don't kill me."

"You're pathetic."

The Piper kicked Redfern in the back of the knees and he crumpled to the floor. Redfern spoke, but his words dissolved into an incomprehensible whimper.

The Piper's intimidation disgusted Scott. He could have intervened, but it wasn't his place. Redfern had to fight his own battle. Scott's gaze moved to the darkened heights. He stared into the darkness and tried to pick Sammy out of the gloom. The sawmill's acoustics bounced Sammy's sobs from wall to wall. Scott strained his hearing to pinpoint the origin. He couldn't be certain, but Sammy sounded as if he was in the farthest corner of the top level, probably in one of the offices.

"Scott, kill him."

The order shocked Scott from his thoughts, striking him with the intensity of a slap. Before he could object, the Piper pressed the gun into his hand. The revolver's chrome finish glinted under the spotlights. A clean weapon for a dirty job.

"C'mon, Scott, don't wimp out on me now." Twisted glee entered the Piper's tone. He'd shoved the blade between Scott's ribs and was twisting it yet again. "You've been a great ally so far. Don't fail me now. Sammy's life depends on it."

Scott looked from the gun to the Piper. A smile stretched the ski mask's opening.

"You can't, Scott," Redfern said.

It was an easy decision for Scott to make, under normal circumstances. But these weren't normal circumstances. If he let Redfern live, Sammy died. As much as he didn't want to kill anyone, he didn't have a choice.

"Scott, are you going to disappoint me?"

Sammy called out, "Daddy."

"I promise you that I will make Sammy suffer."

Scott pointed the revolver at Redfern.

Redfern's eyes went wide. "Scott, no."

Redfern expressed the kind of shock Scott would have expected if they were great friends or brothers, but they weren't. Scott barely knew him. They'd spoken eight years ago and again tonight. He owed Redfern nothing.

"I'm sorry, Mike. I don't want to do this, but I have to do the best for my son."

Redfern went to speak, but a dry heave cut his words off and disbelief spread across his face.

"Scott, you never fail to surprise me," the Piper said.

Scott took a step closer. At this range, he couldn't miss his target.

"I paid," Redfern said. "I served my sentence. My family shunned me. I had to change my name. I work a shit job. I live with the guilt every day. I paid my debt."

Redfern wasn't speaking to Scott or the Piper. He was just getting out what he needed to say before he died. He looked directly at Scott. His tears had dried up. His eyes burned with need. "I paid my debt."

"Scott, shoot this piece of shit. I'm tired of listening to him."

Scott regrasped the gun, working the weapon's ergonomically designed grip into the contours of his hand. It didn't want to fit.

"You'll have Sammy back the moment you pull that trigger."

Suddenly, the gun snapped into place in his hand like it had been handcrafted for him and him alone.

"Please, Scott," Redfern pleaded. "Don't do this."

"Scott, you're overthinking it. Just pull the trigger and all this is over."

The Piper thought he knew people so well. He thought he was the great puppeteer, capable of pulling anyone's strings. He was wrong. Scott swung the gun away from Redfern and aimed the revolver at the mouth hole in the Piper's ski mask.

"Do it," Redfern shouted, struggling to his feet. "Shoot him."

"You're making a big mistake," the Piper warned.

Anger filled his voice. Even face-to-face with a gun, the Piper had the audacity to be angry. After all the misery he'd brought to all those innocent people, he thought he was invincible enough to stop a bullet. The bastard sickened Scott.

"Shoot him," Redfern urged.

"Shooting me will be the biggest mistake of your life, Scott."

"I've already made the biggest mistake of my life. I consider this making up for it."

Scott pulled the trigger—and nothing happened.

Just as the realization sank in, the Piper stepped forward and drove a fist into Scott's face. An explosion went off in his nose and he saw only blinding light before he crashed to the floor.

The Piper snatched Scott's wrist and twisted the gun from his grasp. Redfern swept in to help, but the Piper backhanded him out of the way with the gun. The blow upended Redfern and he hit the floor hard.

The Piper jerked out a second gun from his waistband and jammed it in Scott's face. "You failed the test, Scott. If you'd pulled the trigger, it would have been over for you. You would have played your part and you could have gone home to live happily ever after."

Blood streamed down Scott's face as he struggled to get up, but the Piper forced him back down.

"Now I'm going to have to think of another punishment for you."

Scott's mind leapt to Sammy. He'd made another mistake and Sammy would end up paying the price. It was Nicholas Rooker all over again.

"No," he yelled out, forcing his way up.

"Yes," the Piper said and smashed the gun down across Scott's head.

Scott clung on to consciousness, but his grasp slipped off its slick surface. He heard a scream before a shot rang out, then nothing.

EIGHTEEN

Scott awoke as if ejected from unconsciousness and jerked upright. He half expected to be somewhere else, but he'd been left where he'd fallen. The Piper was nowhere in sight. Redfern lay on his back, shot in his face. The sight of the corpse first stilled Scott, then electrified him.

"Sammy," he yelled, his cry bouncing off the sawmill's cavernous walls.

He scrambled to his feet and bolted for the stairs. His shoes clanged on the steel steps. He called out his son's name over and over.

Sammy didn't reply.

Scott cursed himself for being so stupid. What had he been thinking when he pointed the gun at the Piper? The Piper wasn't going to hand him a loaded gun, leaving himself unarmed. Scott prayed the monster hadn't taken it out on Sammy.

Hitting the top of the stairs, Scott called out, "Sammy, it's Dad. Where are you?"

Still, Sammy didn't answer.

Scott kicked open the first office door in front of him.

The door swung back and crashed into the wall, cracking the frosted glass pane set into it. The office was deserted, long since stripped bare.

"What have you done to him, you bastard?"

Sammy called back. His voice was faint, dampened by fear. His cry came from the end of the mezzanine.

"I'm coming, Sammy," Scott called back. "I'm coming."

It was over. The Piper had gotten what he'd wanted and it was over. The mezzanine shook under Scott's crashing footfalls.

He arrived at the office and heard Sammy whimpering. The door was locked, so he smashed into it with his shoulder. His momentum and the rotten door frame sent him hurtling into the office, robbing him of his balance. He crashed to his hands and knees. Sammy's voice continued to call out to him, but his son was nowhere to be seen. There wasn't any furniture to hide behind, just dirt and leaves blown in through the busted windows.

"Sammy, where are you?"

"Daddy, don't let him hurt me."

Scott followed the sound of his son's voice to the corner of the office. The single red eye of a minidisc player looked back at him. He went over to it and picked it up. Nausea left him light-headed. Sammy had never been here. It was another of the Piper's tricks to torture him. That meant Sammy was somewhere else, alone, hidden away. Scott couldn't imagine how frightened he must be. Anger boiled up inside him. He hurled the minidisc player at the ground and it exploded into pieces, the disc flying out and extinguishing the red eye.

"You piece of shit," he shouted at the Piper.

Scott descended the stairs. Redfern's corpse radiated its presence thanks to the lights surrounding it. Scott approached the man he had abducted.

The Piper had shot him only once. The bullet had entered his head just above the right eyebrow. Its destructive power had shattered the bone, collapsing his eyebrow ridge. A single red bead streaked his temple and disappeared in his hairline. This rated minor damage in comparison to the exit wound. A trail of devastating gore splashed the floor for ten feet beyond where Redfern lay. Luckily for Scott, Redfern lay on his back, robbing him of the sight of what remained of the back of his skull.

Scott couldn't stop staring at the scene and felt his nausea again. He wrenched his gaze to the note resting on Redfern's chest. DISPOSE OF THIS GARBAGE, the untidy line of block caps spelled out.

What had been the purpose? Scott wondered. The Piper had wanted Redfern, and Scott had brought him. Scott hadn't deluded himself about the outcome. He knew Redfern would die at the Piper's hands and he would have to live with the consequences of that. Now Redfern was dead and Scott had to bury the body. He understood that. But the Piper still had Sammy. This wasn't over. What dirty job would the Piper have him do next?

Scott went out to Redfern's car. The pickup was gone, but a shovel lay in its place. He hoped the Piper was on his way to Sammy.

Redfern had spread a blanket across the backseat to cover up the eroded upholstery. Scott yanked it free. The trunk offered little in the way of supplies other than a plastic bag from a supermarket and the duct tape he'd used to tie up Redfern. He took them both.

He stretched out the blanket next to Redfern's corpse. Jerking the plastic bag from his pocket, he knelt by his head. He knew he had to do this, even if every part of his being wanted him to stop. He looked away from Redfern's face and took two deep breaths to steady himself. Trying not to think about what he was doing, he lifted Redfern's head. His hand made contact with his blood-soaked hair. Something shifted within the shattered skull and pressed against his hand. He gagged, but fought back his revulsion long enough to slip the plastic bag over Redfern's head.

Once it was contained, he snatched his hand away. It

came away red. Reflexively, he wiped it on the blanket over and over until Redfern's blood and brain matter were a dim stain in the creases of his hand. Finally, he cinched the plastic bag tight around Redfern's neck and sealed it with duct tape.

With his face covered, Redfern stopped being a person. He was just remains. This made Scott's task only a fraction easier to cope with.

He rolled the body onto the blanket, then rolled it over and over, cocooning it, before duct-taping the blanket in place. Redfern's feet stuck out at one end, as did the top of his plastic-bagged head. It wasn't a perfect shroud, but it would do.

This was the easy part. Disposing of the body was the tough part. He could bury him close to the sawmill, but he wouldn't put it past the Piper to put a call in to Sheils. Then he'd be found digging a grave when the FBI blew in. It would certainly make for a pretty revenge. Maybe the Piper's end game was to set him up for a crime he didn't commit. Sheils would settle for it.

Taking the body somewhere presented its own problems. Driving around with a corpse in the trunk was going to be hard to explain away if he ran into a cop.

Stay or go. That was the question.

Go. He didn't relish hanging out at the scene of a murder longer than he had to.

He gathered up the corpse and bundled it into the Escort's trunk. Redfern returned to his hiding place, this time without complaint.

Scott went back inside the sawmill. There was nothing he could do about the lights and their generator. This was never going to be a perfect cleanup, but he had to do something about the bloodstain. Mopping it up presented as many problems as leaving it. A perfectly clean spot on the floor looked suspicious when years of dirt and grime covered everything else. Disguising the blood was the only solution.

He found a quart of engine oil sitting in the Escort's front passenger foot well. He mixed oil with a shovelful of dirt and scattered it over the bloodstain. He had no idea if the dirt-oil mix destroyed blood evidence, but he hoped so.

When he'd finished covering up the bloodstain, he examined his work. It didn't make for perfect camouflage, but it was good enough. A week of rough weather should do the trick. He killed the lights and ran over to the Escort.

Scott didn't drive far from the sawmill to dump the corpse. He figured if the FBI was alerted to the sawmill and conducted a search for a body, just driving a mile created over three square miles of land to search. That sucked up a lot resources and manpower.

He followed a dirt track down a slope into a wooded area. He tugged the corpse free from the trunk and dropped it on the ground. The blanket-wrapped corpse gathered speed on the slope and disappeared in the darkness.

"Shit."

He didn't have a flashlight, so he turned the Escort around to light his way. The headlights picked out the blanket some two hundred feet ahead. The duct tape had held and the body remained cocooned in the blanket. He grabbed the shovel and jogged over to it.

He decided to bury the corpse where it lay. He wasn't about to lug it somewhere else. He just didn't have the physical or the mental strength. This spot seemed as good as any for Redfern's final resting place. It took him two hours to dig a grave deep enough for the body and fill the hole. With that out of the way, all he had to worry about was being found.

The watch sergeant was waiting for Sheils and Brannon when they walked into the Lebanon Police Department. He escorted them through the station's hallways.

"Where is he?" Sheils asked.

"I've got him in an interview room. He's in pretty rough shape. The Piper worked him over pretty good."

"You bag his clothes?"

"As you asked."

"What about this trucker who found him?" Brannon asked.

Less than two hours ago, Scott had flagged down a trucker in Waterloo, told the driver his name, and asked for a ride to the nearest police station. Scott's release, escape, or whatever the hell had happened last night had taken the heat off Sheils. The bureau looked like a bunch of idiots after Scott's abduction. Now the focus was still on Sheils, but no one was baying for his blood.

"He checked out. We got a statement from him and let him go."

The sergeant opened the door to the interview room. Scott sat at the desk with a mug of coffee cupped in both hands. He was dressed in police department sweats. A Band-Aid covered a gash at his hairline, but not the much larger bruise surrounding it, which was obviously the result of a pistol-whipping.

"I thought we'd lost you last night," Sheils said. "You want to tell us about it?"

"Sure," Scott said.

The sergeant left the interview room, closing the door after him. Sheils and Brannon settled into the chairs opposite Scott. Brannon produced a digital recorder and pressed RECORD.

"Take us through what happened during the ransom drop," Brannon said. "From where you switched cars."

"I drove to the first stop. He called, told me to drown the ransom in the river, toss the cell, change cars, and dump the Camry in the river. I'm sorry about Agent Taggart." Scott gripped the coffee mug so tight he was strangling it. "I didn't have a choice. If I didn't do it, he was going to hurt Sammy. He knew you guys had someone in the car with me. That's why I didn't want anyone riding with me."

"We know," Brannon said.

"Agent Taggart, is he okay?"

"He's fine," Sheils said. "Go on."

"I got into the Buick. There was a cell phone and map in the car. He called me on the cell and told me to drive to Oakridge. I hadn't gotten far when this big truck took me out. At first I thought it was just bad luck that I'd been hit until the driver jumped down from the cab wearing a ski mask, and then I knew it was the Piper."

"Was he alone?" Sheils asked.

"Yes."

"What then?" Brannon asked.

"I handed the money over, but he beat me and shot me up with something." Scott yanked the neck of his sweatshirt down to reveal a puncture wound.

"I want a blood sample for analysis," Sheils said.

"Sure."

Sheils detected a hint of hesitation in Scott's reply. He'd been waiting for a slip. This whole Oregon detour stank. Diverting the ransom drop here made no sense and the abduction even less. Scott shouldn't have turned up alive. The Piper hated Scott enough to kill him. Catch and release didn't feature, unless something else was going on.

"Okay, the Piper dopes you, what then?" Sheils asked.

"I woke up in the back of the Piper's truck."

"Was Sammy with you?" Brannon asked.

"No," Scott conceded. "I don't believe Sammy is even up here. I think this was some elaborate exercise to make us run around like idiots for his sick pleasure."

You said it, Sheils thought. "Did he mention where he's holding Sammy?"

"He wouldn't tell me."

"So you spoke to him?" Sheils said.

Scott hesitated again and a sudden surge of panic ignited in his eyes. The son of a bitch was holding something back from him, but what? Sheils's prejudices said Scott was colluding with the Piper, but that wasn't necessarily the case.

"Yes, I spoke to him in the truck."

"Do you know where he drove you?" Brannon asked.

"No idea. He might have driven around in circles for all I know."

"What happened to your face?" Sheils asked.

"He hit me for asking too many questions about Sammy."

"How did you escape?"

"He beat me up pretty bad. I lost consciousness for a while, but when I came to, I wasn't tied up."

Sheils had expected Scott to hesitate a third time, but he didn't. His reply came instantly, as if it were true—or rehearsed.

"You weren't tied up?" Sheils repeated.

"Maybe he expected me to be out longer, but when I woke up, the truck was moving. I went to the door and tried it. It wasn't locked, so I rolled it up, jumped out, and scrambled to the side of the road."

"That was sloppy of him," Brannon said.

"And quick-witted of you," Sheils said.

Scott looked from Sheils to Brannon and back again. A tinge of panic nicked his expression. "I guess I got lucky. Maybe the Piper is rusty after his eight-year break."

"When you jumped from the truck, did you catch the license plate?" Sheils asked.

Scott sighed. "No. I didn't think."

"Too busy saving yourself and not your son, huh?"

"Fuck you."

"Hey, that's enough," Brannon said. "From both of you."

"I'd like to speak to my wife." Scott jumped to his feet. "Are we finished here?"

"For now," Sheils said.

Scott stormed out of the interview room.

"What do you think?" Brannon asked.

"None of this adds up. We weren't brought up here for a ransom drop. The Piper wanted us up here for a reason and Scott knows what that reason is. There's something he's not telling us."

"Do you want to sweat him?"

"No, I want to see where he leads us. In the meantime, I want his blood tested and his clothes examined. If we find something, we might have what we need to get some truth around here."

"You really think he's involved in this?"

"Something's not right. He did give us one valuable thing, though."

"What's that?"

"If the Piper is up here screwing with us and Sammy Fleetwood is elsewhere, that means he isn't working alone."

NINETEEN

Jane put the phone down, missing the cradle, the shakes getting the better of her. The last twenty-four hours had been the worst of her life. Instead of Scott calling to tell her he had Sammy, Sheils had called to say the Piper had abducted Scott during the ransom drop. The Piper was tearing her world apart. Scott wasn't the only one being punished here—she was too. When Scott had escaped, a piece of her had been returned, but it wasn't enough for her to maintain the facade. She had put on a brave face for Peter and the FBI, even Scott, but the moment she was alone, she felt herself unravel from the inside out. The fabric of her identity was being lost a thread at a time. She clutched herself to keep the remaining threads intact.

Peter picked up the handset and placed it on the rest. He was such a quiet kid. Jane worried about him. He was keeping things from her, just like his father. But it was different with Peter. He lived inside his head. A lot went on in there that he didn't share. She wondered if she should take him to a shrink. Under these circumstances, it might prove to be a good thing. The kidnapping of his father and brother had to be taking its toll on him.

And what of Sammy? He was alive. She truly believed that. She had no doubt that she'd see her son again. Her only fear was how this ordeal would affect him. There would be psychological wounds. But wounds of all kinds could be healed. She'd heal him. If that meant the whole family going into therapy, then so be it. Her family would survive this. She'd see to it.

"When will Daddy be home?" Peter asked.

"Late tonight."

"Can I stay up?"

"No, I don't think so."

Disappointment masked his face.

"But I'll wake you."

Peter smiled, but it didn't last. "When's Sammy coming home?"

Jane was tempted to lie, but it wasn't a time for Band-Aid answers. "I don't know, honey."

Her answer attracted Agent Guerra's attention. Jane had grown to like this woman. She was smart, competent, and thoughtful. Jane expected a friendship to exist after this ordeal.

Guerra stopped her work at her laptop and came over. "Hey, Peter, I've got a job for you. You want it?"

"Yeah."

She held up a menu and a pen. "I need you to get everyone's dinner order."

Peter snatched the menu and the pen and rushed off with it.

"He's a great kid," Guerra said.

"So's his brother." Jane realized how bitter her remark sounded and she softened her tone. "What do you think will happen now? The Piper has his money. He doesn't need Sammy anymore."

"I think we're in the home stretch now. I'm sure the Piper will be in contact to tell us where to pick him up."

Peter came trotting back. It hadn't taken long for him to go around to the handful of agents in the house. Sheils had left only a skeleton crew to watch over them while he carried out the money drop in Oregon. Jane liked the relative peace in the house. Even the TV crews had started losing interest. Their vigil had dwindled since Scott had left for Oregon.

Peter presented Guerra the annotated menu with everyone's meal selections. Guerra added her own. Jane said she'd be cooking for Peter and herself, but when Peter complained, she relented and let him pick something off the menu.

Guerra rang the order in and Peter sparkled when a burger the size of his head arrived. As Jane expected, he didn't come close to finishing it. It was a waste of food, but it gave him a boost. The same couldn't be said of Jane's salad. She only picked at it. A free meal didn't distract her like her son. She wanted to hear from the Piper. He'd been paid. He'd had his fun. Now it was time to give Sammy back.

But he didn't call.

Around nine, Rooker called. "Just checking in. Any news?"

"They're on their way home and should be here in a few hours."

"That's good. I'm sorry I haven't made it over to you today. Duty calls and all that, but I can come by now."

The man's compassion after all that had happened to him left her breathless. She doubted she could be so forgiving or generous. Their families were entwined, but for all the wrong reasons.

"No, it's okay, Charles. I don't plan on staying up much later. I'm hoping tonight is the night I get some sleep."

"Okay, I'll leave you to your houseguests. Are they behaving?"

Jane smiled. "Yes. They're very tidy."

Rooker laughed. "Good. I'll drop by in the morning."

Jane thanked him, said good night, and hung up.

Peter was nestled up against Guerra on the couch asleep. Guerra was lost in a paperback, a political thriller judging by the cover, and was absently stroking his hair.

Jane got up. "I'll relieve you of my little package."

"Oh, he's fine," Guerra said.

Jane knelt in front of her sleeping son. He slept peacefully. She took comfort from this. Maybe he would come through this trauma unscathed.

"I think someone is having his first crush," Jane said.

Guerra colored, but recovered swiftly. "It had to happen, I guess."

Peter stirred when Jane scooped him up in her arms, but didn't wake. She carried him up to his room and put him to bed. She went to bed herself when two of the agents ended their shifts and left, leaving Guerra and Shultz, a cordial but tight-lipped agent.

Jane brought one of Sammy's T-shirts to bed with her and held it to her face. She needed his scent close to her. She'd been doing this since the day of his abduction and without Scott alongside her to comfort her, she needed the T-shirt even more.

She hadn't realized she'd fallen asleep until the sound of a heavy thud woke her. She sat up in bed, not sure whether the noise had occurred in her sleep or the real world. She listened to the house. The digital alarm clocked hummed on the nightstand. A car raced by outside. A wind driven by the Pacific pressed against the windows. None of these familiar sounds soothed her. Instead, they frightened her.

She listened for Guerra and Shultz, but didn't hear them. She wanted to call out to the agents, but a sixth sense stopped her. Something wasn't right.

She slipped from her bed and went to the door. She listened for a moment before carefully opening it. It clicked when she eased it back.

Someone gasped from behind her.

She froze. For a fractured heartbeat, she thought the person was in the room with her, but the gasp was a facsimile. The answer drove a fist into the pit of her stomach.

She turned in the direction of the baby monitor sitting on the nightstand. Peter had objected when she'd dug them out the day after Sammy's kidnapping.

"I don't want you worrying about calling for us," she'd told him, but she'd gotten the baby monitors out for her. Listening to her sons' breathing at night had always soothed her as a new mother and she needed comforting now.

When she'd woken, she'd listened for a sound out of the ordinary, but she hadn't listened for a familiar sound—the sound of Peter's breathing and night mumbles. She didn't hear his breathing now. A noise, a combination of a cry, sob, and howl, left her.

"Jane? Is that you?" a voice crackled on the baby monitor's speaker.

She didn't recognize the voice without its electronic disguise, but she knew who it belonged to. The Piper was in the house. Maybe he was here to return Sammy. It was a lie she would have liked to believe. The Piper didn't return things—he took them.

"Jane, I hoped not to wake you to shield you from this."

She held her belly where she'd grown her babies.

"Please don't cry out. I want to execute my business with the minimum of fuss. Besides, screaming won't help you. Or Peter. I've given him a little something to let him sleep."

She wasn't going to cry. She wouldn't give the son of a bitch the satisfaction, but she couldn't help herself. Tears poured out.

"Come to Peter's room, please."

She eased back the door and stepped into the hallway. Halfway up the stairs lay Guerra, facedown and still. Jane now knew the cause of the thud that had woken her. She guessed Shultz was somewhere in the house in a similar condition.

"She's not seriously hurt," the Piper said from the doorway to Peter's room. "I'm not here for that. Now, this way."

Dressed in black with a ski mask hiding his face, he was a shadow in the night. Jane approached and he retreated into the room, a pistol aimed at her stomach. He told her to stop when she reached the room's threshold. Peter lay on the bed, the covers pulled back. Although in his pajamas, he was wearing his sneakers.

Jane understood and anger burned inside her. "You're not taking him."

"Jane, this isn't a negotiation. Out of respect, I want you to know that I'm taking your son."

The Piper's arrogance infuriated Jane and she charged at him. There was no grace or design to her attack, just raw fury. The Piper dealt with her easily. He waited until the last second to sidestep her flailing arms and brought the butt of the pistol down on the back of her neck. The blow failed to knock her out, but it chopped her legs out from under her. Her momentum sent her crashing into Sammy's empty bed. She bounced off the mattress and onto the floor.

The Piper moved in before she had time to recover. He yanked her hands together and hiked them up until he reached the point of dislocating her shoulders. He pressed a knee into her back, pinning her to the floor. "Please, don't force me to hurt you further."

"No, you're not taking him," Jane moaned. "Take me, but leave him."

"Jane, it doesn't work like that and you know it."

"Why?"

"Scott. He failed me again."

"You knew the FBI was here. We did everything right."

"You're not listening, Jane. The FBI, you, and the media are all doing your part. It's Scott that fell down on the job. I gave him a simple task to do and he screwed it up. Now he must pay the price."

"Not Peter."

"Peter is the price. But all is not lost. Scott can recover from his mistake."

"No," Jane said, the word coming out in a protracted

sob. This wasn't right. It couldn't be happening again, but it was and she couldn't prevent it. The rage that fueled her turned to misery and sucked the strength from her limbs.

"I'm going to let you up now."

The Piper released her arms and removed his knee from her back. She pushed herself onto all fours.

"Please remain on your knees and don't look behind you."

Jane did as she was told. She felt him move in behind her, totally in her blind spot, and press something hard and cold against her neck.

She faced Peter asleep in his bed, his chest rising and falling. No doubt the Piper had choreographed her position this way so that Peter was in full view. She guessed this was supposed to frighten her, but the Piper's plan backfired. If the sight of her sleeping son was to be her final image on his planet, then so be it. To her, there was no better sight.

Jane fought her need to cry, but failed. Peter's still form melted as her tears clouded her vision.

"Just know Scott is to blame for this," the Piper said.

Before Jane could ask why, a bolt of pain shot through her and darkness flooded in to sweep Peter away.

TWENTY

Scott burst through the door. An army of FBI agents filled the downstairs rooms of his house. None made any move to restrain him.

"Where is she?"

"In the bedroom."

Scott tore up the stairs. Sheils yelled after him, but he ignored the agent.

They'd been so close. So close to making it home before the Piper had struck again. Their convoy was tearing through Vacaville when the call had come through that the Piper had snatched Peter. It had taken thirty minutes to cover the fifty miles, but it was all for naught. It didn't change anything. Peter was gone.

The bedroom door was closed. Scott didn't bother knocking. He just called out Jane's name before barging his way in.

She was sitting on the bed while two agents attended to her. They stopped when Scott appeared in the doorway.

"Thank God, you're okay," he said.

"The Piper just tasered and sedated everyone," an agent said.

Jane shoved the agents aside. She raced toward Scott with her arms out. Scott halted his approach. Jane wasn't coming to him in need of an embrace. There was no time to ask questions before she smashed into him.

"What did you do?" she screamed and slapped him hard across the face. "What did you do? He said you didn't do what he told you. That was why he took Peter."

This wasn't the welcome he was expecting and his mind whirled. What had the Piper told her? If he'd told her everything, it was game over. Sheils would find out and there was no way he could help Sammy and Peter. The Piper's next call would direct them to a quiet spot at Golden Gate Park. Was that why the bastard hadn't called with his next instructions during the drive back to California? he thought. He couldn't answer Jane's questions until he knew what the Piper had told her.

She struck him again, this time harder. His face burned white hot with shame. He felt the afterglow of her hand-print on his cheek.

His standing there, just taking the abuse, did nothing to diffuse her anger. Instead, it poured gasoline on an already raging fire. Her hands balled into fists. She pounded on his chest until the agents peeled her from him.

"What exactly did he say, Mrs. Fleetwood?" Sheils said from the doorway.

Guerra came up to Scott. "Are you okay?"

He nodded and sank into the love seat by the window.

"He said Scott was to blame for tonight." Jane stared at Scott while she answered. The hatred on her face forced him to look away.

Sheils took Jane's arm and guided her to the corner of the bed where she sat down. "What else did he say?"

"That Scott had a simple task to do and he screwed it up."

"What is he talking about?" Sheils asked Scott.

Just like the Piper to call killing Redfern a simple task, Scott thought. "I don't know."

"You don't know?" Sheils said.

"You must, Scott," Jane demanded. "You did something to cause this."

"I did everything he told me to do." He jumped to his feet. "He's not looking for reasons to punish me—he's looking for excuses. If I don't jump when he says jump, then I fail his test."

He hadn't said an untrue word and the honesty burned bright when he spoke, protecting the lie for now. He had to maintain the pretense until the Piper called again.

His outburst took the sting out of Jane. The tension in her body that kept her knotted on the corner of the bed unraveled.

"You must, Scott," she said, her tone pleading. "You must know. Think."

There was something he could say to buy him time. It would keep Sheils off his back and pull Jane back to him. He hated that he was manipulating these people, especially Jane, but he had no choice.

"I escaped," he said. "The Piper had the ransom, Sammy wasn't anywhere close, and he wasn't going to let me go, so I escaped. I never thought he'd take Peter because of it."

This explanation left the room quiet for a long moment while Jane, Sheils, and his minions absorbed the information. Scott wondered if they were buying it. Jane seemed to be. The warmth was returning to her face when she looked at him. Sheils remained poker-faced. Scott could have walked himself into a trap and wouldn't even know it.

"Did the Piper say anything else?" Sheils asked.

"That Scott could make up for his mistake." Jane forced out a weak smile.

Scott smiled back. A second chance. The Piper was giving him a second chance, but he'd doubled the stakes. There'd be another challenge. Get it right and Sammy and Peter would live. Get it wrong and he'd surely kill them both.

Sheils examined Scott with a look that could blunt diamonds. "Did he say how Scott could do this?"

That was Scott's question too. Redfern was dead. He

couldn't kill a dead man. No, the Piper had a new challenge lined up. That was why Sammy wasn't at the ransom drop. Redfern was never the end game for the Piper. When Scott looked back on everything so far, he cursed himself for being so blind. It had been child's play to find Redfern, so much so that the Piper with all his skills and resources could have tracked him down years ago and put a bullet in his head. Redfern was only the appetizer. The Piper had been preparing Scott for the main event. But what was it?

"No," Jane said. "He never said."

Sheils turned to Scott. "Got any ideas?"

Maybe the main event wasn't a what, but a who. Redfern and Scott weren't the only flies in the Piper's ointment that had resulted in Nicholas Rooker's death. Sheils was responsible too. He'd been suckered into Redfern's fantasy as much as Scott had. If the FBI agent had recognized Redfern for the hoaxer he was, then everything could have been recovered in time for the money drop to be made and Nicholas to be returned safe and sound, but he'd failed, just like Scott. Was the Piper's next call going to tell Scott to kill Sheils? Sheils had a family of his own. To kill Sheils destroyed the lives of innocents. Scott would die for his boys if the Piper decided that was the ransom to be paid, but could he kill Sheils? He knew the truth. If the call came ordering Sheils's death to save his boys, he would do it. He wouldn't hesitate. Pulling the trigger would be child's play.

Scott shook his head. "Not until he calls."

TWENTY-ONE

The call came in the afternoon. It gave the FBI something to do. The Piper had less than an hour's head start on Sheils, but a multijurisdictional sweep of the Bay Area had failed to locate him. No one knew what they were even chasing. They didn't know his identity or a make on his vehicle. Scott guessed he'd gone to ground within minutes of snatching Peter. The belief was that the Piper was holed up somewhere in Northern California. Scott wondered if he was staying close to home. There were a lot of residences in San Francisco and it would take an army to search every one of them. The Piper could hide in plain sight quite easily.

Until the phone rang, defeat hung in the air. FBI heads had dropped with the second kidnapping. The electricity that had buzzed around the agents fizzled. Peter represented their ninth Piper kidnapping, tenth if someone wanted to include Scott, and the odds of catching the Piper looked slim to none.

Their defeatism was hurting Jane. It was eroding her faith. It would be eroding Scott's too, if it wasn't for his alliance. The feds couldn't do anything for his sons, but he could. The Piper was going to give him one more shot. Scott didn't fear the Piper's demands. The only thing that mattered was saving his boys.

The phone rang and Scott and Jane sat down together on the couch.

"Play it just as we discussed," Sheils said.

Scott nodded and squeezed out a smile for Jane before answering the phone.

"Scott, are you ready to do this all again?" the Piper's distorted voice asked.

"Yes."

"Good."

The technician gestured to Scott to stretch out the conversation like he'd been told. Scott didn't see the point. The FBI hadn't managed to trace the call so far and he doubted they would now.

"Is Peter okay?"

The technician flashed him the thumbs-up.

"Both your boys are fine."

Jane wept at this news. Guerra moved in to comfort her.

"What do you want?" Scott asked.

"Cooperation."

"You have it."

"I can rely on you to do exactly as you're told?"

Scott read between the lines. "I'll do exactly as you tell me. You have my word."

"And the FBI?"

"They'll behave," Scott said.

"They won't, but I applaud your conviction."

"I'm not interested in your games. I just want my kids back. What do you want?"

"Scott, I get the feeling you might be learning after your previous mistakes." The Piper paused, but Scott said nothing. "Okay, we're going to try and do this right this time. Two million in nonsequential bills."

Several of the agents groaned out loud. Sheils dropped his head. Jane buried her face in Guerra's shoulder.

"I'm going to be generous this time. I realize another two million will be hard for you, so take a few days. Just know the longer you take the longer it will be before you see your kids again—if ever."

Jane uncoiled herself from Guerra and lunged for the phone. She snatched the receiver from Scott's hand. "If you hurt my children, I'll kill you," she screamed. "Do you hear me?"

What the Piper had heard was hard to say. By the time Jane paused to listen to his reply, he'd already hung up.

"Jane, it's going to be okay." Scott rounded the coffee table and pulled her to him. He pried the phone from her and handed it to Sheils. "Don't let this bastard get to you. That's what he wants. He wants us to feel helpless. That's what gives him power. Do you want to give him that power?"

"He doesn't have any damn power over me."

"Good," he said and kissed her. "We're going to get through this."

Where Jane felt pain from the ransom demand, Scott felt relief. The dummy ransom was in and he could expect a call from the Piper soon with the real one.

Sheils conferred with his team before coming over to them. "We need to talk about this new ransom. I can get a bank to provide the two million, but I'm going to need guarantees that you can cover the money. I'm not trying to pressure you, but I need to know where you stand."

"We don't have it," Scott said. "We can cover about half, but that's it."

"Maybe we could get the Piper to give us more time or negotiate the amount," Jane said, but she lost faith in what she was saying before she finished saying it. They all knew the Piper wasn't going to budge, not with them. Scott couldn't imagine leaving Sammy and Peter in the

Piper's charge for weeks while he and Jane raised the ransom.

"Can I make a suggestion?" Sheils asked. "Go to Charles Rooker."

"We lost two million of his money already," Scott said.

"I know, but if he's willing to advance you the money, I can get it moving."

"We can ask," Jane said.

Scott knew it was their only option, but he hated it. The Piper had destroyed Rooker's life once. Losing the two-million-dollar ransom added insult to injury. Now to beg another two million was kicking him when he was down. But it was money to save Sammy and Peter. Scott had to try.

"We'll call," Scott said.

Sheils left them alone while Jane called Rooker about the second ransom. He didn't give her time to explain before he told her he would pay again.

They met at the bank an hour later. Rooker arrived early and rushed up to them the moment they set foot inside. He engulfed Scott and Jane like they were his own lost children.

"I'm just sick about Peter," Rooker said.

"We're going to pay you back this money," Scott said.

"I told you before, there's no need."

Scott pulled out the check the *Independent* had paid him and held it out to Rooker. "That's yours."

Rooker made no attempt to take the check.

Scott couldn't profit at this man's expense. "Name a charity. I'll sign it over to them."

Rooker smiled. "That's very generous. We'll worry about that when this is all over."

Jane took Rooker's hand and placed it between hers. When she smiled at him, tears spilled out. "You're a very good man."

"I'm not. Not really. I'll be honest with you. I'm helping

you for selfish reasons. The Piper robbed me of my son." His eyes shone with tears. "I was thinking only today that he would be graduating this year and thinking about college—his life before him still waiting to be written. But it wasn't to be."

"Don't torture yourself, Charles," Jane said.

"He shouldn't have died. I had the money and I had no problem paying it. But circumstances . . ." Rooker trailed off when his gaze fell on Scott. "Look, I had the good fortune to be able to pay my son's ransom, but never got the chance." Suddenly, anger gripped him and his voice rose. "The Piper took my son and killed him, for no reason." His anger subsided. "Giving you the money lets me pay the ransom that I never got to pay for Nicholas."

Scott imagined he hadn't shared this pain with anyone before. There were few people who could understand it. He and Jane were unfortunate enough to be in that select group.

"You've paid. You don't have to pay again," Scott said.

"I've made a good living. Money, I have. Money, I don't need. There's no one to pass it on to. Besides, I'm not paying for Nicholas, I'm paying for your boys."

Jane palmed away her tears. "Thank you. There's nothing else I can say except, thank you, Charles."

Rooker said nothing, accepting the compliment with good grace.

"Would you like to have dinner with us?" Jane asked.

"Actually, I was wondering if I could take you two somewhere," Rooker said. "If that's okay with you, Agent Sheils?"

Sheils looked uneasy.

Rooker smiled. "I promise to have them home before curfew."

"Okay, but I need you to remain in contact in case of developments," Sheils said to Scott and Jane.

"We have our cell phones," Jane said.

Reluctantly, Sheils let them leave with Rooker. By the time they got into Rooker's Mercedes, rush hour was in full swing.

"Where are we going?" Jane asked.

"Hopefully to someone who might be able to help."

Rooker pulled up in front of Four Embarcadero Center. He checked in with reception and they rode the elevator to the ninth floor. The elevator doors opened up on an office floor belonging to Friedkin International Investigations.

Rooker waved to a trim man in his late forties with salt-and-pepper hair. The man waved back, but his expression was grim. He was stretched across the reception desk with a phone pressed to his ear. His call seemed to be the reason for his displeasure.

Rooker and the Fleetwoods approached, but they stood a respectful distance from the man while he talked.

"Okay, I'll find out where he is. In the meantime, I'll assign another of my investigators to your case. Thank you. And I apologize for the inconvenience." The man handed the phone to the receptionist.

"Problems, John?" Rooker asked.

"Only a small one." The man put out his hand to Scott and Jane to shake. "I'm John Friedkin, Mr. and Mrs. Fleetwood. It's a horrible thing that's happened to your children. I can't imagine what you're going through."

Scott wondered if Friedkin knew them from their faces splashed across the TV or from Rooker.

Friedkin said to the receptionist, "Rebecca, see if you can get a twenty on Alex Hammond. I want an explanation for his no show."

Rooker had assured Scott and Jane that Friedkin was the best, but his staffing issues didn't instill confidence in Scott.

"This way, please," Friedkin said.

The investigator walked them through a modern office complex and into a corner office with a view of the piers and the Bay Bridge. It was very impressive, but Scott guessed that was the point. This was no sleazy gumshoe operation and neither was Friedkin, judging by the suit he wore and the Rolex on his wrist.

Everyone sat around a conference table. Friedkin and Rooker sat with their backs to the million-dollar view.

"Why are we here?" Scott asked.

"I told you I had selfish reasons for helping you," Rooker said. "Never paying Nicholas's ransom was one. The other, the main part really, is that I want the Piper caught."

"The FBI is doing that," Jane remarked.

"It's what they're trying to do," Rooker corrected.

"Maybe I should explain," Friedkin said. "The FBI is a well-trained organization with excellent personnel. They have resources and contacts that as a private investigation firm we don't."

"Then why are we here?" Scott asked.

"The FBI, like any law enforcement agency, is constrained by laws that I'm not. I'm not burdened by such things as probable cause."

"After Nicholas died, I waited for the FBI to catch the Piper," Rooker said. "I expected and believed they would. When it became obvious they wouldn't, I turned to John."

"And obviously, you didn't get any further than the FBI did," Scott said to Friedkin.

"No, but the kidnapping of your sons gives me a fresh line of inquiry, which is something I've never had before."

"I'm hoping you'll allow John and his people to work the investigation alongside the FBI," Rooker said.

"What do you mean by work alongside?" Jane asked.

"Give me access to information that comes your way," Friedkin said.

"Will the FBI allow that?" Jane asked.

"The FBI won't like it, but they can't stop you from going to a private investigator. You're a private citizen and you can call upon anyone you wish."

"I don't know," Jane said. "Like you said, the FBI has better resources."

Rooker reached across the table and took Jane's hand. "That's the way I thought before Nicholas died. Please don't make the error I made."

Jane looked over at Scott. He knew Rooker was attempting to corner them, using fear to sell them this bill of goods, but in some ways, it was a friendly corner. Sheils had yet to make any inroads on the Piper, and Rooker just wanted justice.

"There is no risk to you. I would be covering all fees," Rooker said. "I want this man caught just as much as you do. I hope you understand that."

"We do, Charles," Jane said.

"Can we chat this over between us?" Scott said.

"Of course," Friedkin replied and walked Rooker out of the room, closing the office door behind them.

"What do you think?" Jane asked.

"It's going to piss off Sheils."

"Do you care?"

"Not as long as he keeps doing his best for Sammy and Peter."

"Sheils is driven." Jane glanced over at Rooker, who was in muted conference with Friedkin. "Just like Rooker. They're both desperate for the Piper. There's no danger of Sheils not doing his best."

"You want to do this?"

"Don't you?"

Bringing Friedkin in could only help the investigation, but he would be another person Scott would have to deceive. It was getting harder and harder to play the Piper's game with so many observers. Sheils had gotten suspicious in Oregon. How long before Friedkin felt the same way? But to deny Friedkin's help raised red flags. He couldn't see how he could say no.

"I just don't want to make things worse for the boys," Scott said.

"You won't."

He called Friedkin and Rooker back in.

"We want you to help us," Jane said.

Rooker hugged Jane and pumped Scott's hand. "You don't know how much it means to me."

"We do have one stipulation," Jane said.

"Name it," Friedkin said.

"You share any developments with the FBI."

"You have my word."

Friedkin produced paperwork for them to sign. Rooker explained that Friedkin would be sharing information with him as well. Once the bureaucracy was out of the way, Friedkin talked about himself and his firm. His background was military intelligence. Mainly, he conducted background checks, fraud investigations, industrial espionage claims, and criminal defense investigations. His investigators possessed the backgrounds to cover the wide-ranging specialties the agency offered.

"I'll be in touch," Friedkin said. "I need to get what I can from you about the kidnappings."

"Just let us know when," Jane said.

The Piper's cell phone vibrated against Scott's thigh. This was it—his new assignment. The Piper would ask him to perform the impossible. Scott's heart pounded like it was out of balance.

In his head, Scott fumbled for a reason to excuse himself, but the phone's buzzing could be heard quite clearly within the confines of the office. Everyone stopped to look at him. The air-conditioned room felt a lot hotter than the seventy-one degrees the thermostat showed.

"Do you want to take that?" Friedkin asked.

"It's probably the *Independent* wanting an update. They can wait."

"It could be Sheils," Jane said.

Scott reached into his pocket and pulled out the Piper's phone. "Yeah, it's the *Independent*."

"We're finished. You're welcome to take it in here," Fried-kin said and ushered Rooker and Jane out of the office.

Scott answered the phone. "Yes."

"Did Jane pass on my message?" the Piper asked.

"Yes, she did."

Scott kept a grip on his emotions. The room might have been soundproofed, but it was all glass. He rounded the conference table to face the city below, turning his back on anyone looking in. "You took Peter, you bastard."

"That was your fault. You defied me. I gave you a simple task and you blew it."

"You asked me to find Redfern. You said nothing about killing him."

"Typical," the Piper said with disdain. "You knew what I would do with Redfern when you delivered him and you had no problems sending a man to his death as long as you didn't have to pull the trigger. I believe that's the definition of a coward."

"I pulled the trigger on you, didn't I?"

"Only when you thought I was unarmed."

"Even if you had a gun, I would've shot you."

"You sound brave. I'm bringing out the best in you."

"How are my boys?"

"They're fine."

"If you hurt them . . ."

"Yeah, yeah, yeah, I know the cliché."

Scott tossed a glance Jane's way. Friedkin was showing them framed commendations on the wall. Scott smiled at her. She didn't smile back.

He held up his hand, spreading his fingers wide, and mouthed, "Five minutes."

She nodded at him.

He turned to face the view again. "I want to speak to them."

"They're not here."

"You can't leave them alone."

"I'm not operating a day care. They're safe. That's all you need to know. You'll see them again, if you do as I tell you."

Scott stared out the window. He caught sight of his reflection in the glass. A haggard and distressed man stared back at him. "What do you want?"

"I want you to find me. Do it and you'll get your kids back."

"Are you serious? The FBI hasn't found you with all their resources after two decades and you're expecting me to find you?"

"The FBI doesn't have the incentive you do. I have a lot of faith in you, Scott. I think you can do this."

Why the theatrics? Scott thought. "Just tell me where you are and I'll come. We'll finish this."

"Scott, that's too easy. You have to work for this one. This one is for your kids. The challenge has to meet the reward."

"It's going to take time to find you."

"I can wait."

"The FBI can't. We have the new ransom."

"Charles Rooker again?"

"Yes."

"The FBI won't be a problem. I'll slow them down. But I can't wait forever, Scott."

Scott's stomach clenched.

"You've got until Monday. After that, I'm going to have to kill one of the boys."

Scott fought to keep his hand gestures and body language relaxed. He was supposed to be talking to the *Independent*, after all.

"A week," Scott murmured. He wasn't agreeing to the Piper's terms. He just needed to hear the time period out loud. A week, just seven days, sounded so small when stacked up against his task.

"I might get impatient, though. If I feel you're slipping, I'll cut the deadline—and a throat."

"I'll do it. Give me the week."

Scott recognized the defeatist tone in his voice. It would have been so much easier if the Piper had asked him to assassinate the mayor or start a revolution. Finding the man who'd yet to be caught was a task beyond him.

"A week it is. Tick-tock, Scott. The clock starts now."

TWENTY-TWO

"The bastard," Sheils barked and thumped his desk.

Brannon sat opposite him back at his office. They were supposed to be getting dinner, but once he told Sheils about the Fleetwoods hiring a private investigator, dinner was suspended.

"I should have seen it coming," Sheils complained. "He suckered us all with his generosity."

"Technically, the Fleetwoods hired the PI, not Rooker."

"Yes, but my money says Rooker is paying the bills."

"He is," Brannon conceded.

"Son of a bitch."

Professional pride. That was what fueled his annoyance. Rooker had coerced the Fleetwoods into taking on a private investigator. What did that say about the FBI and him? It said they weren't up to the job. And if he was being honest, who could blame them? How many times had the Piper slipped through his fingers? Peter Fleetwood had been snatched out from under his protection. The Fleetwoods were entitled to bring someone on board. His annoyance left him with a sigh. "Who'd they hire?"

"Friedkin International Investigations."

Sheils knew John Friedkin by reputation. Friedkin was good. His moral compass still had the needle pointing in the right direction. Sheils doubted he would be a problem.

"At least they went to someone good," Sheils admitted.

"What do you want to do about Friedkin?"

"I'll pay him a visit and establish a few ground rules."

Brannon dropped a report on Sheils's desk. "The report on the Fleetwood house."

Sheils flipped through the pages without reading. "Give me the Cliff's Notes version."

"No prints, fibers, or hairs. The Piper gained access via the patio slider in the rear yard. No signs of force. He used a key."

"That means one of two things."

"He either stole a key or someone gave it to him."

His prejudice for Scott Fleetwood bubbled to the surface again. Had he given the Piper the key? Sheils still struggled with this. He couldn't believe a father could do that to his children. As much as he didn't like Scott, he didn't believe Scott could be that callous.

So the key was stolen. The Piper was meticulous in his preparations. He could have swiped a patio key from the house months ago. That presented a chilling proposition. The Piper had snatched Sammy from school. That meant he didn't need a patio key, unless he had always intended on kidnapping both Fleetwood boys.

The mood at the house turned subdued after Sheils left for the evening. Jane didn't want quiet. Quiet reminded her of her children. She missed their constant chatter. Even when Sammy and Peter slept, the house thrummed with their energy. That energy had waned after Sammy's abduction. Without Peter, it had been extinguished. Without their boys, Scott's and Jane's energy had been sapped. Scott hadn't spoken a word to her since they'd come home from Friedkin's. He'd retreated into his bedroom office.

The four agents left behind to babysit them milled around in the background. They purposely tried to blend in with the wallpaper. Jane wished they wouldn't. She wanted their noise to distract her from thinking about what she'd witnessed at Friedkin's office. She knew what she'd seen. Known it was wrong. If Peter were here, maybe it wouldn't be on her mind. Without him, it ate away at her. She couldn't let it rest. She had to talk to Scott.

She went into the living room. Two of the agents were watching TV while the other two watched the house from the front and rear.

"Can I get you guys anything?"

"No, ma'am," came the reply.

She climbed the stairs. Her feet felt progressively heavier with every step, but it didn't deter her. Scott's door was closed. She knocked and went in without waiting for permission. He sat at his PC, staring blankly at the information on the screen, a framed picture of the boys on his lap.

"We need to talk."

He straightened in his seat. "I'm a little busy."

"I don't care. Tell me what's going on, Scott."

"What do you mean?"

She needed him to be honest with her. It didn't matter how bad or how ugly it was, she could live with it, as long as he told her.

"I know you're hiding something from me. From the FBI."

Panic lit up in his eyes.

"I won't tell them. Not if you don't want me to."

He got up out of his chair and embraced her. "I don't know what you're talking about."

"Don't you?"

"No."

She stuffed her hand in his pocket and grabbed the phone. She yanked it free before he could stop her.

He took a step toward her. "Gimme that."

"No." She backed up. "This isn't your phone, Scott."

Scott thrust out a hand and stepped forward again. "Give it back."

"Scott, I swear to God, if you don't tell me where this phone came from, I'm going straight to Sheils."

The threat halted him. Jane was glad of it. Fear was burning up her strength. "Where did this phone come from?"

"It's not what you think. It's a business phone."

Her breaths came fast and shallow. This wasn't what she wanted to hear. The lies were killing her.

She flipped the phone open. "If I hit redial, who would I get, Scott? Someone from the *Independent* or someone else?"

She flipped through the phone's functions.

"Don't." His plea was made of glass. "Please."

"Tell me, Scott. I can't turn my back on this."

"I can't tell you."

The answer wasn't good enough. A tear raced down Jane's cheek. "I'm calling."

She pressed buttons on the phone's keypad.

"All right. I'll tell you. Just give me back the phone."

She held out the phone and he swept in to snatch it from her hand. He examined it like it was a lost artifact, checking for damage. When everything looked to be okay, he returned it to his pocket. The anxiety left him.

It didn't leave Jane.

He moved in close to her. She took an involuntary step backward, but he continued to crowd her.

"You can't tell anyone," he whispered. "He'll kill the boys."

It was everything she feared but was too afraid to believe. "I won't tell."

"The Piper slipped me the phone."

She went cold. The chill started at her head and spread all the way to her feet. She slumped against the bureau and he steadied her.

"He didn't give me a choice."

Scott dropped to his knees before her and poured out

the entire story. He was in such a hurry to tell her, events slopped out of him as if spilling from an overfilled bowl. The things he told her didn't follow in chronological order, but it didn't matter.

It was more convoluted and far crueler than she expected. The revelations struck her like body blows, but she couldn't betray his confidence. The price was too high. Her children were at risk.

"He took our boys," Scott said and broke into tears.

She pulled him to her stomach to muffle his sobs from prying ears. She felt the warmth of his tears soaking through her blouse.

His words dissolved into mumbles. She stroked his hair and shushed him. "It's going to be okay."

And it was. She didn't exactly feel his burden lift, but she felt part of it rest on her shoulders. They would work together from now on.

Scott pulled away from her. She helped him up and sat him at his desk.

She nodded at the Web page on the computer screen. "What are we going to do?"

"We?"

"Yes. How do we find him and get our boys back?"

Friedkin saw Sheils and Brannon out of his offices. Everyone thanked everyone for their time, although none of them meant it. Sheils had read him the riot act. He wouldn't allow a PI to interfere with an important federal investigation, blah, blah, blah. Brannon said little, providing an extra layer of menace. None of this fazed Friedkin. He'd expected the visit and respected it. He had no intention of "poaching the glory" as Sheils had put it. He'd witnessed firsthand the damage the Piper did to his victims. He wouldn't wish what happened to Rooker on anyone.

He'd cut Sheils's argument off at the ankles by insisting he'd share any and all findings with the bureau, as long as his clients gave their consent. That robbed Sheils of the bite that went with his bark.

Friedkin returned to his office, fell in his chair behind his desk, and revisited the real reason for his staying late at work. He opened up Alex Hammond's personnel file. He removed the letter of termination and set it to one side. He read through the documentation he'd gathered that would save his butt in a wrongful dismissal case. He wasn't making sure he had all his bases covered. He was searching for a reason not to fire Alex, but didn't find one. Unreliability had crept into Alex's work over the last six months. He took time off without notice, came in late and left early, and didn't have his eye on the ball when he was at work. His failure to show up for a surveillance assignment today was the last straw. Friedkin picked up his pen and signed the termination letter.

It seemed a shitty way to end a professional and personal relationship. He liked to think he could have saved the situation if Alex had just answered his damn phone. No one could argue he hadn't tried. He put the letter in his out tray for mailing.

As he was putting Alex's file away, his cell rang.

"John Friedkin."

"Mr. Friedkin, it's Scott Fleetwood."

"Scott, I was about to call you. Special Agent Sheils just paid me a visit. He wants access to all findings pertaining to your case."

"Let him have it," Scott said, sounding weary.

"Is that why you were calling?"

"No, I have a different request. With the length of time you've been working for Mr. Rooker, I'm guessing you've generated quite a file on the Piper."

"Yes. Over the years, we've compiled a sizeable chunk of data on him. Sadly, it hasn't led to identifying him. Do you want me to share this information with the FBI? The information is private, but I can't see any harm in sharing it."

"No, it's not that. I want to read the file. Would it be possible for me to see a copy?"

Friedkin raised an eyebrow. "Can I ask why you want this information?"

"I just want to try to understand what kind of man I'm dealing with."

"I see," Friedkin said skeptically. "I don't think that will be a problem. I will need Mr. Rooker's approval."

"Sure."

"Is there anything else you need from me?"

"No. I think that's it for now."

Friedkin pressed END on his cell and tossed it on his desk. He couldn't imagine the pain the Fleetwoods were going through right now. If he were in their place, he wouldn't be able to function. At that moment, he realized he'd do everything he could to get these people their children back.

But the fate of two kidnapped children had to come second to the needs of his other client. He retrieved the phone and dialed Charles Rooker's number. Rooker answered.

"He called," Friedkin said.

"When?"

"Just got off the phone with him. He wants to see everything I have on the Piper. I told him I needed your permission. Do I have it?"

"Of course. Whatever he needs, give it to him. You don't have to check with me first."

When Rooker had come to him after the Piper murdered his son, a heartfelt need to help another human being in pain had driven Friedkin to help him. Friedkin judged that decision as a mistake now. Business drove business. Not vendettas. Vendettas were messy, sticky things that never ended well. Poor judgment ran vendettas and he'd made a number of questionable decisions. When Rooker needed him to cross a line, he crossed it, because it was for the good of the case.

"Do you still want me to put Scott under surveillance?"

"Yes. I want to know where he goes and who he sees."

"Do you really think he's in contact with the Piper?"

"I'm not taking any chances. If he is, I want to know."

"What about Fleetwood's kids?"

"What about them?"

"Do you want me to find them?"

"No. That's the FBI's job."

TWENTY-THREE

"How have you gotten on with that second ransom?" the Piper asked.

By now, Scott had gotten used to the monitored phone sessions with the Piper. Too used to them. "I've got it. When can I give it to you?"

"Monday."

"I have the cash now. There's no need to wait until Monday."

"Scott, be patient. This isn't just about you and your family. The safe return of your boys depends on my escape. Haste over prudence will lead to my capture and Sammy and Peter's deaths."

Jane slapped a hand over her mouth and rushed toward the doorway as if to leave, but hesitated, then returned. Scott understood. He wanted to get away too, but that meant abandoning their children.

"I need to have some mechanisms in place before the exchange goes down. Monday is the day."

"Can I speak to my boys?"

"No."

"I need to know they're okay."

"They are. You have my word."

"Your word?"

The Piper pounced on Scott's accusation. "Yes, Scott, my word. I've always stuck by my word. You do as I say, all is well. Don't and people die. I said if I wasn't paid on time, I would kill Nicholas Rooker and I stuck by my word."

Scott glanced over at Charles Rooker standing in the doorway to the living room. Upon hearing his son's name, Rooker let his gaze fall to the floor. He hesitated for only a second before disappearing into the hallway in the direction of the kitchen.

"Don't forget that you and the FBI ignored me. I tried warning everyone but no one listened. Do as I say and your boys will be returned unharmed."

"What happened before won't happen again," Scott said.

"I'm glad to hear it. I will get in contact at ten p.m. on Monday. Don't be somewhere else. You won't hear from me until then."

The line went dead.

"None of this makes sense," Brannon said. "What the hell is this guy playing at?"

"He's rewriting the book on kidnappings," Dunham said.

"He's writing a bad book," Sheils corrected. "He's giving us too much time."

The FBI's confusion failed to warm Scott. As much as lack of progress helped him with his task, he wanted Sheils and his team to find the Piper first.

Jane leaned over and hugged him. He held her tight.

"Do you think Sammy and Peter are okay?"

Her question carried extra weight today. Now that they were both working for the Piper, she needed to know if the kidnapper could be trusted.

"Yes, I do. He won't harm the boys—not if we keep following his script." He hadn't wanted to add the modifier to the end of his sentence, but he couldn't lie to her.

Scott noticed Rooker gesturing to him from the doorway. He took Jane's hand and led her over to him.

"I'm sorry you had to hear some of that," Scott said.

Rooker waved it away. "I'm used to his rhetoric. I refuse to let it get to me. Look, I have some people coming to my home tonight that you should meet."

"Who?" Jane asked.

"People who'll understand and may even be able to help."

"I don't think we can leave," Jane said.

Scott watched the organized chaos around them. "I don't think they'll miss us."

Sheils was knee-deep in a conversation and Scott didn't feel like interrupting. Sheils could find him if he tried hard enough. On the way out, he left word with the nearest agent that they were leaving with Rooker.

Rooker drove them out to his home in Pacific Heights. It was a typical Victorian mansion that was relatively commonplace in San Francisco.

Rooker's guests had already arrived. The house sat on a corner lot and several cars ate up curb space along its two sides. Rooker parked in the garage.

He guided them through the house toward a burble of voices coming from a ballroom-sized living room. Rooker didn't have to introduce his guests. Scott recognized them. In order of Piper kidnappings sat Dan and Carol Fairweather, Gilbert and Rosa Rodriguez, David and Linda Cho, William and Toby Gottfried, and Frank and Janet Rudolph. Michael and Chloe Rodgers were the only ones not present.

It looked to be a casual affair until Scott and Jane's arrival turned it formal. The group sat clustered around a long marble coffee table that held three decanters of wine. Everyone had glasses in hand. No one made any move until Gilbert Rodriguez put down his glass, came over to Scott and Jane, and shook their hands.

"I'm sorry for what you're going through."

"Thank you," Jane said.

"I think everybody knows everyone," Rooker said. "And why we're all here tonight."

Scott and Jane sat down in a love seat.

"Maybe I should explain who we are," Carol Fairweather said. "When the Piper took Gilbert and Rosa's daughter, Sophia, Dan and I saw they were going through the same hell we'd gone through when the Piper took our daughter, Camille. We contacted them and offered our support and love."

"It helped us survive," Rosa Rodriguez said.

"And it helped us heal," Dan Fairweather said.

"We came together again when the Piper kidnapped David and Linda's girl, Annabel," Carol said. "By then we realized we had a support group for families victimized by the Piper. We welcomed a family into our group with each successive kidnapping."

"That's amazing," Jane said.

"Are Michael and Chloe Rodgers not part of the group?" Scott asked.

Rooker reached across the coffee table to pour himself a whiskey. "The Rodgerses didn't want to meet you."

Scott could guess why. The grudge against him for Nicholas Rooker's death extended further than just Sheils. Strangers still shunned him, so victims of the Piper came as no surprise.

"They should have come," Gilbert said. "We promised to support all victims."

"They have their reasons," Rooker said. "Let's respect those reasons."

"And you've been meeting ever since?" Jane asked.

"Only as needed," Linda Cho said. "More around the time of a kidnapping. Less when everyone is home safe and sound." Her voice faltered and she looked apologetically at Rooker.

"We haven't met in seven years." Rooker smiled at

Linda. "These people helped with the grieving. But once that was over and the FBI wasn't going to find the Piper, we stopped meeting. Until Sammy and Peter, that is."

"We understand better than anyone what you're going through," Carol said. "We're here for you. If there's something you want to get off your chest, say it. If you want to cry, we've got shoulders for that too." She finished with a smile aimed at them.

The support group presented Scott with a golden opportunity. He needed information about the Piper and he had families of six of the kidnappings in one room. They had to know something.

"I just have questions," Scott said. "The Piper hasn't let us speak to the boys. I want to understand what's happening to them. Could I speak to your children?"

The warmth in the room turned cold. David Cho, who'd yet to speak, glared at Scott. According to reports in Friedkin's investigation, Cho had become a possessive father since his daughter's release. Scott could understand that. He knew when he got his boys back, there'd be changes when it came to their security. He hoped he could appeal to Cho's wife for help.

"For what purpose?" Toby Gottfried asked.

"I want to know if the Piper looked after them."

"And not as part of a story to splash across the pages of the *Independent*?" she asked.

"I've imaged every kind of hell these past few days," Jane said. "I caught the Piper stealing Peter. I begged for his life. He made me think I was about to die. If he could torture me like that, then what's he doing to my babies?"

Scott could have kissed his wife. Her heartfelt appeal took the sting out of the parents. Toby lost her steel-hard aggression and relaxed in her seat.

"He never harmed Camille," Carol said. "She said he was very kind to her."

"Can I speak to her?" Scott asked.

"She's in college. Duke. I'll give you her number."

Carol's generosity unlocked the doors and all the parents agreed to provide phone numbers as long as their kidnapped children agreed. Only Rooker had nothing to give. Nicholas had no tale to tell. Scott watched the property tycoon retreat from the conversation. He got up with his wine in hand and wandered over to the window to pretend something out there interested him.

Cho held out a business card with his daughter's contact information written on the back. When Scott took the card, Cho didn't release it.

"Your interference eight years ago contributed to Nicholas's death, Mr. Fleetwood. We're exposing our families to you. Can we trust you?"

The chill returned to the room.

Rooker whirled on Cho. "Of course we can trust him. He's the father of two kidnapped children. He has twice as much to lose as we ever did."

Cho released the card.

"Mr. Cho, I made a mistake eight years ago and I'm being made to pay for it. The last thing I'm interested in is making a name for myself."

Scott didn't like lying to these people, especially Rooker. When it all came out—and it would, he had no doubts about that—they would forgive him. If they were in his shoes, they would have little choice but to follow in his footsteps.

The passion went out of the group after that. They exchanged past experiences for about an hour, then called the proceedings to an end. Rooker saw them out.

"I hope you found that useful," Rooker said to Scott and Jane.

"Yes," Jane said. "Very helpful."

"I'll drive you home."

Scott stiffened when the Piper's cell phone vibrated in his pocket. Jane caught his reaction and came to his rescue.

"Would you show me your house first?" Jane asked.

"Of course," Rooker said and led Jane upstairs.

Scott answered the Piper's call.

"How are the feds doing with their search for me?" the Piper asked.

"Not very good."

"And you?"

"Let's end this now. Tell me where to find you. I'll come alone with the money. The FBI won't know. You can take me and release my kids. I don't care what happens to me. Just let my kids go."

"You're just as clueless as the feds."

"Can't we just end this?"

"You still don't get it, do you? This isn't about money. This is about you learning something. You don't learn if someone gives you all the answers."

This was pointless. The Piper was going to keep turning the screws.

"Tell me one fact you've learned about me. If you're correct, I'll let you speak to one of your kids."

"I don't know anything yet."

"Then we've got nothing to say."

"When I find something, then can I talk to them?"

"I'm feeling generous. I'll call you at seven tomorrow night. Impress me."

TWENTY-FOUR

Michael and Chloe Rodgers still lived at the same Palo Alto address they had when the Piper kidnapped Ryan. Mr. Rodgers had made his money in the high-tech boom and held on to it after the bubble burst. Scott pulled up in front of the house just after nine the next morning.

Sheils had given Scott permission to visit the Rodgers family as long as Guerra came with him. Before he opened the car door, he said, "I'd like to do this alone."

Guerra frowned but agreed.

"Thanks. I appreciate it. If Sheils gives you any shit, send him my way."

"Don't worry, I will."

Scott smiled.

He jogged across over to the Rodgerses' house. Their reluctance to attend the support group didn't bode well, but he felt he could open them up in person. He pressed the doorbell and waited.

No one came to the door.

A Nissan Murano sat parked on the driveway. Someone was in. He wouldn't take no for an answer. He pressed the doorbell again. This time, he kept his thumb pressed on the button.

Thirty seconds later, footsteps struck the tiled floor in the foyer. Chloe Rodgers opened the door as far as the security chain allowed.

"Mrs. Rodgers."

She cut him off. "I don't want to talk to you, Mr. Fleetwood."

"This is for my children."

"I don't care."

How could she not care? Hadn't she gone through the same trauma? How could she be so callous toward his pain?

She pushed the door to close it, but Scott jammed his foot in the way. Panic flared in her eyes. She leaned hard on the door, crushing his foot. "Leave. Now."

Chloe pressed on the door with all her weight. Luckily for Scott, she was a small woman, no more than five feet tall and slender. Scott had a considerable height and weight advantage over her. He leaned into the door, easing it back despite her best efforts. She conceded defeat and stepped back from the door, disappearing from Scott's view. Wanting to show he meant no harm, Scott took his foot from the doorjamb, but kept a hand pressed against the door to keep it cracked open.

"I'm calling the police." Her voice bordered on a shriek.

"Please, Mrs. Rodgers, I just need to ask you a couple of questions. The Piper has both my boys."

She stepped back into view.

"This isn't like when he took Ryan. He isn't interested in the money. He's not going to return them unless I get to him first."

For the first time, she didn't look at him like an adversary. Concern and passion filled her face.

"The Piper almost ripped my family apart and we hadn't done a thing to him," she said. "You brought this upon yourself."

"Don't you think I know that?"

"We're done with the Piper. We paid and got Ryan back. Our slate is clean with him. If my family helps you, we put ourselves back in harm's way. I won't do that. I'm sorry. Please leave."

Scott understood this woman's fear and he was sympathetic. She was only protecting her family, but goddamn it, where was her compassion? Where was her humanity? Surely, she couldn't just close her eyes to what was going on.

"Think about this, Mrs. Rodgers. If someone could have helped you when the Piper had Ryan, wouldn't you have wanted them to help?"

"But there was no one."

"But if there was?"

"But there was no one," she repeated.

Scott felt his grip on her slipping. He was at the point of begging. "Maybe this is something you should discuss with your husband?"

"My husband feels the same way."

"Mrs. Rodgers, please."

"No one has caught this man and I doubt they will. I don't want him finding out that we helped you."

A young man appeared behind her. "Mom? What's going on?"

"Nothing, Ryan. Stay there."

"Ryan. I'm Scott Fleetwood," he said in a rush before Chloe could cut him off. "The Piper has my children. I want to ask you some questions."

"Don't listen to him, Ryan."

Shock and confusion swept across Ryan's face. He rushed toward the door.

"Stay right there, Ryan," Chloe ordered.

"Mom, let him in."

"No."

"Ryan, I just need five minutes of your time. I need to ask if you have any recollections from your time with the Piper. Do you remember him?"

Chloe hurled herself at the door to slam it shut. Scott reacted just in time. He put his shoulder to the door and got his foot back in the jamb. Her momentum smashed the door against his foot, but he bit back the pain.

"Get out of here," Chloe shouted.

Ryan rushed up behind his mother and put his hands on her shoulders. "Mom, it's okay. I don't mind talking."

She shook him off. "Ryan, call the police."

"Mom, no."

"Do it."

With her focus on her son and not on Scott, her pressure against the door waned. Scott used his weight to force the door open. He reached for his wallet, tugged out a business card, and tossed it through the door. "Ryan, call me. Anytime."

He didn't see the kid pick up the card. He seemed stuck, frozen between his loyalty to his mother and his own will.

"Get out," Chloe screamed.

"Scott," a voice called from behind him. "Step away from the door."

Scott glanced over his shoulder. Guerra was racing across the lawn toward him. Her suit jacket flapped open. Her gun remained holstered. At least she wasn't going to shoot him. Not yet anyway.

"She won't help us," Scott yelled at Guerra.

"Step away."

Chloe Rodgers continued to squeeze the door shut, regardless if Scott was still in it or not.

Scott glanced back at Guerra. She pounded up the short flight of steps leading to the door. "Tell her—"

The next thing he knew, he was in the air. He struck the manicured lawn on his face and Guerra was on top of him, her knee in his back.

"Hold still, Scott," she said.

Scott didn't fight her. Still, she snapped a pair of cuffs on him.

As she helped him to his feet, Chloe Rodgers finally opened the door. She ventured outside, Ryan at her side.

Guerra pulled out her identification. "I'm sorry for any inconvenience."

"I want him off the property."

"I'm doing just that."

"Guerra, ask her to help with the investigation."

"I'll run it past Agent Sheils." Guerra walked Scott over to his Honda. She opened the door, powered down the window, and recuffed him through the window frame. "Wait here while I clear this up."

Guerra returned to the house. She went inside with Chloe and Ryan Rodgers. He hoped she was asking questions, but she left the house less than two minutes later.

Uncuffing him, she said, "You're lucky. I talked them out of pressing charges."

"Thanks."

She pocketed her cuffs, produced a business card from the same pocket, and handed it to him. It was the business card he'd tossed through the door to Ryan.

"Stop pushing, Scott. Stunts like these aren't helping. Put your faith in us. We'll get your boys back."

If you only knew the truth, Scott thought. He rounded the car and got behind the wheel.

She slipped into the passenger seat next to him. He gunned the engine and pulled away. He noticed Chloe watching them from her doorway. "Are you going to tell Sheils about this?"

"Hell, no."

"Thanks."

"I'm not doing it for you. If he finds out I let you harass Chloe Rodgers, he'll skewer me as well as you."

"I wasn't harassing them. I just wanted to talk to them."

"About what?"

"Ryan's experience with the Piper."

"You should have asked me to come with you. Scott, you're a good guy, but you've got to keep it together."

Guerra's exasperation was hard to ignore. This woman had taken to his family, especially Peter. Scott liked this

about her, but he guessed there was an additional factor
that had caused her frustration. She'd been on guard duty
when the Piper had snatched Peter. There was a lot of guilt
lurking beneath the surface. Guilt he could understand.
"You're right. Thanks. And thanks for not telling Sheils."

"You're welcome. Now where?"

"Back home."

They weren't more than ten minutes from the Rodgerses'
house when Scott's cell rang.

"Mr. Fleetwood?"

Scott sat up in his seat. "Ryan?"

"Yeah." The kid spoke in a hushed tone. Obviously, his
mother wasn't too far away.

Scott had to give the kid his due. He understood the importance of the situation. "How'd you get this number?"

"I saw it on the card. I memorized it before Mom took it."

"Just like that?"

"I've got a good memory for details."

Scott hoped his skill extended beyond just remembering
numbers.

"Look, I want to talk, but I can't really speak with Mom
and all. Can we hook up?"

"Sure. Where and when?"

Stanford University's campus provided a pleasant back-
drop for the Starbucks they were waiting for Ryan in. Scott
spotted him walking toward them. He'd grown into a
good-looking kid. Tall to the point of lanky, he would have
been gawky if it weren't for his athletic build. He carried
himself with a confident air. Seemingly, the Piper had
failed to scar him with any lasting effects. Scott hoped the
same would be true of Sammy and Peter.

Ryan walked in and cut his way through the crowded
seating area.

"Thanks for coming, Ryan," Scott said. "It means a lot."

"No worries. I wanted to help."

Ryan buzzed with nervous energy. Scott guessed talking

about the Piper was bound to make anyone a little edgy. "Can I get you something?"

"A latte would be cool."

Guerra slid off her stool. "I've got it covered."

She joined the line of customers and Ryan asked, "Who's she?"

"FBI," Scott said. "Like American Express, I can't leave home without it."

Ryan smiled and slipped onto Guerra's stool.

"So I'm guessing your mom isn't to know of this."

"Yeah. I'm sorry about Mom. She means well, but she's scared. Y'know?"

Scott nodded. "How'd you duck out?"

"I go to school here." He jerked a thumb in the direction of the campus. "I was only stopping by home to pick up some books I needed for a class."

Considering Chloe Rodgers's protectiveness, Scott wondered if she'd chosen Stanford for Ryan based on its proximity to home. "So, why'd you defy your mom?"

"Like I say, I know they mean well and they want to protect me, but I couldn't ignore you. I know what your kids are going through. I wouldn't wish it on anyone. If I know something and it helps the FBI get them back, then I want to help."

"You're a good kid, Ryan." He removed a digital recorder from his pocket. "Do you mind if I record this?"

Ryan shook his head.

Guerra returned with the latte. She handed it to Ryan, then parked herself in a corner of the shop with a newspaper. She looked over at Scott and he raised his coffee cup as a thank-you for her considerateness.

"Can you tell me anything about the Piper? Did you ever see him? Was there anything distinctive about him? Tall? Short? Fat?"

Ryan sipped his latte before answering. "He was a giant with no face. I was nine and doped up, so everything about the kidnapping was a haze. He seemed larger than life. He wore a ski mask and kept me in some sort of basement with no windows and little lighting. He kept to the shadows. The darkness blotted out his ski mask and he looked like the Headless Horseman. I haven't told Mom that I still dream about him."

Ryan seemed to sink into himself. Scott hated himself for raking up the traumatic memories, but Ryan was volunteering this information to help Sammy and Peter. Scott gave him a minute before going on.

"You say you were in a basement. Can you tell me anything about it?"

"It was dirt."

"Unfinished, then?"

"I guess. I just remember a dirt floor."

"The Piper spoke to you."

"Yes."

"Do you remember if he spoke with an accent or used a certain word or phrase all the time?"

Ryan shook his head.

This wasn't going the way Scott had hoped. Asking Ryan specifics wasn't going to yield a unique fact that would satisfy the Piper, so Scott changed his approach. If Ryan's ability to recall the cell number demonstrated his attention to detail, Scott needed to focus his attention. Instead of asking specifics, Scott talked Ryan through events leading up to the kidnapping, during his abduction, and his subsequent release. He used Friedkin's notes as a guide.

The approach worked. Scott noticed how relaxed Ryan had become. Just talking things through had dispelled his nerves. Ryan blotted out the distraction from the customers and staff in the Starbucks. He was no longer at the coffeehouse, he was nine again and the Piper's sixth victim.

Little details made themselves apparent. Ryan recalled the sneakers the Piper wore when he'd snatched him from the soccer tournament he was competing in. The drive to the Piper's hideaway remained a blur. Ryan had been sedated at that point. The Piper's use of a sedative to keep

GET UP TO 4 FREE BOOKS!

You can have the best fiction delivered to your door for less than what you'd pay in a bookstore or online—only $4.25 a book! Sign up for our book clubs today, and we'll send you **FREE* BOOKS** just for trying it out...with no obligation to buy, ever!

LEISURE HORROR BOOK CLUB

With more award-winning horror authors than any other publisher, it's easy to see why CNN.com says "Leisure Books has been leading the way in paperback horror novels." Your shipments will include authors such as RICHARD LAYMON, DOUGLAS CLEGG, JACK KETCHUM, MARY ANN MITCHELL, and many more.

LEISURE THRILLER BOOK CLUB

If you love fast-paced page-turners, you won't want to miss any of the books in Leisure's thriller line. Filled with gripping tension and edge-of-your-seat excitement, these titles feature everything from psychological suspense to legal thrillers to police procedurals and more!

As a book club member you also receive the following special benefits:

- **30% OFF** all orders through our website & telecenter!
- **Exclusive access to** special discounts!
- **Convenient** home delivery **and 10 days to return any books you don't want to keep.**

There is no minimum number of books to buy, and you may cancel membership at any time. See back to sign up!

*Please include $2.00 for shipping and handling.

YES! ☐

Sign me up for the Leisure Horror Book Club and send my TWO FREE BOOKS! If I choose to stay in the club, I will pay only $8.50* each month, a savings of $5.48!

YES! ☐

Sign me up for the Leisure Thriller Book Club and send my TWO FREE BOOKS! If I choose to stay in the club, I will pay only $8.50* each month, a savings of $5.48!

NAME: _____

ADDRESS: _____

_____

TELEPHONE: _____

E-MAIL: _____

☐ **I WANT TO PAY BY CREDIT CARD.**

☐ VISA   ☐ MasterCard   ☐ DISCOVER

ACCOUNT #: _____

EXPIRATION DATE: _____

SIGNATURE: _____

Send this card along with $2.00 shipping & handling for each club you wish to join, to:

**Horror/Thriller Book Clubs
1 Mechanic Street
Norwalk, CT 06850-3431**

Or fax (must include credit card information!) to: 610.995.9274.
You can also sign up online at www.dorchesterpub.com.

*Plus $2.00 for shipping. Offer open to residents of the U.S. and Canada only.
Canadian residents please call 1.800.481.9191 for pricing information.
If under 18, a parent or guardian must sign. Terms, prices and conditions subject to change. Subscription subject
to acceptance. Dorchester Publishing reserves the right to reject any order or cancel any subscription.

JOIN NOW!

the kids docile came with an added bonus. Keeping the kids drugged up reduced their memories to mush. The things Ryan told Scott amounted to a jumble of confused details.

"I'm not helping, am I?"

"You're doing great. Really, you are."

"I thought I would be able to come up with something tangible. It sounds good in my head, but when I say it, it sounds like I'm describing a dream."

"Don't worry about it. Tell me about leaving the basement and when he released you."

"I remember the light hurting my eyes when he took me out of the basement. It was noisy on the way to the van."

"What do you mean?"

"Animals." Ryan got excited. "Lots of animals. I didn't remember it before."

"What kind of animals?"

Ryan put a hand to his mouth while he mined for memories left buried for a decade. Scott gave him the room to mine and remained silent. He didn't want to disturb a breakthrough, should it come.

He glanced over at Guerra. She had her cell phone to her ear. The news wasn't good, judging from her expression.

"This may sound stupid, but I'm thinking horses."

"Any other kinds of animals? Cows? Sheep?"

Guerra hung up and walked toward them. Scott guessed his Q&A with Ryan was about to end.

"No, just horses. I remember the smell of horses. I hate that smell."

Scott thought about the dirt basement the Piper had kept Ryan in. Ryan mentioned the basement had no windows or vents. Normal building codes wouldn't have allowed that. "Ryan, do you think you were held captive at a ranch?"

"Yeah, it could have been a ranch. I don't remember other houses. A farm or a ranch, yes. It makes sense now."

A farm or a ranch. Scott smiled. He had something to tell the Piper when he called.

Guerra appeared behind Scott. She leaned in close. "We have to go. Sheils wants you back at the Federal Building."

"We'll be finishing up in a few."

"No. Now."

"What's going on?" Ryan asked.

"We have to go, Ryan," Guerra said. "Thanks for your time."

"Come on, Guerra," Scott pleaded. "I just have a couple more questions."

"I'm sorry I have to do this, Scott," Guerra said and pulled out her cuffs. "Sheils's orders."

TWENTY-FIVE

Instead of a two-way mirror where others could watch unseen, the interview room featured a less than discreet video camera high up in the corner of the room. A red light glowed next to the camera lens. Scott wondered how many people Sheils had watching the video feed.

No one had read him his rights, so he wasn't under arrest, but he felt his grip on freedom was a tenuous one. Obviously, Sheils believed he had something on him. Scott eyed his watch.

"Am I keeping you?" Sheils stood underneath the video camera.

Just from the Piper, Scott thought. The Piper's next call was at seven. He had twenty minutes to talk his way out of this room. He didn't see it happening. On the drive over, he'd taken the precaution of stuffing the Piper's cell phone between the seat cushions of his Honda. "Just from my wife. Does Jane know I'm here?"

"Yes," Brannon said. He sat across from Scott with a folder on the desk before him.

"Is she here?"

"No."

The folder remained closed. Neither Sheils nor Brannon seemed in a hurry to kick-start the interrogation.

"What's this about?"

"Inconsistencies," Brannon said.

"Lies really," Sheils said.

Scott didn't have time for this. It had to end, and fast. The Piper would be calling and for once he had something for him. Something that would get him a word or two with Sammy and Peter. Sheils had touted the importance of proof of life. Well, he was on the verge of getting it—if he could get his butt out of here. "Tell me about them."

"This is your chance to tell us," Sheils said.

They either had something on him or they were fishing. He flicked through his catalog of deceptions since the Piper had press-ganged him into service. Half the time he'd been forced to conjure something up on the fly. Most of it was watertight, but airtight? He doubted it.

"Look, my children are missing. You should be focusing your efforts on finding them, not hauling me in here for some spurious reason."

"I know my job," Sheils said. "I wouldn't bring you here for spurious reasons. I have good grounds to question you."

"Really? What are they?"

Brannon opened the folder. "We'd like to go over a few things about the ransom drop in Oregon."

Oregon was Scott's Achilles' heel. He'd had so little time to concoct a plausible story that the holes were there, if someone cared to look. Scott had relied on Sheils having more pressing lines of investigation to occupy his time. They'd found something up there—but what—Redfern?

"Walk me through what happened," Brannon said. "From the moment we put you in the car to when you flagged down the truck after your escape."

"You have my statement. This can wait. My children can't. Find them and stop wasting my time."

Scott's tantrum failed to cut the interrogation short. Brannon removed a copy of Scott's statement.

"No one has given the Piper the slip before," Sheils said. "That makes you unique."

"Just lucky."

"Luck doesn't come into it with the Piper. Let's discuss your capture. The Piper kept you confined to the unlocked cargo hold of his truck, but you weren't gagged or bound. Correct?"

Scott nodded despite the weakness of his claim. "I was drugged."

"He shot you up once. A shot of that size wouldn't have kept you sedated long."

"So what are you saying—the Piper let me escape?"

Sheils shrugged. "That's one idea. If you weren't bound or gagged, why didn't you bang on truck walls or scream out for help?"

"He would have killed me."

"Reasonable, I guess. Gutless, but reasonable."

"Hey, screw you, Sheils."

The slur bounced off Sheils. "The Piper held you captive for twenty-four hours, but you escaped less than fifty miles from where he ran you off the road. He could have gotten to Canada in that time. Why didn't he?"

"Didn't you have roadblocks in place?"

Sheils didn't have an answer, but Scott didn't feel like he'd won a point. They were toying with him, eating into his time. He fought the urge to check his watch. It couldn't be seven yet. Missing this call meant missing the chance of speaking to his kids. The Piper would know something was wrong. He guessed it was around quarter to seven. Still time to talk his way out of here.

"We got the analysis back on your clothes," Brannon said.

"It proved very interesting," Sheils said. "We discovered blood. Your blood and someone else's."

Both agents paused for Scott's reaction. Any confidence

he had about leaving the room before the seven o'clock deadline disappeared. He scrabbled for something to shove suspicion away from him.

"That's probably the Piper's blood. Can you trace him with that?"

"Not yet, no," Sheils said.

Brannon flicked through the file. "Did you know Waterloo, where you escaped, isn't far from where Ray Banks lives in Lebanon?"

"Who?" Scott said without any hesitation.

Christ, he was right. They had found Mike Redfern. That was the bombshell they'd come to drop on him.

Sheils marched over to the desk and tossed the open file at him. It skidded across the desk's slick metal surface. Reflexively, Scott slapped a hand on a single eight-by-ten head shot of Redfern lying on a stainless steel autopsy table. The blood and dirt had been washed away, but his cleanliness only highlighted the ravages of decomposition and the bullet wound. Scott recoiled from the photo like his hand was actually touching the corpse.

"Recognize him now?" Sheils asked.

Scott said nothing. His gaze remained on the picture of Redfern, no matter how hard he tried to wrench it away.

How had they discovered him? Scott wondered. *The Piper? Did the son of a bitch sell me out? How the hell am I going to juggle a murder charge with finding the Piper?* He wondered what else the Piper was going to load on his shoulders. Redfern had gotten off easy.

"Talk to us, Scott," Brannon said.

Sheils clamped his hands to the edge of the table and leaned in over Scott. Scott felt the FBI agent was gearing up for the kill. "I don't know him."

"Scott, I'll make it easy," Sheils said. "This is all about the Rooker kidnapping. The Piper sucked us back into this. We're only missing one other person." Sheils rapped on Redfern's lifeless image. "Mike Redfern."

Scott tore his stare away from the photo and looked up

at Sheils. He tried his best to sound confused when he said, "Redfern?"

Sheils smiled, a nasty little thing without an ounce of humor. "That's right. That's Mike Redfern."

Sheils pushed himself away from the table and circled it like a bird of prey. "I have a hard time with coincidence, Scott. The Piper arranged for a ransom drop in Oregon. Very odd, but I can sort of believe it. It forces us to work on the fly. It's a smart tactic." Sheils smirked. "I can almost respect the son of a bitch for it."

Sheils stopped and slammed his hand on the table. Scott flinched in his seat.

"Then some forestry guys stumble upon a corpse. That corpse turns out to be Mike Redfern, the fly in the Piper's ointment in the Nicholas Rooker kidnapping. He's been shot in the face and he died sometime during your abduction. Not only that, it all happened within an hour's drive of where you were." Sheils stopped circling. "Now, that's not coincidence. That's choreography."

Sheils waited on Scott for a response.

Scott's heart pounded. They had him. Eventually, when they ran the blood on his clothes, they'd tie him to the murder. Right now, Sheils had a theory and he was putting it to the test.

"So the Piper killed Redfern, so what?" Scott said.

Sheils snapped his fingers and pointed at Scott with overdramatic flare. "That's what I thought, but it doesn't make sense. Why arrange to kill Redfern in the middle of a ransom drop with the FBI around? That's just asking for a screwup."

"He's showboating," Scott said. "He wants to show the world how good he is. He shows you up yet again, turns my life to hell, and assassinates his number one fan all at the same time without dropping a step."

Sheils exhaled. "Nice theory. You want to hear mine?"

He didn't give Scott time to object.

"You and the Piper are working together. The pair of

you orchestrated this whole thing to extort money and dispose of Redfern."

Sheils didn't know how close he was to the truth. If his grudge wasn't blinding him, Scott felt he would have guessed by now what was really going on.

"Cat got your tongue?"

"It's an allegation unworthy of a response."

"Is that right?"

Brannon rifled through his file again. "Local police entered Mike Redfern's home. They found signs of a struggle. Currently, the place is being checked for fingerprints and trace evidence."

Scott knew they'd find proof to tie him to the house. He hadn't cleaned the place down. He hadn't had the time or the opportunity. He felt the noose tighten.

"We also have an eyewitness," Brannon said. "A neighbor of Redfern's remembers speaking to someone matching your description at the time of your abduction. Would you be available for a video lineup?"

"It doesn't make sense," Scott said. "You said as much yourself. It's overly complicated. Diverting the ransom drop so that it occurs in Redfern's backyard just to kill him is crazy. It could have been done a lot more quietly."

"And to quote you, 'He's showboating.' You both are. You two think you're smarter than us."

"You're crazy."

"Was Redfern part of your act eight years ago?"

"You might not believe in coincidence, but you sure believe in fantasy."

It had to be close to seven now. Scott could play the lawyer card, but not in time to meet the seven o'clock call, and it would only buy him a day. By tomorrow, Sheils would have enough for an arrest. He couldn't find the Piper while he was behind bars. He needed to stay out of jail until Monday. He didn't feel any closer to finding the Piper, but he still had five days. A lot could happen in five days. Christ, Sheils had almost pieced it together in a day.

Scott had to keep the faith that he would find the Piper by Monday. But he couldn't do it if Sheils kept him pinned down here.

"What time is it?" Scott asked.

The question threw both Sheils and Brannon.

"Excuse me?" Brannon asked.

"Time. What's the time?"

Brannon checked his watch. "Six-fifty."

Ten minutes. There was no shaking Sheils off in ten minutes without forcing his hand. He'd lost. There was no other way around it. Maybe this was for the best. He would have liked to run it by Jane, but they had him.

"I can't do this anymore."

TWENTY-SIX

When a case split and the hard shell of lies fell away, a flush of excitement always ripped through Sheils. This time was no different. Adrenaline coursed through him, leaving him shaky and on edge. But this time, his excitement lasted only a minute, because Scott sucked it from him.

"I'll talk to you and only you," Scott said to Sheils.

"It doesn't work that way."

"It does this time or I'm leaving. The only way you'll stop me is if you shoot me."

The hard edge to Scott's words unnerved Sheils. He meant it. He wasn't going to get anything from Scott unless he complied. What did it matter if Scott spoke off the record? It would end up on the record eventually.

"You're wasting time," Scott said.

Sheils nodded to Brannon and Brannon left the room.

"Kill the eyes and ears too," Scott said and nodded at the camera.

Sheils flashed the camera a kill-it gesture. The red light next to the camera lens went out.

"What's the time?" Scott asked. "The exact time."

Sheils checked his watch. "Seven minutes to seven."

"What I tell you doesn't leave this room. Understood?"

Sheils didn't like the turn this interrogation was taking. He'd seen crap like this before when a suspect tried to save his neck, but that didn't jibe here. Scott was vibrating with fear.

Sheils slipped into the seat vacated by Brannon. "I'm not making any promises until I've heard what you've got to say."

Scott shot out a hand and snared Sheils's arm from across the table.

"My kids' lives depend on this and I have minutes to save them." Scott's eyes were wide. "I'll tell you everything, but I need your word."

Sheils knew he was making a mistake, but he wanted to hear what Scott had to say. "You have it."

Scott released Sheils's arm. "I've been working for the Piper against my will. The ransoms have been a cover for his personal vendetta for the screwup with Nicholas Rooker."

"Is that the best you can come up with?"

"I'll prove it. He's calling me at seven on a cell. He's going to let me speak to Sammy and Peter. Let me take the call."

Sheils checked his watch again. Five minutes to seven. Five minutes for Scott to hang himself. It was worth the indulgence. "Where's the phone?"

Sheils guided Scott through the building and to the parking lot. Sheils held on to the car keys just in case this was a scam.

In the parking lot, he chased Scott over to his car and unlocked it. Scott yanked open the back door, stuffed his hand between the seat cushions, and jerked out a cell phone. He powered it up, but it didn't ring.

Sheils imagined the Piper sitting somewhere secluded, phone in hand, waiting for the clock to change from six fifty-nine to seven. He eyed his watch. "It's two minutes to. Let's get you inside."

The phone vibrated in Scott's hand in the middle of a corridor.

"Not yet," Sheils warned.

"I can't hold off. He knows I'm going to be waiting by the phone."

Sheils cursed. He wanted this call taken in a controlled environment. He would have liked to trace it but there was no time for that. If Scott was telling him the truth, as long as they maintained the Piper's belief that Scott still worked under the FBI's radar, they'd have other calls. When those came, he'd be ready. He shoved Scott into a copy room and closed the door.

The phone had rung four times. Scott answered it before it rang a fifth time.

Sheils leaned in to listen. He heard the Piper's electronically disguised voice.

"What have you learned about me, Scott?"

"You keep the kidnapped children at a farm or ranch. Some place with horses."

Sheils flashed Scott a look. Where the hell had he gotten that information?

"How did you come across that tidbit?" the Piper asked.

"From one of the kidnapped children."

"Which one?"

"I'm not saying."

The Piper laughed. "Just like a reporter to protect his sources. Scott, I'm not going to punish your source. I told you I want you to find me. I'm just interested who remembered horses."

"It wasn't part of the deal. Now I want to speak to my sons."

"I said you could speak to one of them. Don't get greedy. Now, which one? Who's Daddy's favorite?"

The perverse pleasure the Piper took from teasing Scott disgusted Sheils.

Scott squirmed. Sheils saw the dilemma. Regardless of which of his sons he chose to speak to, the other would take it personally, especially if the Piper had the boys within earshot. It was the kind of remark that would leave a scar.

"Peter. Let me talk to Peter."

"So Daddy likes Peter more."

"Fuck you. It isn't like that."

The Piper laughed. "I'll get Peter."

Scott sagged. Sheils squeezed his shoulder and gave him the thumbs-up sign.

Distant fumbling noises came over the line. The Piper spoke in the distance. Sheils guessed he wasn't using a cell phone.

Scott stiffened when a boy shrieked. The Piper barked something and the shriek turned to crying.

"Take it easy, Scott," Sheils whispered. He needed Scott to hold it together. "He's not going to hurt them. He still needs you."

The crying increased in volume as the Piper returned to the phone with Peter. Sheils hoped the Fleetwood boys were holding up well. He'd seen Peter and understood why Scott had chosen him over Sammy. Peter needed the reassurance. No kid was built for this kind of trauma, especially Peter. Sheils would hate to see the kid permanently damaged by all this.

"I'm putting Peter on. Don't say anything stupid," the Piper said. "Peter, it's Daddy."

Peter's sobs dried enough for him to speak. "Daddy?"

Scott's knees buckled. Sheils moved in to save him. Scott regained his footing and Sheils released him. All doubt about Scott's claims left Sheils.

"Yeah, buddy. How are you and Sammy?"

The kid sounded tired, but not drugged. That excited Sheils. If Sammy and Peter were undrugged and conscious of their surroundings, they'd make great eyewitnesses, better than the other kids in the Piper kidnap club.

"We're okay."

"He feeds you okay?"

"Yeah."

"And you're not hurt?"

"No. Is Mommy there?"

"No, sorry, bud."

Peter sobbed. "I want Mommy."

"Not this time. Next time. That's a promise."

The Piper snatched the phone from Peter. "I think that's enough. It's starting to get sickening. I'll be in touch."

"When?"

"Tomorrow at five. Tell me something else about me and you can speak to Sammy."

"I will."

Sheils had the Piper. The dumb bastard had gotten too smart for his own good. He would lead him all the way. Sheils made a fist and punched the air. His elbow connected with a plastic cup with pens in it. The cup and pens clattered to the floor.

"Is someone with you, Scott?"

Scott's heart stopped. "No."

"Where are you?"

Scott thought fast. "In a Burger King."

"So you aren't alone?"

"I'm alone in the way you mean."

"What are you eating?"

"A Whopper," Scott said without any hesitation.

Sheils wondered if Scott had realized his critical save. When people lied, they rarely thought beyond the initial lie. Someone says they went to the movies and when they're asked what they saw, they don't have an answer. The Piper had tested that lie by asking what he'd ordered. Most people would have hesitated trying to remember a menu item. Scott hadn't hesitated.

"Do you know how many grams of fat are in those things? You're heading to an early grave eating that crap."

"Not if you put me in one first."

The Piper laughed. "Ain't that the truth? So what happened?"

"A guy knocked his drink over."

"Let me speak to your clumsy friend."

"What?"

"Just do it."

Sheils pointed to himself and nodded. Scott shook his head. Sheils understood Scott's hesitance. The Piper knew his voice. If he recognized it, it was all over. He grabbed two sheets off a Post-it notepad and stuffed them into his mouth. He gagged on the treated paper and glue strip. He chewed fast, working his saliva into the paper to soften it.

"Okay," Scott said and walked across the copy room to Sheils. "My friend wants to talk to you."

"What?" Sheils sounded as if he'd been caught mid-chew, his face stuffed with food.

"My friend wants to talk to you."

"Fuck you, fag. Tell your homo friend to go fuck a pipe wrench."

The outburst created the desired effect. Scott listened to the Piper talk, then hung up.

Sheils spat the chewed wads of paper into a trash can. "Did he buy it?"

"I think so. He said, 'Sounds like you found a real knuckle dragger there. No wonder he knocked his drink over. I doubt his thumbs have had a chance to develop.'"

"Thank Christ. I'm sorry."

"Believe me now?"

"Yes."

"So this stays between us?"

"Yes. Does anyone else know about this?"

"Jane does."

"Okay, I want to talk to you two, but later. I need to square this here. Now go home. Stay there. I'll be along in a couple of hours. Okay?"

Scott looked uneasy, but nodded.

Sheils hustled Scott out of the building. On the way back to his office, Brannon stopped him in a corridor.

"Where's Fleetwood?"

"Gone."

"Gone? We had him. What's going on, Tom?"

Sheils had hoped to gather his thoughts before having to launch into an explanation. "Who was observing?"

"Just Guerra and Dunham."

"Tell them it was all a mistake. Then I want you in my office."

Brannon faltered. "What happened in there?"

"My office in five."

Sheils got to his office and closed the door. He called Travillian at home. He'd gotten as far as telling him there'd been a new development when Brannon knocked at the door. Brannon came in and Sheils put Travillian on speaker.

"So, what did Fleetwood tell you?" Travillian asked.

"I can't go into details but the Piper is monitoring this investigation. I want him to keep believing he has the upper hand. In the meantime, I want permission to run a second investigation outside of this office to follow up on what I've learned tonight."

"You're asking a lot, Tom," Travillian said.

"I know."

"You've got to be shitting me. You haven't believed a word Fleetwood has said since the day you met him, but suddenly, you believe what he told you tonight?" Brannon said.

"Yes, I do."

Brannon shook his head in astonishment.

"Then you have my blessing," Travillian said. "This meeting never happened."

Brannon frowned before answering. "What meeting?"

"Good," Travillian said. "Can you give Tom and me some privacy, Shawn?"

Brannon got up from his seat and left Sheils's office, closing the door after him.

"Tom, you're risking a twenty-five-year career on this."

"I know."

"Would you do this if this weren't the Piper?"

"Oh, c'mon, Bill, I don't know."

"Tom, you should know. If this play hits the wall, not only will you be damaged, so will the Fleetwoods and the Sheilses. So think damn carefully before deciding."

Sheils had tried to ignore the consequences. If he kept one eye on the rearview mirror, he'd never arrive anywhere. But Travillian was right. If he failed, many people would suffer the repercussions. Was he being selfish? Was he so focused on catching the Piper that nothing else mattered? He liked to think not, but he felt the grip of the Piper pulling at him. If he didn't go after this, he'd always regret it. It was true that no one could win them all, but he felt he could win this one this time.

"I know what I'm doing. I know what I'm risking. I can get him, Bill."

"Then you'd better do it."

TWENTY-SEVEN

Interesting, Friedkin thought as he watched Scott leave the Federal Building. Rooker had called him with the news that Sheils was bringing Scott in. He arrived in time to see Scott riding in the back of his own car, driven by one of Sheils's agents. Less than an hour later, he was leaving of his own accord. That said a lot. Sheils's investigation must have taken a shift.

Scott's Honda emerged from the building's underground parking lot and drove past Friedkin's Mercedes C-class. Friedkin waited until Scott was half a block ahead before pulling into traffic. Traffic was light enough to speed, but Scott observed the speed limits, so he wasn't in a rush to be somewhere. Scott crossed a light just as it turned red. Friedkin lagged too far behind to run it and had no option but to stop. He cursed under his breath.

The light switched to green and Friedkin punched the gas. He guessed Scott was heading home and guessed right. He picked him up two streets later. He grabbed his cell and entered Rooker's number.

"Any developments?" Rooker asked.

"I'm not sure. Sheils released Scott. Whatever he thought he had on him, he's dropped. Scott's on his way home. Did you call Fleetwood's wife?"

"Yes, but she knew nothing."

"Look, I'd like to bring more people in on this one. Something's changed in the last couple of hours and I'd like to cover all the bases."

"No. I want to keep this just between you and me. We're playing with fire. Bringing more people in is likely to start one. I realize your limitations, but I'll use my inside position to direct you."

Friedkin didn't understand Rooker's resistance to assign a full surveillance team. It wasn't the money. The man had paid him hundreds of thousands over the years. A team of watchers for a couple of days wouldn't hurt his pocketbook any more than it had already. Friedkin would even do it for cost. He hated doing second-rate work and Rooker was forcing him to do that, but Rooker was the boss.

"Okay. I just wanted you to be aware that I can't be in two places at once."

"I realize that and accept it."

"Putting a tail on Sheils could reveal something."

"Just Scott for now."

Friedkin surrendered and ended the call with "I'll call you back with updates."

Rooker concerned Friedkin. He wouldn't describe him as a friend, but he knew the man well enough to see changes. When Rooker had first come to him, he was a father seeking justice. Friedkin understood that. He couldn't imagine the state he'd be in if someone murdered his son. Now that justice-seeking father was gone. Rooker was on a crusade for revenge. *What does that make me?* Friedkin wondered. *Lancelot to Rooker's King Arthur? Hardly the makings for a happy ending.* The quest seemed to have intensified since Rooker's wife's death. He lost his compass when the cancer claimed Alice.

Scott made a turn. The truck between Scott and Friedkin carried on. Friedkin made the turn as well, but lagged back.

Until the Piper had resurfaced, Friedkin always considered his search for the Piper as a form of rainbow chasing. The FBI hadn't caught this guy with all their resources. His firm was good, but they were no match for the bureau. He didn't feel that he was taking Rooker's money on false pretenses. He thought he might dig up something on the Piper, but the FBI would beat him to the punch. But his assumption was changing. He had a feeling about the Piper this time. He would be caught. And what then? What would Rooker have him do for him then?

Friedkin slowed when Scott reached the cordon around his home. Friedkin stopped short and watched Scott pull into his garage.

He should bow out of this, but if he did, someone else would replace him. Possibly, someone without the same moral responsibilities. He was in this for the long haul. Lancelot picked up his cell and dialed King Arthur's number.

"You told him," Jane said.

"I had to," Scott said. "It was the only way he'd let me go."

He'd gotten her alone in their bedroom. The FBI detail had viewed him with suspicion when he walked through the door. The bureau grapevine worked as fast as any other workplace rumor mill and his sudden reappearance, unescorted, defied comprehension. None of the agents looked happy about it, but he didn't care the moment Jane came rushing over to him.

"The Piper called while I was with Sheils. That's how I got him to believe. He heard him."

Jane fixed him with a stare that said she hadn't made up her mind that he'd done the right thing. He said something to change that.

"I spoke to Petey."

He stunned Jane into silence.

"He said he and Sammy were fine."

Tears filled Jane's eyes. "Thank God."

"He sounded so scared. I'm scared. So far, I'm keeping up with the Piper, but I'm frightened I'm going to fail."

He couldn't play the tough guy any longer. It was shredding him from the inside. Jane pulled him to her. It all came out—all his fears. He told her everything he couldn't share with Sheils, Friedkin, the Piper, not even himself until now.

"We'll get them back," Jane said when he had talked himself out. She pulled away from him. "You hear me?"

Scott nodded and went into their bathroom. He ran a damp washcloth over his face and neck. It reminded him how soiled the rest of him was. He stripped off his shirt and wiped the washcloth over his chest. As he toweled off, Jane threw him a T-shirt.

"Can we trust Sheils?" she asked.

"I think so. He had enough to nail me, but he didn't."

They lay on the bed in each other's arms until an agent knocked at the door. "Mr. and Mrs. Fleetwood? Agent Sheils is here and he wants to talk to you."

"Okay," Scott answered. "We'll be down in a minute."

Jane frowned.

"We're about to find out if we can trust him."

They found Sheils sitting at the table in the kitchen, alone. All the other agents were gone.

"Where is everyone?" Jane asked.

"Dinner break," Sheils said. "We've got a lot to talk about."

Someone let themselves in the front door. Scott jumped to his feet.

Sheils put out a hand. "It's okay. He's with me. We're in the kitchen, Walter."

No one answered. Footsteps cut through the house. A black man with close-cropped gray hair stopped in the doorway. Although in his sixties, he showed no signs of frailty. He carried a fearsome build that filled the doorway.

"Good evening. I'm Walter Jones."

Scott couldn't believe it. Sheils had promised to keep silent and he'd already betrayed him. He aimed a finger at Sheils. "You promised to keep this between us."

"You said we could trust him, Scott," Jane barked.

Sheils held up his hands. "I know. I should have told you, but I didn't have time."

Jones took a couple of exploratory steps into the room. "Look, folks"—his voice oozed calm—"your confidence hasn't been breached. I'm not with the FBI. I'm retired."

"Walter worked the first two Piper cases with me. He's familiar with the Piper's methods," Sheils said. "We need an outsider for this to work."

"Why?" Jane asked.

"We can't tip our hand to the Piper. For all intents and purposes, it's FBI business as usual. We don't have any leads or clues. Walter can work the leads without alerting anyone."

It made sense. Scott just wished Sheils had run it past them first. He regained his cool and sat at the table. Jones took this as an all clear and joined them.

"We don't have much time," Sheils said. "I don't want my people seeing Walter. I need you to tell us everything that's happened since the Piper conscripted you."

The details poured from Scott. He recalled the stages with perfect clarity. His journalistic background had nothing to do with it. The events masterminded by the Piper had been burned into his memory. Waking up to find Redfern's corpse would never become a distant memory. Those events would be with him until the day he died.

Both Sheils and Jones scribbled notes on legal pads. Scott hoped those notes were the forefathers to plans that would bring down the Piper.

When he was finished, Jane slipped an arm around his shoulder and squeezed him.

"That was good," Sheils said.

"Now what?" Scott said. "We need to come up with something to give the Piper tomorrow. If we do, he'll let me talk to Sammy."

"I'd like that cell phone for a start," Sheils said. "I'd like to put a trace on it."

"Will he be able to tell if you're tracing the call?"

"No."

"I don't think it's imperative that we find anything out by tomorrow," Jones said.

"It is to us," Jane said.

"I realize that, but tracing the Piper's location may be all we need to track him down."

"But if we don't track him from his call, that's another day wasted," Scott said. "I have until Monday to find him and go to him. We have to be doing something to find him. If Monday comes and we haven't found him, I don't know what comes next."

"I want everything Friedkin gave you today," Sheils said. "I want to know if those guys found anything out on the Piper."

Scott was about to tell Sheils not to bother. Friedkin's investigators hadn't dug up much after eight years. Then it struck him. Someone else had done a far more thorough investigation.

"Do you have access to Mike Redfern's place in Oregon?"

"Yeah," Sheils said.

"When I was at his place, he had box files full of stuff he'd put together on the Piper. I didn't get a chance to read it all, but he had a lot."

"We got everything when we busted him," Sheils said.

"I'd say you didn't from what I read."

"I'll check this out," Jones said.

"Go now," Sheils said. "I'll clear the way so you don't have any problems with access."

Jones rose. He thanked Scott and Jane and shook their hands before leaving the way he'd come—quietly and without fuss.

"What do we do?" Scott asked.

"For once, we work together," Sheils said.

TWENTY-EIGHT

Annabel Cho lived and worked in Napa. She was a sales manager for a prestigious vineyard. David Cho had called the day before to say his daughter was willing to speak about her kidnapping experience. The tension in Cho's voice indicated that this was a reluctant concession. Jane wondered if Rooker had twisted his arm. Cho had one stipulation. Only Jane could meet with his daughter. Scott wasn't happy with the concession, but he understood it. Out of all the Piper's surviving victims, Annabel had it the hardest. It had never been reported in the press, but Friedkin's file and Sheils's confirmation revealed mistreatment. Annabel had returned home with a broken arm. The girl insisted that the Piper had treated her well. Supposedly, the broken arm was the result of an accident and the subsequent sepsis an unfortunate side effect. Either way, the Piper delivered a very sick child to her parents after they paid one and a half million dollars.

As Jane crossed the Bay Bridge, a weight lifted from her shoulders. The Piper had turned her city into something oppressive and ugly. She prayed the oppression would leave when they got Sammy and Peter back. She hoped her boys would blind the town with their brightness. If not, she wasn't sure she could live there anymore.

She hadn't shared this feeling with Scott. There was too much on his shoulders already. He was willing to sacrifice everything for the boys' safe return. She knew it was more than just parental instinct that drove him. Getting their boys back and toppling the Piper was also Scott's way of shedding his guilt. Destroying this monster would never resurrect Nicholas Rooker, but it would bring his killer to justice. She felt her love for Scott swell. She forgave him for what he'd done in the past and for the deception when the Piper had inducted him. He hadn't done this out of spite, malice, or for profit. How could she hate him for that?

Jane reached Napa by ten-thirty. Annabel had specified they meet at the winery itself. Jane found the place easily enough. Its marquee name made it a tourist spot as well as a working winery. Bus tours stopped every day to see how the vineyard and winery operated. The restaurant and gift shop just underlined its popularity.

She parked and followed the signs to the restaurant. They'd agreed to meet there. It wouldn't be open this early in the day and they would have the place to themselves. The restaurant door was locked and she knocked on the windowpane. A striking Asian woman emerged from a booth. She waved and unlocked the door, but showed no warmth at Jane's arrival.

"Mrs. Fleetwood?"

"Yes." Jane smiled, hoping to melt the ice between them. "Call me Jane."

Annabel nodded and led Jane over to the booth.

"Thank you for seeing me," Jane said. "I think you're one of the few people who understand what we are going through."

"My parents can." She kept the remark on the right side of polite. "I have more in common with your sons."

"Yes, you do. So for my boys, I thank you."

"How can I help you, Jane?"

"I'm trying to learn something about the Piper. I'll be candid with you. The Piper's drive this time isn't monetary as it was with you and the other children he kidnapped. It's personal. He wants to inflict maximum damage on my family."

"He's not like that."

Annabel's remark was reflexive and threw Jane. "What do you mean?"

"The Piper was never mean to me."

Jane noted a hesitation when Annabel said the Piper. She could have sworn Annabel had almost called the Piper by his name.

Annabel moved quickly to say, "He was anything but. He was a gentleman."

Jane threw out the game plan she'd walked in with. She had to play it careful. There was something wrong here. Annabel was holding back. "But this *gentleman* broke your arm."

"Not on purpose," she snapped.

Jane sipped her water to give Annabel time to cool down. "How did you break your arm?"

"He was carrying me down a ladder and he slipped and fell. He did his best to protect me, but I landed awkwardly on my arm and his falling weight broke it."

"It was an accident."

"Yes." Her answer was emphatic with no room for misinterpretation.

"But he made no attempt to take you to a hospital."

"He was hardly about to do that considering he kidnapped me."

"It was a compound fracture. Anything could have happened. He was risking his reputation and your health by holding on to you. A smart move would have been to leave you at a hospital and cut his losses."

"He knew how to take care of me."

"He had medical training?"

"He wasn't a doctor, but he knew how to take care of the break."

Jane doubted that. Friedkin's file indicated that Annabel had undergone numerous procedures to reset her arm to prevent necrosis and deformity. She guessed the Piper knew only rudimentary first aid. "But your health deteriorated. You went into septic shock."

"He did his best with what he had."

"Ryan Rodgers remembers being kept in a cellar or basement. Is this what you remember?"

"I remember a room without windows. I couldn't swear to it being a basement, but I wasn't there long."

"He moved you?"

"When I got sick."

"To where?"

"A bedroom."

Jane struggled to contain her excitement. Was this another lead? Another break? After feeling so impotent for so long, she was getting somewhere. "A bedroom—where? In a house? An apartment? A ranch?"

The mention of a ranch halted Annabel. "Why did you say a ranch?"

"Ryan Rodgers mentioned a ranch. Do you remember a ranch?"

Annabel's expression tightened as she tried to squeeze out a recollection. "I don't think so."

"Are you sure?"

"I'm sorry. I don't really know."

Jane could feel Annabel selecting facts before answering. "Horses. Do you remember horses? Did you hear them or smell them?"

"I don't remember a ranch."

You're pushing too hard, Jane, she thought. Her excitement was getting the better of her and Annabel was binding up. Her hand trembled when she picked up her water glass, so she put it down. "Did you mention to the FBI that the Piper moved you?"

Annabel uttered a disgusted laugh. "Your boys are going to see the other side of the FBI when they come home. They badgered me like I was a suspect. I didn't know what was going on. I was eleven years old. I didn't make sense of what went on until much later."

Jane felt sympathy for Annabel. She'd seen how Sheils had treated Scott. Sheils's drive to capture the Piper was relentless. "Why didn't you mention it to them later? The Piper kidnapped other children after you."

"My family drew a line after my return. They weren't going to subject me to more FBI interrogations."

It was a selfish attitude, but Jane could empathize. Sammy's and Peter's lives were at stake. No one else mattered. She'd crawl over anyone to save her babies. "Do you remember the drive at all?"

"No."

"It's always been a matter of some uncertainty whether the Piper worked with accomplices or alone. Did you ever see or hear others?"

"Just him."

"Ever see his face?"

The question took Annabel by surprise. This had been Jane's intention. This woman was holding out. Jane got the feeling she'd gotten close to the Piper. Too close.

"No. Never. He kept his mask on at all times."

"I don't believe you."

"I don't care what you believe. I'd like you to leave. I only agreed to this meeting because my father asked me to. I think I've given you more than enough of my time. I hope your children are returned to you unharmed."

Annabel slid out from the booth.

Jane grabbed her arm. Annabel attempted to wrestle it free, but Jane clung on. She pulled Annabel toward her until their faces were inches apart. "The Piper killed two people. It's more than likely he'll kill my sons."

"I don't know anything about that."

"You know more than you're saying. I suggest you say it."

"I don't know anything. Now leave."

Jones stretched his back out. He'd been at Mike Redfern's files for five hours straight. He got up and walked around Redfern's living room.

"Coffee break?" the young officer assigned to him asked.

Sheils's words had gotten Jones through the door, but not out of it with Redfern's files. The locals were okay with an outsider rummaging through Redfern's things, but only under their supervision. Cooperation was one thing. Rolling over for the feds was another.

"Yeah," Jones said. "I'll make the run. You want anything?"

"A latte. Low fat. No whip."

"Son, I'm getting coffee, not a cocktail. Coffee comes one way—black and hot, like Angela Bassett."

The kid smiled. "Then I'm good."

Jones frowned. "I'm betting you don't want a doughnut either."

"You have to keep a handle on the carbs or they'll have a handle on you."

Jones frowned. "You dishonor the brotherhood. I'll be back in ten."

He drove out to a doughnut place he'd seen on his way to Redfern's. He bought two coffees and a couple of pastries the kid wouldn't like. He should know his roots.

On the drive back, he thought about Redfern. He had to hand it to the guy, he'd been resourceful. How the holy hell he'd gotten official police reports, phone records, and all manner of documentation was beyond him. The case file he'd put together was impressive. They could have used his insight during the investigation.

Redfern had put together a map. It showed the snatch

sights of all the kidnapped kids. It made a pattern. All the kids had been kidnapped within thirty minutes of a central point. In Redfern's notes, he clung to the notion that the Piper kept the kids somewhere in the East Bay, probably Oakland. Jones gave it six out of ten with an A for effort. He saw something that made a lot more sense to him. The central point Redfern pinpointed wasn't the Piper's hideout—it was his escape route. The central point was within spitting distance of five freeways—I-80, I-580, I-680, I-880, and I-980. Those freeways sent him in every direction. His hideout could be anywhere.

The only thing that reined in the hideout location was the Rodgers kid's claim about the ranch. The ranch restricted things. Jones couldn't see the Piper straying too far from the action because he needed to be close to the ransom drops. If he were the Piper, he wouldn't want to be more than three hours away from the Bay Area. Dollars to doughnuts, the bastard never had the kids with him during the ransom drops. Dozens of cities were clustered around the Bay Area making it difficult to possess a secluded ranch with horses, so he surmised the Piper's ranch was within two hundred miles of the Bay Area.

He pulled up in front of Redfern's house and carried in the coffee and pastries. His young cop looked less than impressed when he plunked down a cup of scalding-hot coffee and something sweet and sticky.

"Get that down, son. Put some fat on those bones. It'll help slow down a bullet."

Jones carried his coffee around the house and poked about. Redfern lived a meager life and it depressed the shit out of Jones. The second bedroom was an office and was Redfern's nerve center for Piper operations. Five years of prison hadn't managed to rehabilitate him. Jones knew that Redfern had taken a few beatings during his stretch and still the guy kept a hold of this junk. Suddenly, Jones's coffee tasted bitter and he set it down on the desk.

He looked around the room, taking it in. It was unimpressively decorated. Painted in the color of two-day-old snow, it wore its drab colors with pride. The paint looked somewhat fresher where the maps and note boards had hung. Dirt rings outlined their positions. The place needed a home makeover.

Then again, maybe it had gotten one already.

His gaze fell on the wall where the map had hung. He went over to the wall and ran his hand over the surface. The shades of paint differed not because of exposure to dirt or light, but because that section of wall had been painted at a different time than the rest of the room.

He stood back from the wall and the answer presented itself. A new section of drywall had been installed.

The reason could easily be termites or dry rot. The Oregon environment was a prime candidate for either.

But Jones had dealt with enough compulsives to know they held on to their prized possessions like a drowning man does a life preserver. Redfern would be no different. When Redfern was busted, he'd let Sheils find what he wanted him to find. He wouldn't haven given up the good stuff. If he had something precious, he might just wall it up and never look at it again. Jones thumped the wall.

"Come in here, quick," he yelled out.

The kid ran in. "What?"

"There's evidence behind this wall."

"How do you know?"

"Twenty-seven years chasing scumbags like Redfern."

"I'll call it in."

Jones raised a hand. "That's where we have a problem. I don't have time for you to call it in. I don't have time for a warrant. I have until tonight to find something on the Piper."

The kid looked nervous and understandably so. His

future career hung in the balance. "I don't know about that."

"I'm going to make it easy for you. I'm not an FBI agent anymore. If I break that wall down, that's vandalism. A misdemeanor. If you break it down, it's inadmissible in a court of law. So I suggest you go buy your low-fat latte with no whip and come back looking suitably shocked."

Jones shoved the weight of the decision on the kid's back. The young cop struggled with the load.

"What's it going to be?" Jones asked.

"I think I'll stop to get a biscotti to go with that latte."

A ranch, Annabel thought. It completed the part of the puzzle that had been missing all these years. She remembered the road. Saw the road sign. She'd driven that road so many times in search of him. In search of Brian. But she never knew what to look for. Now she did.

She roared along CA-128 in her BMW 5-Series. She'd been driving with her foot firmly planted since she'd hit the road. At first, anger had fueled her race car speeds. Jane Fleetwood thought she knew everything, just like the FBI. The Piper was a villain. The Piper was evil. They were out for blood—and themselves.

If they'd only seen him with her. Seen his compassion. His concern. In her head, she played through those days she'd spent with him. She remembered the fear when he took her from her school recital. She didn't know what was going on. One second she was going to the bathroom, the next, powerful arms were restraining her. She'd screamed in the van, but he'd stilled her with his voice. He didn't bark orders or threaten violence. He just spoke to her in that tone of his. The one that said he could be trusted. When he said, "I'm not going to hurt you. It's going to be okay, Annabel," she believed him.

Unconsciously, she touched her arm where the bones had speared her flesh. The break had been a serious one.

The doctors had repaired her arm with no ill effects, except for the scars around the long-since-healed wound. The scars left her self-conscious and she never wore short sleeves out in public. She would around him, though. He wouldn't mind.

She remembered how he'd panicked when he fell down the steps with her in his arms. He drew her into him to protect her from the fall. It had been an instinctive reaction. A loving thing to do. She was to blame. She'd fought him, panicked by the fall. She'd gotten her arm free and when they hit the ground, his weight had broken it.

"Oh, Christ, oh, Christ," he repeated and lifted her mangled arm.

Strangely, his panic had calmed her. The pain knifed through her when she made the smallest of movements and the tears flowed from her without cessation, but she wasn't scared. She watched him with fascination as he hurried to repair her arm. He fed her that drug that left her drowsy and numb, but the kisses he left on her cheeks as he set and bandaged her arm did more for her than any tranquilizer.

He stopped wearing his mask after he moved her from the basement to the bedroom. He came to her after he'd given her antibiotics. He probably thought she'd be asleep. He leaned in to check her temperature by placing his hand on her forehead. She opened her eyes and he jerked away from her.

"It's okay," she said. "I won't tell."

Things changed after that. He didn't bother with the mask. He sat with her most of the time, instead of simply locking her in the room. He read stories to her.

When he told her he was returning her to her parents, she'd asked, "What's your name?"

He'd hesitated before answering. "Brian. My name is Brian."

If Jane had heard the tenderness in his voice when he said his name, then she wouldn't believe he was evil.

Recalling all this took the sting out of her anger. Excitement filled the void. Her foot remained pressed on the gas pedal. She knew where to find him. Fifteen years after he took her, she was on the verge of meeting Brian again.

She stopped the BMW at the road sign she'd spied all those years ago. When Brian had returned her, he hadn't bound her up. He'd just told her to stay still in the back of the van, but she had gotten up and peeled back the drapes to see out the window. She'd murmured the street names and he'd whirled on her.

"Get away from there. What did I tell you about moving?"

It was the only time he'd ever raised his voice to her.

She slipped from the 5-Series and went over to the crossed road signs of McKinley and Walnut. She visualized that moment in the back of Brian's car. Not much had changed in fifteen years. It was a crossroads flanked by fields and trees and little else to define it. She oriented herself with her position when she'd peeked out the window. Brian had turned off McKinley onto Walnut. She hurried back to the BMW and sped away, kicking up dirt.

She'd driven down this road a dozen times, maybe two dozen. Every time, she drove blind, driven by the slim hope that Brian would emerge from his driveway or be strolling to the mailbox.

Annabel scanned the properties on both sides of the road. Unwittingly, Jane had bridged the gap in her memories for her. Annabel had no idea where Brian had kept her. Even when he loaded her into his car to take her home, he'd covered her head with a blanket. But it had been the mention of horses that had done it. She'd never seen the horses, but she'd heard them. A ranch made sense. That explained the hay in the cellar and the wet grass smell that permeated the air.

She knew what she was looking for this time.

A ranch house loomed on a rise on a sizeable section of land to her left. No horses roamed the land, but it was

Brian's place. There was no doubt in her mind about the fact. She jumped on the brake. The BMW came to an untidy stop on the narrow road.

A pickup with an enclosed flatbed sat out front. He was there.

Nerves set in. Her hands shook and she felt hot within the car's air-conditioned cool. Her foot remained on the brake.

This is crazy, she thought. *Why am I doing this?* She'd wanted this moment for years and now she wanted to pull a one-eighty.

Brian was only a few hundred yards away. It would be stupid not to drive up to his door. If not for herself, for him. The FBI was closing in. He needed to be warned—and helped. She would help him if he asked.

She turned into his drive.

"Okay, what have you got?" Sheils asked.

Scott sat in Sheils's car parked across from the field office on Golden Gate Avenue. He had his cell phone plugged into a hands-free unit. Jones's voice came through a tinny speaker mounted in the top corner of the windshield. Sheils didn't want to conduct this covert business in front of his agents, even behind closed doors.

"It's a series of paparazzi-style black-and-white eight-by-tens featuring the Piper, or someone who I assume is the Piper. He's wearing a ski mask. Redfern must have been on top of the guy to take these. Shit, the Piper is supposed to be uncatchable, but this crackpot got these without the son of a bitch knowing."

"Christ," Sheils murmured.

"Are the pictures dated?" Sheils asked.

"You bet. He wrote the dates on the back of each shot. The dates correspond with Ryan Rodgers's kidnapping."

In that moment, Scott lost all sympathy for Redfern. When he'd caught up with him in Oregon, he was a pathetic figure, broken by his own stupidity. It was hard to despise someone like that. Not now, though. Redfern had gotten within arm's reach of the Piper before Nicholas Rooker's murder. He could have prevented the boy's death if he'd come clean and not gotten carried away with his damn fantasy. Not to mention the karmic fact that if he'd gone to the cops, the Piper wouldn't have put a bullet in his face.

"I hope that fucker is burning in hell," Sheils said.

"Ditto," Jones said. "Now, the photos don't help us a whole bunch. They show the Piper walking through a park. We don't see a vehicle or anything incriminating. We have a physical description, but no clear shot of his face."

"So the pictures are useless," Sheils said.

"Not so fast, quick draw. The Piper must have been feeling pretty cocky at the time."

"Why?"

"He's not wearing gloves and I can see a ring. Right hand. Pinky."

Sheils smiled. "School ring? College ring? Super Bowl ring? Something we can trace kind of ring?"

"Don't have to. I have the ring."

Sheils exchanged a look with Scott. "Tell me you're not joking."

"No joke. Christ only knows how Redfern got a hold of it."

"Sure it's not a replica?" Scott asked. "Redfern was all for aping the Piper. Taking secret pictures of him and buying a ring just like his wouldn't be in the realms of fantasy."

Scott wasn't trying to rain on anyone's parade here. He wanted this to be real. He wanted it to lead them all the way to his boys. He wanted to jam the damned ring down the Piper's throat and choke the fucker on it, but he had to be sure they weren't chasing after ghosts.

"I don't think so," Jones said. "He walled this thing up with the pictures. The ring was stored in a nice case. This was special."

"What kind of ring is it, Walter?"

"Signet ring. Black onyx with the letters BG stamped in it. Now, I know BG could stand for anything, but I'm betting it's his initials. This ring looks like something a proud parent would give."

"Shame they didn't shell out for an inscription," Sheils said.

"Them being cheap is the last thing they need to worry about when it comes to their parenting skills. Their little boy grew up to be the Piper," Jones said. "Look, I want to try something here. I'd like to run a property search for someone with the initials BG who owns a ranch within a three-hour driving radius of the Bay Area."

"That's going to generate a lot of names," Sheils said. "Let's cross-reference with people who own homes in the Bay Area counties. This guy will be local."

"Cool," Jones said. "But I want to stick around here. There's still a bunch of notes I want to go through."

"No problem," Sheils said. "Don't touch the ring. We might get lucky on prints or get DNA off it."

"Amen to that," Jones said. "I need you to take care of something else. I have a babysitter, courtesy of the sheriff's department."

"You want to lose him?"

"No, he doesn't know dick about coffee, but he knows right from wrong. Now, the shit's going to hit the fan when you explain how I just happened to punch a hole through Redfern's wall to find his stash. I just don't want any spray hitting the kid."

"I'll take care of it. Hang tight. I call back in fifteen." Sheils hung up and turned to Scott. "I need to follow up on this. Can you disappear for an hour?"

"Sure. I need something to eat. I've got my cell. Call me when you're finished."

They both got out of the car. Scott watched Sheils race across the street. Scott headed toward Market Street.

Jones's breakthrough excited Scott. It brought them a step closer to the Piper and not the way the Piper expected. The son of a bitch wouldn't even know he was losing at his own game. Developments were far from heading to a simple conclusion. The Piper wouldn't go down without a fight. Regardless, things were breaking Scott's way. For once, he felt optimistic. That is, until Jane called him.

"Scott," she said, her voice filled with concern. "I think I wrecked things with Annabel."

Brian opened the door.

Annabel's heart fluttered in her chest and she lost the ability to breathe. She'd guessed right. Surely, that had to be a sign, didn't it? Out of all the homes on this road, she'd picked right the first time.

Time had treated him well. He'd aged, but in a good way. His hairline had crept up his forehead and silver dominated his dark hair. The lines around his mouth and forehead had deepened, giving him a distinguished look. His trim build helped keep him looking vibrant.

Seeing him again warmed her, but he eyed her with suspicion and looked over her shoulder at her BMW. "Can I help you?"

He didn't recognize her. There was no shame in that. She'd been eleven when he'd last seen her. She was a woman now.

"You don't recognize me, do you?"

He shook his head. "No. Should I?"

"It's been a long time."

"I don't mean to be rude, but I have some business to attend to and I don't have time for a sales pitch. Sorry."

He went to close the door.

"Brian, it's me. Annabel Cho."

The mention of his name, not hers, stopped him from closing the door. His gray eyes went wide and he scanned the landscape behind her.

"It's okay, Brian. You have nothing to fear. You're safe with me," she said, then pushed the door open and stepped inside.

He closed the door after her. "What do you want?"

"To see you. You're in the news again. I remembered how kind you were to me." She flushed. "I never stopped thinking about you."

"Let me see some ID."

She delved into her purse and pulled out her wallet. He snatched it from her and removed her license and credit cards. He examined the license photo, then Annabel.

"I'm all grown up." She did a little pirouette for him. "I'm a woman now."

"How did you find me?"

"I sort of always knew where you were. Remember when I peeked out of the car window? I saw the road signs for McKinley and Walnut."

He still retained a note of caution in his voice. She put it down to shock. He wasn't expecting her. But he would relax. He just needed a minute. She would get things started. She wandered over to a love seat and settled into it. Room for two.

He remained standing.

"You didn't just happen to find me from a couple of road signs."

"No, I had help."

"Help? From whom?" Panic edged his tone. He went to the window and stared out from behind the sheer drapes.

"From Jane Fleetwood. You have her boys. She's beginning to work things out."

He whirled. "What do you mean?"

"She doesn't have much and I didn't tell them anything, but something she said connected the dots and I knew where to look for you. I felt I should warn you. Help you, if you'll let me."

She patted the spare seat next to her. He sat, handing her wallet back to her.

She took his hand and placed it between hers. It was warm and dry. Hers were ice cold. All the heat in her body was in her chest trying to contain her pounding heart.

"Why have you come here?" he asked. His tone was soft and soothing, just like it had been all those years ago.

Her nerves melted away. "You were so kind to me during the kidnapping, especially after breaking my arm. I never felt kidnapped. I felt like I was with a friend. No one ever treated me with the tenderness you did."

"Surely, your parents did."

Images of her father drumming into her what was expected of her while her mother turned a blind eye filled her mind. She shook her head.

"Boyfriend?"

"Boys always wanted something. You were the only one who loved me for who I was." She put her hand to his cheek. "You don't know how upset I was when you returned me to my family. I wanted to stay here forever."

He smiled, took her hand, and guided it back to her lap. He let his hand rest on top of hers. His warmth radiated through her hand to warm her thigh.

"I don't know what to say," he said. "No one has ever expressed themselves to me quite like that before. And you've felt that way all these years?"

"Yes."

He patted her hand softly, then stood. He went to the window and peered out before turning back to her. "And you want to help me?"

"Any way I can."

He smiled again. "And nobody knows you're here?"

She joined him at the window. "Of course not. No one understands how I feel about you."

"I doubt they do."

"I want to help you with the boys. I know you work alone, but if you let me help, I can half your work and double the FBI's."

He drew her into an embrace and she slipped her arms

around his waist and laid her head against his chest. His heart beat at a steady, calm rate. He wasn't afraid. He'd make this work.

"You're right. The boys would appreciate a woman's touch. C'mon, I'll show you."

He took her hand and led her out of the house. He pointed toward the barn.

"Where are the horses?" she asked.

"I didn't have the time to take care of them, so I sold them."

"Maybe with me around, you'll have time for horses again."

He looked down at her. "Maybe I will."

They walked toward the barn. It meant nothing to her. Even if she'd remembered it, it still wouldn't have bothered her. He had never intended to harm her.

"Are they in the cellar?" she asked.

"Of course. No one gets special treatment."

She smiled. "Except for me."

He smiled back. "Except for you."

The barn doors were padlocked. He removed the lock and uncoiled the thick length of chain binding the two doors before swinging them back. Light penetrated the gaps in the siding to cut through the gloom. It was enough to illuminate the trapdoor at the center of the floor.

"Ladies first," he said and gestured.

She grinned and walked inside the barn. Her heels sank in the soft earth. She wished she'd dressed for the occasion. It didn't matter. She could pick up a new wardrobe later.

"Annabel."

Hearing him say her name invoked a smile. She turned to face him. His smile tightened into a grimace as he smashed her in the face with the chain. A bomb detonated inside her skull. Blood filled her mouth and spilled down her chin. She flew back, colliding with the soft dirt and spraying blood.

He stood over her, the chain swaying in his grasp. She

looked up and saw a monster hidden in the shadows. The shadows bled into the light, turning everything black. She couldn't keep her head up any longer and it crashed to the ground.

"You've ruined everything," he said.

TWENTY-NINE

"Where are you?" the Piper asked.

"The *Independent*," Scott answered.

He wasn't. He and Jane were at Sheils's home with Sheils and a technocrat named Charlie Pitts. Pitts had jerry-rigged a system that linked up to the phone company to triangulate the Piper's location. Scott's cell was plugged into a unit with handsets that allowed Sheils and Jane to listen in.

They had the house to themselves. Sheils's wife had welcomed Scott and Jane into her home like they were old friends. Seeing Sheils's kids reminded Scott about the size of the hole in his life. As soon as Sheils's wife made sure everyone had a drink in their hands, she bundled the kids and herself out the door, leaving them to their business with the Piper.

"Writing up your next installment?" the Piper asked.

"It keeps the FBI off my back. They don't bother me when I'm here."

"The story's getting cold, though."

It was true. The media were losing interest. Too much

was happening behind the scenes and not in front of the camera. The hordes at his door had dwindled. They needed a body or an arrest to bring them back.

"Not the money-spinner you thought it was going to develop into," the Piper said.

"I didn't come looking for this. You came to me."

"That's true. But you must have thought all your Christmases had come at once when I took Sammy. You know this has book and movie potential."

The Piper was baiting him. He wanted to provoke a fight, but Scott wasn't in the mood. The taunts had lost their effect. The Piper had torn through his life with a chain saw. The insults were cheap by comparison.

"I think you're in it for the fame more than I am."

The Piper chuckled. "Not in the mood to play?"

"I just want to speak to Sammy."

"And you will. So what have you got for me today?"

"Your initials are BG."

"How did you dig up that particular nugget, Scott?"

Scott's palms were perspiring and he tightened his grip on the cell before he dropped it. "Is that important?"

"It is if you want to speak to your son."

Scott had to play it cool. He couldn't tell the truth about Jones's discovery today and he had to keep the lie convincing. He'd hoped not to go this route, but he and Sheils had invented a cover story.

"Mike Redfern. The cops never got all his notes. I got them from his mother. He'd stashed them at her house."

"And how did he find out?"

"If you hadn't put a bullet in his head, I could ask him."

The Piper laughed. "My shortsightedness will be my undoing."

No, Scott thought, *I will be*. "I want to speak to Sammy now." His words came out in a rush. He hated how desperate he sounded.

"In a minute. You're making great inroads. I'm interested in how you're doing it."

"Sammy first."

"Impress me and I'll let you speak to both your boys."

Suddenly, Pitts smiled and put his thumb up. Sheils rounded the desk and looked over the technician's shoulder at his laptop. He pulled out his cell and punched in a number.

Sheils scrawled something on a sheet of paper and handed it to Jane. She read it. Her expression tightened with worry. She showed it to Scott.

It read: WE'VE GOT A LOCK ON HIS LOCATION. HE'S IN THE CITY. I'M GOING AFTER HIM. KEEP HIM TALKING.

Scott's stomach clenched. Everything hung in the balance. One wrong move from Sheils and it was all over for his boys. He shook his head.

Sheils mouthed the words "Yes. It has to be now."

"I'm waiting, Scott."

Sheils used the Piper as a distraction and left the room. Scott went to stand, but Jane put a hand on his arm and shook her head. He settled back in his seat. Pitts looked embarrassed to be caught in the middle of this.

"You moved Annabel Cho from the basement after she got sick," Scott said.

"Is that right? Who told you that?"

"Annabel."

"Wow. I'm impressed. You've achieved a lot in the last couple of days. How close are you to finding me?"

A couple of days, Scott thought. Was that all it amounted to? Just a couple of days? It took the second hand a long time to make a revolution lately. "Pretty close."

"You'll know by Monday?"

"If not sooner." Scott felt incredibly tired. It was taking all his strength to hold the phone to his ear. "Can I speak to my boys now?"

"Get any outside help?"

Scott went cold. The Piper had heard Sheils in the copy room. Scott had detected the skepticism in the son of a bitch's voice at the time. He'd hoped he put enough doubt in the Piper's mind to dismiss it, but had he just deluded himself? It was all going off the rails, just as it seemed it was coming together.

"Christ, no."

The color drained from Jane's face. Her grip on his forearm cut into his flesh.

Scott wanted to reassure her and tell her the Piper was bluffing, but he couldn't. He knew things weren't airtight. The deceptions weren't holding up under the pressure. The Piper could know everything.

"I thought I made it pretty apparent what would happen if you betrayed our confidentiality agreement."

"You did and I haven't. No one knows." Scott didn't like the panicked tone in his voice. He sounded like every movie stoolpigeon begging for his life.

"I'll go get Sammy."

The sound of the Piper putting his phone down echoed through the line to Scott.

Jane went to speak. Scott put a hand up to her mouth to silence her. He hadn't heard the Piper move away. He wouldn't put it past the bastard to trick him to confirm his suspicions.

A few seconds later, he heard the Piper moving away from the phone. He returned with Sammy a minute later.

"Sammy, Daddy's on the other end of the line," the Piper said. "Say hi to your daddy."

Jane clapped a hand over her mouth. Tears burst free and trickled down her face.

"Daddy?" Sammy said.

Hearing his son's voice tore a hole inside Scott. It was the best and worst moment of his life. "It's Daddy, Sammy. I'm coming for you and Peter real soon, okay?"

Sammy broke into tears. "Come now, Daddy."

Scott couldn't hold back his tears. "Oh, Sammy, we're doing everything to get you guys home as soon as possible, but you've got to hang in there. You and Peter have to be strong, you hear?"

"That's interesting," the Piper said. "What you said there."

What had he said? What mistake had he made?

"You said 'we.' *We're* doing everything to get you guys home. Who's we, Scott?"

He needed a fast answer. His mind spun its wheel, struggling for traction. "His mother and me. I don't want him thinking I'm acting alone."

The Piper didn't answer.

The Piper was sweating Scott. Scott fought the urge to speak. Anything he said would be a lie.

"I don't believe you. You've made too much progress in too little time to be working alone. Who knows?"

"No one."

"Tell me the truth and I'll spare one of your sons."

"No. Don't hurt them. I'm working alone."

Sammy's shriek cut through Scott. He found he couldn't breathe.

Jane jumped up. She had a trapped animal look in her eyes. She wanted to bolt, but she couldn't, not when her children were under threat. She retreated to the corner of the room and sobbed silently.

The color had left Pitts's face.

"Do I have to break Sammy's arms and legs before I get an honest answer from you?"

"No."

"Good. Let's review. Today, you dug through previously undiscovered files held by Mike Redfern and you spoke to Annabel Cho. That's pretty amazing considering the FBI doesn't let you go anywhere without an escort."

How did he know about the escort? Had he been watching him?

"I know you're good, but you aren't that good. You need help for that. Now I'm going to ask you one last time, who knows? Lie and I'll kill Sammy. Right here. Right now. So choose your answer carefully."

Would the Piper do it? He'd been so compassionate with

Nicholas Rooker. Now he was threatening to kill Sammy in cold blood. Was it all a bluff? It could be, but Scott couldn't take the chance.

"People know." His words tasted like rust on his tongue.

"No, Scott, no," Jane shrieked.

"My wife and Sheils know."

"Jesus Christ," Pitts said.

Jane charged across the room. She slammed into him and his chair tottered back but rocked back onto its feet. She thumped at his chest. He didn't bother defending himself. He deserved this. He deserved worse. She soon lost her strength and collapsed against him, sobbing. He stroked her back and shushed her, while he kept the phone pressed to his ear. That was the important thing. To maintain the lines of communication to keep his boys alive.

"What have you done?" she moaned.

He'd bought his sons time, but he couldn't bring himself to say the words.

"Thank you, Scott. I appreciate the honesty. I can't say I'm happy about it, but you told me and I respect that."

Scott had trouble speaking. His words caught, forcing him to clear his throat. "What happens now?"

"Punishment."

"Please don't say that. Not Sammy. Not Peter."

"I'm sorry, Scott. You betrayed me. Again. Sammy has to pay your price."

"Don't hurt him. Please. He's just a kid."

"Sorry, Scott. Not this time."

He couldn't control the sobbing, but he was out of tears. He emitted a noise, harsh and ugly. It was the sound of him dying inside.

"Say good-bye to Sammy now."

"No. Stop. A trade. A life for a life."

"I'm not interested in you, Scott. I'm going to have you later."

Jane leaned up from him. "Me," she said.

No, he couldn't do that to Jane. If anyone were to survive this, it would be her and the boys. Everyone else was expendable.

"Tom Sheils knows where you are. He's coming for you. Now."

There was silence for a long moment. It was as if Scott had been struck deaf. The Piper didn't speak and Scott's admission left Jane and Pitts shell-shocked.

"You just saved Sammy's life. Well done."

The Piper's cell was transmitting from an address on South Van Ness, only minutes from Sheils's home. Sheils drove like a madman and parked on a cross street two blocks from the property, a two-story mixed-use building on the corner of South Van Ness and Sixteenth with a clear view of anyone approaching.

Sheils's business suit and necktie clashed with the neighborhood. He stripped off his tie for a more casual look, but he needed his suit jacket to hide his weapon. It wasn't a great disguise but it did give him the appearance of an office worker on his way home. He rounded the corner and approached the building.

His cell rang and he answered it.

"We've got a problem," Pitts said.

"What?"

"He knows you're coming."

He stopped short. "How?"

Scott came on the line. "He knew I was working with someone. I had to tell him. He was going to kill Sammy. I had to trade you for Sammy."

Scott's explanation faded into white noise. The revelation kicked Sheils in the guts. Surprise was the only thing he had going for him and it had been snatched away. Now he was walking into a trap and he didn't see any way to avoid it. Sammy and Peter were in worse danger than before. He had to go in.

"Tom, he knew," Scott said, using Sheils's first name for

the first time. "I'm so sorry. I had no choice. You have to believe me."

The forced betrayal was eating Scott up inside, but his pleading grated on Sheils's nerves. Sheils needed to figure out how he was going to piece this mess back together again. He couldn't do that with Scott bleating in his ear.

He talked over Scott's incessant prattle. "You did the right thing. The situation isn't blown. Is he still there?"

Pitts came back on the line. "After he got what he wanted, he hung up and powered the phone off. I've lost the signal, Tom."

"When did you lose him?"

"Three minutes ago."

The building looked derelict with its whitewashed windows. Sheils looked for signs of movement from within and saw none. Vehicles lined the street next to meters. A couple of vans made for prime transport vehicles, but none had a guy loading kids into them.

"I'll call for backup," Pitts said.

"I'll take care of it. Just be ready if this bastard calls back," Sheils said and hung up before Pitts could object.

He stopped in front of the building. The door to the commercial downstairs section looked fragile enough to give way if he breathed too hard on it. A padlock hanging from the outside said go away.

He stepped back from the building and turned onto Sixteenth. He dialed Brannon's number.

"Shawn, it's Tom."

"Yeah."

His tone was harsh. Obviously, he was still sore about being cut out of the investigation.

"I've got the Piper cornered. Get to the southeast corner of South Van Ness and Sixteenth."

"I'll send up a flare."

"No. Just you and Dunham. I can't explain right now."

"Tom, I don't like this."

"Neither do I. Just get here. I'm going in. I'll stall him until you get here."

"Are you crazy?"

"No. Just out of options," he said and hung up.

He estimated it would take Brannon and Dunham ten minutes. He hoped he could last that long.

He went to the rear of the building. A narrow alley, less than three feet between the building and a chain-link fence, provided access to a rear door. He edged his way to the door. He listened for movement and voices and heard nothing. He tried the doorknob. It wasn't locked.

I'm expected, he thought.

Entering the building without backup was a mistake. The Piper wanted him to enter the building through this door and he'd pick him off the second he charged inside. But if he waited for Brannon and Dunham, he'd have the Piper cornered along with two human shields. If the Piper saw no way out, those boys didn't stand a chance. He had to go through that door alone and shift the Piper's gun barrel from those boys to him.

He unholstered his Glock and snapped back the slide. He inhaled and exhaled to scare away his nerves. He put his back against the wall and twisted the doorknob, giving the door a shove.

No gunshot punched a hole in the half-opened door. So far so good.

He sneaked a look inside. A narrow corridor led into the derelict storefront. A thick layer of dirt dusted the floorboards. Fresh footprints ruined the perfect filth layer. The prints led into the store and he followed them, his Glock leading the way. He stopped at the end of the corridor to listen for a whimper or a muffled threat.

Nothing.

The area was deserted, but the door leading upstairs sat ajar. Sheils had to hand it to the Piper. He liked to tempt and tease. The bastard had left him another invitation. He crept over to the door.

Sheils pulled back on the door. The staircase disappeared into darkness. He aimed his weapon into the gloom and placed his foot on the first step. It didn't creak, but his footfall on the wood was unmistakable.

The time for stealth was over and he pounded up the stairs. With no flashlight, he trusted the next stair would be there to take his weight. He reached the door at the top and twisted the knob. It didn't turn. He was backing up to throw his weight against it when someone called his name from behind him.

The trap had been sprung. He knew it had to come at some point. All he could do was work with it. He whirled and a flashlight beam struck him in the face, turning his vision into a snowstorm. Reflexively, his non–gun hand went to his face to shield the light. That insignificant action was all the edge the Piper needed and he fired twice. Both bullets struck Sheils in the chest. His legs went out from under him, sending him tumbling down the stairs.

He never felt the fall.

THIRTY

The sound of footsteps roused Sheils. It took a second for him to piece the world back together. He lay on the floorboards at the bottom of the stairs. His gun lay three feet from his right hand with the barrel pointed toward him. He was lucky the thing hadn't blown his face off.

The Piper was gone. Sheils didn't have to do a search to know the bastard had left before his head had struck the bottom stair.

"In here," he called out.

Brannon and Dunham stormed into the room, weapons drawn. Their expressions turned grave when they saw he'd been shot.

"Christ," Brannon said, falling to Sheils's side.

"He's gone," Sheils said.

"I'll clear the place," Dunham said. He edged his way past Sheils and clambered up the stairs.

At least someone was playing it by the book.

"I'm getting an EMT," Brannon said, holstering his gun and reaching for his phone.

"We don't have time. Help me up."

Brannon looked grave.

"Just do as I tell you. You can tell me what an idiot I am later."

Brannon took Sheils's arm and hoisted him to his feet. Sheils's body screamed out where the two bullets had pounded his chest. Getting kicked by a rhino couldn't have hurt any worse.

"You're damn lucky you were wearing your vest," Brannon said.

"Luckier that he didn't go for a head shot."

He ripped open his shirt. The slugs lay buried in the Kevlar armor. He peeled off his jacket, shirt, and vest, leaving him in a plain white T-shirt. "We've got our first ballistics evidence."

Dunham came trotting down the stairs. "Clear."

Sheils picked up his Glock and holstered it.

"What now?" Brannon asked.

Sheils handed Dunham the vest. "Get that to someone who can tell me if those bullets match anything. I need to pick up the Fleetwoods."

"What about this place?" Brannon asked.

"Secure it and I want to know who owns it."

Sheils led the way out of the building. His chest ached every time he breathed and his footfalls drove a spike into his brain. His earlier remark about not needing a doctor felt like bravado now. He took extreme care when he stepped from the doorway into the alley but almost puked. He sucked in a lungful of alley air to chase away the nausea.

Brannon placed a hand on Sheils's shoulder. "Tom, you should get checked out."

"Later. We need to move fast."

A '78 Camaro slid to a halt in front of the building. Scott and Jane clambered out of the car.

"You shouldn't be here." Sheils's bruised rib cage prevented his remark from sounding like a reprimand.

"When you stopped answering your phone, we had to come," Scott said.

"You could have gotten yourselves killed."

Jane grabbed Sheils's arm. "Sammy and Peter?"

He shook his head. "He got away. I'm sorry."

"Shit," Scott said.

Jane sagged. Then she noticed Dunham holding Sheils's battered Kevlar vest. Her gaze went from the vest to Sheils. She examined him, noting his disheveled condition and his pallor. "What happened?"

"Ambush. He knew I was coming. We knew it would go down that way."

"And you still went in?"

"I had to."

Scott rounded the car. He checked out Sheils's condition and ran a hand through his hair. "Christ, I nearly got you killed."

"You played it the right way."

Sheils felt Brannon's and Dunham's stares. They wanted an explanation, but they weren't getting one for now. Not everything was in ruins. The Piper now knew he was involved, but he didn't know about Jones. Jones could still work in the open unseen. It left a back door open. He could still nail the bastard.

"We need to get you home," Sheils said. "Now."

"Why home?" Jane asked.

"We nearly had him, so he's going to accelerate things now. He'll strike out to keep us distracted."

"Strike out at the boys?" Jane asked.

"No. He still needs the boys. Now let's go."

Scott pointed at the Camaro. "What about the car?"

"Lock it and leave it."

The lights changed and Sheils hustled them across the road in the direction of his Crown Victoria. Dunham jogged off toward his car, the Kevlar vest tucked under his arm. Brannon stayed to secure the scene.

"That's Pitts's car. He doesn't let anyone drive it," Sheils said.

"We persuaded him," Scott said.

Sheils couldn't see Pitts doing him any favors any time soon.

Sheils tossed his car keys to Scott. He wasn't up to driving. He stretched out in the front passenger seat. His chest hurt less when he didn't bend. Scott sliced through traffic. His driving left Sheils nauseated and he powered down the window to get some air.

"What's the Piper's next move?" Scott asked Sheils.

"He'll regroup, get your boys to another safe house, then call."

They arrived outside the Fleetwoods' home to confusion. Two of Sheils's agents were restraining an Asian man, while an Asian woman tried to pry the agents off him.

"That's David and Linda Cho," Jane said.

All three of them got out of the car and David Cho turned at the sound. His angry expression turned enraged when he saw Scott and Jane. He tore himself free of the agents and raced toward the Fleetwoods.

"What did you do to my daughter?" he yelled at Jane.

Sheils stepped in front of Scott and Jane to block Cho's path.

Cho called out his question again and lunged for Jane, but Sheils restrained him long enough for the other two agents to catch up and take over. Linda Cho begged them to release her husband.

"Mr. Cho, I'm Agent Sheils. Remember me?"

The question distracted Cho and took some of the fury from him. "Yes, I remember you."

"Tell me what's going on."

"They wanted to talk to my daughter. Mrs. Fleetwood saw her today." Cho couldn't have injected any more repugnance into her name if he tried. "Now Annabel's missing."

"Missing?"

"Yes," Linda Cho said. "She left work earlier, but she's not home and isn't answering her cell phone. No one knows where she's gone."

Cho turned on Scott. "I warned you, Fleetwood. She's a

delicate girl. I didn't want all this getting dragged up again. It's not good for her. You hurt her to save your children."

Then the rage and the strength went out of Cho. He sagged and only the two agents holding him prevented him from striking the pavement.

"I just want her back. Do you know where she is?" he pleaded.

The crazy bitch, the Piper thought, *what the hell was she thinking?* At first, he'd thought Sheils had found him and sent in a decoy Annabel Cho to unbalance him. He should have known it was no such thing. If Sheils knew where to find him, he wouldn't bother with a pantomime. As soon as Annabel had called him Brian, he knew she was the real deal. Kneeling by her side, he cleaned the blood from her unconscious face.

He couldn't believe she thought something existed between them. Had she really been holding a torch for him for over a decade? It sure looked that way. Casting his mind back to her kidnapping, he thought her fascination made sense now. She was a strange kid. She seemed to welcome the kidnapping as a vacation. Allowing his emotions to get the better of him hadn't helped. When she started getting really sick, he feared his perfect system had crashed. Falling down the ladder with her was a stupid accident. Her catching him without his mask just added to the stupidity.

Well, if her wish was to rejoin him, he'd grant her wish. He put her in the same cellar he'd put her in fifteen years ago.

He finished clearing her nostrils. Blood turned the gauze red.

She'd ruined everything. His escaping the U.S. hinged on liquidating the ranch and his house. That wasn't an option now. Annabel knew the ranch. County records would tell Sheils who owned it. Tax records would lead them back to his Half Moon Bay house. He had his liquid assets to fall back on, but losing the real estate funds limited his options. It was all going wrong again. How crazy was that?

Killing Annabel was the simple solution, but it might not be necessary. If no one knew she was here as she claimed, there was no need to kill her. What she said in the next few minutes determined if she lived or died.

He tapped her swollen cheek, the bruising already distinctive and ugly. It took a hard tap to rouse her. Her eyes flicked open, then slid shut.

"Hey, Annabel. Wake up. We need to talk."

Her eyes opened again and rolled. He spoke her name and she fixed on his face. A smile developed, then morphed into misery as memory leaked into her consciousness.

"You hurt me, Brian." Her broken nose made her sound like she had a cold.

"Yes. You know the position I'm in. You came at the worst possible time."

He couldn't believe he was having this conversation with this woman. It was like he was explaining to a kid why she couldn't have candy with her dinner. In effect, he was. Annabel was still the same eleven-year-old he'd snatched. Her wiring had gotten crossed up somewhere along the line, probably long before he'd entered her life.

"I thought I meant something to you." She went to encompass him in a hug, but the shackles confining her to the bed stopped her well short of her aim. "I thought we meant something to each other."

He considered softening the blow, but he didn't have time for it. If this woman had screwed him, then he needed to know now. "There is no us. Never was. Do you understand that?"

She broke into her little girl sobs. He didn't bother to wait for her to cry herself out. He turned her head so that she looked him directly in the face. "I cared for you, because I didn't want to see you hurt. I kidnap, but I don't hurt people."

"You killed that boy."

The remark took the sting out of him. Nicholas Rooker had been a necessary kill. That was what he told himself. Nicholas's death had preyed on him over recent days. He'd killed to make a statement. A point had to be made to the FBI, the public, and the other Mike Redferns out there.

"Yes. I killed that boy. I have to kill sometimes."

He softened his tone and leaned in so close that his breath brushed her ruined face. "It's very important you answer me truthfully. This isn't a time for games. Do you understand?"

She nodded stiffly. Even though he was tender with her, she feared him. He felt it radiating off her. It was a good thing. He needed her scared. "Good. Did you tell anyone about this place?"

His hand went to the small of his back, where he curled it around the pistol. His finger looped inside the trigger guard. He wouldn't enjoy killing her, but he'd do it. He waited for her answer.

"I didn't tell anyone." Excitement rushed from her and she sat up as best she could.

He leaned back from her. "What about your family? You tell them?"

"No. No one."

His hand remained firm around the pistol. "What about Jane Fleetwood?"

"She knows something about this place."

He eased the pistol from his waistband, but kept the gun out of her line of sight. "She knows?"

"She and her husband know you have a ranch. Ryan Rodgers remembered the horses."

He snapped off the pistol's safety. The dry click failed to register with Annabel. "They know where to find me?"

"No. They know you have a ranch. They don't know where. I remembered. I remembered the road signs. McKinley and Walnut. It was easy to find after that."

"You didn't tell Jane Fleetwood?"

"No. I'm not helping her. I want to help you."

Annabel, you just saved your life, he thought. He put the safety back on and tucked the pistol into his waistband.

"Okay," he said. "You rest up now."

She smiled. "You do care."

What was the point of trying to break her perceptions? They were too deep seated. "Yeah, I care."

He stood up and crossed over to the ladder. Things weren't as bad as he feared. Annabel was an unfortunate nuisance, but his plan still remained intact. He could escape at his pace. He'd wrap up his affairs, sell the house and ranch, then leave. Of course, he'd have to accelerate things now that the Fleetwoods knew about the ranch. The good thing was that he was the only one who knew Annabel was here. He still might have to kill her, but not just yet. He had climbed two rungs when she stopped him.

"Brian, you have a gun. Why?"

He hadn't expected her to notice in her drugged-up state. "It's to keep the bad guys out."

She smiled and drifted back into unconsciousness.

He continued climbing the rungs. He had some things to take of.

THIRTY-ONE

Sheils had gotten the Chos inside and calmed them down. He told them not to worry about their daughter. She probably wanted some time alone. With the Piper back in the news and Jane's questioning, it was bound to open up old wounds. He was about to bundle them out the door when Scott and Jane pulled him to one side.

"I'm worried about Annabel," Jane said.

"Why?"

"I got a strange vibe off her. She was holding back." She frowned. "I think she knows his name. Maybe even where he lives."

Sheils had shoveled down a fistful of Motrin to kill the pain from the shooting. They had started to work, but suddenly he felt worse. He took a deep breath and exhaled. "How sure of this are you?"

"Sure on the name. She nearly said it. As to where he lives, not so sure. It's just a feeling."

"Do you mind answering some questions, Mr. and Mrs. Cho?"

Sheils ushered the Chos and Fleetwoods into the kitchen. The table only sat four, which was fine with Sheils. It hurt to sit. Cho apologized for his earlier behavior. Sheils closed the kitchen door and leaned against the countertop.

"Some disturbing aspects came to light during Annabel's discussion with Mrs. Fleetwood and I want to address them," he said. "Now, between both families, I think we can help each other."

Cho looked at his wife. Sheils felt them knot up, but they didn't object.

"How well did your daughter know the Piper?" Jane asked.

"I object to that question," Cho said.

"This isn't a courtroom," Sheils said. "We leave our baggage at the door. Honesty will help me find Annabel."

"She knew him as well as any of the other kidnapped children did," Linda Cho said. "She was only with him five days."

"Friendships can be made in five days," Scott said.

"What are you saying?" Cho asked.

"I remember your daughter's kidnapping," Sheils said. "It was a touch-and-go affair. Annabel got seriously hurt. If the Piper hadn't looked after her, I don't like to think how things could have gone differently."

Cho lost his grip on his temper. "Looked after her? Do you know how many operations she had on her arm? How long she was in the hospital? Do you?"

"A long time. I remember. But the question still remains, how well did she get to know the Piper?"

"Did she ever mention her time with him?" Jane asked Linda, mother to mother.

Linda hesitated. "No, not really."

Cho rushed to cover his wife's hesitation. "Of course she mentioned him."

Annabel wasn't the only one who kept secrets. Sheils remembered the Chos as the most difficult Piper parents. Interviews had to fit to their schedule. They denied access to Annabel on health grounds. But not all wounds were physical.

"Did your daughter ever see a psychiatrist or psychologist?" Sheils asked.

Hesitation. Cho's earlier need to object to every question deserted him. It was as good as an admission.

Sheils didn't follow up. He let that one question hang in the air, giving it time to fester. The Fleetwoods picked up on it and allowed it to grow. The pressure was on the Chos. They were distraught. Finally, the silence broke them.

"Yes," Linda conceded eventually. "She saw a psychologist for a number of years. Post-traumatic stress disorder."

"Totally understandable," Scott said. "I'm sure Sammy and Peter will have to go that same route. I'll do anything to make this all a memory."

"That's what we tried to do," Linda said.

"Tried?" Jane said.

Sheils sat out of the conversation. He liked how this was going. More would come from the Q&A if it was perceived as a chat between parents instead of an FBI interview.

"The counseling never really worked," Cho said. "The psychologist cataloged Annabel's post kidnapping issues. Nightmares. Abandonment issues leading to panic attacks. Counseling helped cure the symptoms, but not the root cause. Annabel never opened up about the Piper."

"She wouldn't even tell us," Linda said. "Her parents."

"I think she knows his name," Jane said.

"She does," Cho said. "The psychologist got her to admit that, but never managed to get the name from her."

"I think she idolized the Piper," Jane said.

"Are we talking Stockholm syndrome?" Sheils asked.

Cho shook his head. "I don't know. Possibly. The psychologist was leaning that way."

"Jesus," Sheils said. "Why didn't you tell me?"

"It took two years to find out," Cho said. "You'd moved on. Besides, if she wouldn't tell us, she certainly wouldn't have told you."

"Do you think she's been in contact with him?" Scott asked.

"No," Linda said. "If she had, I think she would have gone to him." It looked to be a tough admission to make about her daughter.

"Then you don't think she knows where he lives?"

Linda shook her head.

Jane turned pensive. "I think she does now."

"What are you saying?" Cho asked.

"She may have gone to be with the Piper," Sheils said.

The Chos broke down, but were able to give Sheils Annabel's credit card numbers and the license plate to her BMW before he left them to their fears. He didn't mean to be cold, but he didn't have the time to hold hands. Things were happening too fast.

He handed off Annabel's details to Guerra to get them into the system. He was hoping for a hit on the credit card. A gas fill-up here and a meal there gave him a trail to follow.

Guerra handed him a sheet of paper. "Ownership records for the South Van Ness building. The property belongs to a Mitch Harrison. The mailing address is a private mailbox in New Mexico."

No BG, then, Sheils thought. It was too much to hope that the Piper owned the place. "I doubt this guy knows his place was being used by the Piper, but find him and ask him."

Taking out his cell phone, Sheils cut through the house to the backyard. The security night-lights burst into life the moment he set foot on the deck, obliterating his need for privacy. He punched in Jones's phone number. Jones picked up on the second ring.

"Where are you?" Sheils asked.

"Still in Oregon. I'm having dinner."

"How'd you get on with BG?"

"Good. I've got twenty-nine males with the initials BG owning a ranch or farm property within a two-hundred-mile radius of the Bay Area. Tomorrow, I start hitting the addresses. If you and the Fleetwoods want to do a little legwork, we can divide and conquer."

"Not an option. Things have changed in the last few hours." Sheils paced a tight circle on the deck and filled Jones in on recent events.

"Christ, man. You were shot. You should be at home."

"That's what everyone keeps telling me."

"And you should be listening. Do you want me back there?"

"No. I've got it covered. I want you to check out these addresses. The Piper will have to retreat somewhere. Besides, I might be able to narrow your search for you," Sheils said, and told him about Annabel.

"That girl is screwed if she finds him."

"I know. I hate to say this, but I hope she finds him." Sheils stopped pacing. "The Piper won't have planned for this. I'm hoping he'll get sloppy having to juggle the Fleetwood boys and Annabel."

"Amen to that. This is the kind of thing that'll bring him down."

"By morning, I hope to have credit card activity."

"I'll call you when I hit the road."

"Thanks, man," Sheils said and hung up.

The moment Sheils hung up, Scott slid back the kitchen slider and joined him on the deck. He came over with his hands stuffed in the pockets of his jeans. His shoulders were hunched against the cold. "I didn't want to disturb your call."

"You could have. It was Jones. He's narrowed his search to twenty-nine BGs in the area."

"That's great," Scott answered, but didn't sound excited

by the news. "Look, I wanted to talk to you about today."

Sheils held up a hand. "I've already told you there's nothing to worry about."

"I know, but I just wanted to say thanks." Sheils tried to brush the gratitude away, but Scott kept at him. "I called you before you entered the building. You didn't have to go in there. You took two bullets for my kids. No matter how many times I say thank you, it won't be enough. So thank you."

Sheils searched for something to say, but all he found were John Wayne clichés. Instead, he said the only thing he could say. "You're welcome."

Scott held out his hand. Sheils took it and shook.

"Now, I know you don't have a high opinion of me and that's fine. I don't expect us to be buddies or anything when this is all over, but I want you to know that if you ever need anything from me, you just have to ask."

Sheils's opinion of Scott had changed. He didn't see Scott as a friend, but he didn't view him as a lowlife anymore. After Scott confessed that the Piper had been using him, Sheils found he understood Scott for once. The guy had thrown himself on a spike for his family. Scott didn't care what happened to him as long as he got his boys home safe and sound. Sheils couldn't fault the nobility in that. He would do the same for his kids. It was the reason he went into the South Van Ness building alone, knowing full well the Piper had the drop on him. If he stopped the Piper, it might dissuade someone from thinking they could get away with similar crimes.

"Thank you. I will. Now let's get out of the cold."

They hadn't been back inside five minutes when the call came. Food was just arriving for the evening meal. Agents were picking over the delivery when the phone rang. It stilled everyone in the house.

After his talk with Sheils, Scott's mood had lightened. Things were still dark for his family, but he could see light breaking through. They'd almost caught the Piper today. By tomorrow, it could be over. They'd have the boys home for the weekend. He'd done the right thing cutting Sheils in when he had. Together, they were getting somewhere. But the sound of the ringing phone killed his mood. Even though he'd expected this call, he still dreaded it. He replaced his food on the pile and crossed the room.

Jane caught up with him halfway. "It's going to be okay."

They sat next to each other on the couch. Sheils stood on the opposite side of the coffee table like he had on all the previous occasions. The scenario was all too familiar.

"I expect this one to be messy. He's rattled and he's going to scare you to make you fall into line. Think beyond threats. We're really on to him now." Sheils turned to his technician. "We good?"

The technician nodded and Scott answered the phone.

"Scott, you betrayed me, and to Sheils." The Piper's tone smoldered with contempt. "I'm insulted."

"What do you want?"

"To tell you that the rules have changed."

Scott's stomach fluttered. He tried to cling on to Sheils's advice and think beyond the threats. They might be closing in on the Piper, but he only needed a moment to kill Sammy and Peter.

"How?"

"Monday is off."

"No, you gave me until Monday. I can still find you by then."

The agents shot Scott and Sheils confused looks. From Brannon's expression, he was piecing together the secrecy over the last twenty-four hours.

"You can't do this," Scott said.

"I can, Scott. You switched sides. You didn't honor the agreement, so why should I?"

"Please."

"Don't demean yourself in front of all those bureau agents around you."

"What happens now?" Scott dreaded asking the question. Ignorance felt so much better.

"A change. I'm stepping up the schedule. It all happens tomorrow."

"I have to find you by tomorrow?"

The Piper laughed. "No, we're beyond that. Have the money ready. Tomorrow, we meet."

THIRTY-TWO

Only nine. Sheils had gotten lucky with the credit card. A credit check revealed Annabel had filled her car at a gas station in Vacaville. That gas station wasn't on the doorstep of any of the twenty-seven BG-owned properties, but it did rule out eighteen of them. Unless Annabel was taking some bizarre detour to prevent anyone from following her, then she was heading northward and Jones was following her.

He'd been on the road five hours, having checked out of the motel before dawn. He wouldn't get to all nine properties before Scott had to leave with the ransom, but he estimated he'd get to at least four. He was batting close to .500 with those stats. He stood a good chance of nailing the Piper before Scott left the house.

The credit card transaction gave him a good feeling, but it worried him too. There were no other transactions since the gas station. No restaurants. No hotels. It looked as if Annabel had found her man.

The signs for Red Bluff flashed by. He pulled off I-5 at the next off-ramp. There wasn't time to conduct surveillance. He had to take a direct approach. He had his line of bullshit worked out to get him through the door.

Barry Gordon's farm was the nearest, in Red Bluff. Jones stopped short of the property. He removed his .38 revolver from his glove box and slipped it into his windbreaker pocket. He got out his cell, dialed Sheils, and got voice mail. He didn't need to speak to him. He just needed Sheils to know where he'd visited. If the Piper got to him first, then Sheils would know who'd stopped him.

"Let's do this," he said to himself and drove onto the property.

The Gordon house was set back and the land rose steeply, so the house couldn't be seen from the road. It would make the perfect Piper hideout.

Jones felt exposed as he pulled up in front of the house. It was a single-story ranch-style house with at least a three-thousand-square-foot footprint. Low and flat, it looked as if it was peeking out from the ground.

As he approached the house, he felt twitchy. It had been a decade since he'd retired and he'd gotten used to not having to walk into hot zones. He stuffed his hands in the pockets of his windbreaker, keeping one hand on the gun.

He scanned the field behind the house for horses. He didn't see anything. That didn't mean anything in itself. Ryan Rodgers remembered horses, but that was nine years ago. Things changed.

The door to the house opened as Jones reached the stoop. A man around sixty stepped out. Sixty put this guy in the age range for the Piper. The estimate had been that the Piper was in his thirties at the first kidnapping; add twenty years since then and sixty hit the mark. He was tall and wiry. He had the height of the man pictured in Mike Redfern's candid shot, but not the build. Jones's tension ebbed, but not on the trigger.

"Mornin'," Jones called out.

Barry Gordon raised a hand and Jones knew he wasn't the Piper. Gordon's raised hand was riddled with arthritis, reducing it to a knotted ball. Those weren't the hands of the man who'd pulled a trigger on a gun that had killed Mike Redfern. Jones released his grip on his revolver.

"Can I help you?" the arthritic man asked.

Jones had no intention of prolonging a foregone conclusion. He used a lost traveler line and asked Gordon for directions. He pretended to listen to the directions Gordon gave. He had all he needed. He just needed confirmation before he crossed this man from his list.

"You have a great place, Mr.?"

"Barry Gordon."

Official. Strike Barry Gordon.

"Thanks again, Mr. Gordon."

Jones returned to his car and got back to the road. Once on the move, he checked in with Sheils to let him know Barry Gordon wasn't the Piper and he was on his way to Brett Grafton's place in Paradise.

Jones arrived to find Grafton's place unoccupied. Jones wouldn't get a physical ID on Grafton, but he could look the property over. The house and a barn fit the bill, but considering the unkempt condition of the place, Grafton hadn't visited in a long while. Jones's tire tracks were the first to disturb the dirt drive in months. Jones jimmied the door to the house. The utilities had been disconnected and the air inside was stale. The place smacked of an unwanted inheritance. Jones had seen enough. Grafton wasn't the Piper.

Ben Garrett came next. He ran an organically operated farm outside Oroville. He didn't match the Piper's build and was five years too young for Piper consideration. Jones used the lost tourist act again to excuse himself, but not before he received a fifteen-minute recitation on the importance of organic farming.

Brian Givens came next on Jones's list. It took him two hours to get to Winters where Givens lived. Jones was done for the day and he smiled when he stopped at the three-way stop at McKinley and Walnut. He just had to make this turn onto McKinley and drive for a couple of miles and he was there. Retirement had robbed him of his stamina. The combination of sleep deprivation and hours cooped up behind the wheel of his car was getting to him. Ten years ago this legwork wouldn't have fazed him.

This gig was proving to be a stark reminder to get his sorry ass off the couch and do something with his life. Retirement was easing him into an early grave. He owed Sheils one for the wake-up call. Things would change when he got back. He'd check into consulting gigs. There was more to be made working one day a week as a consultant than he ever did busting his hump for a week. Alternatively, he could go private. It was clichéd to become a private investigator, but if he angled it right, he could pick up and put down work when he wanted.

Givens's property loomed on Jones's left and he slowed to a crawl. He took in the lay of the land. It was a Craftsman-style, two-story in good condition perched on a rise with a tin-roofed barn a short walk from the house. It looked like the perfect place to keep horses. The barn could easily double for a stable. Before turning up the driveway, he left his customary voice mail with Sheils.

He pulled up behind a Ford F-150 and got out. A man came out from the barn. His lean build and height matched the man in Mike Redfern's picture. At around fifty, he was the right age group too.

"Hi there," Jones called out, walking toward the man. The barn door was open and he tried to sneak a peek inside, but in the fading afternoon light, all he saw was shadows.

The man wiped his hands on a rag and stuffed it into the back pocket of his jeans. He closed the distance between Jones and himself swiftly.

Jones put out his hand. "I'm Walter Jones."

The man eyed Jones with suspicion, but shook his hand. "Brian Givens. Can I help you?"

"Yes, I hope so," Jones said with a smile. "Are you the property owner?"

"Yes."

"Great. I'm from WJ Property Development and I'm scouting for new sites. There's a great demand for second homes in this area. San Franciscans want their getaway homes and don't care how much they pay. I think your place has plenty of potential. Have you considered selling?"

Givens put up his hand. "Not interested."

"I haven't said how much I'm willing to offer."

Givens smiled. "Not much considering that ten-year-old Century you're driving."

Jones glanced back at the Buick, his retirement gift to himself. Yeah, Givens was right. It didn't fit the image he was trying to portray. "That's my scouting car. I can't just turn up in my Mercedes. You see Mercedes, you think big bucks. That wouldn't do me any favors when it comes to negotiations, now, would it? Can we discuss terms?"

Givens shook his head. "Thanks, but no, thanks."

Jones strode past Givens and leaned against a paddock fence. The spot let him look over the land and gave him a better angle on the inside of the barn. "You know you're sitting on a gold mine here. There's room for twenty luxury cabins."

Givens moved in next to Jones, blocking his view of the barn. "I'm not interested and I'd like it if you left now."

"Mr. Givens, I'm willing to make you a very attractive offer."

Givens grabbed Jones's biceps. "I said, I'd like you to leave now."

Jones raised his hands in surrender. Givens released his grip.

"I'm sorry if I've offended you. My exuberance got the better of me. May I use your bathroom? Too much coffee."

"There's a strip mall about two miles further up. Use theirs."

Givens shadowed Jones all the way to his car. He stood over Jones while he got into his Century and fired up the engine. Jones smiled and waved as he backed onto the road. Givens just nodded and didn't head into his house until Jones drove away.

Jones drove only a few hundred yards before pulling over. He'd struck a nerve with Mr. Brian Givens, but which kind? Did this guy have something to hide or was he just a privacy freak? Jones wasn't leaving until he knew which.

The Piper watched Jones drive off and went inside the house. He didn't believe for one second the man was a property developer. He rang as true as the Liberty Bell.

He went into the living room and gripped the back of the sofa. They'd caught up with him. He slammed a fist into the sofa's seat cushion.

But how? Had Annabel lied to him? He didn't think so. She was too crazy to sell him out, but she was blind enough not to notice a tail on her. Either way, it was over for her. He had to leave. Now.

He retrieved his pistol from the den. He yanked back on the slide, putting one in the chamber. He hurried through the house and stopped when he reached the door.

Jones—who was he? He wasn't a fed. He was too old and out of shape for that. He might have been once, but not now.

The Piper had the same thought as he'd had the day before when Annabel arrived. If a tactical strike team sat in hiding a mile down the road, they would have stormed the house by now. Jones had no one behind him. He was probably a PI hired by the Chos to find their daughter.

He climbed the stairs and went into his bedroom. He looked out the window across his property. Jones's Century sat parked a quarter mile up the road. He picked up a pair of binoculars and zeroed in on him. Jones got out of his car and looked back up the road at him. The watcher was being observed by the watched.

"Who are you really, Mr. Jones?" he murmured. "Shall we find out?"

The Piper left the house. He locked the doors, but left a

window conveniently open for Jones to find. He didn't
bother locking up the barn. No doubt Jones wanted to see
inside. The Piper would let him. He got into his F-150,
drove to the road, and turned in the opposite direction
from where Jones had parked.

He drove to the market and picked up a few things.
While he stood in line at the checkout, he stared at the wall
clock. Jones would just be entering his property now. He
wouldn't have risked driving. He would have walked. The
question was whether he'd enter the house or go straight
for the barn. The Piper guessed the barn. Jones would find
Annabel's BMW, but it would take him time to find the
floor hatch. It wouldn't be enough time for him to raise
the alarm.

The Piper paid and drove back home. He parked the
F-150 short of driveway and went the rest of the way on
foot. He circled around the back of the house. A line of eu-
calyptuses provided nice cover for him to come onto his
property unseen.

The sound of an engine bursting into life from within
the barn told the Piper Jones's location. He rounded the
rear of his house and dropped to his stomach as Jones reversed Annabel's BMW out. Jones jumped from the car,
leaving the engine running, and raced back inside. He
moved with a kind of agility the Piper wouldn't have cred-
ited him with possessing.

The Piper jumped to his feet and sprinted toward the
barn. He took a wide arc to stay in Jones's blind spot
should he look out. His footfalls made noise on the dirt
track, but the BMW's engine masked it. Jones was making
it so easy for him.

When he reached the barn, he stopped to listen. The
barn wasn't substantial. It was easy to hear inside. He
peered through a gap in the siding.

Jones flashed across his vision. He dropped to his knees
and scraped at the ground. It didn't take him long to find

the hatch under the dirt and hay. Jones mumbled something the Piper couldn't understand.

This was the perfect time to move in. Jones was occupied. The Piper could rush in and put a bullet in his head and the dumb bastard would never know what hit him, but he didn't want to spoil his fun. Jones had worked so hard for his prize. He should at least see it even if it were only for a moment.

Jones yanked the hatch up. He brought out a flashlight and snapped it on.

Annabel's voice leaked up from the depths.

"Jesus Christ," Jones said and clambered down the ladder.

The Piper moved with fast, efficient steps. His pace was swift, but his footfalls never made a sound. He crept up on the open hatch and pointed his pistol inside.

The sight inside the cellar took Jones's breath away. His flashlight beam lit up Annabel stretched out on a cot, her face a bruised and swollen mess. He clambered down the ladder and swept the cellar with his flashlight. His beam failed to pick out the Fleetwood boys. The Piper had to be storing them somewhere else.

Jones knelt over Annabel. "It's okay. I'm here to help you. It's okay."

She writhed on the cot. "Where's Brian? I need Brian."

Her words came out slurred. She was heavily medicated. Not a surprise. He examined her broken nose. She'd be in a world of hurt without the drugs. He wasn't about to attempt any first aid. Just get out and get her somewhere safe. Sheils could do the rest.

The Piper had cuffed her wrists and ankles to the cot. There was enough slack for her to move, but the hard steel had cut into her flesh. He needed a bolt cutter for the cuffs, but not the cot. It wouldn't take much to cut through the aluminum frame.

"Where are Sammy and Peter? Have you seen them?"

"No. I asked about them. Brian didn't show me." A lazy smile leaked across her face. "There's Brian."

The sucker punch turned Jones's guts to water. He'd fallen for a rookie trick. The bastard had driven around the block to catch him with his hand in the cookie jar. Damn, he had gotten too old. Now the Piper was behind him. There was only one thing left to do.

He spun around. Brian Givens, the Piper, stood on the ladder with a pistol pointed at his chest. Jones reached for his revolver in his windbreaker pocket, but lost his balance on the soft dirt. He clipped the cot and fell on his back, flailing for his gun. He snatched the butt and yanked at the revolver, but the weapon snagged on his pocket. He hit the dirt hard and the .38 bounced from his pocket and stopped just out reach of his outstretched arm.

The Piper had him, dead bang. He didn't move a muscle.

"Who are you?" Givens asked.

"Walter Jones." Jones eyed his revolver, just two inches from his grasp.

"Don't make me shoot you," Givens said. "That .38 might as well be in Mexico for all the good it's going to do you."

"Where are Sammy and Peter Fleetwood?"

"I'm the one with the gun. I ask the questions."

Jones eyed his gun again.

Givens fired a shot into the dirt just short of the .38. The gun boomed in the cellar confines. The noise left Jones's ears ringing. Annabel wailed and writhed on the cot.

"Forget the gun and answer my questions. Now, who are you working for?"

"I don't work for anyone."

Givens shot Jones in the thigh. Pain knifed through his body. He clutched at his leg, cursing.

"My head," Annabel moaned. "Brian, you didn't have to shoot him."

"Sorry. Had to. He's not a friend," Givens said. "Jones, I don't have time to play games. Tell me who you're working for."

"Tom Sheils."

"You're not FBI."

"I'm retired. I'm working a separate line of inquiry."

The Piper climbed down the remaining ladder rungs. "Does anyone know you're here?"

This was a lose-lose question. Answer yes, he was dead. Answer no, he was dead. It didn't matter. His thoughts turned to Lucy. It was going to be hell for her living without him. She called his retirement their golden years. Golden years were meant to last longer. "No one knows I'm here. I haven't had the chance to call in."

"That's good."

"Where are the boys?" He prayed the kids weren't dead and already buried deep in the paddock someplace.

Givens smiled. "If I told you, I'd have to kill you."

THIRTY-THREE

Scott felt the way he did when he'd run track back in school. Those final minutes before competitors were called to the starting blocks were the worst. But the moment the starter pistol fired, his nerves evaporated, seared into extinction by adrenaline. He prayed that would happen tonight when the Piper called.

The world centered on the kitchen. Two million dollars again sat on his kitchen table. It was surreal to see that much cash in his home. Two million bought dreams with plenty to spare. Tonight, it might not be enough to save his children.

Brannon and Sheils slotted bound stacks of hundreds into a large backpack to ensure an even load. Sheils had sprung for a top-of-the-line pack with padded shoulder straps and a backrest. If the Piper sent Scott on a long chase, that two million in hundreds would weigh every ounce of forty-four pounds. Brannon checked the pack's weight and zippered it up.

"Try it on for size," Sheils said.

Scott slipped the pack on. It failed to knock him off his

feet, but it was a dense weight. He adjusted the straps and settled into the shape and feel of the cash. "It's fine."

He looked at Jane. As nervous as he felt, he squeezed out a smile for her and she sent one back.

Rooker stepped into the kitchen. He'd asked to be here for the ransom drop. No one had objected. He had as big a stake in all this as anyone. It was his money again. He deserved to be here when they caught the Piper. He gave Jane a hug.

Scott slipped the backpack off and Brannon set it on the table.

"Will you reconsider?" Sheils asked Scott.

"Reconsider what?" Rooker asked.

"I'm playing it straight," Scott said. "No undercover cars tailing me. No monitoring devices. No dye packs."

"Why?" Rooker demanded.

This had been the crux of an argument that had raged all day. Sheils wanted Scott to employ every form of human and electronic surveillance available. Sheils only backed down when Scott threatened to cut the FBI out. He knew Scott would go his own way if cornered.

"The Piper isn't going to take any more shit from us," Scott said. "He isn't stupid. He'll know if I'm followed or wired up. As soon as he does, he'll kill Sammy and Peter."

Jane didn't flinch at his stark portrayal. She was desensitized to it all. So was he. They would feel the pain and anguish if the worst happened, but they were numb to the realities of the if-then scenarios.

"I won't take that risk with our sons," he said.

"Scott, think about this. He could get away again. Do you want that?" Rooker asked.

He'd thought about nothing else. The Piper wouldn't get away again. He wouldn't let him. Plain and simple. He would stop the Piper tonight by whatever means it took.

"I know the risks, Charles. If you're worried about your money, I will repay it."

Jane had dug out his life insurance policy this afternoon.

There was a million of Rooker's money right there if he died tonight.

Rooker stormed across the kitchen and thumped the table. "I don't care about the money. I care about two things—this family and nailing the Piper."

"I'm sorry," Scott said.

"Damn right, you are."

"I'm still doing this my way."

"His way. Not yours."

Scott shrugged. "His way, then."

Rooker turned to Jane. "Are you going to let him do this?"

"Yes."

He threw his hands in the air. "I can't believe I'm hearing this. You guys are crazy."

"He won't be totally alone," Sheils said. "We'll have a helicopter in the air tracking him."

Scott had allowed this minor concession. From up there, they could see everything they wanted, but they'd be too far away to prevent anything from happening.

"At least that's something," Rooker said, his cool returning, "but we're still dancing to this maniac's tune."

No one disagreed with him.

The Piper called at seven minutes to ten.

"Here are your instructions. Follow them and everything will work out fine. Ignore them and you know what will happen. Understand?" The Piper kept his tone clipped to the point of sounding aggressive. His playfully cruel banter was absent.

"Yes. I understand."

"Good. Drive to the cable car terminal at Powell and Market. Go to the pay phones there. One phone will be ringing. You have twenty minutes. If I get a whiff of FBI, I'll kill the boys."

Scott looked over at Sheils. "There won't be any interference from the FBI. You have my word."

Sheils frowned.

"Your word means nothing. Just do as I say."

The line went dead.

Scott put the phone down.

Jane came over and hugged him. "Bring them back. You hear?"

He felt her tears against his face.

"I will," he said and released her.

Rooker shook his head. "Good luck, Scott."

Sheils followed Scott to his Honda and held the door open for him. Scott slung the two-million-dollar backpack on the passenger seat and got behind the wheel.

"I can put a detail on you. He would never spot them."

"Thanks, but no, thanks. I think we both knew this would come down to a showdown between him and me. Just keep your helicopter in the air. When he's got the money and I've got Sammy and Peter, he's all yours."

Sheils nodded and shut Scott's car door. "Look after yourself. He's looking for an excuse to take it out on those boys of yours. Don't give him a reason."

"I won't."

Scott started the Honda and reversed out onto the street. Twenty minutes from his house to the cable car terminus was tight. He could do it if he ran a couple of lights.

He felt like a first-time driver at the wheel. He gripped the wheel too tightly and his feet were clumsy on the pedals.

"Get a grip," he told himself.

He had to be sharper than this. The Piper was calling the shots and would be at least one step ahead of him. If he didn't pull it together, the Piper would screw him again.

With his thoughts on the Piper, his driving improved and he reached the cable car terminus. He dumped the Honda on Ellis. He yanked the keys out of the ignition, dragged the pack out with him, and slammed the door, not bothering to lock it.

The cable cars had long since stopped running for the day. The drive system's incessant grinding and the cable car's bell ringing was absent. The sound of a pay phone ringing half a block away traveled on the air with ease.

Scott sprinted toward the phone while pulling on the backpack.

He weaved in and out of the night owls on their way to another nightspot. They looked at him like he was a maniac.

His adrenaline kicked in. He covered the ground in seconds, eating into the distance between him and the phone.

It was still time enough for the ringing phone to catch someone's attention. A young black kid sporting an urban look split from his two buddies to answer the phone.

"Leave it," Scott bellowed.

"Fuck you, bitch," the kid snarled.

Scott snatched up the phone before the kid could grab it. The kid backed off, but tossed insults Scott's way.

"I'm here."

"You took your time," the Piper said. "Two more rings and I would have hung up. You've got to be quicker."

"What now?"

"There's a cell phone taped to the underside of the *S.F. Weekly* kiosk behind you. Get it and get on BART. Get off at Glen Park. Hurry. There's a Millbrae-bound train at ten twenty-five. Be on it."

Scott hung up. He flipped the *San Francisco Weekly* kiosk over, tore off a cell phone taped to the underside of the steel box, and raced down into the Powell Street BART station.

Scott waited on the platform, his adrenaline hurtling through his system. Sweat poured off him. The sprint for the phone had been the perfect shock to his system. He was ready for this.

He powered up the phone the Piper had left him. The display revealed a picture of Sammy and Peter shoved together, their hands and wrists bound. They looked terrified. Anger ripped through him.

"Bastard," he growled under his breath.

He expected a call, but one didn't come. Couldn't come. No signal made it through to the subterranean train. It was a smart move on the Piper's part. He'd cut Scott off from the world. Scott couldn't call out and no one could call in. He was alone. The way the Piper wanted him.

The tone in the house was tense, but restrained. Scott's insistence that the FBI keep their distance left them impotent. The helicopter was the only thing keeping them in the game. Everyone sat clustered around Sheils's walkie-talkie listening to the pilot and observer's commentary. The situation reminded Sheils of a space movie where mission control was sitting around with their thumb up their butt when disaster hit. His Houston-we-have-a-problem was about to strike.

"Fleetwood is out of his car," the helicopter observer said.

"Where?" Sheils asked.

"Ellis at Powell. He's running toward the cable car terminus. Looks as if something's happening."

"What?"

"He's answered a pay phone."

The Piper was going old school. He was going to have Scott run from pay phone to pay phone to see if he was being tailed. "Which one?"

"Bank of four. Second from the left if you're facing the phones."

Sheils said to Dunham, "Get SFPD down there. I want that phone secured. Then I want techs all over it. They might get something off it."

Dunham yanked his cell phone out and punched in a number. He excused himself from the living room to make the call.

"Something odd's happening," the observer said.

"What?" Sheils said.

"Fleetwood just tipped over a newspaper kiosk and tore something off the bottom. It's small. Could be a cell phone. Yeah, I think it's a cell. Oh, shit."

Jane gasped. Rooker put an arm around her shoulder and told her it was okay.

"What's happening?"

"Fleetwood's just gone into the BART station."

Putting Scott on BART was the worst thing that could happen with no ground surveillance teams. Most of San Francisco's BART line was subterranean, which meant they had no way of knowing which train he was on or which direction he was heading.

"Shit," Brannon said. "We've lost him now."

"Not yet, we haven't," Sheils said. "Someone pull up a BART map. I want to know which trains are leaving and when and where BART hits daylights after Powell."

"Depends which way he's heading," Brannon said. "If he's going to the East Bay, it's West Oakland, to the South Bay, it's the Oakland Coliseum, and if it's the airport he'll ride it all the way to Millbrae."

The gravity of Brannon's remark hit everyone in the room at once. What if the Piper was at San Francisco International with the kids? If Scott handed the Piper money there, then the bastard was on the next flight to Rio.

"The next train arriving at Powell is a Millbrae train," Guerra called out from her laptop.

"He's going to skip," Brannon said.

Sheils didn't think so. It was too obvious. The Piper was anything but obvious. Besides, he was far from finished with Scott. He had plenty of blade twisting left to do.

"What do you want us to do?" the helicopter observer asked.

"Circle," Sheils said. "Make sure Fleetwood doesn't go in and come back out again."

"What are you going to do?" Jane asked Sheils.

Panic was sinking its teeth into her, but Sheils expected a rough ride. The BART system was small and self-contained and that would work to his advantage. There weren't a lot of travel options. Even if it took them ten minutes to establish Scott's location, the chopper was capable of catching him in minutes.

"Brannon, get a hold of BART police. Tell their guys to

check the platforms for Scott. I want a visual. They aren't to make contact. No heroics."

Brannon didn't have to be told twice and got on the phone.

"Guerra, tell the TSA and security at SFO and Oakland International to be on the lookout for Scott and a guy with two boys matching Sammy and Peter's descriptions."

"Yes, sir," Guerra said.

That was it. There was nothing left to do until they caught a break. Sheils stood up and moved away from his radio.

Jane moved in with Rooker behind her.

"Scott's on his own, isn't he?" Her tone was accusatory.

"Steady, Jane," Rooker said.

"Scott wanted it this way," Sheils said. "Don't worry, though. I might have lost him for now, but I've got the bases covered. I'll pick him up again. Just trust me. Okay?"

Jane exhaled. "I'm sorry. You're right. I'm just so scared."

"Just know Scott isn't in any danger for now."

"How do you know that?" Rooker asked.

"The Piper has put Scott on BART to lose us. He won't attempt anything there. There are cameras in all the cars. He won't risk getting ID'd and he can't contact Scott while he's underground."

"What about when he gets off BART and you haven't found him again?" Jane asked.

She knew the answer. She was testing him to see whether he had the guts to tell her the truth.

"Unless Scott has a guardian angel, he'll be at the Piper's mercy."

A horn blared from deep within the train tunnel. A slug of air tainted by the stench of oil and grease swept over the platform moments before the Millbrae-bound BART train roared into the station. A smattering of people stepped from the train before Scott and his fellow passengers filed inside.

He found an empty bench seat and sat down with the

pack still on his back. The last thing he needed was a thief snatching it from him.

He parked himself in the middle of the seat to prevent anyone from sitting next to him. Several of his fellow passengers stared at him. He knew he looked like an antisocial freak. Good. He wanted to be unapproachable. No one was to screw with him tonight except for the Piper.

The train's doors slid shut and it accelerated out of the station, plunging into darkness. The windows turned into black mirrors reflecting the faces of everyone aboard the car. Scott eyed the other passengers. Any one of them could be the Piper.

The Piper could be amongst them or waiting at the next station or the one after that. Scott wouldn't know. He felt they'd gotten close to the Piper over the last few days. They'd managed to unearth things about him in the last forty-eight hours that the FBI hadn't in the last decade, but one fact still eluded them. His identity. The man five rows in front of Scott with his head buried in a paperback could be the Piper. He wouldn't know.

The train pulled into the Civic Center station. The man with the book got off. Another man replaced him. Another possible Piper candidate.

Scott followed the Piper's instructions and got off at the Glen Park station. Riding the escalator to street level, he pulled out the Piper's cell phone. The reception bars appeared and the phone rang. As he exited the station, he put the phone to his ear, ignoring a panhandler.

"I like BART," the Piper said. "It's predictable. It makes things like this very easy."

"Where do I go now?"

"Bus ride. Take the 23 westbound."

"Where do I get off?"

"I'll tell you where."

Scott caught the bus and found a seat. He wasn't much in a talking mood, but the Piper instructed him to remain on the line. Scott guessed it was to keep him from calling Sheils.

"Sheils let you go without any babysitters?" the Piper asked.

"I didn't give him a choice."

The Piper laughed. "Well done. I might even forgive you for telling him."

"Not for Nicholas, though."

"No forgiveness for him. We wouldn't be here otherwise."

No, Scott thought, *we wouldn't.*

"I wouldn't put it past Sheils to put someone on your tail."

Scott remembered the surveillance chopper up there somewhere. He peered through the window up at the sky and saw nothing but stars and night. No doubt he'd lost his shadow the moment he'd descended into the BART station. Sheils would be scrabbling for answers about now. "How are my boys?"

"Good under the circumstances. They take strength from each other."

Scott clutched his stomach. It hurt to hear the Piper talk about his children in such a blasé manner. He held his tongue and spent the bus ride listening to the Piper babble.

Ten minutes later, the Piper said, "You must be coming up on the zoo about now."

"Yeah. Another couple of stops."

"Get off there."

Scott couldn't see the exchange happening there. The zoo was closed at this time of night. The Piper was capable of many things, but taking over the city zoo wasn't one of them.

Scott got off the bus at Sloat and Skyline. No one got off with him.

"I'm here."

"Good. You're looking for the south entrance. It's on Herbst, off Skyline."

He headed along Skyline toward the zoo's entrance. He

and Jane had brought the boys here numerous times. As zoos went, San Francisco Zoo wasn't in the same league as San Diego or Denver, but the boys loved the place, especially Peter.

Turning onto Herbst Road, Scott was aware of how vulnerable he was on the empty street. The northern tip of Lake Merced provided his only company. He kept close to the streetlights. He wanted to be visible, even if it were only to himself.

"Why am I here?" Scott asked.

"So I can see you."

He stared hard over at the grounds attached to the recreation center across the street from the zoo. Was the Piper hiding there?

"I want to make sure you're alone."

"I am."

"You'll forgive me if I don't believe you, Scott. You have a habit of lying to me."

Scott prayed Sheils had kept to his word. He hadn't seen a cop car, marked or unmarked. That didn't mean there wasn't one, but if he couldn't see it, then the Piper might not see it either. Road noise was virtually nonexistent. He strained to listen for the whump-whump sound of rotor blades, but couldn't be sure he heard anything. He didn't dare look up to check in case he alerted the Piper to the chopper's presence.

He stopped in front of the zoo's south gate. "I'm here," he said into the cell.

"So I see."

He stared deep into the shadows and forced his eyes to penetrate the night, but all he saw was darkness. He couldn't tell the difference between twenty or two hundred feet.

"Don't bother, Scott. You'll never pick me out."

"Sammy," he bellowed. "Peter."

His boys didn't or couldn't answer.

The Piper laughed.

Scott heard his voice on the phone, but not out in the open. He had to be close enough to see him, but not close enough for his voice to travel.

"Nice try, Scott. All you need to know is that I'm close. Close enough to see you. Close enough to get to you. Close enough to kill your boys. But you're too far away to stop me."

"Let's finish this." Scott felt his grip on his temper slipping. "I've got the money here. I'm not being followed. I'm not wired. Let's end this now."

"Watch your tone," the Piper snapped. "I call the shots. You follow them. I'll tell you when the exchange happens. Go back to Skyline. You'll see a triangular median island. There's a motorcycle waiting for you. Tell me when you find it."

Scott darted across Skyline. He found a fairly new dirt bike along with a helmet hidden in the long grass. He yanked the bike free of the foliage and wheeled it to the road.

"I've got the bike."

"Ride over to AT&T Park, but I want you to take the following route." The Piper reeled off a long-winded set of directions to get to the San Francisco Giants Stadium.

"Why do I have to take the scenic route when I could straight-line it across the city?"

"I still have to see if you're playing straight with me. If you have tails, they will expose themselves sooner or later. And stay on the line. I don't want you calling anyone."

Scott didn't bother arguing. He climbed aboard the bike and got on the road. He found his way to the Great Highway and sped along the ocean road. The frigid wind streaming off the Pacific cut through his sweats. The bike tottered when the wind gusted. It had been a long time since he'd ridden a motorcycle and his rustiness showed. He lost his rust by the time he reached the Presidio. The time was edging toward midnight and traffic was light. It didn't take him long to pick up the Embarcadero and get to Giants Stadium. He stopped on the street and dismounted.

"I'm at AT&T Park."

"Good."

Scott walked toward the stadium's locked entrance. "Why the bike? You gone cheap?"

"No. You can't conceal anything on a bike. Both hands are needed to operate it. You can't do anything except ride."

"No one's with me. Satisfied?"

"Yes."

The answer surprised Scott. He expected more tests, more hoops to jump through.

Fear-fueled excitement lit up inside him. If the exchange was to take place now, Sammy and Peter had to be close. This was almost over.

"Walk to the Caltrain station on Fourth Street."

The station was only a few blocks away. He'd be there in minutes. He broke into a jog. He was getting his kids back. The two million on his back had never felt lighter.

His euphoria ended the moment the station came into view. This was all too easy. The Piper wanted him to pay a price. The two million in the backpack and the two million the Piper had taken in Oregon were a big price, but it hadn't cost Scott a penny. Rooker had footed the bill. The Piper knew that. More than a money drop would go down at the Caltrain station. He'd enter the station to see the Piper execute Sammy and Peter. He tried to blot out the image filling his head. His hand trembled when he reached for the station door.

"I'm here," Scott said, entering the lobby.

"Do you see the luggage lockers?"

"Yes. Where are you?"

"Don't worry about me. Go to the lockers. You're looking for locker 203."

Scott found the locker. It was big enough to stow two large suitcases or two small boys. His stomach clenched and his voice withered to a whisper. "I'm here."

"Reach above the lockers. You'll find the key taped there."

He reached up, felt along the ledge, found the key, and ripped it free. "Got it."

"Open the locker."

Please don't let the boys be inside, he thought. He slotted the key in and twisted. He hesitated before easing the door open.

It was empty.

The rush of air escaping his lungs hurt his chest.

"Now put the money inside, lock the locker, and put the key back."

Scott did as he was instructed. "Done. Now where are my boys?"

"Got a pen?"

THIRTY-FOUR

This was the last leg. The ransom had been paid. Scott just had to ride to Vallejo to collect the boys.

Sending him out to Vallejo was obviously a diversionary tactic. While he raced out to this address, the Piper was unlocking the luggage locker. He didn't let it worry him, as long as he got to his boys first.

The Bay Bridge loomed over AT&T Park. It took minutes for Scott to reach the on-ramp. He weaved in and out of bridge traffic on the bike. People flashed headlights and leaned on horns, but they fell into the past the moment he passed them. His recklessness carried him through Emeryville and Berkeley, but came to an abrupt halt as he approached the Carquinez Bridge. If an unobservant driver clipped him, he could end up dead. Even with the surveillance chopper skulking in the clouds, no one knew where he was heading. If he got killed, Sammy and Peter's location died with him. His hand eased on the throttle.

The Carquinez Bridge toll plaza blocked the freeway on the northern side of the bridge. Scott didn't stop for it. He blew through one of the unmanned FasTrak toll booths.

An enforcement camera snapped a shot of his license plate on his way through. It was a futile gesture considering the bike was probably stolen.

He took the off-ramp two exits after the toll bridge. The Piper's directions took him into an industrial section that used to serve the naval shipyards before they closed. He slowed his speed. Rubble and debris lay strewn across the private road and potholes marred the surface.

The bike's headlight swept across a broken sign for GJK Machining. The boys were being held at GJK. Scott sped through their parking lot and stopped in front of a pair of hangar-style doors. Using the bike as a flashlight, he guided its beam across the doors until it illuminated a big red X daubed on the doors in spray paint. X marks the spot. The Piper's little joke. Very amusing.

Other than the cross, nothing highlighted this place as the right location. A row of broken windows ran underneath the eaves. No light flickered from within. It didn't concern him. The Piper couldn't risk the light attracting someone's attention.

"Sammy. Peter. I'm here. Daddy's here," he called out.

No answer.

Propping the bike on its kickstand, he ran up to the red X. "I'm coming," he yelled out. "Daddy's coming."

He yanked back on the doors and the headlight lit up the interior, casting grotesque shadows off the abandoned machinery. Neither the boys nor the Piper welcomed his arrival.

He called Sammy's and Peter's names again. They didn't reply.

A chill ran over him, encasing him in his fear. He forced out the images filling his head. He didn't want to believe them.

He remounted the bike and rode it onto the shop floor. He eased the handlebars to the left, then to the right in a slow arc to light up the vast expanse. Shadows shifted and light reflected off an object hanging from a radial crane.

He jumped off the bike and tore off the object clipped to the crane hook. At first, he thought it was a sheet of paper, but from its feel, it was a photograph. In the gloom, he couldn't make out its image. He raced back to the bike and stuck the photo into the headlight's glare. The captured image took his breath from him. He bent over and closed his eyes to blot out what he'd seen, but his memory reprinted the photo in his mind. The eight-by-ten shot pictured Sammy and Peter back to back, bound together at the wrists, their arms over their heads, dangling from the crane where he'd just removed the photo. The look of anguish on his sons' faces knifed through him.

"No," he yelled out. His plea rebounded off the aluminum siding to slam back into him.

The cell phone in his pocket rang.

Scott yanked it out. "You bastard. I'll kill you. I'll fucking kill you."

"Temper. Temper," the Piper said, his voice calm yet mocking. "That's no way to speak to me."

Scott curbed his rage as best he could. His hand was a knot wrapped around the phone. "What have you done with them?"

"Nothing. Yet."

"What do you mean?"

"The locker where you left the two mil is a bank. You've made a deposit. Deposits take time to clear."

"Take it. It's there. I want this over."

"And it will be. As soon as I collect the money and leave with it unmolested."

"How long will that take?"

"Not long. A few hours at the most. Just don't let anything screw it up."

Headlights carved tunnels in the darkness and the night blinked with red and blue lights. A legion of FBI vehicles poured into GJK's parking lot. They skidded to a halt in front of Scott. The haste was impressive, but he couldn't see what good it did. He got up from his sitting position in the open doorway.

Scott spotted Jane in a car with Sheils. She shouldered the door open and raced over to him. She struck him with so much force he took a step back to steady himself.

After the Piper had hung up, Scott had called Sheils and told him where to find him. While he waited for them to arrive, he filled Sheils in about the drop and where he'd left the money. When he had nothing left to say, he repeated it all for Jane. Where he told Sheils facts, he told her his fears. That morning, he'd felt confident they would get the boys back, even catch the Piper. Not now. Now he was scared. The only way he'd get Sammy and Peter back was to tear them from the Piper's grasp.

"I'm sorry," he said to Jane. "I'm so sorry."

"It's not your fault," she said.

She was wrong. It was. He'd led them to this point. His children's lives depended on him doing the right thing and he hadn't. He'd screwed up. He didn't want forgiveness and understanding. He wanted someone to point a finger at him and tell the world he was to blame.

Sheils came over and placed a hand on his shoulder. "Scott, we need to talk."

"Not right now," he answered.

Sheils went to say something, but bit it off. His expression softened. "Five minutes. Okay? But I need the photograph."

Scott held out the photo facedown so Jane didn't see it. Sheils held out an open evidence bag and Scott slotted the photo inside.

Scott took Jane's elbow and guided her away from the melee around them. He walked her to the edge of the parking lot. GJK sat close to the Mare Island Strait. The night was clear enough to see across San Pablo Bay to the Marin County shoreline.

He stood in front of her, blocking her view of the water. He held her hands in his, the way he had when he'd proposed to her eleven years ago.

"I thought I'd get them back tonight," he said. "I really did. You have to believe me."

"I do."

She tried to hug him, but he backed away.

"But I was wrong. I can't do anything to stop him."

He unraveled. His ability to hold it all together deserted him and he burst into uncontrollable sobs. His legs buckled. She caught him, but he was too heavy for her. They both collapsed to their knees in the dirt, crying.

"This is all my fault. I waited too long to tell the police when Redfern contacted me. I played the Piper's stupid games when I should have told you and Sheils. And it's got Sammy and Peter kill—"

"Don't say it. Don't you dare say it," she interrupted.

He knew why she'd pounced on him. If he said it, it could never be taken back. And if it ever came true, he could never live with himself.

"You made mistakes. Everyone has."

"My mistake cost a boy his life."

"No." Her reply crackled with electricity. "He killed that boy out of spite. The same applies to Redfern. He killed him. Not you. Say it. Tell me you weren't responsible for anyone's death."

"I wasn't responsible," he told Jane. And for the first time, he started to believe it.

"Have you at any time not done your best for our boys?"

"Of course not. I've done everything I can to get them back."

Jane's harsh tone softened. "Then you aren't to blame."

He fought hard to believe her, but he couldn't rid himself of the guilt until he got Sammy and Peter back.

"Scott, if you lose faith, then I'm lost. You'll take me down with you."

He couldn't allow that. "I won't give up."

"You'd better not."

Sheils strode across the weed-ravaged parking lot

toward them. Scott and Jane got up and walked toward him, hand in hand.

"Sorry to interrupt," Sheils said. "I know you probably want more time to yourselves, but I need an important decision from you."

"It's okay," Jane said. "What decision?"

"I have a team inside the Caltrain station."

"Are you crazy?" Scott said. "What if the Piper spots them?"

"He won't. I'll make sure of it."

"Okay," Scott said. "What's the decision you need?"

"When the Piper comes, I want to take him down at the station."

"No," Scott said.

"Scott, I don't need your blessing."

"Then why ask?"

"A courtesy. I've indulged you more than I should. It's time the FBI took control."

"Not yet. Let him take the money and he'll release Sammy and Peter."

"Will he?" Sheils said. "Let's say we let him take the ransom. Then what? He'll only come back with another demand. We can't pass up this opportunity."

"He's right," Jane said. Her expression left no room for doubt.

He tried to fault their logic and found he couldn't. Deep down he knew the Piper wasn't finished with him. The bastard wanted to inflict the maximum pain and he still had a ways to go.

"Okay," Scott said. "Do it. But get it right."

THIRTY-FIVE

Friedkin hummed the tune to Elvis Costello's "Watching the Detectives." From behind a pair of night-vision binoculars, he watched the FBI swarm over the abandoned factory. He surveyed the action from a quarter mile up the hill looking down on the old industrial section. His binoculars propelled him into the thick of the action. He recognized Sheils and several of his agents. Scott and Jane were off in the distance.

Friedkin was glad he was back in the hunt, no thanks to Rooker. The man's insistence that he work Scott's surveillance alone had almost botched his assignment. Rooker called him to tell him the ransom drop was tonight and to stick close to the house. He picked Scott up easily enough when he left the house in his car. The lack of an FBI tail worried him. How the hell had Scott talked Sheils into letting him go alone?

The shortcomings of his solo surveillance showed themselves when Scott went into the Powell Street BART station. If Rooker had allowed him to use a second investigator, Friedkin could have made it work easily, but alone, he was at a distinct disadvantage. When Scott descended into the station, he had no choice but to follow, dumping his car. When the train arrived, he slipped into the car next to Scott's. He stood by the doors instead of sitting, ready to hop off the moment Scott got off the train. He noticed BART cops at every stop. Placed there at Sheils's request, no doubt. When Scott got off at Glen Park, he fell in behind him.

Street level was where a second investigator would have saved the day. A second person could have driven to meet him there. Instead, the situation forced him to get on the bus with Scott where he risked being spotted. Luckily, Scott seemed too intent on the situation to notice him. He stayed on the bus after Scott got off and waited until it had gone half a dozen blocks before crying for the driver to let him off. The "missed stop" line worked every time.

His luck ran out when Scott emerged from Lake Merced with a motorcycle. Talk about caught with your pants down.

He wasn't about to let Rooker's need for privacy ruin his surveillance. Rebecca, his office manager, lived a dozen blocks from the lake. He called her to pick him up, but by the time she'd arrived Scott was long gone.

Castrated by Rooker's stupidity, he was forced to default to his fallback position and return to the Fleetwood house. He gave Rebecca his car keys and cab fare and told her where to find his car. Her look threatened to strip paint, but she did as she was told. He'd have to make it up to her in the morning, especially as he had her car now. Flowers and a night out on the company credit card were in order.

When Sheils and company had leapt into action, he tailed them. He peeled off when they turned into the industrial section in favor of higher ground where he could watch.

He wished his binoculars came with sound. He could read between the lines well enough, though. The Piper had screwed them again. It was a ransom drop with no exchange.

The Piper wasn't working to his usual m.o. this time, but

then again, this wasn't a usual Piper kidnapping. He felt for the Fleetwoods. Their kids were going to wind up dead. The Piper was stringing them along, but nothing but misery waited for them.

Sheils was on the move. He crossed the factory parking lot to where the Fleetwoods stood. Friedkin zoomed in on their faces. He tried to read their lips but only made out the odd word here and there. He turned to the agents at work. Without a view into the factory, he couldn't see much.

He pulled the binoculars away to rub his eyes. Eyestrain was killing his vision. Everyone was taking on a blurry edge to them. He scanned the sorry set of buildings surrounding the factory. No doubt some developer would come in soon to turn the abandoned shipyards into marina property.

A flash of something caught his eye. A dot of light reflected off the building opposite from the FBI. He stared hard, not sure if he'd really seen something or if it was just eyestrain.

There it was again. No eyestrain. Something was catching the light on that rooftop.

He trained his binoculars on the spot. His breath caught when he focused on the source of the flicker. A man clad in black from head to toe, his head covered by a ski mask, lay flat on the top of the building with a night scope aimed at the factory.

"Shit," he cursed. "The son of a bitch is watching them."

As if his words carried across the air, the Piper edged back from his position before getting to his feet and backing away. The bastard had gotten his jollies watching everyone run around like idiots.

"I don't fucking think so."

Friedkin raced back to Rebecca's car. He yanked out his cell phone and punched in Rooker's number. "It's Friedkin. Tell Sheils the Piper is watching him from another building."

"Are you serious?"

"Yes, I'm cutting him off."

"Which road are you on?"

"Don't know. Tell Sheils to listen. I'll be making some noise."

Friedkin hung up, got behind the wheel of the Chevy, and floored the gas. A main service road encompassed the shipyard industrial park. The Piper had to use it to get back to the freeway. Friedkin would be meeting him head-on. He doused the headlights and held the wheel steady.

A sedan rounded the corner ahead at a sedate speed with its lights off. Friedkin had gotten lucky. The Piper hadn't spotted him watching from the hillside.

But he spotted him now.

Suddenly the sedan accelerated. The high beams ignited, bathing Friedkin in blinding light. Friedkin returned the favor, switching on the Chevy's high beams. Rebecca's dirty windshield refracted the light to create a total whiteout. He aimed the car at the light.

The light intensified. He glanced at the speedometer. The needle nudged sixty. A head-on collision would be nasty. He tugged on the seat belt to tighten it against his chest.

The light in front of him jerked to his right. He jerked with it.

The light jerked back and he mirrored the move. The Piper wasn't escaping this shipyard.

The headlights seared his eyes. He held up his hand to block the light. The ghost image of the car swelled before him.

The Piper killed the lights. Friedkin's eyes saw nothing but starbursts and afterglow against the darkness.

The Piper jerked the car out of Friedkin's path. Friedkin didn't notice until the cars skimmed each other on the drivers' sides, shearing off door mirrors. Exploding glass clattered against the window.

Driver's door to driver's door, Friedkin was the closest anyone had come to the Piper. If the cars had been stopped, he would have been close enough to grab him by the throat. He stared into the car to see the face of a child killer, but saw only a blur.

The impact rocked Rebecca's Chevy and it fishtailed. Friedkin fought to control the car, but overcorrected. The tires clawed at the asphalt but lost their grip and the car spun out. He yanked on the emergency brake to provoke a faster, tighter spin. The Chevy whirled around, coming to an untidy halt with its back end tight against the curb.

Friedkin yanked the selector into drive and chased after the disappearing sedan. The alignment had taken a pounding and the steering wheel shimmied in his hands.

The Piper was way ahead of him now. He accelerated but failed to cut into his lead.

His night vision returned to him steadily. He glanced over at Sheils and his people at the factory. He hoped to see them flying into action. Instead, they remained focused on the crime scene. Obviously, Rooker hadn't gotten through to Sheils yet.

Friedkin chased the Piper over the connecting roads. The Piper knew how to handle a car. Friedkin's high-performance driving training gave him an edge, but he fought to keep up. He pushed Rebecca's Chevy to the breaking point just to maintain the gap.

The Piper joined the road heading back to I-80. Friedkin didn't stand a chance of keeping up once the Piper hit the freeway. There was no traffic to slow him down at this time of night.

The Piper roared through a signal light that turned to red by the time Friedkin reached the intersection. An eighteen-wheeler, a pickup, and a couple of cars on the cross streets lurched forward. Friedkin had no intention of stopping for them and jammed his hand down on the horn and flashed his brights. The cross traffic hesitated in confusion. Without lifting his foot off the gas, he slalomed between the moving targets. He hoped he wouldn't have to do that again.

He closed on the Piper as the kidnapper slowed for the

westbound I-80 on-ramp. He left his braking to the very last second to slice into the Piper's lead, then stood on the brake pedal. The Chevy's antilock braking system worked overtime to prevent a skid and gained him two hundred feet on the Piper.

The Piper joined the interstate with a healthy lead on Friedkin, but it was the closest he'd gotten to the kidnapper. They both weaved in and out of the scant traffic at over a hundred miles per hour. Their speed scared the traffic out of their way. They shifted to the fast lane unhindered. Friedkin glanced down at the speedometer to see the needle wavering over one-twenty. The Piper's sedan inched away from him. Traveling at two miles a minute, Friedkin watched his advantage ebb away.

A siren split the air a second before red and blue lights splashed the night. Friedkin looked in his mirror. A Highway Patrol cruiser peeled out from the Carquinez Bridge toll plaza. The CHP Crown Vic ate up the road behind him.

"Shit," Friedkin cursed. He knew the cop had locked on to him. It wouldn't occur to the cop to go after the leading car. He would see him as the aggressor.

The Highway Patrol cruiser was two miles behind him. Friedkin estimated he had less than five minutes before the officer caught up with him. Five minutes to make a difference. Five minutes to stop the Piper.

The CHP's siren and lights affected the traffic. Everyone got religion and clung to their lanes, forcing both Friedkin and the Piper to swerve around them. Their speeds dropped below a hundred. CHP might have been reeling him in, but he was also reeling in the Piper.

"Just a little more time," he murmured.

The eighteen-wheeler sealed the deal for Friedkin. The investigator would have kissed the man if he'd gotten the chance.

The trucker spotted the Piper racing up behind him in the empty fast lane. As the Piper came up on the trucker's left, he drifted his big rig over. The Piper's lane narrowed to a sliver and he jumped on his brakes to avoid being crushed between the truck and the center divide.

"Thank you, Mr. Trucker," Friedkin said and closed onto the Piper's tail. He got close enough to read the license plate, but not to see the driver.

His euphoria didn't last. His five minutes were just about up. They hurtled past another on-ramp and a pair of CHP cruisers joined the chase.

The Piper dropped back from the truck, jerked right, then accelerated hard. The lumbering big rig lurched to block, but the Piper had three open lanes, agility, and horsepower on his side and blew by the eighteen-wheeler. He was off and away.

Friedkin sneaked by on the truck's left with the three CHP cruisers snapping at his heels. The Piper began to ease away. Friedkin looked at the Piper for an ID. He made a partial profile. White. Brown hair.

That was all he got before the impact from the rear. CHP were all over him. They were attempting to box him in and squeeze him against the median. Standard highway procedure. Except the cruiser behind him moved in before the other two had positioned themselves to create the box. The thump destabilized the Chevy's rear. It shimmied and bumped the second cruiser coming up on his right. The car pinballed off the cruiser. The rear wheel slipped off the smooth highway and onto the uneven shoulder. The Chevy bucked on the rough surface and smacked into the second CHP cruiser again. The bucking grew into a fishtail at ninety-five, and Friedkin lost control of the car.

The CHP cruisers dropped back to let physics do its worst to Rebecca's Chevy and Friedkin, now a passenger at the wheel. The car's rear end snapped out. Friedkin attempted to correct, but it was too late. The tires lost traction and momentum took over. The car spun around. Friedkin feared the Chevy would roll, but the front end connected with the median first.

The windshield fractured as the hood concertinaed. The

driver's-door window exploded, spitting diamonds of glass over him. The airbag detonated into his face before the coupe snapped back to spin in the opposite direction, pirouetting three times and crossing all four lanes.

Just as it looked as if the Chevy was losing its steam and the incident was coming to an anticlimactic end, one of the CHP cruisers slammed into the car. Both vehicles came crunching to a halt, half on the shoulder and half in the slow lane.

Friedkin didn't move. Couldn't move. Too dazed, he was welded to his seat.

Systems check, he thought. He recounted the Piper's license plate. He was good.

The CHP officers were out of their cars, weapons drawn.

"Hands up where we can see them," a voice ordered.

The flashing red and blue lights scorched his eyes and he couldn't see who issued the order, but he wasn't about to argue and raised his hands.

An officer rushed in, his weapon extended. "You okay?"

"Yeah."

"You shouldn't be, you dumb son of a bitch."

Friedkin took in the extent of the wreckage. He owed Rebecca much more than a bunch of flowers and a night out on the company credit card.

THIRTY-SIX

Agent Richard Jessup did a damn good impression of looking bored, because he was bored. He made up part of a three-person team inside the Caltrain station waiting for the Piper to claim his money. He and Guerra pretended to be passengers waiting for the next Caltrain to arrive. Dunham patrolled the station dressed as an employee. All were positioned in different locations, but each had a clear view of the luggage lockers. Jessup covered the main entrance to the station. The Piper would have to pass him to get to the lockers.

That simple fact kept him charged. He, a new boy at the bureau, would literally be the first law enforcement officer to come in contact with the notorious kidnapper. This had been the reason he'd joined the FBI. He wanted to take bad guys off the streets.

As yet, he hadn't been on the front line of any major busts during his eleven-month tenure at the San Francisco field office. This was the closest he'd been and he couldn't see anything coming of it either. Not tonight.

"Lone male approaching the station. Blue jeans. Hoodie.

Slim build. Approximately six feet in height. He's coming your way, Jessup," a voice said over his earpiece.

"Got it."

He mainlined the adrenaline his body fed him. The lethargy from an eighteen-hour workday evaporated. He was awake and sharp. He was ready.

The automatic doors slid back and Jessup's excitement left him as quickly as it had entered. The lone male was in his twenties. The Piper was in his fifties and athletic by all accounts. This guy was skinny and looked like a bum or a junkie.

The guy shuffled by Jessup.

He whispered into his mic, "Suspect does not match the Piper's description. Repeat. Does not match the Piper's description."

As he was saying this, conviction left his words. The lone male, instead of going to the ticket kiosk or bumming change from the waiting passengers, headed toward the luggage lockers. Jessup's breath caught in his throat as the suspect looked the lockers up and down.

"Suspect has gone to the lockers," Jessup said. His words scraped his dry throat.

"Guerra, Jessup, move in," Dunham said. "Take him down when his hands are on the ransom. He'll be vulnerable."

Jessup rose to his feet. He moved with speed and stealth, making sure he kept in the guy's blind spot. He opened his jacket. His hand rested on his weapon.

The lone male stopped in front of the locker with the ransom inside. He reached above the lockers for the hidden key.

"He's going for the key," Dunham said. "Watchers cover all exits. He doesn't leave the station."

The suspect inserted the key, unlocked the locker, and opened it.

Jessup swooped in fast. In his peripheral vision, he saw Dunham and Guerra speeding across the station to cut off any escape routes. Jessup removed his weapon from his holster.

The suspect reached inside the locker and tugged out the backpack with the two million packed inside.

Jessup reached him first and aimed his weapon. "Freeze. FBI."

Dunham and Guerra arrived a second later, blocking off his only avenue of escape.

Shock and confusion masked the guy's face. Without being told, he dropped the backpack and raised his hands.

"You're under arrest," Jessup said.

The Piper went down as simple as that.

Sheils didn't have to be told they hadn't captured the Piper. He knew just by looking on the video monitor from the viewing room. Barrington "Baz" Reagan sat alone in the interview room vibrating from nerves.

"I'm going to talk to this clown," Sheils said to Dunham. "Keep the Fleetwoods occupied. I don't want them getting their hopes up on this one."

He'd brought Scott and Jane back with him to the field office. He left Brannon to oversee the crime scene in Vallejo. The Piper had stretched them thin tonight. Sheils's people were now spread out in three locations. If something else broke, he didn't have the resources to cover it.

Sheils traipsed down the corridor to the interview room. The seemingly never-ending series of failures had drained his energy. He shook the fatigue off before entering the interview room.

"Hello, Mr. Reagan, I'm Agent Tom Sheils."

"Can I go?" It was a plea, not a question.

Sheils didn't need to be a specialist in body language to read Reagan. The guy was wound tighter than a clock spring. He bounced his right knee with such vigor his whole body trembled. He beat a tattoo on the floor with a sneaker-shod heel. Sheils sat at the table across from the Piper's unwitting pawn.

"No, you can't go. May I call you Baz?"

"Yeah. Sure. Call me Baz. I hate Barrington. I got my butt kicked throughout school because of it. All the firstborn sons in my family are called Barrington. Shit, I sound like a duke."

"You're a bicycle messenger for Bay Bike Messengers?"

"Yeah."

"Good job?"

"Great one. I bike for a living. Shit pay, though. Didn't used to be. Traffic sucks in this town at any time. A bike was the answer to gridlock."

"Was?"

"E-mail. No one uses couriers much. It can be done with the click of a mouse."

The banal chat helped pacify Reagan. He still bounced his leg, but it had lessened to a steady bob.

Sheils opened the file with Reagan's brief statement and his DMV record. "So is that why you took two hundred bucks to collect a ransom?"

"Hey, I didn't know the guy was the Piper. He just told me to come to the Caltrain station, take a bag from a locker, and hand it off to him."

"At two in the morning? You didn't think there was anything suspicious in that?"

Reagan's bouncing knee ramped back up to two hundred beats a minute. "Okay, okay, I didn't think I was picking up his forgotten luggage, but I didn't know he was the Piper."

"So what did you think you were collecting?"

"I don't know. Didn't want to know. Drugs. Guns. Dirty money. Stolen kittens. It wasn't any of my business."

"Not very smart of you."

"No shit, Sherlock."

"You said it, Einstein."

The remark stopped Reagan in his tracks. His leg ceased bouncing and he leaned across the table with his hands out in a help-me gesture. "Look, I'm not saying I'm an angel, but I don't know where those kids are and I don't know anything about the Piper."

"I disagree, Baz. You know a lot. You're the first person who's encountered the Piper without a mask. I think that makes you very important."

The color drained from Reagan's face. Sheils guessed the realization had just sunk in. Reagan's foot bouncing restarted.

"How did you get this gig?"

"He approached me."

"Through Bay Bike Messengers?"

"No. At the Mechanics' Memorial on Market and Battery. A lot of us messengers hang out there between jobs."

"Were there many of you around at the time?"

"Three or four," Reagan said and reeled off names.

"Did he offer the job to all of you?"

"No. Just me."

"Why you, Baz?"

Reagan shrugged his shoulders.

Sheils could hazard a guess. Reagan looked as if he'd do anything as long as cash came attached.

"What did he ask you to do? Exactly. Word for word."

Reagan thought hard. "He asked if I wanted to earn two hundred bucks. I said yes. He said he needed the contents of a locker at the Caltrain station on Fourth brought to him. I asked when and he said he'd call with details, but expect it to be a night job."

"After you collected the backpack, then what were you supposed to do?"

"Go to Fort Mason."

"Were you supposed to call first?"

"No. Just go there."

Sheils wasn't sure if a window of opportunity had just closed up on him. A catch-and-release approach with Reagan might lead him to the Piper, but the Piper had to know Reagan had been waylaid. He knew just about everything they did. They would have been better off letting Reagan collect the ransom and following him to wherever he took it. Sheils cursed himself. He should have known the Piper would pull a stunt like this.

The best he could hope for now was to milk Reagan for all he could get.

"Can you describe the man who approached you?"

"Sure."

Friedkin hit a wall with the CHP officers. They weren't in the listening mood when it came to the Piper. They wanted to know why he was driving like a madman on I-80 endangering lives in a vehicle that didn't belong to him. Mentioning he was snooping on the FBI while they worked a crime scene didn't help either.

Rebecca changed matters when they contacted her about her now deceased Chevy Cavalier. She confirmed Friedkin's account, but it failed to loosen their grip on him. Rebecca realized the seriousness of the situation. She called Friedkin's lawyer and he knew the right people to wake up. Within twenty minutes, Sheils had a fast and dirty version of events over the phone, and in another thirty, officers escorted him through the doors of the FBI field office.

Sheils met Friedkin as he stepped off the elevator. The FBI agent looked less than ecstatic to see him.

"I can do without the granite stare. I've had enough of that with the CHP boys," Friedkin said.

Sheils sighed. "I think it's been a long day for everyone."

Friedkin followed Sheils to his office. He expected other feds to be in on the meeting, but it was just the two of them. Sheils fell into the chair behind his desk. Friedkin lowered himself into a visitor's chair. The effects of the car crash were making themselves known.

"You hurt?" Sheils asked.

"Yeah."

"Good. I told you to stay out of this."

It's going to be one of those meetings, he thought.

"Do you want to explain what you were up to tonight?"

Sheils asked. "Did the Fleetwoods have any knowledge about your plans?"

This was where it got tricky. Telling the truth meant betraying his client. Privacy was what his clients paid for and expected. Breaking that fundamental trust would destroy his reputation, but he couldn't avoid it. The lives of two boys were more important than Rooker's business.

"The Fleetwoods had no knowledge."

"But they're your clients."

Friedkin squirmed, but Sheils wanted him to squirm. Mission accomplished.

"Rooker is also my client. He wanted me to tail Scott—see where he went, who he spoke to."

Sheils leaned back in his chair with a mug of coffee in his hand. He didn't offer Friedkin any. "For what reason?"

"Rooker hopes Scott will lead him to the Piper."

Sheils leaned forward onto his desk, the coffee mug held in both hands. "Does he think Scott is colluding with the Piper?"

"Don't know. He just wants to find the man who killed his son."

"Okay. Scott leads you to the Piper. What was the plan then?"

Friedkin shifted in his seat. The move set off the headache he'd been trying to suppress.

"I'll make it easy for you," Sheils said. "You were going to do your citizen's duty and come straight to me to tell me where I could find the Piper."

"Agent Sheils, I have vital information and we're wasting time."

"Okay, tell me about this guy on the roof."

Friedkin outlined what had happened from when he'd spotted the Piper on the roof until he totaled Rebecca's Chevy.

"As soon as you saw this bastard, why didn't you contact me?" Sheils demanded. "I could have alerted CHP and they could have shut him down without the carnage."

"I did. I called Rooker and told him to call you."

"He never called."

Why hadn't Rooker called? Friedkin thought. It would have put him in an awkward position with Sheils, but so what? Catching the Piper outweighed the embarrassment factor.

"What makes you think this guy on the rooftop was the Piper?"

"I have a hard time believing it was coincidence. Someone wearing a ski mask just happens to be on a rooftop in the early of the morning across from a building where two kidnapped children were kept? I don't think so. Do you?"

Sheils said nothing.

"Did you run the plate?"

"The car's a rental. We'll get a name and face when the rental company opens for business. In the meantime, there's an alert out on the car. SFPD are combing the streets for it now."

"I know the car was last seen heading west, but what makes you think the Piper will return to the city?"

"He sent someone to collect the ransom from the Caltrain station."

The news hit Friedkin hard. The Piper had gotten too cute for his own good and the balance was tipping to Sheils. The Piper's options would be narrowing, just the way they had with Nicholas Rooker's kidnapping. If the Piper was smart, he'd do what he'd done eight years ago and cut and run. But cutting and running left bodies behind.

A knock came at the door and a man entered Sheils's office holding a thin stack of printouts. "I thought you'd want to see the digital rendering we got out of Reagan as soon as it was ready."

Sheils took the printouts and studied the face. He looked up at Friedkin after a minute. "Did you get a good look at the guy in the car?"

"Just a partial profile."

Sheils slid a copy of the picture across the desk. Friedkin

picked it up. It was a head shot, in color and fairly lifelike. The face looking back at him drove a fist into his gut. He recognized the reconstructed face. The hair color was wrong—dark when it should have been blond. He'd probably worn a wig to disguise his identity, but the wig failed to disguise the face. Friedkin knew it well. It was Alex Hammond, his AWOL investigator.

"Do you recognize him?" Sheils said.

"No. I've never seen him before."

THIRTY-SEVEN

"When is someone going to talk to us?" Scott asked Guerra.

"Soon. Just let us do our jobs. Relax."

Relax. What a joke. He and Jane had been cooped up in the windowless room since returning from Vallejo. For the last hour, Guerra had been babysitting them. Dunham had poked his head through the door now and again to make sure things were okay, but things weren't. A suspect was being detained in this very building. They'd been told he wasn't the Piper. They learned these two facts on the ride back with Sheils. Since then—the mushroom treatment.

"Would you like more coffee?"

"No. I've drunk so much I need the bathroom," Scott said. He got to his feet. Guerra stood with him.

"I don't need company."

Guerra backed down, raising her hands and moving back. "You know the way."

She held open the door and watched him stride down the corridor toward the restroom. When he reached it, he glanced back. Guerra had returned to the boardroom. He doubled back in the direction of Sheils's office.

Dunham came out of the copy room and expressed his dismay at seeing Scott wandering the building unescorted.

"Save it," Scott barked. "You blew your chance to explain. Now I want the boss."

"Mr. Fleetwood, please return to the boardroom," Dunham said.

"When I've got an answer."

Dunham nipped at Scott's heels all the way to Sheils's office. Scott didn't bother with knocking and barged in. The office was empty.

"Damn it."

Sheils appeared from behind them. "Scott, what's going on?"

"That's what I want to know. We're going crazy in that room."

"I apologize, but things are happening very quickly. Good things. I can explain. Let's return to Jane."

Sheils and Dunham escorted Scott back to the boardroom. Sheils eyed Guerra with disappointment, but it was momentary. He took a seat at the table and Scott returned to his seat next to Jane.

"I apologize for keeping you in the dark, but I want to bring you up to speed and ask you a question," Sheils said. "Agents Dunham, Jessup, and Guerra picked up a man who attempted to collect the ransom from the Caltrain luggage locker. The Piper paid him to collect the backpack and bring it to him."

Scott didn't like how this sounded. It hadn't made sense why the Piper wanted him to put the money in the locker and leave it. The locker would be staked out when he came to collect the ransom. It was stupid, unless . . .

"This guy was a sacrificial lamb," Scott said. "The Piper knew you'd bust whoever came for the ransom. This was a test to see if I'd play by the rules. He knows I sold him out."

"Not necessarily," Sheils said. "Remember the accident we passed on I-80?"

Scott nodded.

"John Friedkin followed us to Vallejo. He chased after a man watching us at the crime scene."

"Watching us?" Jane asked.

"Yes, it looks as if the Piper had the Vallejo factory staked out to see what happened."

Scott wondered how long the Piper had been watching. Had he seen him break down when he found the photograph of Sammy and Peter? He couldn't imagine the Piper missing that dose of pure misery.

"What I'm hoping is the Piper doesn't know his bagman was picked up and he believes you fear him enough to tell us about the factory but not the location of the money," Sheils said to Scott.

"That's a big what-if," Scott said.

"What does this have to do with John Friedkin?" Jane said.

"He pursued the Piper and got a license plate before getting into a wreck," Sheils said. "Unfortunately the car's a rental, but we'll know who rented it in a couple of hours."

"So you still don't know who the Piper is," Scott said, hoping for better news than what Sheils had given up.

"No, but I know what he looks like." Sheils slid a computerized image of a man across the table. "The bagman described him."

Scott held the image. At last he was face-to-face with the kidnapper of his children. The man was in his mid-forties, which was younger than Scott expected.

Jane examined the picture. An involuntary whimper escaped her lips. Scott leaned over to hug her.

"Do you recognize him?" Sheils asked.

Both Scott and Jane shook their heads.

"We have a man without a name," Scott said. "What now?"

"I'm releasing the bagman to go through with his exchange."

"You have nothing to fear. At no time will you be out of sight of an agent," Sheils said. "Smile, Baz. You're working with the good guys now."

Reagan found it hard to smile, all things considered. He'd only agreed to turn on the Piper to ensure that he didn't get any splash-back when they charged the kidnapper. He'd convinced Sheils he was an unwitting party in the Piper's plans, but he was still an accessory to a bunch of felony raps. Prison or the Piper? He couldn't decide which was more dangerous. He tried not to think about it.

Two of the agents who'd busted him replaced the ransom in the backpack he'd taken from the locker with wads of paper. The two million bucks was elsewhere. Shame. He'd never seen that much cash. It occurred to him that he'd been a multimillionaire for about three seconds. That would be something to tell his grandkids—as long as the Piper didn't slice his balls off.

He was still in the interview room. The room felt small and tight. Prison would kill him. God knew how many hours he'd have to spend cooped up in a cell. No, he'd take his chances with the Piper.

"Do I get a wire or something?" Reagan asked.

"Not necessary. We've got you covered," Sheils said. "Besides, I don't want to tip the Piper off if he frisks you."

It felt decidedly sketchy. It didn't matter how much these guys played nice and told him not to worry. He was risking his ass.

The agents packed the last of the dummy cash into the pack, zippered it up, and helped him put it on. The load felt good. After ten years as a cycle messenger, he was used to heavy loads.

They took him down to the parking lot and drove him out to where he'd left his bike a couple of blocks from the Caltrain station.

"You know what to do," Sheils said. "Just do as you would have done if we hadn't interrupted you. Don't think about us. Don't look for us. You might not see us, but we're there. Just focus on the job the Piper paid you to do. Okay?"

Reagan perched himself on his saddle, jammed a foot onto the pedal, and locked it in place. "Yeah. Sure. Solid."

Sheils clamped a hand on the crossbar. "Don't even think about riding off. I'll find you and mail you to the Hall of Justice."

Cops. They're all the same. "Never crossed my mind."

Sheils removed his hand. "Make sure it doesn't."

Reagan cycled away before the feds could issue any more threats. He threaded his way down to the Embarcadero. He ignored a red light and turned left toward Fisherman's Wharf.

It felt good to be on his bike again. The night air cut through his clothes straight to his skin, invigorating him. To the east, a faint glow rose up from the horizon. This was why he rode a bike—for moments like this—and he'd nearly thrown it all away for two hundred bucks. He couldn't believe he'd been dumb enough to take a job to collect a bag from a locker. He was lucky it turned out to be the Piper. The guy could have been a terrorist and he could have turned himself into an unwitting suicide bomber.

Two hundred bucks, he thought. *How long would that last me? Two weeks—tops.* He needed to get out of the bike messaging business and into something that paid a living wage. This debacle was a wake-up call for him. No doubt.

He seemed to be the only soul on the road. If Sheils's guys were out there, he didn't see them.

He reached the end of the Embarcadero and cut along the sidewalks to get to Fort Mason and the location for the exchange. Two million dollars for two hundred bucks. He needed to learn to negotiate better. He cycled up to where McDowell met Battery, the agreed rendezvous point.

He dismounted and leaned his bike up against a tree.

The Piper was nowhere to be seen. He scanned his sur-roundings and saw no one. No feds. No kidnapper. The ride had warmed him up, but the wait chilled him.

"C'mon, where are you?" he murmured.

The Piper failed to answer his plea then or an hour later. The fucker wasn't coming. It was a washout, but he had no way of telling the feds. They should have wired him for sound. No one ever listened to him.

An SFPD cruiser crept up the private road toward him.

He groaned. Not more cops. He could do without ex-plaining himself.

The cruiser stopped in front of him. Two of San Fran-cisco's finest took up the front seats. The window came down on the passenger side.

"We're FBI, Baz. Agent Sheils says it's over. He's a no-show. You've done your part."

The curse on his shoulders lifted. He was Piper- and cop-free.

"Now point toward the city," the fed said. "We have to make this look convincing in case the Piper's watching."

Reagan pointed at the Transamerica Building. The feds dressed as cops got out of the cruiser and made a loud fuss. He was loitering. Did he want to go downtown? He played his part, pretending to be misunderstood. The feds patted him down, put his bike in the trunk, and bundled him into the back of the cruiser.

They drove him to his studio on the edge of Japantown. He got them to drop him off two blocks short. He didn't want his neighbors getting the wrong idea.

He climbed the stairs all the way to the fourth floor with his bike slung over his shoulder and let himself into his apartment. The moment he closed the door, he smelled aftershave. Not quality stuff. His intruder was a Rite-Aid bargain shopper. His hand went to the light switch next to the door, but he hesitated. He didn't want to see his visitor.

"Do we have to sit in the dark?" the voice said.

He flicked on the light. The man who'd offered him two hundred bucks at the Mechanics' Memorial sat on his sofa bed. His dark hair was now blond. A silenced automatic rested on his lap. His fingers were loosely curled around the weapon.

"Where have you been, honey?" the man asked in a mocking tone. "I expected you home hours ago."

Reagan wheeled his bike into the kitchenette and stepped into the small living room. He tried to keep the desperate sound from his voice, but failed.

"I got tied up. I've been waiting for you for hours at Fort Mason like you asked, but you didn't show."

The man raised the gun to silence him. "Baz, where's the backpack?"

Reagan felt the curse fall back on his shoulders. The feds had taken it from him at Fort Mason.

"You haven't peeked inside, have you?"

"No, no, no," he said, fumbling for an answer. "I took it back to the locker. Returned it. I guessed you'd get back in touch with me."

"That was thoughtful of you."

Reagan shrugged. "You know, I try."

"I'm sure you do." The man's words slipped out on a thin layer of oil, sounding smooth and convincing. "Cops got in your way, did they? FBI to be exact."

"What? FBI? No. What makes you think that?"

The man aimed the gun straight at him, cutting Reagan's babble short.

"Please don't insult my intelligence, Baz," he said with restrained anger. "I am a professional at what I do. I take precautions, and you're one of them. Do you understand?"

"Yes."

"Good. Lie to me and I'll know."

Reagan wasn't in any doubt of that. This guy knew the FBI had busted him. He knew everything.

"Did the FBI pick you up?"

Sorry, G-man, it's time for me to swap sides again, he thought. "Yeah, the feds picked me up. They have the money."

"Thank you," the man said and shot Reagan in the face.

THIRTY-EIGHT

Friedkin pulled up in front of Alex Hammond's home in Daly City. The house sat silent and dark pressed up against its neighbors. That wasn't surprising at four in the morning. Friedkin liked to think Alex was asleep inside with no connection to the Piper and the kidnapping of Sammy and Peter Fleetwood, but he knew it was fantasy. So what did he hope to find here? Sammy and Peter? He didn't really know. He just hoped to find an explanation.

He slipped out from behind the wheel of his Mercedes. After Sheils had released him, he'd caught a cab to Rebecca's. He apologized for wrecking her car and after giving him some grief, she handed him his keys back. He crossed the street, went up to Alex's window, and peered inside. He saw and heard nothing.

He ducked down the narrow side yard to the rear of the house. The yard was overgrown. A gas barbecue sat knee-deep in the grass and a garden hose disappeared into the dense thatch. Friedkin couldn't count the number of times he'd been here and it was always immaculate. Alex prided himself on his yard, his family, and his home.

That had been until the trial separation. Kerry had moved out a couple of months ago, taking Jack with her. Friedkin didn't know the details, but he should have. Not because he was Alex's boss, but because the man was his friend. When he saw the drop-off in Alex's work and the change in his demeanor, he should have asked questions instead of firing him.

He tried the back door. Locked. He eyed the houses on either side of him. Nothing stirred. He counted his blessings that neither neighbor owned a dog while he brought out his picks and worked the lock.

Even if Alex's life was going down the tubes, it didn't explain why he was in Vallejo watching the FBI work a crime scene. Alex wasn't the Piper, so what was he doing there? That one question created a drift of other equally difficult questions. How did he know to be in Vallejo at the exact same time as Scott Fleetwood? Was he working for someone? Friedkin didn't like where his thoughts were taking him. The lock clicked and he was in.

The kitchen stank. He snapped on his flashlight and shone it over the countertops. Rancid takeout containers sat in piles. Yesterday's date appeared on top of a delivery slip taped to a pizza box. Alex would be back.

He went into the living room. His flashlight beam swept over papers covering the dining table. He flicked on the light switch and groaned. Photographs of the Fleetwood family were pinned to the walls. One wall featured individual shots of Scott, Jane, Sammy, and Peter. A sheet of paper with their names hung above their respective candid photos. A character profile hung below their shots. It consisted of a bullet point list of information written at different times in different inks. Their habits. Their likes. Their dislikes. The Fleetwood family had been reduced to a Cliff's Notes companion.

Four files sat on the dining table with the names Scott, Jane, Sammy, and Peter written on each cover. Inside, he found daily logs dating back months detailing the Fleetwoods' movements. Friedkin struggled to believe his friend had any involvement with the Piper, but the wealth of evidence before him pushed him toward that conclusion.

How had this happened? How had he let this happen? He flicked the lights off.

He returned to the kitchen and checked the answering machine. The new message light blinked and he pressed PLAY.

The machine's mechanical voice time stamped the first message a week ago last Tuesday.

"Alex, it's Kerry. Why aren't you returning my calls? I know you're going through a tough time right now. I'm not trying to punish you. Call me. Please."

The second message came three days later, again from Kerry.

"Alex, please call. I'm worried. You missed our appointment. I understand if you don't want to see me, but don't shut Jack out. Please call, just let me know you're doing okay."

Kerry's third message came yesterday. Concern filled her previous two messages. Fear contaminated the last one.

"Alex, I came by the house today. You've changed the locks. No one has heard from you in days. I called your office. They said they let you go. What's going on? Call me, even if it's just to say I'm a rotten bitch. It'll tell me you're alive." Kerry ended her call with a sob.

Friedkin wiped his hand across his mouth. His friend was in serious trouble. He felt very old and very tired.

His cell phone rang in his pocket. Alex's name appeared on the display.

"Why are you in my house, John?" Alex asked.

Friedkin went to the kitchen window. He didn't see Alex. "What makes you think I'm in your house?"

"Your car parked out front."

Friedkin cursed his stupidity. He was a professional and he wasn't thinking.

"If I were to enter my home to find you there, skulking

in the dark, I would be within my rights to shoot you thinking you were an intruder—which you are."

Friedkin took the threat seriously. "If you were to shoot me, you'd be shooting a friend."

"Friends don't break into friends' houses in the middle of the night, John."

"It was with the best of intentions. Kerry and I are worried about you."

"Have you two been talking behind my back?"

"No. I just know she's worried."

He cut through the house back to the kitchen. He pocketed the flashlight and tugged out a paring knife from a knife block. There were bigger knives, but they were unwieldy in a fight. The paring knife came as close to a street weapon as he could get.

"Why were you watching the FBI in Vallejo, Alex?"

"I was working."

The house wasn't a safe place. It was going to be Friedkin's tomb if he didn't get out. He opened the back door, then sped through the house and unlocked the front door. He cracked the door an inch. If he needed to escape through the front door, just a quick tug and he was out.

"Are you the Piper?"

Alex exploded into laughter. "No, I'm not the Piper. Damn, John, I thought you were better than this."

Friedkin moved to a point midway between the front and rear doors. No matter which door Alex entered, he had a head start.

"What am I supposed to think, Alex? Your living room is a testament to premeditation to a double kidnapping. If I take this to the FBI, they'll come after you."

"But you won't. You've got the reputation of the agency to consider."

"Reputations can be rebuilt."

"Friendships can't."

Alex was right. The reason Friedkin had lied when Sheils showed him Alex's composite was out of friendship.

He wanted his friend to explain himself and give himself up if he'd had any part in the Fleetwood kidnappings.

"Maybe our friendship isn't supposed to last."

"Maybe," Alex said with resignation. "I'm hanging up now. I have an intruder to stop."

This was it. Alex was coming for him. His breathing quickened as he listened hard for footsteps. Front or rear? Front or rear? Which way would Alex come? The front door shifted a fraction and Friedkin bolted for the rear. He hurtled through the kitchen and out the back door. He charged down the side yard for the front. He wanted to turn the tables and trap Alex in the house.

He rounded the front of the house expecting to see Alex bursting inside, but Alex wasn't there. He slowed and approached the door with caution. The wind had nudged the door. Not Alex.

He looked up and down the street for Alex or his car. Neither was anywhere to be seen.

THIRTY-NINE

Sheils sat at the Fleetwoods' kitchen table eating the breakfast Scott and Jane had made for his team. He'd yet to go to bed, but he'd gone home for a shower, a change of clothes, and the opportunity to hug his family. It went a long way to recharging his sleep-deprived batteries.

The same couldn't be said of Scott and Jane. They had no one else to turn to for solace. They needed good news, and soon.

Sheils wasn't sure how he was going to get it for them. The ransom drop had left them no leads. His team was working the places where Scott had stopped the night before, but he didn't bank on them finding anything. Baz Reagan had looked to be their best chance of catching the Piper and that turned out to be a bust. The license plate Friedkin got off the rental car was their remaining lead. It would turn up an identity and an address. He expected it to be a bogus identity, but it would start a trail leading to the real one. Proactively, that was all he had going for him. Reactively, he expected a call from the Piper. It had to come soon and it would be bad.

He finished the last of his eggs and pulled out his cell phone to check his voice mail. Jones dominated the voice mails. He left a message before and after he approached each BG suspect on the list. Jones added his own flavor to each report, waxing lyrical about each BG as he eliminated him. He added how much his butt hurt from sitting in his car all day. Sheils smiled at the extraneous commentary, but his smile slipped when he listened to the messages for Brian Givens.

"Tom, I've just left the property for this Brian Givens character. I don't like him. He left me feeling queer and you know how I hate feeling queer. I'm not saying Givens is our guy, but he didn't want me on the premises. Now, he might just not be a fan of the black man or he could be a country hermit who likes his privacy, but he's hinky. He needs a second look. There's a house, barn, and a paddock for horses. I'm going to stake this place out and search it when he leaves. If you have any friendlies up here, I'd appreciate extra help. Call me. I'll call you with progress reports."

But Jones hadn't called. He left his last message just after 4:00 p.m. That was seventeen hours ago. Even if his cell had crapped out on him, Jones would have gotten to a pay phone. Sheils didn't want to believe something bad had happened. He punched in Jones's cell number and the call went to voice mail.

"Jones, call me."

Panic edged his words, drawing Scott and Jane's attention.

"What's wrong?" Jane asked.

"It's Jones. He didn't call in after checking out one of the BG properties yesterday."

He went to his briefcase and yanked out the short list of nine property owner names and addresses. He yanked out Brian Givens's details from the mix.

"Dunham, in here," he yelled.

Dunham entered the kitchen.

"You got anything back from the rental place?"

"Yeah. Just now. Douglas Ritchie hired the car with a

MasterCard using an Ohio driver's license. Both bogus. He's our guy, though." Dunham held out a printout of the driver's license.

Sheils took the printout. Douglas Ritchie's DMV picture matched Baz Reagan's description in every respect except hair color.

He handed Brian Givens's property details to Dunham. "Get me a DMV and whatever else you can on this guy, fast."

"Do you think Jones found the Piper?" Scott asked.

"I don't know."

"But you're worried he did," Jane said.

"Yes," he admitted reluctantly.

He called Jones's number and got voice mail again. He called Jones's wife and she moaned at him for taking her husband away from her. He bantered back and forth with her before asking her if she'd heard from him. She hadn't. He kept the fear from his voice when he told her he'd get Jones to call her back.

Dunham returned with Brian Givens's driver's license details. The man pictured on the California driver's license wasn't Douglas Ritchie.

"Who is he?" Jane asked, looking at Givens's DMV photo.

Sheils had an inkling. At fifty-three, Brian Givens was in the Piper's age range. Douglas Ritchie, or whoever he really was, was on the young side for the Piper. He would have barely been out of his teens when the first victim, Camille Fairweather, had been kidnapped. The Piper came over as a well-organized loner, but his position as team leader couldn't be ruled out.

"The man in the city last night could be an accomplice. When Friedkin followed the rental car last night, he didn't see either of your children with him. Considering the merry dance he had us running last night, he would have been forced to leave Sammy and Peter behind. It's unlikely he left them unattended."

"You think Brian Givens is the Piper?" Scott asked.

"I think it's worth investigating."

"That's not an answer."

Sheils had no direct proof. He had threads, mere strands of information, but those strands wove together to construct a thick enough rope to hang the Piper.

"Yes, I think it's him."

"Then what are you waiting for?" Jane asked.

"We aren't." He returned inside and called his team into the living room. "We have a new player in this game. Brian Givens. He owns property similar to that described by Ryan Rodgers. Annabel Cho and someone I sent in have disappeared in the vicinity of this property. I want to know this man inside and out, financially, criminally, and personally. I want to know if he owned any of the properties used in this case. That includes the store on South Van Ness and the sawmill in Oregon. I want this picture shown to Baz Reagan and the Piper kidnap families. Do they recognize this man?"

The speech invigorated his flagging team. He capitalized on their newfound energy by divvying up assignments. While everyone jumped on their tasks, he called the Yolo County sheriffs and got them to form a half-mile perimeter around Givens's home. They weren't to approach or intercept, just establish his presence and make sure he stayed there. Sheils requested a chopper to fly him and Brannon to Winters.

Scott stopped him on his way out. "I'm coming with you."

"You're staying here in case we receive a call from the Piper."

"Jane can take the call. I'm coming with you."

"I can't allow that."

"If Givens has my children and you squeeze him, he'll kill them, but he might hesitate if he knows I'm there. You'll need a bargaining chip and I'm it."

Sheils looked to Brannon. Brannon showed no signs of disagreement.

"You know Scott's right," Jane said.

"Okay," Sheils said. "You're coming."

*   *   *

The door opened and Kerry Hammond stepped out from her parents' home in Concord. Her son bounded along behind her and she opened the car door for him to get in.

Friedkin had been waiting for this moment and dreading it. He'd been parked outside the house for a couple of hours. Lights came on and movement from within began an hour ago, but he lacked the courage to go up to the door. How could he tell this woman her husband was tied to the Piper? He still didn't have all the details, but he was out of time. He slipped from his car and jogged across the road.

She was fastening the boy into his car seat when he called her name. She looked up, then smiled when she recognized him. "John, what are you doing here?"

Her smile dropped when she took in his disheveled appearance and his grave expression.

"Kerry, we need to talk."

"I can't. I've got to get Jack to school."

"It can't wait, Kerry."

She pretended she hadn't heard him and fussed with the straps on Jack's car seat, but couldn't seem to snap the buckle together. He eased her aside and snapped it into place. She went to the driver's side, but he caught her arm.

"Can't your mom or dad take Jack to school this morning? It's important. It's about Alex."

Kerry's dad appeared on the doorstep. Friedkin released her arm before anything could be misconstrued.

"Anything wrong?"

"No. This is Alex's boss. Dad, can you take Jack to school? He wants to talk to me about Alex."

The news failed to warm Kerry's dad, but he agreed to drive Jack to school.

Kerry led Friedkin into the backyard. They sat at a picnic table away from the house. Kerry's mom fussed in the kitchen, keeping an eye on them.

"I need to find Alex," he said.

"He's at home."

"He's not. I've heard your phone messages."

Kerry sagged. "He changed the locks."

"I know. How long have things been bad between you two?"

"Months."

"You guys have been solid for so long. What happened?"

She laughed without humor. "It feels like nothing now. We separated three months ago. I got tired of him working away all the time. He was putting all these hours in and never got to see us. I wanted him in a nine-to-five job for once. He said he was working a big case for you and didn't have time for us."

Friedkin stopped her. "Did he specifically say the big case was for me?"

The question confused her. "Yes. For you. John, what's going on? Why have you come here?"

"Alex hasn't been working a big case for me, but I think he has been for someone else. Do you know who that would be?"

Kerry shifted in her seat. "He did a little divorce work now and again. Nothing big."

"No, this is someone with money. Did he ever mention someone like that?"

"No. Nobody like that. Why? Tell me what's going on."

"For the last six months, Alex's been working a serious surveillance job. Around-the-clock stuff. Someone would need deep pockets to fund it. Does that jog any memories?"

She shook her head.

"If I wanted to find Alex, where should I look?"

"All we have is that house."

Friedkin berated himself. He should have staked the place out and cornered Alex instead of breaking in. Now he'd scared him off.

"John, you're scaring me. Is he in trouble?"

He could see she was cracking under the load. She knew

Alex was in trouble. He'd heard her concern on the phone messages. She just didn't know what kind of trouble and how bad. He couldn't keep the truth from her.

"Yes, he's in trouble. The FBI is looking for him, but I want to find him first."

"What's he done?"

"I don't know for certain."

"Don't give me that, John. You know. You wouldn't be here if you didn't."

"Kidnapping."

He didn't sugarcoat it. He gave it to her straight and it took her unawares. She mouthed denials, but they were halfhearted and tapered off before she could form a reasoned objection.

"Do you have any way of contacting him? I need to reach him."

Kerry didn't answer. She was lost in her thoughts.

He was losing time and he pressed her. "Kerry, if you can't help me, I have to go to the FBI."

"Don't. Please."

"Then help me."

"He has a cell. We bought the phones as a Christmas present so we could always reach each other. I've called him on it, but he doesn't answer."

"What's the number?"

She recited the number and he punched it into his phone. Alex would ignore his wife's call, but Friedkin hoped he'd answer when his number appeared on Alex's phone. The phone rang for a long time. Friedkin thought the voice mail was going to kick in when Alex answered.

"You must be with Kerry, John."

"Yes, I am. We need to talk. The feds have ID'd you. They're going to find you. Let me help."

"I don't need your help. I'll be out of the country before nightfall, well before Sheils and his crew have it all worked out."

Friedkin had a timeline. Whatever Alex and the Piper

had planned, it ended today. Thoughts of a Nicholas Rooker scenario filled his head for Sammy and Peter Fleetwood. He pushed them from his mind before they blinded him. "Where does this leave Kerry and Jack?"

Alex's blasé tone switched to anger. "My family is none of your damn business."

"But it is. I'm Jack's godfather. I'm not sure I want him seeing his father hunted across the planet, and you will be. If you flee, the FBI will track you. You'll never stop running. That doesn't sound like much of a clean getaway to me."

"You don't know shit."

"You're right. I don't. So explain it to me. Meet me."

"Not a chance," Alex fired back.

"Sheils might not be able to touch you legally, but I can. I swear I'll hunt you to the ends of the earth if you don't meet with me now."

The intensity of Friedkin's statement silenced Alex. Friedkin wasn't bluffing. He meant every word. He couldn't walk away from something that involved him so heavily, both personally and professionally. He took Alex's silence as a sign that Alex believed him.

"Come back to the city," Alex said.

He'd gotten through. "Where?"

"Pier 25. Drive up to the water and honk your horn twice. Don't bring the FBI."

FORTY

The Yolo County sheriffs didn't have a helipad in Winters, so the chopper set down in a field. Uniformed officers crossed the field from their vehicles to meet Scott, Sheils, and Brannon as they clambered from the helicopter. Introductions were brief and carried out on the move. In staccato fashion, the sheriff brought Sheils and Brannon up to speed. Deputies were in position. Givens hadn't left his ranch, but the possible kidnap victims remained unsighted.

This failed to worry Scott. Givens wouldn't be parading his captives unless he was moving them out. They were there. They had to be.

Just as they reached the road, Sheils's cell rang. As he listened to the call, his expression turned grim. He cursed when he hung up.

"Baz Reagan is dead. Shot in the face," he announced, darkening the mood around them.

Scott's secure feeling began to lose its integrity. Sammy's and Peter's lives depended on taking Givens now.

Sheils and Brannon climbed into an unmarked Crown

Vic. Scott went to get in the back, but Sheils put out his hand. "You go with the sheriff, Scott."

"No. You need me. This is all about me."

"I know, but I can't risk Givens seeing you. Your presence will provoke him. Do you want that? Do you want to risk Sammy and Peter's lives?"

Scott angled for an answer. He wanted to be first through the door with Sheils and Brannon. He needed to look Givens in the eye. He wanted to say, "Here I am, you bastard. Now what?" Unfortunately, none of his desires and needs constituted a persuasive argument. There was only one answer. "No, I don't want to risk their lives."

"Good," Sheils said. "I'm keeping you close, Scott, for when I do need you. Right now, I need you to work with me. Okay?"

Scott nodded.

No one gave Scott time to mourn the decision. Sheils and Brannon accelerated after the cruiser leading the way. Scott slid alongside the sheriff in his Explorer, and they brought up the rear.

The motorcade raced along the winding roads without lights or sirens. The sheriff threw the SUV into the bends to keep up with the cars ahead. He told Scott not to worry. He ran a well-drilled team of deputies. The FBI knew their stuff. Givens didn't stand a chance.

It was all nice stuff meant to reassure him, but Scott knew better. The sheriff hadn't driven on the twisted road Scott had traveled to reach this point and it wouldn't straighten out now. Not if Givens was the Piper.

Scott guessed they were close to the ranch when he started spotting sheriff's cruisers tucked away on side roads and pullouts. The three-vehicle convoy slowed to a halt next to a lone cruiser already parked in a neighbor's driveway. One of the deputies briefed them on the current situation, which wasn't much. Givens had been spotted going back and forth from his house to his pickup, loading it up.

Sheils and Brannon stripped off their jackets and shirts to put on Kevlar vests, then redressed. The body armor bulked out their clothes, but their jackets disguised its presence well.

"Okay, I want a group channel on the radio kept open so everyone can hear. You'll know if we need backup," Sheils said. "I want this to go down without fireworks. Is that understood?"

Sheils received a round of nods from his law enforcement brethren. Scott felt compelled to join in. That was it. Scott watched Sheils and Brannon go and there wasn't anything he could do about it.

Sheils parked across the back of Givens's Ford F-150, blocking any chance of a fast getaway. He and Brannon slipped from the Crown Vic prepared for anything and everything. He had a radio set to transmit clipped to his belt. His Glock sat in its holster unclipped for easy removal. If events followed the game plan he and Brannon had worked out during the chopper flight, he expected to take Givens alive. Givens was the only one who could spoil their plan.

Movement came from inside until Brannon rang the doorbell. Givens would be deciding whether to answer the door or play possum. *You can't play possum with your truck parked out front*, Sheils thought. *Come out and say hi.*

Movement from within resumed. Feet pounded the stairs. Did Givens have someone stashed up there? With possibly four people held against their will at this ranch, Givens couldn't afford to keep them holed up together. He risked being jumped by the sheer numbers.

Brian Givens opened the door. Although in his fifties, he was in good shape. He lived well and why shouldn't he, considering all the money he'd extorted over the years? Crime paid well, but for only so long. In his mind's eye, Sheils slid the masked figure in Redfern's photograph over Givens's frame. It was a perfect match.

"Can I help you?"

"Yes, I'm Agent Brannon from the Federal Bureau of Investigation." Brannon produced his ID. "And this is my colleague, Agent Sheils."

Sheils hoped to goad Givens with his presence, but Givens failed to register an emotion at the arrival of the FBI on his doorstep. Instead, he scanned Brannon and Sheils as if he were X-raying them. Alarm bells were ringing in Sheils's head. Could he really have caught up with the Piper?

"How can I help you?" Givens asked.

"We're looking for a suspect who we believe is operating out of this area," Brannon said. "His name is Vernon Neville. African-American. Late fifties. Two hundred and forty pounds. Six foot three in height. More than likely, he would have called himself Jones."

"What's he done?"

"Home invasions," Brannon answered. "He cons his way into the home owners' properties to beat and rob them."

"I see," Givens said.

"Have you seen this man in the area?" Sheils asked.

"No," Givens said.

Gotcha, Sheils thought. He'd caught Givens in a lie. Jones had been there and hadn't returned. After so many years of disappointment and failure, Sheils had the son of a bitch. He maintained his poker face to shield his excitement.

"I'm glad to hear it." Sheils cast a glance over the rest of the property, ending his scan at the locked barn. "You have a sizeable parcel of land, do you mind if we look around?"

"Do you think he'd hide out here before making his move?" Givens asked.

"No," Sheils said.

"Then you have no reason to search my property."

Givens was spooked. Sheils liked that. Jumpy people made mistakes.

"Can we not look around, sir?" Brannon asked.

"Not unless you have a warrant. Do you have one?"

"No," Brannon answered.

"I'm taking your word that you're an FBI agent. For all I know, you could be this Vernon Neville and this is your attempt to invade my home."

"Sir, really," Brannon said.

Sheils didn't buy in to Givens's paranoia, but he decided it was time to back down.

"Maybe we should leave," he said and stepped back from the door.

"Maybe you should," Givens said.

"Thank you for your time," Brannon said. "Sorry for any inconvenience."

Sheils and Brannon backed away from Givens's doorstep. Neither man wanted to turn his back on the Piper.

Givens crossed the threshold of his doorway to watch Sheils and Brannon return to their vehicle. He reminded Sheils of an animal reclaiming its territory, forcing out the weaker animal. Then his body language changed. He stiffened in shock and directed an accusing arm over Sheils's shoulder toward the road.

"What's going on?"

Sheils turned to look.

Scott was crouched next to the sheriff at the side of the road, with a clear view of the house, the barn, Sheils, Brannon, and Givens.

Scott's heart raced while he listened to the mundane questioning on Givens's doorstep and went into overdrive when Givens made his error. He'd lied about meeting Jones. Sheils and Brannon had him. They could take him now.

But they weren't. They were backing off.

This couldn't be happening. How could they come this far only to walk away? It was insane.

"What the hell are they playing at?" Scott demanded.

"They're playing it safe. Building their case."

Playing it safe? Building a case? What bullshit was this? Four people were being held captive. This charade only served to alert Givens. Now he knew the FBI was on to him and he'd have no reason to hang tight while Sheils waited for warrants. As soon as he realized he was screwed, he'd execute everyone and disappear.

Scott couldn't let that happen. Not when he'd suffered so much to get this close. Not when his kids had suffered even more to survive this long. He wasn't leaving without them.

If Sheils needed probable cause to search the property, then he'd give it to him.

Scott leapt from his hiding spot in the drainage ditch, dropping the radio the sheriff had given him. He clambered from the ditch and bolted for the driveway.

The sheriff reacted fast and snared Scott's ankle from his position in the ditch. Scott's momentum carried him forward, but his feet went out from under him and he crashed to the ground on his side. He ignored the jolt of pain running up his spine and tried to shake the sheriff off, but his hold was too tight.

"What do you think you're doing?" the sheriff demanded.

"Ending this farce."

"That's not going to happen, Mr. Fleetwood."

Scott punctuated the sheriff's reply by swinging his foot around to kick him in the face. The sheriff's position in the ditch gave Scott the advantage. Scott's foot connected with the side of his head, dislodging his wrenchlike grip. The sheriff fell back into the ditch holding his nose.

Scott shoved aside any twinge of guilt as he scrambled to his feet and bolted for the entrance to Givens's property.

The sheriff yelled at Scott to stop. Scott glanced over his shoulder. The sheriff was already clambering from the ditch, but Scott had enough of a lead on him and kept running.

The sheriff's cry alerted a nearby deputy on the other side of the driveway. He popped up from his hiding place and charged toward Scott with his weapon drawn. The county cop moved to block Scott's access to Givens's property. He stopped and aimed his gun at Scott's chest.

"Stop," the deputy instructed.

Scott kept running toward him. "Shoot me or help me," Scott called to the deputy. "The decision is yours."

The deputy's features knotted as he fought with his decision, but his aim remained steady.

"Do it if you're going to."

"Shit," the deputy murmured and lowered his gun.

Scott called out a thank-you as he ran past the deputy and charged up the driveway. The lazy incline from the street to the house took the strength out of his legs. He got his second wind when he saw the barn Ryan Rodgers had been held captive in with all the other children. His children. They should have brought Ryan with them for identification purposes. Too late now. Well, they'd soon know whether Brian Givens was the Piper or not.

Givens spotted him and jerked out an arm in his direction. Sheils and Brannon turned, disbelief and anger spread across their faces.

"What's going on?" Givens bellowed. "You have no right."

"Scott," Sheils yelled. "Get out of here."

Realization crept into Givens's expression. He recognized Scott.

That's right, you bastard, you didn't think I'd find you, Scott thought. "I'm here," he yelled. "This is what you wanted. You wanted me to find you. I've found you. The game's over."

Givens bolted for Scott. Sheils blocked his move, putting his body in Givens's way. Givens had several inches of height difference on his side, but Sheils used his lower center of gravity to keep him from breaking away.

Brannon sprinted after Scott. To Scott's relief, he made no move for his weapon, but the FBI agent moved with real speed to intercept. Scott changed his direction to run on the far side of the parked vehicles, forcing Brannon to go the long way around. It bought Scott vital seconds to elude the agent.

The sheriffs stormed the property, including the deputy

Scott had talked into not shooting him, but were too far back to catch him.

Givens bridled at Sheils's attempt to restrain him. Sheils told him to calm himself. The FBI was taking care of it.

Brannon came in at Scott from his right. With his speed, his agent would cut him off long before he reached the barn. Brannon's expression said he intended on stopping him.

They failed to understand Scott's intention. The law bound them, but if he ripped open the barn door to expose vital evidence, it was admissible. If they let him reach the barn, they had Givens. Unfortunately, that wasn't going to happen. Brannon came at Scott, spreading his arms to show him he had nowhere to run.

Scott did. The agent should have just tackled him instead of trying to cut him off. Scott dropped a shoulder and drove it with all his momentum into Brannon's stomach. Brannon realized too late and didn't have time to react. He doubled over onto Scott from the impact. His deadweight came down on Scott's back, but Scott's speed drove him forward, dislodging Brannon's falling body.

Brannon flailed for him, catching his pant leg and tripping him. He came down hard on his hands and knees, but picked himself up and broke into a run again. Brannon attempted to follow, but Scott had winded him enough to slow his pursuit. He'd reach the barn now.

Sheils shouted and Scott turned in time to see Givens shoving him aside. Sheils lunged to restrain Givens, but Givens jerked out a gun from his waistband at the small of his back. As Sheils went to grab him, he pistol-whipped the agent across the cheek. Sheils fell to his knees and Givens bolted after Scott.

Elation ripped through Scott. Givens had dropped the facade. There was no going back. The Piper had unmasked himself. His reign ended today.

Givens raised his gun. Scott felt its aim settle on his back. *Not now*, he thought. He couldn't die before he got to see Sammy and Peter. It wouldn't be fair.

Calls to freeze came one after another from Sheils and Brannon. Both agents had their weapons out and trained on Givens.

Scott ran on. Gunplay could be the edge he needed to reach the barn.

Sheils issued a final warning to Givens.

Givens squeezed off a shot at Scott, then dived to the ground. The bullet missed Scott and struck the barn, but felt damn close.

Sheils and Brannon opened fire. They each fired twice before finding cover. Sheils took refuge in the doorway to the house. Brannon had nowhere to go in the open and lay flat on the ground to reduce his target area. Sheils opened fire again, two bursts of two shots. Brannon saw the shots as an opportunity to take cover behind his vehicle, but Givens fired and hit Brannon low in the back, his vest stopping the bullet. Brannon went down on his face and crawled to safety behind the vehicles.

The gunfire drew the sheriff's limited might. Three cruisers roared onto the property and stopped short to prevent Givens's escape by road and provide a second line of defense for Sheils and Brannon if the need arose. No doubt the sheriff's other men were closing in from other directions with more on the way. Givens wouldn't escape. It was over for him, but there was still plenty of time for him to take others down with him.

Scott slammed into the barn's double doors. The doors bowed against his weight but held fast against their chain and padlock. He peered inside and made out two cars inside before another shot struck the barn to the right of his head. He hit the ground and scurried around the side of the barn.

Scott yelled his sons' names through the gaps in the siding. A faint cry came from within the barn interrupted by the crack of gunshots.

"Boys, are you there? It's Daddy. It's okay. Make noise for me."

More muffled cries came from inside, but he saw no movement. They had to be in the cellar.

Scott jogged around the edge of the barn. The windows had been boarded from the inside. The only way in was through the double doors in clear view of Givens. Scott snatched up a rake propped up against the barn and ran out into the open again toward the main doors.

"Have my back, Sheils," Scott murmured over and over.

He jammed the rake handle through the loop of chain held in place by the padlock and yanked down on it. Its wooden handle cracked and split under the load. A third bullet struck the door. The next one would surely hit him. Scott put all his weight on the rake, jamming his foot against one of the barn doors. The chain and padlock remained intact, but the screws holding the latch didn't. They sheared off in the rotted wood. The door swung outward and Scott struck the ground on his back.

Two more shots hit the barn in quick succession before covering fire pinned Givens down.

Scott scurried inside the barn on his hands and knees before collapsing on his face. He yelled Sammy's and Peter's names again. He heard muffled voices coming from the ground. He made out the trapdoor in the dirt, but a Buick covered it.

He slid behind the wheel. The keys were in the ignition. He gunned the engine and reversed out into daylight before skidding to a halt. Bullets struck the car and shouts continued. He leapt from the car, raced back inside the barn, and yanked up the trapdoor. The stink of stale air wafted up at him. Two forms, too big to be children, moved in the gloom.

"Sammy? Peter?"

"No," Jones replied. "They're not here."

They had to be here, Scott thought. *Givens was the Piper. The Piper put his kids in the cellar. That's how it worked.* But not this time. Fear knifed through him. Givens had stashed Sammy and Peter somewhere new. Givens couldn't die in the shoot-out. If he died, so did Sammy and Peter. Scott charged out of the barn with his hands up.

"Don't shoot. They aren't there. We need him alive."

"Get down, Scott," Sheils barked. "Get down."

Givens swung his aim at Scott.

Scott stood in the open with nothing to protect him. Givens's arm stopped its arc. The weapon's muzzle was in direct line with Scott's chest.

"Don't shoot," Scott said more to the law enforcement officers than to Givens.

No one listened.

Sheils fired a fraction of a second before Givens did. The bullet struck Givens in the neck. An explosion of red mist erupted from the wound. Givens fired, but his shot struck the ground.

A new nightmare began for Scott. He ran to where Givens lay, ignoring Sheils's order not to approach. Scott fell to his knees at Givens's side. Sheils's shot had torn through the artery. Blood jetted from the ragged wound. Givens raised his weapon at Scott to shoot. Scott slapped the weapon from his hand and clamped his hands over the hole in Givens's neck to stanch the bleeding. He made a difference, but not much. Blood pulsed between his fingers. Givens didn't have long left. Neither did Scott's sons if he didn't get answers.

"You're the Piper, yes?"

"Yes," Givens croaked.

Sheils, Brannon, and the sheriff's people arrived in time to hear the confession. Sheils gathered up Givens's discarded weapon.

"I found you," Scott said. "I did as you told me. Now where are my boys?"

Givens didn't speak. He just shook his head.

"Tell me," Scott demanded.

Givens shook his head again.

Blood didn't seem to be exiting Givens as fast as before. His pallor had changed from white to gray. He had seconds.

"Don't do this to me. Don't take it out on my kids. I did everything you told me to do. It's not fair. It wasn't my fault. Tell me. Please."

"It wasn't me," Givens said. "I kidnapped seven children, I killed Nicholas Rooker, but I never took your kids."

"You're lying," Scott hit back.

"No."

A bomb went off in Scott's head. *This can't be happening.* "If you don't tell me, I'll let you bleed out, you son of a bitch."

Givens forced a smile. "I'm dead already."

"Who's got them, if you don't?" Sheils demanded.

"I don't know," the Piper said before dying.

FORTY-ONE

While the piers around Fisherman's Wharf and the Ferry Building were the hub of tourist activity, many others weren't. Pier 25 fell into that category. Friedkin turned off the Embarcadero and pulled up to the entrance. He expected it to be locked, but the large double doors hung ajar. He pushed the doors inward and drove his Mercedes through.

A series of arrows spray-painted on the ground directed him through the warehouse and out onto the pier itself. He parked at the end of the pier and went to honk his horn twice as instructed. Before he got the chance, a black Ford Fusion reversed out of the warehouse and skidded to a halt across the back of his car. Alex leapt from the Ford with a pistol aimed at him.

Friedkin had hoped this meeting would be less adversarial, but under the circumstances, it wasn't a surprise. Alex was mixed up in the Fleetwood kidnappings up to his neck. He was looking at a lifetime in prison, even if he did the right thing and gave himself up. Friedkin slipped from his car with his hands raised.

"There's no need for the gun, Alex," he said.

"Maybe not, but I'm just taking precautions. Hands on the roof."

Friedkin put his hands on the roof and spread his legs.

Alex came behind Friedkin, pressed the pistol's muzzle against the back of his head, and frisked him. He left Friedkin's wallet in place but took his cell phone, pocketing it.

"I don't want you phoning a friend." Alex stepped back, pushed the pistol hard against Friedkin's skull, and tossed a pair of handcuffs on the car's roof. "Put those on."

Friedkin cuffed his hands in front of himself and took a step toward Alex.

"That's close enough," Alex said.

Friedkin froze. Alex was afraid of him. He raised his cuffed hands in compliance. "Whatever you say, Alex."

"You've got a minute. Make your case."

"I don't have a case to make. You're mixed up with the Piper. You know you're screwed. Come with me. We'll go to Sheils and you can tell them where the Fleetwood kids are and cut a deal."

"That's it?"

The contemptuous tone in Alex's voice pissed Friedkin off. He marched over to Alex, ignoring his repeated warnings not to come any closer. He walked into the gun aimed at his stomach and continued walking. Alex put up no resistance and his arm buckled, pinning the weapon between them and forcing Alex against his car.

"Alex, you changed sides. You've thrown in with the worst kidnapper in California history. Your future is fucked. If that weren't bad enough, you've screwed up Kerry and Jack's futures too, and you don't seem to give a shit."

"Back off, John. I'm warning you."

"Screw your warning. You owe me an explanation."

"Get off me."

Alex shoved Friedkin hard. With his hands cuffed, Friedkin struggled with his balance and lost. He staggered back before toppling and striking the asphalt hard on his tailbone.

Alex rushed in with the pistol outstretched. He jammed the muzzle into Friedkin's cheek. "Don't make me shoot you. I don't want to kill anyone else."

Friedkin's breath caught. His brain seized, jamming on Alex's admission. He dreaded the answer, but he had to ask, "Who have you killed, Alex?"

"It doesn't matter," Alex snapped.

"It does. You're not a killer."

"I am now." The enormity of his claim seemed to drain his energy. He lowered the gun until it hung slack at his side. "That's why there's no going back."

Friedkin's stomach clenched at his next thought. "The boys. Sammy and Peter. Please tell me you didn't kill them."

"How can you even think that, John?"

Friedkin rolled over and struggled to his feet.

Alex aimed his pistol at Friedkin. "Stay where you are. Please."

Alex's finger tightened on the trigger, but Friedkin ignored the threat. He stepped forward.

"Where are you going?"

"To finish this."

"It's not yours to finish."

Alex turned his back on Friedkin to get behind the wheel.

Friedkin charged at him. He covered the short distance before he could circle around, aim, and shoot. He slammed into him, driving him into the side of the car. The impact knocked the pistol from Alex's grasp and it bounced across the ground, stopping under his Fusion.

Friedkin looped his cuffed wrists over Alex's neck. He jerked the short chain connecting the cuffs against his windpipe. Alex let out a strangled gurgle. Friedkin pulled back harder, gripping Alex's neck for greater leverage. Alex exhaled in nasty ragged breaths. He elbowed Friedkin in the gut to dislodge him. The impact winded him and his legs buckled, but his deadweight around Alex's neck pulled the cuffs tighter.

Alex elbowed him again and again, taking turns with each elbow. Friedkin's cuffed wrists exposed him to attack. He clenched his stomach muscles and tried to twist out of the way, but Alex's elbows found their mark every time. He struggled to breathe with each successive blow and he staggered back.

Alex tangled a leg between Friedkin's and tripped him. Both men fell and Alex's weight broke at least one of Friedkin's ribs. Friedkin yelled out in pain, but scrabbled over to Alex's pistol underneath the Ford. He clutched the weapon, but Alex grabbed him by the waistband and yanked him back. He whirled around, ready to shoot. Alex snapped out a foot, kicking the weapon from Friedkin's hands. It skittered across the asphalt, off the pier, and into the water.

Alex stamped down on Friedkin's stomach and all the fight went out of him. He hoisted Friedkin to his feet and put him in a headlock. Friedkin struggled to free himself and Alex tightened his choke hold.

"Stop or I'll keep squeezing," Alex said.

Friedkin stopped and Alex loosened his grip. Friedkin panted hard to get air into his lungs.

"You're not going to let this go, are you, John?" Alex asked.

"You know I can't."

"Then I'm going to have to let you go."

Alex released his hold and shoved Friedkin in the back. He tottered toward the edge of the pier, struggling to regain his balance, his cuffed hands throwing him off. His momentum carried him forward, pitching him over the side. The water swallowed him up and Alex disappeared.

The impact forced his mouth open, sending water gushing in. The ebb and flow of the water surging against the pier tossed and turned him. He kicked with his legs to stabilize his body, but he needed his hands free for that. He used his cuffed hands for an awkward doggy paddle and his natural buoyancy carried him upward.

He broke the surface coughing and spluttering. He drew in nasty, ragged breaths, his broken ribs knifing him. He tried to tread water while he caught his breath, but he couldn't maintain his balance.

The sound of squealing tires echoed off the buildings surrounding the pier. He glimpsed the streaking profile of Alex's Ford Fusion racing toward the street.

Alex wouldn't get far. Friedkin wouldn't let him. He powered toward the pilings, driving himself forward with his legs and steering with his hands. It wasn't pretty but he made it.

He grabbed a piling. It was slick with algae, seaweed, and pollution. His hands slipped, but after several attempts he got a firm purchase. He secured his position by jamming his feet onto the cross-ties jutting from the pilings.

The cat's cradle of pilings and cross-ties proved to be a helpful climbing frame. He developed a slow but effective climbing system, using his hands for purchase and his legs to power him up. He even used the cuffs to hang himself off any hook or protrusion he could find. It took him at least twenty minutes to make the fifteen-foot ascent, but he made it and clambered back onto the pier.

He gathered himself up and raced over to his car. He fumbled inside the console between the two seats and yanked out his personal cell phone. He punched in the office number. Rebecca answered.

"Where the hell are you? The place is crawling with cops."

"Let them crawl. Trace my cell."

"Don't you have it?"

"No, it's in a vehicle. I want to know where that vehicle is heading."

"What's going on?"

"Just do it, Rebecca. Please. It's important."

"Okay. Hold on."

Friedkin had signed up with a cell phone tracking service for all the cell phones registered to his business. At any time, he could log in to a secure Web site, enter the cell number, and a GPS tracking map would tell him where the phone was transmitting from. It provided secondary backup for his investigators in the field and improvised tracking in a clinch. Alex had unwittingly placed a bug on himself when he took Friedkin's phone. As long as he hadn't remembered to power it off, Friedkin would know his destination.

Rebecca came back on the line. "Your phone is at a fixed location."

Friedkin cursed. Knowing his luck, Alex had thrown the phone out the window. "Where is it?"

The address Rebecca read off left him sick to his stomach.

FORTY-TWO

Sheils watched the coroner's people load Brian Givens's corpse into a body bag. The Piper could no longer harm anyone. It was over.

Oddly, he felt no elation. After nearly twenty years of chasing the Piper's trail, he'd believed if he caught him, he would feel complete again. He could close the case on the man who'd ruined so many lives, including his own.

An ambulance lit up its lights and siren and roared off with Annabel and Jones inside. Both would be okay in time. Jones was a mule and a single gunshot wound wouldn't slow him down for long. Sheils feared more for Annabel's mental condition than her physical one. She'd cried foul at the sight of Givens's corpse, declaring her love for the Piper.

"You got him," the sheriff said and slapped a hand on Sheils's shoulder.

Yeah, he'd gotten him, but who had he gotten? Givens confessed to the earlier kidnappings, but not those of Sammy and Peter Fleetwood. It could just be a lie to twist the blade between Scott's ribs. If Sammy and Peter's location died with Givens, it would leave Scott with a living hell. He would spend the rest of his life wondering where his kids were. It was a cruel epitaph to leave behind, but Sheils didn't believe it. Before the paramedics took Jones away, he confirmed Givens's account. He had confessed to kidnapping seven children and killing Nicholas Rooker, but swore no involvement in Sammy's and Peter's kidnappings. The ranch fit Ryan Rodgers's description. Sammy and Peter should have been in the basement or in the house. They weren't. Nothing suggested that they'd ever been there. This left one conclusion. For the second time, someone was pretending to be the Piper.

The coroner's people lifted Givens's bagged body onto a gurney.

"I think it's time to celebrate," the sheriff said.

Sheils couldn't. He'd taken down the Piper, but he hadn't rescued Sammy and Peter. There'd be no celebrations until they were reunited with their parents.

"Excuse me," Sheils said.

With all the commotion surrounding the Piper, securing the crime scene, and collecting evidence, Scott had distanced himself from everyone. He sat on the dirt with his back up against a fence. He had a cell phone to his ear. Sheils walked over to him.

The idiot had screwed it up again. Givens was dead because of his latest stunt. Brannon was lucky to be alive. Sheils should be bawling him out, but there wasn't time for it. Whoever did have Sammy and Peter would know about Givens's death soon. He eyed the news chopper in the air.

"I love you," Scott said and hung up.

"Was that Jane?" Sheils asked.

Scott got to his feet. "Yeah. I wanted her to hear it from me."

"What did you tell her?"

"That the Piper is dead, but he didn't have Sammy and Peter. Was he telling the truth?"

"Yes, I think so."

Scott leaned against the fence post. "So who is behind this?"

Sheils had been thinking the same thing. Givens had the trinity—means, motive, and opportunity—but it never quite rang true. If he'd wanted to take his revenge on Scott and Redfern for interfering with Nicholas Rooker's kidnapping he could have done it years ago without all this fuss. Whoever had put together this three-ring circus really had an axe to grind. He wanted maximum devastation to Scott's and Redfern's lives. Sheils couldn't help feeling he was just a cog in this person's machinery.

"Whoever's doing this is connected to the Piper, either directly or indirectly."

"Do you think we've got another Redfern on our hands?"

"I hope not." Sheils prayed this wasn't a power struggle. Perhaps someone wanted to take on the mantle of the Piper and a new cycle of kidnappings would begin.

"At least something makes sense now."

"What does?"

"When the Piper told me to find him, I thought he wanted a showdown. But he really wanted me to find Givens." Scott indicated the scene before them. "Whoever is doing this wanted this to happen. This all goes back to that damn note Givens pinned to Nicholas Rooker's body. You're to blame. You, me, and Redfern. We're to blame."

"And the Piper. You're forgetting he had a piece in this too."

"Yeah, and we're eliminating each other while this sicko sits back and watches it all unfold."

Does Scott realize what he's saying? Sheils thought. An answer was forming itself before them. He was beginning to see it, even if Scott wasn't.

The coroner's truck started up and drove toward the road. Everyone stopped to watch the Piper's corpse leave for the morgue. It wasn't out of reverence, or even contempt. It was more out of disbelief. Finally, the monster was dead.

"I want to go back home," Scott said.

Sheils did too. The answer to this puzzle was back in San Francisco. He left Brannon to manage the scene after paramedics saw to him. The sheriff drove him and Scott back to the chopper.

In the air, Sheils checked his messages. His cell had been ringing off the hook. He paged through his missed calls. His cell rang again. Guerra's name appeared on the display and he answered the call.

"Sir, I've uncovered the ownership information you asked for."

In all this melee, he hadn't reassigned half his people. He'd forgotten about Guerra and the paper chase he'd sent her on. "It's not important now. Givens is dead. I need you elsewhere."

"No, you don't. You need to hear this."

The strength of her reply stopped him in his tracks. "Excuse me?"

"You're going to want to hear this. The out-of-state guy, Douglas Ritchie, who owned the South Van Ness property, also owned the factory in Vallejo and the sawmill in Oregon."

Guerra had his attention. "Go on."

"I checked this guy out. He doesn't exist. It's a front."

"For Givens?"

"No. For Charles Rooker."

FORTY-THREE

Rebecca met Friedkin two blocks from Rooker's house. She pulled up behind him in a rental car and slipped into the front passenger seat alongside him. Her jaw dropped when she took in his condition and his cuffed hands resting on the steering wheel. "What happened to you?"

"Never mind me. Did you bring what I asked?"

She nodded. She produced the handcuff key and uncuffed him. While he examined the angry welts and wounds left behind by the cuffs, she held out a 9mm pistol. He took the Glock from her and chambered a round.

"What's going on, John? Why do you need a gun to see Charles Rooker?"

Lies. Betrayal. Manipulation. Revenge. He had his pick.

"Just stay here, okay? Give me fifteen minutes. If I don't come out, call Sheils."

He opened the car door to get out, but she caught his arm. "John, don't. Call Sheils now."

"I just need to confer with my client first."

"With that?" She pointed to the Glock.

"Okay. Give me ten minutes," he said and left to her protests.

Alex's Ford Fusion sat in front of the house. If he was inside, Rooker was inside. Friedkin approached the house in clear view. He wanted to be seen and seen to be alone. He didn't want to spook Rooker and Alex.

As he climbed stone steps to the front entrance, the door eased back. He stopped when he reached the threshold. Alex stood off to one side, a gun aimed at Friedkin's chest.

"I'm here to talk, Alex."

"I bet you are. Step one foot inside and I'll shoot."

"Let him in," Rooker called from the stairs. A gun hung loose in his grasp. "Come in, John. Close the door after you."

Friedkin did as he was told.

"Are you armed?" Rooker asked.

"Yes."

"Slide it over to me," Alex said.

Again, Friedkin did as he was told. The pistol raced across the tiled floor. Alex stopped its progress with his foot and picked it up.

"Come up to my study," Rooker said.

Friedkin followed Rooker into his study, a gun trained on his chest and his back. He'd been in this room many times. He'd given updates, made promises, and felt sorry for Rooker in this room, but not anymore. Pity was the last thing he felt.

Rooker lowered his weapon and leaned against his mahogany writing desk. Alex blocked the doorway. He pointed Friedkin's own gun at him.

"Where are the kids?" Friedkin asked in a calm and level tone.

"Not here."

"You used me."

"That's your job. Cop for hire. Get used to it."

"I tried to help you and you lied to me."

Rooker shrugged. "Bad things happen to good people."

"Like you. You were a good person and a bad thing happened to you. The same way a bad thing happened to Nicholas."

Rooker jerked his pistol up. His hand trembled, but the wavering muzzle still stared Friedkin in the face. "Don't you talk about my son. You have no concept of my pain."

"So because your family suffered a tragedy, it's okay for you to inflict the same on others? Pay it forward, is that it?"

"Why not?" Rooker tapped the gun. "It makes the pain go away."

Friedkin was wasting his time. Rooker was too eaten up with hate to see reason.

Friedkin turned to Alex and took a step toward his friend.

"Don't take another step, John. Don't make me shoot you."

Friedkin halted. "You're going to have to shoot me anyway. Does it matter when?"

"I suppose not."

Alex's answer lacked the conviction of someone dedicated to Rooker's cause. Friedkin saw this as his way out. He needed to force a wedge in the gap and bust the two of them apart.

"What happened to you?" he asked Alex. "You have a wife, a child, a job. You had a life and you tossed it away for this." He jabbed at finger at Rooker. "For his blood crusade."

Alex looked to Rooker for a response and got none. He was cornered and like any cornered animal, he lashed out.

"Yeah, I had a life, but I never got to live it. I spent my days and nights working for you. I let my life slip from me while I spent it picking apart other people's lives. I went days, sometime weeks, without seeing my son awake. And for what? To help you build a business that made you rich. For that, my wife no longer wants to be around me and my son looks at me like I'm a stranger."

Friedkin felt for his friend, but he couldn't condone his

actions. "You had choices, Alex. You took the easy way out. How much is he paying you?"

"Fuck you."

"How much? How much to buy you? How cheap do you come?"

The tendons in Alex's neck popped out. His finger tightened around the trigger, but not tight enough to unleash a bullet. "One million."

"You undersold yourself."

Rooker laughed. "Can't you see what he's doing, Alex? He's stalling. While he plays the bleeding heart, the FBI is moving in."

Friedkin turned to Rooker. "You're wrong."

A fist slammed Friedkin in the back. The pain dropped him to his knees. Alex shoved Friedkin onto his face and pinned him to the floor. He pressed the pistol to his skull. "Did you sell me out?"

"No, but they will come. It's over. They've worked it all out. I came here to get both of you to see sense."

"I've seen sense," Rooker said. "Sense is not taking a backseat to the FBI's ineptitude."

"It's done," Friedkin said. "You've made your point. You've made others miserable. Now it's over. Tell me where to find the kids and this meeting never happened. I just want to help those boys."

Rooker put down his gun, picked up the remote from his desk, and switched on the flat screen on the wall. A cable news network in midstory appeared. The picture showed a ranch filmed from the sky. An off-screen voice babbled excitedly. The caption at the bottom of the screen read THE PIPER IS DEAD?

The news sucker punched Friedkin. Rooker's crazy plan had worked. He'd brought down the Piper, but Sheils wasn't any closer to finding Sammy and Peter.

"You're right about one thing," Rooker said. "It is over. I've gotten what I wanted. You no longer matter. Get him up."

Alex yanked Friedkin up by his collar. Friedkin pushed

back off his heels, slamming into him and crashing down on top of him. Pain flared from his broken ribs, but he bit it back. The Glock bounced from Alex's grasp. Friedkin rolled off Alex and grabbed the weapon. He snapped to a shooter's stance, ready to shoot either man.

Ready wasn't good enough. Rooker didn't hesitate. He grabbed his gun, aimed, and fired. Friedkin didn't see him shoot. He just felt the bullet rip through his right shoulder. His strength exited with the bullet. He collapsed, the Glock slipping from his hand.

Alex rushed over to snatch up Friedkin's Glock.

"Go," Rooker told Alex.

"What about you?"

"I wired payment to your account. You don't have to worry about me. Kill the twins and you're done."

"I'm sorry, John," Alex said and ran for the door.

"The kids," Friedkin called out.

Alex stopped at the doorway.

"Let the kids go. Ignore him. You're paid and he's finished. Let them go."

Alex hesitated.

"Go," Rooker barked.

Alex cast a final look Friedkin's way before disappearing, his feet beating a tattoo on the stairs.

Friedkin shifted on the floor, rolling on his side to get up. Rooker knocked him on his back with his foot. He stood over Friedkin and aimed the gun at him.

FORTY-FOUR

Scott was riding in the back of an FBI car with Sheils when news came of shots fired at Rooker's home. The FBI had been waiting to pick them up when the helicopter touched down at the Hall of Justice. They hadn't been on the road five minutes when Sheils's cell rang. He asked for a three-block cordon around Rooker's home and requested backup from SFPD, but they weren't to approach the house without his say-so. Sheils ended his call with one last instruction—no lights or sirens.

They parked one block from Rooker's house. The FBI agents put on their vests. Sheils still had his on from the ranch. He handed a spare one to Scott.

"Put this on," he told him.

After the carnage at Givens's ranch, Scott expected to be locked into the car. His surprise leaked into his expression.

"I want you with me, but I won't tolerate a repeat of this morning. I'll need your help with Rooker, but you don't step inside without my okay. Is that understood?"

Scott nodded and pulled on the vest.

"Don't make me regret this."

"I won't."

They moved as a unit toward Rooker's house perched on its corner lot. Sheils and his team approached with weapons drawn. The agents watched the doors and windows for signs of movement or a gun barrel. Neither appeared.

Sheils broke the team up when they reached the house. He sent two pairs of agents to cover the exits. Scott went with Sheils and an agent named Beatts up to the front door. It stood open, as if inviting them in.

Sheils ordered Beatts to keep Scott back. Beatts kept a firm grasp on Scott's arm.

With his weapon stretched out in front of him, Sheils peered through the open doorway. "FBI, Mr. Rooker," he shouted.

"Come in," Rooker shouted back. "We're upstairs."

Scott's heart beat rabbit-fast. Rooker had said *we. Does he have Sammy and Peter up there?* Reflexively, he pulled forward, but Beatts tightened his grip around his biceps.

"Wait here until I give the go-ahead," Sheils said and went inside.

He crossed the hallway, climbed the stairs, and disappeared from Scott's sight. Sheils announced himself from the top of stairs, then went silent. Scott strained to hear voices, but heard nothing.

The silence was agonizing. It could mean Rooker had Sammy and Peter and all was well. Silence could also mean his boys were dead and Sheils didn't know how to break the news. Scott wanted to burst in there, but he'd seen the carnage that action could cause. If Sammy and Peter were up there with Rooker, he wasn't going to risk their lives. He'd play by the rules.

Two minutes later, Sheils gave them the all-clear.

Beatts led the way and Scott followed. Nervous energy coursed through him, but climbing the stairs to the second floor drained him. He was clinging to the banister by the time he reached the second-floor landing.

Sheils held a shooter's stance at the entrance to one of the rooms off to his right. His body blocked Scott's view inside the room and he feared the worst. The nastiest of hostage situations might lie in that room. They could be a trigger squeeze away from disaster.

"Wait here," Beatts said to Scott. He darted ahead to join Sheils.

When Sheils had his backup, he ventured inside. "Scott, come in here. He wants to speak to you."

Scott rushed forward. The stink of cordite in the air chilled him. He pushed by the agent to enter the room.

Friedkin lay slumped in a chair with a vicious bullet wound to his shoulder. Rooker stood behind with a gun pressed to the private investigator's head. Sammy and Peter weren't there.

Sheils calmly said, "Scott, stand to my right. Remain behind me."

Scott understood the request and slipped in behind Sheils. Even though Scott wore a bulletproof vest, Sheils was using his own body to shield him. Rooker wouldn't leave this house a free man, but he wasn't finished. He still held Sammy's and Peter's lives in his hands and he could still put a bullet in Scott if he was feeling vindictive.

"Where are my boys?" Scott asked.

"Not here."

Rooker sounded triumphant, but didn't look it. Every time Scott had encountered the property tycoon, he'd looked resilient, in command, but not now. It looked as if it took all his energy to press the gun against Friedkin's skull.

"One of my ex-investigators has them," Friedkin said. "Alex Hammond."

Rooker backhanded Friedkin with the pistol, snapping his head around. "Keep your mouth shut."

"Rooker," Sheils barked. "Take it easy."

"He needs to know his place," Rooker said. "You all do."

"You're in charge here," Sheils said. "We understand that. There's no need to hurt anyone else."

Rooker's eyes sparkled at Sheils's remark. "Isn't there?"

"Where are they?" Scott pleaded.

"Why should I tell you?"

"Because I found the Piper. His name was Brian Givens."

"I know. I've seen the news."

"Then I've done all that you asked. I found Redfern and I found the Piper."

"No, you haven't done what I asked." Rooker's reply was bitter and harsh. "You were told to kill Redfern. You didn't. You were told to find the Piper and he's dead."

"Does it matter? You wanted the Piper dead, didn't you? Does it matter who killed him?"

"Yes, it does matter," Rooker barked. "I wanted to kill the Piper. That was my right as a father."

Silence filled the room. No one had anything to say. Revenge was a dirty business. Scott couldn't blame Rooker for wanting his revenge, but wished he hadn't chosen it.

"Why now?" Scott asked. "Why wait eight years to initiate this?"

Rooker pointed at a photograph of himself and his wife knocked askew on his desk. "Alice made me promise to. She believed in you, Sheils. She believed you would catch the Piper."

"She was right," Sheils said.

"But not if I hadn't started this. Without someone else's kids' lives on the line, Nicholas would have remained an unsolved case."

Sheils said nothing in his defense. It was true. Sammy's and Peter's kidnappings were the fuel that had ignited a new investigation.

Rooker smiled. "How did it feel to put that animal down? Fantastic, I imagine."

"Empty. I wanted him alive. I wanted him to suffer in jail. Instead he got off easy," Sheils replied.

Rooker frowned. He tightened his grip on Friedkin's neck. "Give it time, Sheils. You'll change your mind."

Scott looked at this man he'd harmed. The Piper had killed Rooker's son, but he had helped tip the balance, sending Rooker into a downward spiral of hate. He'd inspired the man to embark on a deadly game of revenge. The guilty had been punished, but the innocent too. Sammy and Peter didn't deserve to be hurt. Still, he owed Rooker one thing.

"I'm sorry," he said.

Rooker looked surprised by the apology.

Scott came out from behind Sheils. Sheils darted forward to get back in front of him.

"What are you doing, Scott?"

"Apologizing. I should have and I never did."

Scott's move unnerved Rooker. He swung his gun away from Friedkin and aimed it at Scott and Sheils.

"Take it easy, Rooker."

Scott held the balance of this moment and he halted. Sheils resumed his position as a human shield.

"I'm sorry," Scott repeated. "I hurt your family. I can't undo what I did and you've had your revenge, but it's over. The Piper and Redfern are dead and I've broken enough laws to separate me from my family for years. Now it's time to release Sammy and Peter. They aren't part of this."

"Neither was Nicholas, but it didn't save him."

"So Sammy and Peter have to die?"

"Why not? It's a fair trade. Your children for mine."

"Trades are open to substitution. What do I have to do to save my boys?"

Sheils tensed. "That's it. You're out of here, Scott."

Scott pushed by Sheils. "C'mon, Charles. What do you want for Sammy and Peter? What can I give you to let them go?"

Sheils holstered his gun and grabbed Scott. Scott fought him, but he easily restrained him, knotting his arms under

Scott's arms and around his neck. The agent at the door rushed in with his weapon aimed at Rooker to protect Scott and Sheils. With Sheils's weapon holstered, they were sitting ducks if Rooker opened fire. Rooker didn't need to shoot. He stopped the commotion with a single word.

"Okay."

Sheils froze with Scott in his grasp. "What?"

"I'll trade Sammy and Peter for Scott."

"Deal," Scott said.

"Not a chance in hell," Sheils said.

"I'll do it."

Sheils jerked Scott back and toward the door. "No, you won't."

"Don't be a spoilsport, Sheils," Rooker said. "I'll even throw in Friedkin. Three lives for the price of one. You won't get a better deal."

Scott fought Sheils's hold but got nowhere. Sheils hauled him out of the room and onto the landing. Scott spun around. Sheils pressed a hand against Scott's chest and pointed a finger in his face. "There's no way I'm turning you over to him."

"It's the only way we're going to get Sammy and Peter."

"He'll kill you."

"I don't care," Scott said. "It's what I want. Every minute we waste is another minute this Alex Hammond has to hurt my kids."

Sheils exhaled. "I can't believe you're talking me into this."

"Thank you," Scott said. "I owe you."

Scott followed Sheils back into the room, but didn't venture farther than the doorway. "Release Friedkin and tell us the location of Sammy and Peter Fleetwood and you can take Scott as a hostage."

"Good," Rooker replied.

"But you get me too."

Scott went to tell Sheils this wasn't his fight, but it was. Both of them were trying to put wrongs right.

"The more the merrier."

Rooker released Friedkin and the private investigator slumped forward. Rooker moved out of the way, stopping next to his desk. Sheils nodded at Beatts. Beatts swept in, gathered Friedkin up, and carried him out of the study.

"I want two in here to replace you," Sheils said to the agent as he went past.

Sheils had his weapon trained on Rooker. Rooker had switched his aim to Scott.

"Okay, you've got what you wanted," Sheils said. "Tell us where to find Sammy and Peter."

"Come closer," Rooker said to Scott.

"Stay where you are," Sheils ordered.

Scott ignored Sheils. He crossed the room to Rooker.

"Goddamn it, Scott."

He stopped in front of Rooker, blocking Sheils's shot. Sheils switched to a new position to regain a kill shot on Rooker.

"Kneel," Rooker ordered.

Scott kneeled.

Rooker pressed the gun to Scott's forehead.

"Rooker, don't even think about it," Sheils warned.

"Kill me, Sheils, and you'll never find those kids."

"It's okay," Scott said.

Sheils cursed. Scott felt sorry for him. He was doing his best, but he was realizing he was excluded. This was between Scott and Rooker, like it should have been from the beginning.

"You destroyed my life," Rooker said. "Not you alone. I understand that. But you played your part."

"Don't you think I know that?" Scott said. "I've lived with the guilt every day, but my children don't deserve to die for my mistake."

"Location, Rooker," Sheils demanded.

Rooker ignored Sheils. He needed to say what had been festering inside him for eight years.

"You didn't just kill Nicholas. You killed Alice too. Nicholas represented the last chance at motherhood for her. We'd struggled to conceive. We'd both given up hope when one day, without the intervention of medical miracles, she fell pregnant with Nicholas. Nicholas's murder stripped us of our family. We weren't even husband and wife. I watched Alice's soul whither. I believe the cancer came as a result of Nicholas's death. It sounds crazy, I know, but I truly believe that. She wanted to die and to die in pain." Rooker squeezed out a sad smile. "She got her wish."

"Please spare my boys." Scott hoped he was appealing to the last remnants of Rooker's humanity.

"You would die for them, wouldn't you?"

"Rooker, take it easy," Sheils said, an edge of tension in his voice.

"Yes, I would. I would die for my children."

Rooker smiled and nodded his approval. "I'm glad to hear it. Given the chance, I would have gladly given my life for Nicholas."

Rooker's finger tightened on the trigger. Scott kept his eyes open. He'd surrender to Rooker when he knew where his children were and not before.

"Don't do it, Rooker," Sheils said.

"Where are they?" Scott asked.

"You think a noble sacrifice will save your children, don't you?"

"Yes."

"Goddamn it, Rooker," Sheils said. "Nobody needs to die."

"They do, Sheils. Misery needs victims."

"Spare them," Scott said. "You have the power."

Rooker smiled. Scott saw compassion in his face. The man was a father, not a monster. Then Rooker's expression changed. Hate-fueled cruelty twisted his features.

Scott recognized Rooker's solution to his problem a fraction too late. He lunged for the weapon, but Rooker jerked out of the way and kicked Scott back. He jammed the pistol under his own chin.

"Now you'll know my pain, Scott," Rooker said and pulled the trigger.

FORTY-FIVE

Scott held Rooker's dead body in his arms. A single bullet had dispatched any chance of answers, understanding, and reconciliation. How could Rooker have been so cruel? Did he really hate him that much? Scott wished he could have talked to the man without the threat to his children, without the disguise of the Piper to mask his motives. If they'd talked, maybe something good could have happened. In a twisted way, Rooker had been successful. The Piper had been unmasked and killed. Redfern had been killed. Scott's children were in dire peril. What more could Rooker have asked for? Scott tried to feel something for the man. Hate. Pity. Disgust. It didn't matter which. Anything would do. But Rooker's act of selfish cruelty left him numb.

"He's dead, Scott. Leave him," Sheils said. "We have to think about Sammy and Peter now."

Scott nodded. He took a last look at Rooker's face. A ragged hole, scorched by the muzzle flash, stained the underside of his chin and blood had spilled from his mouth. The top of his head was a ruined mess. His stare stretched into the distance, but his expression was one of pleasure. Victory. With his last act of revenge, Rooker believed he'd won.

"You haven't won yet," Scott said. "Do you hear me? You haven't won yet."

"C'mon, Scott."

Sheils dragged Scott away and Rooker slid to the floor.

Two of Sheils's agents burst into the room with weapons drawn. The tension went out of them at the sight of Rooker's corpse and they lowered their weapons. Sheils issued them instructions, but as he was finishing, Beatts rushed back in.

"Sir, you'd better come with me."

Sheils and Scott chased after Beatts to where Friedkin lay slumped against the doorway to the house. Friedkin held a towel to his shoulder wound.

"I know where he's going," Friedkin called across the hallway.

"Where?" Sheils asked.

"Call my office. My cell is in the car with Alex. He's driving a Black Ford Fusion. The cell's transmitting its location. You can track it through a Web site. My office manager is parked across the road in my car, a Mercedes. She can help you."

Beatts volunteered to check and ran off. Sheils took the towel from Friedkin and applied pressure to the wound.

"What's your story here?" Sheils asked. "And where does Alex Hammond fit in?"

"You know my story. Rooker wanted me to find the Piper. Like you, I couldn't find him. When Sammy and Peter were kidnapped, Rooker changed tack. He wanted me to follow you, Scott. Me working for you was a sham. I'm sorry."

"Doesn't matter," Scott said. "Why follow me?"

"You'd gotten close to the Piper. He hoped you'd get close to him again."

"That doesn't make sense," Sheils said. "Rooker and Alex kidnapped Sammy and Peter."

"Yes, it does," Scott said. He'd slotted it all into place. "Rooker kidnapped my boys to stir up the Piper. He hoped I would find the Piper or the Piper would find me. Rooker wanted me to be his bloodhound."

"And his sacrificial lamb," Sheils added.

The remark chilled Scott for a moment. He couldn't deny the truth of the statement. If he had tracked down the Piper and managed to keep Sheils out of it, Rooker would have risen up from the shadows to reveal himself, his intent, and probably would have killed them both.

"And when you found the Piper, I would be on hand to tell him where," Friedkin said. "Christ, what a mess."

"What about Hammond?" Sheils asked.

"He was one of my investigators," Friedkin answered. "He went rogue on me the week before Sammy's abduction. He got sloppy on the job so I let him go. I never thought it was because of this."

"You knew nothing of his connection to Rooker?" Sheils demanded. An edge had crept into his tone.

"No. I didn't know about Rooker until my tracker brought me here."

"But you knew Hammond was connected. You recognized him from the digital mug shot," Sheils said.

"Yes," Friedkin admitted. "I was trying to get him to turn himself in."

Sheils shook his head in disgust. He snapped his cell phone off his belt clip and dropped it in Friedkin's lap. "Call your office."

One handed, Friedkin punched in a number, talked for a minute, and waited for the person on the other end of the line to log on to the Web site.

"He's on I-80, heading east."

"Keep them on the line. I'll alert CHP. I need another phone," Sheils said.

Scott gave Sheils his. Sheils punched in a number.

Beatts returned without Friedkin's office manager.

"Where's Rebecca?" Friedkin asked.

"There's no one in your car."

"She arrived in a rental, a white compact. It was parked behind my car."

"There's no vehicle parked behind yours."

"Shit." Friedkin put his phone to his ear. "I'm hanging up. Stay on the tracker. Call this number if the course deviates from the freeway."

"What's wrong?" Scott asked.

"Nothing, I hope."

Friedkin hung up and punched in another number. "Rebecca, where the hell are you?" He cursed when she answered. "Has he seen you? Okay, stay back and observe. The FBI is on this now. Don't approach him. Don't go hero on me." He smiled. "Yeah, yeah, not like me. Look, I'm staying on the line with you."

"What's going on?" Sheils asked, the cell pressed to his ear.

"My office manager is in pursuit. She saw Alex leave after Rooker shot me, called 911, and followed."

Scott reined in his excitement. Minutes ago, he couldn't see any way they would find Sammy and Peter. Now they were being led to them. It was good news, but they were a long way from recovering his children.

"You're sure Alex is going to kill my boys?" Scott asked.

"Yes," Friedkin answered. "Rooker told him to."

"Okay," Sheils said. "Let's get after him."

Sheils had a car brought around. He and Scott took the car, leaving the rest of the team to secure the scene and watch over Friedkin while the ambulance arrived. Sheils sliced through traffic with his lights and sirens on.

Scott balanced Sheils's laptop on his knees. He'd logged on to the Web site Friedkin had given him to track his cell phone. A red dot on a map of Northern California blinked close to Fairfield, giving Alex a thirty-five-mile head start.

Sheils burned minutes on his cell. He corralled his agents and enlisted support from other jurisdictions. CHP had sighted Alex's Ford Fusion on the freeway. Sheils made one thing clear. Everyone was to leave Alex alone. No one was to approach or apprehend him. He was leading them to Sammy and Peter.

While Sheils rallied his multijurisdictional task force, Scott stayed on his cell with Rebecca.

"Can you still see him?" he asked her.

"Yes. He's about three hundred yards ahead."

"I want to thank you for what you're doing for my boys."

"I don't want them to get hurt. I can't believe Alex is involved in this. He's a nice guy with a wife and kid."

Scott thought of Rooker. He'd been a nice guy with a wife and kid too.

"I just want this to work out," she said.

"We all do."

If he got Sammy and Peter back safe and sound, he'd be indebted to a lot of people for life.

"Where is he now?" Sheils asked.

Scott tracked the red dot on the laptop. "He's still on I-80, approaching Sacramento."

Sheils called Guerra. "Lucy, I need to know what properties Rooker owns either in his own name or under his false identity near Sacramento. He's been using his properties to run this show so far. He'll be using one to hold the kids captive. Get back to me when you have a list."

He hung up on Guerra and drove hard. He took the cell from Scott and talked Rebecca through her tailing techniques. His calm tone soothed Scott as well as her. Everything sounded in control.

It all seemed to be coming together. All Rooker's best-laid plans were falling part. His legacy consisted of Alex Hammond, and Sheils had him in his sights. They had visual and electronic confirmation of Alex's location. Law enforcement was in a position to take him down at any

time. But none of it allayed Scott's unease. Time was working against them. If they'd arrived a few minutes earlier,
Sheils and his people could have apprehended both
Rooker and Alex, negating their need for a high-speed
pursuit. They couldn't afford to give Alex enough time to
kill Sammy and Peter. Scott didn't want Sheils arresting
the man for the murder of his children. He willed Sheils to
drive faster.

Scott watched the dot on the laptop. Sheils was reeling
Alex in. As the dot curved north around Sacramento,
Sheils's triple-digit speed had closed the gap to within six
miles. Sheils cut the sirens at that point. He didn't need to
give Alex a heads-up. He nixed the lights when he got
within three miles of the red dot and slowed to a sane
speed when he got within two. He moved with stealth to
close within half a mile of Alex. Scott dispensed with the
laptop and strained to see the Ford Fusion ahead. He
didn't see it, but he spotted what he thought was Rebecca's
white Pontiac G6. He took the cell from Sheils.

"Rebecca, I think I see you. Are you in the right lane
with a gray Dodge pickup in front of you?"

"Yes."

He looked to Sheils and nodded. Sheils took the phone
back. He told her they had it covered. She cut her speed
and Scott waved to her as they sped by.

Sheils closed the gap on Alex to within three hundred
yards. They had a clear visual on the car. Scott's mouth
went dry. This man was leading them to his boys. They
couldn't screw up this time.

The Placerville/Grass Valley exit came up and Alex
took the off-ramp. Sheils floored the gas, but made sure
there were a couple of vehicles between them and Alex.
Sheils reached the off-ramp as the lights turned green and
the vehicles surged ahead. Alex turned left toward Grass
Valley. Sheils accelerated and made the light just as it
turned red.

Sheils lagged back. He maintained visual contact, but remained a sufficient distance behind not to stick out. Alex would have the comfort of knowing he had the jump on the cops, but he might be on the lookout for a tail.

Sheils stuck his cell in the hands-free dock and called Guerra again. "We're off the freeway, heading toward Grass Valley. What have you got for me?"

"Then I know where you're heading. Rooker owns the Imperial Mine. It's a mined-out gold mine."

"Where?"

Guerra reeled off directions.

"Okay. Tell Brannon and wake up the locals. This guy is getting into the mine. He's not getting out."

"Will do," Guerra said and hung up.

Alex pushed the speed limit, staying an acceptable five to ten miles per hour over the posted signs. The vehicles behind Alex and ahead of Sheils matched them. Scott estimated they were twenty minutes out from the mine. The proximity excited and scared him. He tied himself to the belief that he would see his boys alive in half an hour.

Things looked good, but Scott feared Sheils's car would give them away. A Crown Vic with its conservative dark blue shade screamed *government car*. To Scott's relief, Alex seemed not to notice them. He maintained his speed and did nothing erratic.

Then ten miles out, the status quo crumbled. The vehicles between them and Alex peeled off to leave them exposed. Sheils maintained his distance, but only bad eyesight would prevent Alex from spotting them.

"He'll see us," Scott said.

"Don't worry about it. He knew we were coming."

Scott didn't like their frail grip on the situation. Circumstances had spread them thin and forced them to react without the time for preparation. They were in prime slipup country. It wouldn't take much for unnecessary deaths to occur. He shut out the image of Nicholas Rooker's body lying in the rain.

Sheils closed in on the rear of Alex's sedan, slowly at first, then more swiftly. Scott eyed the speedometer. Sheils hadn't increased his speed.

"Shit. He's seen us," Scott said. "What do we do?"

"We go around. He doesn't know we know about the mine."

Alex's brake lights came on and Sheils reeled the kidnapper in. He took his foot off the gas as a precaution and eased the Crown Vic over to pass.

"Don't acknowledge him," Sheils said. "We're going about our business. We're not interested in his."

Scott's hands were slick with sweat and his respiration was elevated. He noticed his condition and exhaled slowly to calm his nerves.

They were within a hundred feet when the Ford Fusion's reversing lights came on. Alex stamped on the gas. His car leapt backward, then accelerated fast. Sheils jumped on the brakes, but he couldn't avoid the impact.

The Ford's rear slammed into the Crown Victoria's front. The jarring impact threw Scott and Sheils into the exploding airbags. The Fusion's higher profile worked to Alex's advantage. The Ford climbed up the Crown Vic's hood, the back wheels smashing through the windshield. The safety glass splintered, showering Scott and Sheils in diamond-sized fragments. The conjoined cars slithered to a grinding halt.

The Fusion rolled forward off the Crown Vic. Alex stamped on the gas, burning rubber and dragging his shattered rear bumper.

The Crown Vic's engine had died. Sheils twisted the ignition. The engine turned, but didn't fire. "Start, you bastard," Sheils snarled.

Scott sat dazed, less from the impact than from Alex's audacity. He watched their tenuous hold on the situation slip with Alex's disappearing vehicle.

An approaching sedan slowed at the sight of Sheils's crippled car blocking the road. It would have to stop. Scott kicked open his door.

"Bring your gun and your badge."

Sheils looked at him in confusion.

Scott stood in the way of the sedan, waving his hands. The car stopped and an elderly couple climbed out.

"Do you need us to call 911?" the man asked.

"No, we need your car."

Sheils held his shield in the air. "FBI. We need you to stay with this vehicle and turn yours over to us."

The couple, too stunned to argue, stood by as Scott and Sheils took their vehicle from them. Sheils reversed hard and spun the sedan around to point in Alex's direction.

Sheils drove with his cell pressed to his ear. He yelled instructions to Brannon. He and his team were still ten minutes behind, but would take care of the elderly couple when they caught up with them. He told Brannon to brief the locals. They were to seal off the mine the moment he and Scott reached the property. Whatever happened, Alex wasn't to leave.

Sheils drove hard until they reached the mine, then slowed going through the entrance. They followed the winding gravel drive that snaked around a crumbling mansion to the mine behind. Alex's damaged sedan sat in the open, hemmed in by the remains of the foundry, the winch house, and other shop buildings. Sheils stopped the sedan and cursed.

"What's wrong?" Scott asked.

"We're sitting ducks. He's got his choice of cover and we're stuck out in the open."

Scott reexamined the layout with informed eyes. The frontier architecture and the narrow strip of dirt flanked by buildings on all sides reminded him of every western movie ever made. He pictured the black hats hiding behind the parapets while the white hats walked down the middle of Main Street with every gun barrel trained on them. Alex could be hidden amongst any of the shattered windows with them in his sights.

"What do we do?" Scott asked.

"Wait for backup and pin Alex in."

"We can't. You corner this guy and you take his choices away. He'll go down and take Sammy and Peter with him. We have to go in now, while he still thinks he has an out."

Sheils pursed his lips and exhaled. "I know."

Sheils peered at the open windows and rooftops for Alex. "He'll pick us off."

"I don't think so. He can't shoot us and juggle Sammy and Peter. He knows he doesn't have time. He'll go for the boys."

"So we're going in?"

"Loud and proud. He knows we're coming. Let's tell him we've arrived."

Sheils called Brannon on his cell. "Alex's at the mine. We're going to make contact. Get here as quick as you can."

Sheils eased the sedan forward. No bullets perforated the windshield, but Alex failed to identify himself. Sheils rolled up on the rear of Alex's sedan and stopped. Nothing happened. No shots. No hailed warnings. Nothing.

Scott leaned across Sheils and thumped the horn three times. He didn't wait for an answer and flung the door open. Sheils told him to stay in the vehicle. Scott clambered from the car to stand in the open.

"Alex Hammond? It's Scott Fleetwood. I want to talk."

He scanned the buildings surrounding him. He looked for movement or a face. He didn't feel fully exposed since he wore the Kevlar vest Sheils had given him. He didn't know how accurate a handgun was over distance, but felt Alex stood little chance of a head shot from one of those busted windows. He called out to Alex, but got no reply.

Sheils climbed from the car. "Stunts like that are going to get us killed."

Scott ignored the remark.

Sheils jogged over to Alex's sedan. He opened the driver's door and jerked the keys from the ignition. He stuffed them into his pocket and jogged back to Scott.

"I'm going to search for him. Stay here. When Brannon arrives, fill him in."

Sheils didn't get ten feet before a whine emanated from the winch house. Scott locked gazes with Sheils. They both understood. Alex hadn't shot at them or answered Scott's shouts because he'd gone down into the mine to fetch Sammy and Peter. They ran for the winch house.

The winch house was nothing more than a simple enclosure protecting the mine shaft from the elements. The rusted carcass of the head frame that supported the hoist system for lowering and raising the men and materials jutted through its roof. The original winch system no longer existed. In its place, a power winch had been bolted onto the head frame.

Sheils pointed to a small office off to one side, presumably belonging to the shift supervisor. "In there," he ordered.

Scott ducked inside the office and knelt on the dirt floor. He peered through the window frame, the glass long since smashed.

Sheils pressed himself up against a wall to the right of where the elevator spilled out. The majority of the room's lighting came from the open doorway. A couple of naked bulbs hung from a limp cable nailed to the ceiling, but only one bulb worked. Shadows easily hid him. Scott heard, rather than saw, the FBI agent remove his weapon from his holster.

The elevator system was nothing like Scott had seen before. It was a primitive product of frontier times. The shaft descended at a steep incline instead of vertically. Skips rode a pair of narrow-gauge rails along the incline pulled by the winch. Scott stared at the steel cable coiling around the winch drum. Each turn of the cable brought his sons closer to the surface.

"I've got this," Sheils growled at Scott. "I'll take care of Hammond. Is that understood?"

Alex's voice echoing up from the depths prevented him from answering. The distance reduced the kidnapper's shouts to ghostly whispers. The weaker echoes of sobbing followed. Relief swept over Scott at the sound of crying. If his boys could cry, they were alive.

He listened to Alex's voice gain strength and lose its echo. He was berating Sammy and Peter. He threatened to leave them to rot in the tunnels if they didn't do as they were told. It took every ounce of restraint Scott had to stop from screaming down to Alex to leave his boys alone. He couldn't give away their position. Sheils needed the drop on Alex. It was all they had.

The skip neared the top. Its wheels squealed on the rails. The cable enveloped the winch drum completely. It had to be only feet from the surface.

Sheils aimed his weapon. He'd have a bead on Alex the moment he stepped from the skip.

Scott's hands tightened into fists, his skin stretching tight across his knuckles. "C'mon, you bastard," he murmured in the dark.

The skip appeared. It was nothing more than an elaborate cart set on the rails. Wooden bench seats were set at an angle so miners could sit for the long ascents and descents. Alex stood. His head appeared to rise from the depths. He held a gun on Sammy and Peter. The two boys, cuffed to each other, cowered on the bench seat next to him. Dirt and grime covered them from head to toe. They were still in the same clothes they'd been wearing when they were abducted.

The sight of his children left Scott giddy. He hadn't expected to see them. They were petrified, but they were alive. Relief squeezed his chest until it hurt, but his fear lifted. He wished Jane were here to see them.

The skip jerked to a halt when it reached its end. Alex grabbed Sammy's wrist and jerked both boys to their feet by virtue of the cuffs connecting them.

"Let's go," he snarled and tugged them off the skip.

Sheils let Alex get two paces before he moved. His gun muzzle was inches from the back of Alex's skull when he said, "Freeze. FBI."

Alex did as he was told. Scott felt an instant of release. It was over.

And it was. For an instant.

FORTY-SIX

Alex sagged as if in defeat, then stiffened. He jerked his gun arm up and back. The pistol smashed Sheils in the cheek. The FBI agent staggered back before falling to the ground, his Glock tumbling from his hand. Alex whirled on Sheils, then aimed to shoot.

Scott jumped up from his hiding place. "Don't."

Alex flinched, jerking Sammy and Peter. Alex looked as if he expected Scott to be holding a gun on him.

Sheils used Alex's hesitation to reach for his dropped weapon.

Alex saw Sheils's move. He jerked Sammy and Peter toward the mine shaft. He whirled them around and the momentum sent them over the edge. Only Alex's grip on Sammy's wrist prevented them from tumbling into the abyss.

"Daddy," both boys screamed.

"Touch that gun and the kids die," Alex barked.

Sheils drew his hand away from the weapon.

"You don't have to hurt them," Scott said.

Alex kicked the elevator descend button. The safe landing spot under Sammy's and Peter's feet disappeared with the plunging skip.

"Take it easy," Sheils said.

"Help us, Daddy," Peter whined.

Light from the open doorway fell on Alex, highlighting the veins standing out on his arm. The man had strength, but how long could he hold on to Sammy and Peter?

"It's okay. Daddy's here." The words caught in his throat.

Sheils went to get up.

"Stay there," Alex barked.

Sheils dropped to his seated position.

Scott counted the minutes. Brannon and his team were moments away. Instead of quelling the fire, their presence would ignite it. Alex would panic. Scott ripped his stare away from his sons

"Give me my boys and go," Scott said.

Alex hesitated. "No. They're my ticket out of here."

"They're not. You don't need them. You've got your money. Just give me the boys and go. No one's going to stop you."

Alex eyed Sheils. "What about him?"

"I won't let him."

Sheils looked at Scott with disgust but said nothing. Scott couldn't fault Sheils's duty. He'd sworn to uphold the law. In addition to that, he'd put his life on the line to stop Rooker and Alex. He'd taken two bullets for Scott's kids at the abandoned store on South Van Ness. He wouldn't let Alex go without a fight. Scott felt for Sheils, he really did, but his kids came first and everyone else came a distant second—Sheils included.

"I'd really like to believe that," Alex said.

"I'll prove it."

Scott came out from the office and snatched up Sheils's

Glock. Alex stiffened. He swung his weapon from Sheils to Scott. Before he squeezed off a shot, Scott pointed the weapon at Sheils. Alex held off on the trigger.

"Go," Scott said. "He won't give you any trouble."

"Scott, you idiot," Sheils snarled.

"I'm sorry, but I have to think of my kids."

Alex edged away from the elevator shaft, heaving Sammy and Peter from the precipice. Blood streaked their wrists where the cuffs had sliced into their flesh. Their screams and wailing subsided the moment their feet touched solid ground.

"Thank you," Scott said.

Alex had yet to his release his hold on Sammy's wrist. "Toss the gun to me and I'll let them go."

"Don't do it," Sheils warned. "He'll kill us all."

Scott had no choice. He tossed the Glock. It struck the ground at Alex's feet.

Alex let go of Sammy's wrist to pick up Sheils's weapon.

Scott rushed to his sons. He dropped to his knees and engulfed them in a hug. Both boys broke down. He kissed both their grubby faces and tasted their tears.

As Alex straightened with both weapons in his hands, the sound of vehicles drawing up outside cut the reunion short. From the open doorway, vehicles belonging to both the FBI and local sheriffs pulled up behind Sheils's Crown Vic.

Alex whirled on Scott. "You lying bastard."

"No."

Alex lunged at Scott and his boys. He came at them with the intention of pushing them down the elevator shaft. Scott shoved Sammy and Peter away from him. Sheils leapt up and snatched both boys out of Alex's path. Scott scrabbled on the dirt to get out of Alex's way, but the kidnapper slammed into him while he was still on his hands and knees.

Instead of knocking Scott toward the shaft, Alex's higher

center of gravity sent him pinwheeling over Scott and he slipped over the edge. He released the weapons in his grasp and snatched at Scott, grabbing his forearm and a fistful of his shirt. Gravity sucked Alex down, taking Scott with him. Scott skidded over the loose dirt and gravel until Sheils pounced on his back to stop his slide.

Alex clung to Scott. Scott felt his shoulder muscles and tendons stretch to their breaking points. The kidnapper's fingernails dug deep into the flesh of his shoulder where he'd grabbed his shirt. Alex flailed, trying to find a foothold on the steep incline.

"In here," Sheils bellowed.

"Take my hands," Scott said.

Alex released his grasp on Scott's shoulder and clamped on to Scott's wrists.

"Help," Sheils cried out again.

Sammy and Peter piled on top of Scott and Sheils to lend their weight. "We've got you, Daddy," Peter said.

"Thanks, guys."

Brannon burst into the winch house with two other men, all with their guns drawn and aimed. They put them away the moment they saw the human pile on the ground.

"Hit the button," Sheils said. "Hit the button."

Brannon punched the button, halting the skip's descent and bringing it back to the surface.

"Hang on," Scott said. "The skip will catch you in a minute."

Sweat beaded from Scott's arms. Alex slid a sickening fraction of an inch, but it felt like a mile.

"It doesn't look good for me," Alex said.

"I'm not going to drop you."

"I don't mean that."

Scott understood. "Kidnapping. Two murders. No, it doesn't look good."

Brannon and another agent pulled Sammy and Peter

aside. The two remaining men gathered them up and rushed them out of the winch house. Brannon and the other agent leaned in to take the strain from Scott.

"Take my hand," Brannon ordered Alex.

He let go of one of Scott's arms and reached for Brannon's proffered hand, but instead of grabbing it, he lunged for Brannon's gun in its holster.

Brannon jerked back. "Gun. He's going for my gun."

Brannon's partner went for his weapon.

Alex swung in the air, held only by Scott's remaining hand. Scott felt his grasp wane. He grabbed Alex's wrist with both hands to halt the slide.

"What the hell are you doing?" Scott demanded.

Alex didn't answer. He tore at Scott's hands. Scott recognized the suicide bid. He'd seen one man kill himself. He wasn't about to see another.

Alex continued to wrestle his hand free, but when Scott's grip proved too tight, he went limp. Scott thought he had him until he reached inside his pocket and brought out a box cutter. He slashed the blade across the knuckles of Scott's right hand. Scott yelled out and snapped his hand open. His remaining hand didn't have the strength to hold Alex and the kidnapper slipped from his grasp. Scott watched openmouthed as Alex Hammond plunged out of sight, swallowed by the darkness. He didn't make a sound until his body broke on the rising skip. It was several minutes before his twisted remains returned to the surface.

"We could have saved him."

Sheils pulled Scott away. "It was his choice. There was nothing you could have done."

Sheils guided him out into the open. All thoughts of Alex evaporated when he saw Sammy and Peter. They sat on the tailgate of an FBI SUV and were being tended to by a sheriff's deputy. She was wiping their faces with a washcloth. Scott broke away from the FBI agent and hugged his sons.

Sheils held out his cell phone to Scott. "It's Jane."

Scott snatched the phone. "They're okay," he said with tears streaming down his face. "They're okay. We're coming home."

FORTY-SEVEN

The spotlight lasted a little over a week. Scott and Jane gave interview after interview under the watchful gaze of the *Independent*. Every time they turned on a TV, if they didn't see their names and faces, they saw Sheils's and Friedkin's. The media wanted answers, but there were gaps. Assumptions and theories filled in the voids, but Rooker took the mystery out of the saga, even from the grave.

Just as the fervor died down and Scott set about rebuilding the stability in his family's life, the call came. Rooker's lawyer needed to meet with him in conjunction with the reading of Charles Rooker's will. The lawyer provided a time and date for the reading.

Scott arrived outside the California Street address at precisely 2:00 p.m. on a mild Tuesday afternoon. Jane wasn't with him. She hadn't wanted to go. He understood why. She'd opened up to Rooker, trusted him, and pitied him. She'd grown to like the man and he'd taken advantage of her kindness to get to her children and husband.

"You go. Whatever he has to say, I don't want to hear."

He gave his name at the reception and was directed to

the offices of Thornton and Barron. When Gerald Thornton showed Scott into his office, Sheils and Friedkin were already in attendance. Thornton gave them time enough for small talk before proceeding.

"Gentlemen, as executor to Charles Rooker's estate, I'm obliged to read this document to you." Thornton cleared his throat before beginning. "If this document is ever read out, then I owe those assembled an explanation."

Thornton plowed through the ten-page diatribe never once faltering. Scott pretty much guessed what was coming the moment Thornton started reading. Rooker pointed fingers. He blamed Scott for interfering, Sheils for failing in his duty, Redfern for his idolatry, and the Piper for his contempt for life. The four of them shared the responsibility for Nicholas's death and needed to pay the price. A plan had festered for eight years while Rooker's wife, Alice, remained alive. She'd known of his intentions and she'd used his love to keep him from taking action. The day she died he felt his promise was no longer valid. Because the eight-year gap cosigned Nicholas's case to cold case status, he needed to ignite a fire under it and did so by resurrecting the Piper through Alex Hammond. In his dealings with Friedkin, he identified Alex as a man of need. While Alex donned the guise of the Piper, Rooker worked the logistics. He bought properties and funded capital expenditures as well as ingratiated himself with the Fleetwoods and the FBI for intelligence gathering.

The revelations failed to shock Scott. He was numb to it all. His error in judgment had been presented to him. He knew it, recognized it, and accepted it. He'd spent eight years hiding his shame. He wouldn't hide it anymore. He regretted his part in Nicholas's death, but it was time to move on and never repeat his mistake. He owed Nicholas that much.

Rooker's statement concluded without apology or remorse. Once the facts were stated, it simply ended. Thornton sighed when he finished reading.

"When was that written?" Sheils asked.

"The day before his death."

"He saw it was all falling apart," Friedkin said.

No, Scott thought, *he knew he'd achieved his objective.* Rooker wanted to hurt the ones who'd failed him. Whether anyone else wanted to admit it or not, Rooker had succeeded.

Thornton picked up a sealed envelope, came around his desk, and handed it to Sheils. "Charles requested you receive a copy. Now, if you'll excuse me, I have Charles's estate to take care of."

Thornton ushered them from his firm. Scott felt no slight. He wanted to leave as much as the lawyer wanted them out. They traveled down together in the elevator.

"How are the kids?" Friedkin asked Scott.

Sammy and Peter were coping with their ordeal well. The first night home was shaky, with tears and nightmares. He and Jane sat up with them and listened to them talk about their ordeals. Scott's chest hurt listening to them. Letting them vent helped. A night back in their own beds and all seemed to be forgotten. Scott noticed anxiety creep into both of them when they were left alone, but that was already passing. The therapy sessions helped probe the areas he and Jane were too afraid to explore. He expected his boys to bounce back like Ryan Rodgers had.

"You know kids," Scott said. "Made of rubber, mentally and physically."

"That's great. I'm glad," Friedkin said and Sheils agreed.

On the sidewalk, they were about to go their separate ways, but Scott stopped them.

"I want to thank you both. If it hadn't been for you, I don't think we would have been in that room listening to that letter."

Both men tried to shrug the compliment off, but Scott refused to let them. He pulled out his wallet and removed a check the *Independent* had given him for his story. He'd endorsed it, signing away his claim to the money. He held it out to Friedkin.

"I know Alex Hammond had a family. Will you see that they get this?"

Friedkin took the check. "Two hundred and fifty thousand. Are you sure?"

"Very. We've seen where the sins of the father lead."

"Yes, well, Kerry will be very grateful," Friedkin said. "Thank you."

Friedkin made his excuses, blaming a waiting client, and hailed a passing cab.

"That was diplomatic of him," Sheils said.

The investigator had detected the mood. Scott wanted a moment alone with Sheils. He hadn't gotten the chance to speak to Sheils at the mine. Priorities changed for both of them the moment Sammy and Peter were safe. Scott had practiced a speech, but Sheils cut it off before he had the chance to begin.

"That was very generous of you," he said. "I'm sure there will be other checks coming your way."

Sheils spoke without malice and more as a statement of fact. The movie and book people were beating a path to Scott's door again.

"No. I have no tale to tell."

"If you don't tell it, someone else will and they'll get it wrong."

"Let them. It's not important."

Sheils smiled. "What is?"

"My family. You."

The remark caught Sheils off guard. "Me?"

"I want to apologize to you. I didn't make things easy for you. Now or eight years ago. You went out on a limb for me and I didn't treat you well. I'm sorry for that. I don't expect us to be close, but I don't want you walking away today thinking ill of me. I hope you can accept my apology."

Sheils looked away. He followed the progress of a cab running a light. After the cab made a left, he turned back to Scott. "One question. In the mine, when you pulled my gun, would you have shot me?"

Scott deserved this question. It topped the list of wrongs he'd committed against Sheils. He considered ducking the question and massaging his bruised ego with the kind of answer anyone would want to hear, but Sheils deserved the truth, regardless of how palatable. "Yes. If it came down to you or my children, I would have shot you."

Sheils took the answer in his stride. "Okay. Fair enough. I would have done the same in your shoes."

Scott put out his hand and Sheils shook it.

"Good luck," Scott said. "I'm sure you're in line for a big promotion."

"No. I think it's time to bow out. I've got my years in."

Sheils's admission surprised Scott. He couldn't imagine the agent retired. "You could see Friedkin about a job."

Sheils laughed. Scott realized he'd never heard the man laugh.

"No. There are some lines I won't cross. The bureau likes retired agents for instructors."

"Look after yourself," Scott said. He shook Sheils's hand again and walked away.

Sheils didn't let him get far. "My wife wants me to invite your family to dinner tomorrow. She wants to meet Sammy and Peter and she says it's time to bury the hatchet between us."

"What time are we expected?"

"Six-thirty."

"Tell her we'll be there."

Turn the page for an advance look at
SIMON WOOD's next thrilling
novel . . .

WE ALL FALL DOWN

Coming in July 2008

PROLOGUE

The BMW 530i's engine screamed but it was unclear whether it was in agony or ecstasy. Vee8 squashed the gas pedal deeper into the carpet and tipped the balance into the pain barrier. The car accelerated through the narrow road lined with cars, occasionally clipping door mirrors as it sped by.

"Spank it, Vee8. Spank it," Donkey shrieked hysterically and thumped the passenger-side dash with his fist. In chorus, D.J. and Trey seconded Donkey's request from the backseat.

Donkey might have been hung like one but he was sure as shit as dumb as one. Vee8 didn't need Donkey telling him what to do. He'd been jacking cars since he was fourteen and in four years, he'd thrashed, crashed, and cremated over three hundred of them without ever being caught. The cops had chased him across the San Francisco–Oakland Bay Area, but they'd never come close to netting him. Many had tried and all had failed. Several had woken up in the hospital to discover that sorry fact. Like that old-school gangster, Dillinger, Vee8 would be an old man before they ever got their hands on him. He threw the powerful sedan through the left-handed kink.

He'd learned his trade among the sideshow kings of Oakland. He'd been taught by the best, until he was the best. Most of them were now in prison, but in their heyday, they'd shown Vee8 how to make a car dance.

Infineon Raceway was only a thirty-mile burn across the bay and he could have been a legitimate race driver, but why? He didn't have the money or the connections to race. Anyway, they were pussies. Where was the fun in driving on a road where the traffic went in one direction? Oncoming traffic, now, that was racing.

Even though he was eighteen and old enough to possess a driver's license, he hadn't bothered. What did he need a license for? He didn't own a car and why should he? There were too many people like him who would have a set of wheels out from under you before you'd locked the doors. No, if he wanted a car, then he had Donkey take one. They were more frequent than buses, and nicer.

Donkey started up again. "Vee, get off these pissy little streets. If the po-po catch our scent, we're fucked."

Vee8 hated the way Donkey spoke. Donkey came from the Deep South somewhere. Alabama. Louisiana. One of those fuck-your-sister, marry-your-cousin states. His southern drawl intensified when he whined and it grated on Vee8.

"Who's fuckin' driving, Donk?"

"You."

"That's right. Me. When you're driving, you can make the decisions."

But Donkey was right. Tearing strips off the residential streets was asking for trouble. They'd jacked the BMW from the El Cerrito del Norte BART station around noon, before the suit returned home from a hard day of stroking his secretary's thigh. Now that it was after eight, the car would be on the hot list and the cops would be looking for it. But like Cinderella's coach at midnight, it would be a rotting husk by the time they found it.

Although Donkey whined, he was a necessary part of the operation. He was a magician with locks and alarm systems. Cars just opened themselves up to him. Within a matter of seconds and with the aid of a few tools that appeared from his pockets, his work was done. Despite Donkey's talents, Vee8 was the star. Essentially, Donkey got them in and Vee8 got them out.

Vee8 threaded his way through the Sausalito streets avoiding downtown. He didn't fancy a run-in with the cops. He headed for Highway 1. The narrow, coastal road snaked and heaved, and it would put him and the BMW to the test. More than enough thrills for a Wednesday night.

He got clear of the town. The full moon gave Vee8 a clear view of the road ahead well beyond his headlight beams. He brought his speed up to eighty-five. The turnoff to the two-lane highway was coming up on his left.

As he approached the four-way, Vee8 eased the BMW hard over to the curb to get a faster turn-in for the left turn. A Honda Civic sedan approached the intersection from Vee8's right, but it didn't bother him. He was on the through road and had the right-of-way. The Civic would have to stop. Even if he didn't have the right of way, so what? No one in their right mind was going to argue the point when a car was driving at breakneck speed. He smiled.

Vee8 stepped off the gas and jumped onto the brake. Everyone in the car was thrown forward against the seat belts as the BMW dived on its suspension. He watched the speedometer dial sag as the speed was sloughed off and ignored the whoops of his boys.

Vee8's smiled slipped. The Civic wasn't slowing. It wasn't traveling as fast as he was, no more than fifty, but it wasn't going to stop.

"I don't think he's stopping," Donkey said flatly, seeing what Vee8 had seen.

Donkey's words silenced everyone.

Vee8 pressed down on the brake harder and thumped the horn twice with his fist.

The Civic showed no sign of stopping for the BMW. It leapt across the intersection and into Vee8's path. The BMW and the Civic met in the middle of the intersection.

Everyone in the BMW swore and braced themselves for the impact. Vee8 stamped on the brakes and the antilock system went into action. He didn't bother to turn onto Highway 1 as he'd planned. It would have just made the collision worse. The best he could hope for was to T-bone the bastard and do as much damage to him and as little to himself as he could.

For a moment, Vee8 thought he was going to get away with it. The Civic was passing out of his field of vision faster than expected, but not quite fast enough. The BMW clipped the Civic's rear panel and wraparound light cluster.

A deafening bang echoed through the car as sheet steel collided with sheet steel. The Civic wiggled after its glancing blow and carried on its merry way unhindered. The BMW was less fortunate. The car plowed on, veering right, and struck the curb hard. The front wheels jackhammered into the wheel arches and relayed their agony through the steering wheel. Vee8's hands and arms tingled in sympathy. The car leapt the curb and came to a halt in the field beyond the pavement.

"Christ, my head," Donkey whined. He put a hand to his nose, checking for blood. There wasn't any. He touched the dashboard where he'd smashed his face.

Vee8 checked the rearview mirror and found D.J. and Trey were bleeding from where they'd banged heads. Both were looking dumbly at each other and moaning about whose head hurt more. *Christ, what a cluster fuck*, Vee8 thought.

"Am I bleeding?" Donkey asked and jabbed his head in Vee8's direction.

"No, you're not, you dumb shit," Vee8 said.

The BMW had stalled and Vee8 tried to start it. He was greeted by an overlong electronic whine before the engine caught and fired. He jammed the selector into reverse and stamped on the gas. The wheels spun on the soft earth and the car went nowhere. The tires and the engine whined.

"Come on, you bastard," Vee8 hissed.

As if by command, the tires bit into the earth, found traction, and the car lurched back.

"Where are we going?" Donkey asked.

"We're going to get that son of a bitch."

The BMW bumped down off the curb, raced away from the scene of the collision, and joined the coast road as planned. The engine sounded off-key and the steering sucked. Only one headlight cut through the darkness, the passenger-side light obviously lost. But none of this bothered Vee8. The coast road went on for miles with no intersections to any other major roads. He had no doubt that he would catch the Civic driver. It was just a matter of when.

Vee8's passengers were still bleating about their injuries and the accident.

"Shut the fuck up," Vee8 shouted. "Keep your eyes open. Yell when you see that bastard Civic."

Vee8 scanned the fields to his right and the beach to his left. Deep thoughts of what he would do to the Civic driver when he got hold of him clogged his mind. It wasn't the first time he'd used a vehicle as a weapon and it wouldn't be the last.

Vee8 caught sight of his quarry in a twisting section descending toward the ocean a mile a head of him, then lost it when he hit a series of switchbacks. He drove miles without seeing it again. He turned to faith that the Civic remained ahead and his faith was rewarded on the descent into the town of Stinson Beach.

"There it is. Down there." Donkey pointed at the beach falling away from the roadside to their left.

The Civic, with its passenger-side taillight snuffed out, sat untidily on the beach.

Vee8 swung the BMW left onto a private road the Civic had taken. He didn't stop at the road's edge. He followed the Civic driver's lead and drove onto the beach. He bumped the BMW over the curb and the car slithered on the sand, the tires failing to grip the shifting surface. The car tore down the sloping beach before crashing into a sand dune where it leveled out.

Vee8 and his crew flung the doors open, leapt from the stricken BMW, and charged down the beach. The Civic sat cocked at an angle to the rolling waves, with the driver's door open and the engine running. Beyond the car, the headlights picked out its driver, an East Indian, standing at the water's edge.

The broad-shouldered man stood some six inches taller than Vee8. He might have the strength advantage but Vee8 doubted the guy possessed the fighting skills. Not that Vee8 cared. His blood was up. The prick was going down.

"Hey, bitch," Vee8 shouted. "I want to have a word with you."

The man didn't react. He stared out across the darkened ocean with the moon reflected on its surface. Vee8 heard the man mumbling something but couldn't make out what he was saying.

"What's that? I can't hear you," he barked in a mocking tone.

The man took a step forward into the waves. That stopped Vee8 in his tracks.

Vee8 glanced back at his boys and found they'd already given up the chase. They'd picked up the strange vibe early. Vee8 had been too pissed off to see it.

He gestured to his crew for answers. Donkey shrugged at him with a what-the-fuck expression plastered across his face.

The man strode out farther. The water lapped over his knees.

There was something very wrong here. It looked pretty obvious what it was. Vee8 wasn't sure he wanted to be part of this, but he already was. Slowly, he followed the man to the water's edge, but no farther. This guy might get lonely and want to take someone with him.

"Hey, Gandhi," Vee8 said. "What are you doing?"

Vee8 had hoped the slur would provoke a reaction, but the Indian didn't respond. He continued to wade out, chanting his incantation.

"Hey, guy. It don't have to be this way," Vee8 offered. He looked down at his feet. A wave licked at his Lugz's, chilling his toes, and he edged back.

"I think we should get the hell out of here," Donkey suggested.

Vee8 turned to face him.

"He's right, Vee," D.J. echoed.

"I don't think we should get mixed up in this," Trey added.

"But we can't just let him kill himself," Vee8 said.

"Can't we? Just watch me," Donkey said and started to back away. D.J. and Trey followed suit.

Vee8 swore under his breath and chased out into the waves after the guy. He caught his breath the moment the ice-cold water hit him. Its chill climbed up into his core, but it didn't stop him from reaching the Indian. Vee8 reached out and placed a gentle hand on the man's shoulder, which stopped the man in his tracks. The strong surf thrust against them, urging them back to shore. Vee8 hoped the guy would take the hint. He took the man's hesitation as a positive sign.

"You don't have to do this," Vee8 said. "Nothing can be that bad."

The Indian turned to Vee8. "I have done a terrible thing and I can't be forgiven. I must pay for it. This is the only way."

Vee8 could have argued with the man to get him to see sense, but he knew there was no point. He'd seen a lot of broken people. Fathers and mothers beaten down by mistakes. Friends lost to booze or drugs. No matter how far gone they were, they still clung to hope. While they hung on, they could be saved. But not the Indian. He'd let go. Vee8 had never witnessed total hopelessness before, but he saw it in the Indian's eyes. He'd surrendered to whatever haunted him. There was nothing Vee8 could do for him.

"I have to do this," the man said.

Vee8 nodded and removed his hand from the man's shoulder.

The Indian smiled and resumed walking out to sea. Vee8 watched him go. The man's final gesture was hypnotic in its incomprehensibility. But by the time the Indian was waist deep, Vee8 had managed to wrench his gaze away and was heading back to shore.

When he reached dry land, Vee8 glanced back at the suicidal man just in time to see a wave wash over his head.

It was obvious that the Civic driver wasn't turning back.

ONE

The Saturday morning traffic was behaving itself, so Haydn would make good time from Fairfield to San Rafael. He hoped this weekend would be the start of something big. Marin Design Engineering only wanted someone on short contract, but if he impressed, the contract might go from short to long. Not an unusual occurrence for him. He'd built up a solid reputation as a contract design engineer over the last three years, which was a pretty bold move for a twenty-five-year-old. But his rep hadn't gotten him the high-paying gig at Marin Design Engineering, his old college roommate had.

Haydn reached the limit of the radio station broadcasting out of Sacramento and he switched to a San Francisco station. He caught the tail end of a song before the station went to the news. The discovery of Sundip Chaudhary's body was the lead story.

"The body of missing scientist Sundip Chaudhary was found late last night by a jogger on Muir Beach," the newsreader said.

At least they found him, Haydn thought. He shuddered at the thought of the condition of the guy's corpse.

The story had made a stir in the Bay Area. Chaudhary had walked into the ocean three days ago in an apparent suicide attempt. He hadn't left a note, but his car had been found on Stinson Beach with the keys still in the ignition and the engine running.

Family and friends cited no problems in his professional and personal life that would warrant a suicide attempt. If it weren't for an anonymous eyewitness account of Chaudhary walking into the sea, foul play or an accident might have been suspected. Speculation centered on the possibility that the eyewitness had been involved in a fender bender with Chaudhary. Chaudhary's car exhibited fresh damage, and debris from a second vehicle was found on the beach. Speculation ended when it came to what had led up to Chaudhary walking into the Pacific.

"The Marin County Sheriff's Department urges the eyewitness to come forward," the newsreader said.

Yeah, right, Haydn thought. No one was coming forward if they feared any backlash.

Haydn pictured Chaudhary's body on the beach he knew well. Drowning. There were less painful ways of killing yourself. Haydn wondered if that had been Chaudhary's aim. The eyewitness had stated in the 911 call that Chaudhary had insinuated he'd committed an act so severe that he couldn't live with the guilt. The cops had yet to turn up anything to support the claim—or just weren't saying.

The whole subject left Haydn feeling queasy, and his cell phone bursting into song provided the perfect reason to forget about Chaudhary's suicide.

"Where are you?" Shane Fallon asked.

"I just got on Highway 37, so I'm about half an hour out."

"I'm so glad you're coming aboard."

"Me too."

"It's going to be so cool catching up, man." Although

college roommates, they'd lost touch over recent years. Work took them in different directions. Now it was bringing them back together. "This is going to be a great weekend. See you in thirty."

"In thirty," Haydn said and hung up.

Haydn found the upscale gated community where Shane Fallon lived easily enough. He'd known Shane had done well for himself, but not this well. Shane lived in a modest house compared to the monster mansions at the higher end of the price scale, but even so, this was high living and it put Haydn's fifties-built ranch-style home to shame. If Shane's firm treated him this well, they could definitely afford to pay Haydn a hundred bucks an hour for the grunt work they were contracting him to do. He pulled into Shane's driveway.

Haydn was removing his overnight bag from the passenger seat when Shane came out to greet him. Haydn put out his hand and Shane gripped it before crushing him in a bear hug. Shane didn't have much in the way of brawn, but he was tall and possessed a lot of inherent strength.

"Damn, it's good to see you. I can't believe we've let three years pass without getting together."

"Neither can I."

Shane relieved Haydn of his bag and dropped it by the stairs in the hall. "We don't have to be at the Giants game until midday, so we've got a couple of hours until we leave. Do you want coffee or something?"

"Yeah, coffee would be good."

"C'mon through into the kitchen, then."

Haydn followed Shane into a custom kitchen clad in marble and stainless steel. It was all very upwardly mobile. Haydn took a seat at the kitchen table while Shane primed the coffeemaker.

"You've done really well for yourself. I'm impressed," Haydn said, surveying his surroundings.

Shane looked about him. "What can I tell you? Nice things happen to nice people."

"It's a long way from the dorms at Cal-State and that AMC Gremlin," Shane added. "God rest its soul."

"Amen."

Haydn wondered whatever had become of that car—it had probably long since been consigned to the crusher.

"Marin Design Engineering treats you well, then?" Haydn said.

"They do." The coffeemaker stopped wheezing and Shane grabbed the coffees and joined Haydn at the table. "And they'll treat you well too."

Haydn thought of the premium rate they were going to pay him for this short-term contract. "Any chance this'll turn into something longer term?"

"I wouldn't be surprised. MDE takes on specialist design-build projects. No one else can do what they do, so the margins are always high. And because every project is different, they hire a lot of contract folks. You do okay on this one and I'm sure you'll get a recall."

"So, who do I have to impress for future work?"

"Me," Shane answered. "I'm the project manager on this one."

Who said cronyism was such a bad thing? Haydn thought. He raised his coffee mug for a toast and they clinked mugs.

They spent the next couple of hours catching up and reminiscing before Shane drove them to AT&T Park. San Francisco traffic was thick and parking was impossible, but MDE had splashed out on a corporate box that came with reserved parking. They entered the stadium through a private entrance. Haydn could get used to this kind of treatment.

They met with Shane's colleagues from MDE for a pregame lunch in the hospitality suite. A gaunt-looking man wearing a blazer over dress slacks spotted Shane and Haydn approaching and got up from his seat.

"Shane, you made it," he said. "Is this Haydn?"

"Yes, Trevor. Meet Haydn Duke. Haydn, this is Trevor Bellis, Marin Design Engineering's CEO."

Haydn shook hands with Bellis. His grip was surprisingly strong for someone who looked half-starved.

"A pleasure to meet you, Haydn. Please call me Trevor. I've heard a lot about you. I hope you can be of use to us. We'll discuss business after the game. But for now, enjoy yourself," Bellis said.

Shane introduced Haydn to the assembled group. They were a mix of MDE employees and contract staff. Most possessed either engineering or scientific backgrounds. They welcomed Haydn in a genuine manner and he slipped easily into conversation with them. He could see himself working very well with these people.

Haydn noticed an unoccupied place at the table. "Who are we missing?" he asked Shane.

"Our guest of honor, James Lockhart. He's from the governor's office. He's overseeing the project on behalf of the client."

"Who's the client?"

"I can't discuss that until you're signed up for the job."

Lockhart arrived shortly before the meal ended. His arrival brought a subtle change in the mood at the table, but Haydn felt it as strongly as a weather change. Lockhart introduced an air of formality. He was obviously the big man on campus. Bellis looked distinctly nervous in the man's presence. Haydn guessed MDE had a lot riding on this project.

Haydn understood the change at the table. Lockhart didn't look as if he'd come out for a ball game. He'd chosen to power-dress in a tailored suit and tie instead of something more casual. He looked like he expected to be called upon to give a press conference at any moment. During the small talk over lunch, he weighed and measured each answer before giving it. It was very disconcerting.

Game time arrived and everyone went to their seats. Bellis kept Lockhart segregated from everyone else, which lightened the mood. While everyone got wrapped up in the game, Bellis and Lockhart talked. Haydn cast glances their way. Bellis remained tense around the man. Haydn guessed things weren't as rosy at MDE as everyone liked to make out. Maybe it was a good thing he was working a short contract with these people. The last thing he needed was to sign on for something longer term if they were having problems on the business front. In situations like that, the first people to go were the contract staff. He'd think long and hard on any further offers.

After the game, everyone said their good-byes. Bellis put a hand on Haydn's shoulder. "Let's get you on our team now." Bellis's smile had returned once Lockhart had left. "I've got some paperwork at our offices for you to sign."

Haydn and Shane followed Bellis's Jaguar back to the MDE offices in Corte Madera. The building was set into the hills and was clearly visible from Highway 101, making it its own billboard. It was a squat, two-story structure with the second story being octagonal in shape. It smacked of seventies architecture, but it was no less desirable as a working environment.

Bellis beat a light and by the time Shane and Haydn arrived, he had the building unlocked and stood waiting for them in the foyer.

"Welcome to MDE," Bellis said.

Haydn failed to acknowledge the welcome. His focus was on an easel in the foyer, which held a poster-size head shot of an East Indian man in his thirties. At the base of the image was the caption SUNDIP CHAUDHARY, A FRIEND LOST, BUT NOT FORGOTTEN.

"That's the guy they found this morning."

"Yes," Bellis said. "Very sad."

"Am I his replacement?" The thought of filling a dead man's shoes took the excitement out of the position.

"No," Shane said. "He worked here as a chemical engineer."

"Let's talk about this in the boardroom," Bellis said.

Bellis took Haydn and Shane up to the second floor. At

the end of the conference table sat a roll of drawings, a flash drive, and a file folder. Shane and Bellis took seats next to each other and Haydn took one opposite.

"Sundip Chaudhary was a valued member of this company," Bellis said. "Sadly, he let the stress of his work get to him and he took his own life. None of us saw the signs. If we had, then . . ." Bellis let the remainder of his sentence go unfinished.

"That's not what I heard on the news," Haydn said.

"Out of privacy and respect for Sundip's family, we kept the truth from the press," Bellis said.

There'd been no mention of who Chaudhary had worked for in any of the news reports. Haydn wondered who'd pulled those strings—Bellis or Lockhart?

"Is Sundip's death a problem for you?" Bellis asked.

"No," Haydn replied. "It was just a surprise. No one mentioned Sundip at the ballpark today."

"The project we're working on, that Sundip was a part of, is highly confidential," Shane said. "Our client is on the verge of a major technological breakthrough. So much so, they haven't even filled us in on the full purpose of the design."

"Hence the need for privacy," Bellis said.

"And James Lockhart?" Haydn said.

"James Lockhart is acting on the client's behalf to ensure no industrial espionage occurs," Bellis said.

No wonder Bellis was so jumpy around Lockhart. There was probably a lot of ass-covering going on. Chaudhary's death might have prompted the client to consider switching firms. Bellis wouldn't want to lose such a high-profile job.

"Obviously, none of what I've told you leaves this room," Bellis said.

It sounded like overkill to Haydn, but it wasn't his problem. "Of course," he said.

"We'd better deal with the red tape," Shane said.

Bellis opened the file folder and removed a sheaf of papers and put them before Haydn. "This is a nondisclosure agreement. Should you divulge any project details to anyone outside of Marin Design Engineering, the firm will take severe legal action against you. The financial penalties we would seek are significant. In addition, our client would be entitled to take separate action."

Bellis's tone sounded like a threat, albeit dressed up in legalese. Haydn didn't like being pushed around, regardless of how politely it was done.

"We've all had to sign it," Shane said. "It's standard practice in this kind of situation."

"I would recommend you read the document before signing it," Bellis said. "You're welcome to run it by your attorney, but we are short on time."

Haydn had the urge to walk away. He liked to keep business informal and friendly. This was beginning to get a little too serious for his liking. But it was easy work for excellent money. In a couple of weeks, it wouldn't matter. Haydn scanned the twelve-page document. It was pretty much as Bellis had described. If he disclosed any part of his work, MDE would sue—and sue big. The document claimed MDE would seek ten million in damages. Haydn wasn't sure how much was legal bluffing, but it was enough to ensure that he kept his mouth shut. He finished reading the document and decided the job was still worth doing despite the overlitigious contract. Bellis held out a pen and Haydn signed.

With that out of the way, Bellis and Shane spent a half hour going through the marked-up plans before handing them to him along with the flash drive containing the drawings he was to correct. It was all straightforward enough and the meeting broke up. Everyone shook hands and smiled, but the hard sell with the nondisclosure agreement had soured Haydn's mood. The enthusiasm he'd brought with him this morning wouldn't be making the return drive.

Bellis made small talk as he saw Shane and Haydn out.

Lockhart's presence in the foyer ended the small talk. He stood before Chaudhary's image on the easel in deep contemplation. He seemingly failed to register anyone's presence in the room with him for a moment.

"A great shame. Sundip was a very talented young man. We should have done more for him," he reflected. "What's going on here?"

"James, this is Haydn Duke. He's joining the team," Bellis said.

Lockhart shook Haydn's hand. "Good to have you aboard. I look forward to working with you. Now enjoy the rest of your weekend."

Lockhart couldn't have made his point any clearer. It was time for them to leave.

"Thanks for making the trip, Haydn. We'll talk next week," Bellis said, before thanking him one last time and ushering Shane and him out the door.

"Lock the door, Trevor," Lockhart said. "I don't want to be disturbed."

Bellis did as he was told and Lockhart led the way to Bellis's office. He let Bellis sit while he perched himself on the window ledge. He took in the panoramic view and watched Shane reverse out from his parking spot and drive away.

"Do you know anything about this Haydn Duke?" Lockhart asked.

"Not much. He's a friend of Shane's. Why?"

"I noticed him eyeballing us at the game."

"What do you want?" Bellis asked.

"Watch your tone, Trevor. Just remember who you're speaking to."

Bellis said nothing. Instead he fidgeted in his seat.

"I came here to make sure we're all on the same page about Sundip Chaudhary."

"I got the message."

"Did you? I wasn't sure."

"I got it."

Lockhart glanced out the window. Beckerman was out there somewhere watching his back, visible yet invisible. He'd chosen to keep Beckerman out of sight today. He had a habit of agitating situations. Lockhart didn't want things agitated. Today, he wanted things calm. More specifically, he wanted Bellis calm.

"You say that, Trevor, but I feel you have questions. If you have them, ask them."

"Sundip's death."

"Yes."

"It's convenient."

"Convenient, how?"

"Sundip expressed doubts about the project."

"Did he mention his doubts to you?"

"Only that we'd been lied to. He said the products we're designing weren't being designed for the purpose we were told. He wanted to speak to you and now he's dead. Did he speak to you?"

Lockhart came away from the window and settled into a chair opposite Bellis. Bellis stiffened and looked cornered. "I met with him. I thought I'd set his mind at rest."

"Obviously you didn't."

Lockhart sighed. "I believe Sundip was overwrought and he cracked. He was deluded. When I think about it now, my answers didn't help him. I thought the truth would bring him around. Instead, it looks to have pushed him over the edge."

"So you believe it was a suicide?"

"Opposed to what, Trevor?" Lockhart could feel Bellis psyching himself up to ask the big question. He urged the man to have the strength to ask it. He wanted the question out in the open so he could put the subject to rest.

Bellis was silent for a moment, then puffed himself up. "James, did you have anything to do with Sundip's death?"

"How can you ask such a question?"

He fixed Bellis with his gaze. He left him no room for escape. Bellis would need courage if he were to follow this line of questioning.

Bellis sat up in his seat. "I don't think Chaudhary was deluded. I know he had doubts about the project and was becoming a little difficult to control, but I don't think he was suicidal."

"A little difficult?" Lockhart said. "He was becoming a Grade-A pain in the ass. He suddenly got it into his head that what we were doing was wrong."

"I think that's a little harsh."

"More harsh than you accusing me of murder, Trevor?"

Bellis wiped a hand across his face. Finally, the man saw the ridiculousness of what he was saying. Lockhart saw Bellis's courage leave him in that moment and return to the fold. Bellis might have suspicions and doubts, but he wouldn't take them any further. The project remained intact and his clients didn't need to hear of this setback.

"I'm sorry, James."

"That's okay. The last few days have taken their toll on everyone. We've lost someone close and it's shaken us all. Suicide is hard to accept. It's a betrayal to everyone left behind. We'd prefer to have someone else to blame, but in this case, we don't have that luxury. Chaudhary killed himself. There's even a witness who saw him do it."

"You're right. I'm sorry."

Lockhart stood up from his seat and rounded Bellis's desk. Bellis stood to meet him and they shook hands. Bellis's hand was slick with sweat. It had taken a lot for the man to confront him. Lockhart placed a comforting hand on Bellis's shoulder. "Look, Trevor. Next week, come up to Sacramento and we'll have dinner. I'll explain the facts of life regarding this project. There are a couple of little things I've kept from you. It's time I let you in on a few details. How does that sound?"

"Sounds good," Bellis said, squeezing out a strained smile.

Lockhart saw himself out and drove away. He didn't

pick up his phone until he was back on the freeway. He dialed Beckerman's number.

"How'd it go?" Beckerman asked.

"It could have gone better. There are doubts, but the situation is contained for now. Did you find anything at Chaudhary's?"

"Negative. Anything he claimed to have known, he kept to himself."

"Okay. I want you to keep a close eye on MDE. Any more problems, I want to know about them."

THE
WATER
CLOCK

JIM KELLY

A mutilated body found frozen in a block of ice. A second body perched high in a cathedral, riding a gargoyle—hidden for more than thirty years. When forensic evidence links both victims to one crime, reporter Philip Dryden knows he's on to a terrific story. What he doesn't know is that his search for the truth will involve a mystery from his own past. As his investigation gets increasingly urgent, he will come face-to-face with his deepest fears…and a cold-blooded killer.

ISBN 13: 978-0-8439-6000-6

Michael Siverling

The Sterling Inheritance

Private investigator Jason Wilder has the toughest boss in town: his mother. Working in the detective agency his mother founded is always exciting, but sometimes it can be downright dangerous. Like the case he's on now. All he was supposed to do was locate a missing businessman. But when he found the guy in a run-down motel, Jason never expected him to start shooting. He also didn't know the man was wanted for homicide. Now it's too late. Jason is right in the middle of the case, and the only way out is to see it through to the end. His search for answers will lead him down some deadly, twisting roads…and to a dilapidated movie house that people seem willing to fight—and maybe even kill—for.

ISBN 13: 978-0-8439-6002-0

CAILTIN ROTHER

NAKED ADDICTION

A ticket to Homicide.

That was the first thing disgruntled narcotics detective
Ken Goode thought when he found the body of a
beautiful murdered woman. But his transfer became
the last thing on his mind when more victims turned
up—all linked to the same beauty school his sister
attends. With time running out, a killer on the loose,
and the danger hitting too close to home, Goode has to
stop this murderer while fighting his own growing
obsession with one of the very women he's trying to
save.

ISBN 10: 0-8439-5995-9
ISBN 13: 978-0-8439-5995-6

ACCIDENTS WAITING TO HAPPEN

SIMON WOOD

Josh Michaels is worth more dead than alive. He just doesn't know it yet. When an SUV forces his car off the road and into the river, it could be an accident. But when Josh looks up at the road, expecting to see the SUV's driver rushing to help him, all he sees is the driver watching him calmly…then giving him a "thumbs-down" sign. That is the first of many attempts on Josh's life, all of them designed to look like accidents, and all of them very nearly fatal. With his time—and maybe his luck—running out and no one willing to believe him, Josh had better figure out who wants him dead and why…before it's too late.
